DATING YOU HATING YOU

CHRISTINA LAUREN

piatkus

PIATKUS

First published in the US in 2017 by Gallery Books,
an imprint of Simon & Schuster, Inc.
First published in Great Britain in 2017 by Piatkus

1 3 5 7 9 10 8 6 4 2

A CIP catalogue record for this book
is available from the British Library.

TPB ISBN 978-0-349-41751-6

Printed and bound in Great Britain by
Clays Ltd, St Ives plc

Papers used by Piatkus are from well-managed forests
and other responsible sources.

MIX
Paper from
responsible sources
FSC® C104740

Piatkus
An imprint of
Little, Brown Book Group
Carmelite House
50 Victoria Embankment
London EC4Y 0DZ

An Hachette UK Company
www.hachette.co.uk

www.littlebrown.co.uk

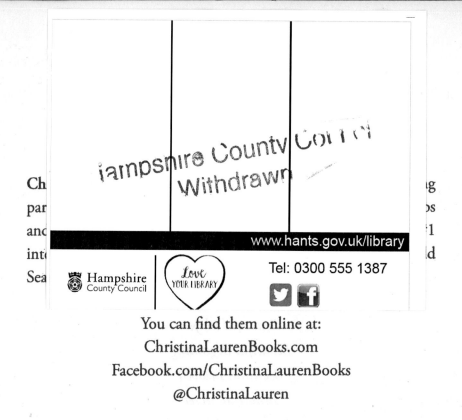

Ch...   ...g
par...   ...s
an...   ...1
int...   ...d
Sea...

You can find them online at:
ChristinaLaurenBooks.com
Facebook.com/ChristinaLaurenBooks
@ChristinaLauren

ALSO BY CHRISTINA LAUREN:

The Beautiful Series
Beautiful Bastard
Beautiful Stranger
Beautiful Bitch
Beautiful Bombshell
Beautiful Player
Beautiful Beginning
Beautiful Beloved
Beautiful Secret
Beautiful Boss
Beautiful

Wild Seasons
Sweet Filthy Boy
Dirty Rowdy Thing
Dark Wild Night
Wicked Sexy Liar

Young Adult
Sublime
The House
Autoboyography

Stand-Alone Romances
Dating You / Hating You

For Kristin,
and all the adventures we have ahead of us.

DATING
YOU
HATING
YOU

chapter one

La Cienega Boulevard is a never-ending hell of snaking concrete, but it's a necessary evil in this town. Running north to south in Los Angeles, it forms an enormous artery cutting through the "thirty-mile zone," also known as TMZ, also known as the Studio Zone—historically containing all the early film studios.

In its heyday, and before other cities began offering tax credits and big incentives to lure filmmakers into shooting on location, this was where most movies were filmed. It's been the center of hundreds of millions of dollars in movie deals over the decades, but I've never heard anyone in the industry throw out "TMZ" in casual conversation. Not in the way you're thinking, anyway. Similar to a tourist shuffling around San Francisco and calling it Frisco, anyone referring to the nexus of Hollywood life as such nowadays would reveal herself as an out-of-towner who'd happened upon a detailed Wikipedia page. It's so archaic, in fact, that many of my colleagues don't even realize that's where the gossip site got its name.

La Cienega looks like most surface streets here in Hollywood: rows of shops and restaurants built at odd angles and crammed into every inch of possible space, palm trees and billboards that shoot for a gray-smudged blue sky, and cars *everywhere*. To the north is the stuff most Hollywood dreams are made of, where a backdrop of steep hills seems to have erupted straight from the asphalt. Multimillion-dollar homes sit like Tetris blocks on the hillsides, their gleaming windows and gated drives towering above the city.

It's one hell of a panorama if you can afford it, but like most people here in Los Angeles, I have my feet safely on the ground, and at home *my* only view is into the apartment across the alley, inhabited by a frequently shirtless Moroccan juggler.

There are worse sights, I suppose.

Although I hate La Cienega and its never-ending gridlock, the boulevard is as much *as the crow flies* as you're going to find through LA. Any local will tell you that driving here is all about timing: leave at two, and you can get nearly anywhere in twenty minutes. Leave at five, like everyone else, and it'll take you an hour to go five miles.

Thank God I'm usually one of the last ones out of the office.

I look up at the sound of a knock and see Daryl in all her blond-haired, blue-eyed glory standing at my door. While I'm the precise amalgamation of my two dark-haired, dark-eyed parents, Daryl Hannah Jordan is the picture of her namesake, and looks more like she just washed up on the set of *Splash* than grew up in San Dimas, three houses away from me.

"The workday ended over an hour ago," she says.

"Just reading this article before I go." My eyes narrow instinctively as I study her. Daryl was in a skirt and sky-high heels just a few hours ago; now she's wearing a pair of scrubs and has her beach-blond hair pulled back into a ponytail. "We have that party at Mike and Steph's tonight. Please tell me that's your costume."

Daryl starts to fidget and becomes increasingly interested in a nonexistent spot on the hem of her shirt, and I know I've been had.

"*No*," I gasp.

"I'm sorry!" She falls dramatically into the chair opposite me.

"You dick. You're flaking?"

"I don't want to! But I forgot I promised my uncle I'd come in tonight. Why didn't you remind me this afternoon? You know that's your job in this relationship!"

I slump back in my chair. Daryl worked her way through college at her uncle's medical spa, and enjoyed the hell out of that employee discount while she was there. She's gorgeous—with tight skin, perfect boobs, and a thigh gap you could watch TV through—but she's also the first to admit that a chunk of that is due to the pioneering efforts of science and her uncle, Dr. Elias Jordan, Plastic Surgeon. Daryl turns thirty this year, and in addition to her job upstairs in the TV-Literary department, she's been doing some extra work for him on the side to pay for all her recent *fine-tuning*. Like most people in this town, she's determined to never grow old.

Thankfully, she doesn't have to worry about that anymore, because I'm going to kill her.

"Well, this day has been comically bad." I check my phone before tossing it into my purse. "Remind me why I love you?"

"You love me because I listen to your endless movie trivia and my passivity complements your need to be in charge all the time."

I wish I could argue, but she's made two good points. I grew up obsessed with movies; it's in my blood. My dad was an electrician for Warner Bros. and my mom did hair and makeup for almost every studio around. By the time I was eight, I'd convinced them to let me ride my bike after school to the neighborhood video rental store—yes, I am old—and then talked the crusty old manager, Larry, into letting me work there for free rentals. When I was in eleventh grade he finally agreed to start paying me.

I've traveled the world, but LA has always been—and will always be—my home. It isn't only because my family is here; it's because my heart resides in the grit and chaos and unspoken rules of Hollywood. It's why I became a talent agent. I've never wanted to be *in* movies, but I've always dreamed of being part of how they were made.

And I do always need to be in charge. She's totally got me on that one, too.

"Fine," I say. "But next time I'm set up on a terrible blind date by a client and can't refuse, you're putting on an Evie face and going in my stead."

"Done." She inspects me with a forced smile. "Not to add fuel to the fire, but is your costume in the car or are you going as a surly but fashionable banker?"

I open my mouth to tell her exactly what she can do with my costume, but I catch movement through the open doorway, over her shoulder.

"Amelia!" I call, and she pokes her head inside. "What are you doing tonight? Please, please tell me nothing, Ms. Amelia Baker, my favorite person alive."

"I'm picking Jay up from camp," she says, "and spending the rest of the night in my pajamas eating ravioli out of the can."

My head drops to my desk.

I work in Features, representing actors and actresses; and Amelia is the second in command in HR. Because she got a start in adulting earlier than most of us around here, Amelia is also proud mommy to the smartest, handsomest twelve-year-old boy in the world.

I am verging on desperation. "Any chance you could get a sitter?"

Amelia steps inside and sits on the arm of Daryl's chair. Her hair is cut close to her scalp. As much as I'd like to be able to pull off a style like that myself, it's never going to happen—but on her, it shows off her bright smile, luminous dark skin, and cheekbones for days.

"On a Friday night?" Her tone carries an undercurrent of *guffaw*. "Not a chance. Why?"

"Because Daryl is the worst friend, and you're the best friend?"

Her laugh tells me to give it up, and I groan.

"You have big plans?" With completely unmasked sarcasm, she adds, "It's not like I expected you to have a date or something, but you know, one can hope."

I sit up and point dramatically at Daryl. "I was supposed to go to a party with that one."

"It's true," she says guiltily, "but I forgot and promised Uncle Elias I'd go through his accounts."

Amelia points a mom finger at her. "You are *not* having something else done to your face."

Daryl immediately waves this off. We rarely comment on anything Daryl has done—she's a grown-up, and as perfect as we think she already is, she's doing it because she wants to and, well, it's really none of our business. Still, even I'll admit she's been a bit . . . overzealous lately.

"Just a little light dusting." Daryl gives a prim flourish of her hands and then turns back to me. "Speaking of, I need to get going."

"I guess I'll head out, too. No sense prolonging the inevitable." I move to slip some work files into my bag, but then I remember what I'd been reading. "Hey, real quick: did either of you see the article about Brad in *Variety*?" I lower my voice and look out into the empty office. "Wait, is he still here?"

Amelia peeks out and down the hall toward the office of Brad Kingman—vice president of Price & Dickle, head of Features, and asshole extraordinaire—and returns, shaking her head. "Just us and Dudley, I think."

I point to my computer screen, and the two of them huddle behind me, reading. "It wasn't *about* him, exactly." I point to the article in question. "Just a mention of how he was seen having dinner with Gabe Vestes." Gabe is an A-list movie star who's signed with our rival agency, CT Management. And, funny thing: everyone knows Brad and Gabe hate each other, although no one really knows *why*.

Daryl straightens, unimpressed. "That's it? I thought this was going to be something tawdry and scandalous."

I give her a little growl and look back down at the article. I'm not reassured by her certainty that this is meaningless; suspicion itches at me.

"Maybe they patched whatever up?" Amelia offers.

I hum, unconvinced. "I don't think that's a thing that happens to Brad unless there's money involved."

"You go ahead and think on that, Nancy Drew," Amelia says, "but Jay is waiting, so I gotta jet." She turns to leave but stops just shy of the door. "And before I forget, a memo ran by my desk today—it'll probably hit your box this week, Evie—Brad is postponing your department's annual retreat, so you can take it off your calendar for now."

"Postponing? Did it say why?" My spidey senses are heightened now. Brad has held our Features department retreat in Big Bear the same week every November for as long as anyone can remember.

"Didn't say," Amelia tells us. "All I know is that it's been delayed indefinitely and I'm sure I won't hear you complain about skipping an entire weekend in the woods with that guy."

· · ·

When you're my age and living alone in an apartment with a common entrance, endless hallways, and tiny buzzers on the doors, you forget that creeping hopelessness you get walking up to a real house. A house with a porch, and a Craftsman door, and a knocker that tells you a little something about the people inside.

An iron dragon.

A brass rose.

Maybe a copper gargoyle.

I stare at the perfectly tarnished cherub on Steph and Mike's front door and scowl, suddenly feeling a lot less satisfied with my life than I did only a few hours ago. They're six years younger than I am and they're already knocker people. Front door people. *Homeowners.*

I can't commit to the yearly plan for Netflix and don't even own the car I just parked two blocks down the crowded street. I am a terrible adult.

I glance at my black robe, at the burgundy-and-yellow tie, at the wand in my hand, and wonder why I ever agreed to this. I'm thirty-three years old and at a costume party dressed as a teenage Hermione Granger.

Jesus, Evie.

Damn you, Daryl.

And it takes some bravery, let me tell you, to come here alone, dressed like a teenage Hogwarts character. There's this instinctive panic, that Bridget Jones tarts-and-vicars-induced anxiety that the door will open and everyone will stare at me with jaws agape and Steph will whisper in empathetic mortification, *Didn't you get the email saying we weren't doing costumes?*

At least with Daryl at my side that outcome would be funny, and we could drink and tease each other about how we ended up here on a Friday night. But alone? Not so much. Here's to hoping the *Come As You Are* theme held, because a girl who needs a time turner to get everything done each day is a perfect alter ego for a single woman working in Hollywood.

I lift the knocker with some effort—using both hands. It's surprisingly heavy.

When I let it go again, it doesn't make the soft, deep knock I imagine, and instead strikes with a deafening metallic crack against the wood. The sound reverberates in the tiny brick court-yard and for a single, terrifying heartbeat the giant cherub wings wobble on their hinges as if they might crash to the ground.

Jumping back, I notice the perfectly normal doorbell on the outside wall: clean, obvious, and to all appearances, completely functional.

So . . . not a knocker then.

The door flies open, letting out a roar of laughter that, from the way everyone is staring at me, seems to be directed at the racket I've just caused. Steph steps forward, bringing a waft of her Prada perfume with her. With a graceful, manicured hand, she stills what is obviously, in hindsight, a metal door decoration.

"Evie's here!" She pulls me into a hug. "You're here!"

I like Steph. We used to work together at the Alterman Agency when I was a young, shiny new agent and she was an in-tern. She's still there, a full agent now, and to this day she holds the honor of being the colleague—past or present—whom I least frequently wanted to strangle. She's warm, she's accomplished . . . but once I step inside, I'm reminded again that she is frantically trying to cling to her teenage aesthetic even though she's neck-deep in her twenties. Case in point: her costume. I'm pretty sure she's dressed as "Wrecking Ball"–era Miley Cyrus in a cropped white tank and a white bikini bottom with boots. Also? I spy a table in the corner with an artful arrangement of Red Bull cans and a selection of fancy vodkas.

Ushering me in, she says—too loudly—"That thing is just decorative, you goose! You scared everyone! And oh my God! Hermione! You look amazing. You are so great for coming alone. My brave little Evie!"

Brave?

The sound you heard? The one that sounded a little like tires screeching? That was my confidence, coming to a standstill just inside the door.

I look around at an assortment of expectant faces wearing polite smiles, waiting for introductions.

A friendly looking redhead dressed as Ariel, with her arm around the waist of a tall Hispanic Prince Eric.

An aloof brunette dressed as a vampire, whispering something to her vampire boyfriend.

A few couples across the room who had been engaged in a group convo but are now staring at where I've just brought singledom into a party clearly meant for pairs.

"Everyone, this is Evie-slash-Hermione! Evie, this is . . . everyone!"

I wave, muttering to Steph out of the side of my mouth in my best Bogart, "You didn't tell me this was a couples thing."

"It's not, really. It just ended up that way!" she chirps, pulling me deeper into the living room. "I promise it will be great."

For a second, when I spot two women dressed as Beyoncé and Nicki Minaj snuggling on the couch, I think she might be right. This is an open-minded group, and I am a strong female choosing to embrace her independence and attend a party alone. Nothing to feel out of place about here.

But then she steers me past the main cluster of guests and parks me at the Red Bull–and-vodka table.

So that's how it is.

"Is Morgan at least here?" I ask hopefully, happy to entertain Steph and her husband Mike's toddler all night if it helps me look even a fraction less awkward.

She looks at me with a dramatic little pout. "At the sitter's. How's work, by the way?"

My shoulders sag, resigned. "It's fine. Tyler—the Broadway actor I signed in March? He isn't here full-time with his wife and kid until the end of November, so I told him I'd check on them. I basically spent the day in a Child Sensory Training and Integration seminar where babies play with cooked pasta in giant plastic bins for seven hundred dollars an hour."

There's an understandable beat of silence before Steph leans in closer. "You didn't."

"I did." And talking about it again, I remember how incredulous I was when we walked in. A group of tiny women in white jeans with their perfectly dressed, smudge-free children staring excitedly at giant bins of cooked noodles. But as the hour went on, and I saw Bea's joy over the naughtiness of playing with her food for fun, my cynicism over the ridiculous parenting extravagance lessened, and I started to feel like, *Yeah, this is pretty awesome.*

But that is exactly how your brain gets corrupted in this town. Seven *hundred* dollars an hour to squish noodles in their chubby fists. These kids could have an awesome time playing with macaroni in their bathtub at home for a buck fifty.

"You aren't her nanny," Steph reminds me with gentle outrage.

"No, I know. But I adore Tyler, and his landing the lead in *Long Board* was a huge coup for us both." A coup I sort of needed, and Steph knows it, too. "I'm happy to check in on his family, obviously, but yeah. Not a nanny. How about you? Things are good?"

"Yeah. Ken's been acting a bit weirder than usual, but—" She mimes tipping a bottle back dramatically and I laugh. The office cocktail hour with Ken Alterman—my old boss—was always an adventure.

Someone catches Steph's eye from across the room, and despite my pleading headshake, she gives my shoulder a reassuring squeeze and says, "Hold tight, I'll be right back."

And then she's gone.

You'd think I'd be used to this sort of thing by now—navigating a room full of matched-up people, alone—but somehow it never really gets easier.

I pull my phone out of my robe pocket, quickly texting Daryl.

> Jerk. I am the only singleton.

> It was a couples party? I didn't know!

> Neither did I.

> I would have faked diarrhea in traffic.

> Actually, that might have been more pleasant.

With a mental groan, I glance covertly at the time before tucking my phone away again. I can stay for forty-five minutes, right? That seems like a length that communicates, *I value your friendship and am so glad I came!* and *No, I am absolutely* not *rushing out the door so I can continue slipping into spinsterdom in peace.* I feel like there should be a clear rule: if you're unmarried at my age and have been a bridesmaid more than seven times, you should be automatically allowed an early exit from any couples event without ever being deemed an asshole.

With this decided, I inspect my vodka choices, pulling the most expensive one from an array of multicolored bottles.

"Is this the third-wheel table?"

Because I'm midpour, I answer without turning around. "The one with all the booze?" I ask. "It should be. I mean, it's the least they can do."

"Then I'm sorry, but I need to ask you to leave," the man says sternly, and just as I turn in surprise, I feel him lean in a little behind me to say more quietly: "I was assured I was the only single person hired to work this event."

He's closer than I expected, and so my laugh is cut off when I see him.

Is he kidding? He's single? No way am I this lucky. His hair is dark, longer on top, and as I watch him bend to inspect some of the bottles, he pushes it back from his forehead. Not like he's fixing it in any way—quite the opposite, because now it's standing straight up—but like that's an unconscious thing he does. I immediately notice how comfortable he seems in his skin, loose and easygoing enough that it's a solid guess *he* wasn't just planning a bout of fake intestinal distress to make a dive for the nearest exit.

He smiles again, and when I look down to what he's wearing, I have to close my eyes to stifle a laugh.

"Did Steph put you up to this?" I ask.

"What?" He follows my gaze. It's subtle, but with the hair,

green eyes, and glasses I can tell where he was going with the white shirt and loose tie beneath a gray zip-up jacket. Harry Potter. The lightning-bolt scar drawn on his forehead helps; that probably should have immediately tipped me off.

His brows furrow. "Oh my God." He takes in my robe, the tie, the wand, the wild dark hair I teased to within an inch of its life while I sat in traffic. "Are you kidding me? The only two single people at this party and we match?"

I can't stifle the laugh this time, and it tears from me, surprising him as it does everyone who has ever heard it. I am small but my laugh is mighty.

He stares at me with a slow-growing, amused grin. "*Wow*."

"Hi." I hold out my hand. "I'm Evie."

"Is that short for Evil?" He pretends to be scared as he tentatively returns the handshake. "Are you sure you're Gryffindor? Your laugh makes me think you have a secret lab and are building an apocalyptic robot dog that's going to eat every smug person here. Slytherin for sure."

"It's short for Evelyn. The cackle is my gift. It keeps the delicate ones away."

"I'm Carter." He points two thumbs at his chest. "Not delicate, I promise."

Is he . . . flirting? I consider the rolling tumbleweeds of my dating life and marvel that I can't even tell anymore.

Carter is sort of dorky, despite being hot. The glasses look real, dark and thick-framed. He's taller than me, but not too tall—which is a bonus in my book—with eyes that are a startling green, hair deep brown and thick . . .

I blink out of my inspection and back down to his face, realizing how long I've been staring at the top of his head. "Nice to meet you."

"You too." He points to his own costume again and smiles. "This was about the best I could do on half-assed motivation and an uninspired closet." He looks me over again. "You're an *amazing* Hermione, though. Harry and Hermione. Perfect. I ship it."

My stomach does another little tumble. "My friend Daryl was supposed to come along as my Ron, but she had to bail at the last minute. She's dead to me."

Carter's laugh comes out as a loud, surprised guffaw before he pops the tab on a can and takes a long, slow drink.

Honestly, I'm trying to stay cool and not look too closely at him, but failing.

Living in LA, and especially working in Hollywood, I meet beautiful people every day, even dated a few. But in a town full of pretty faces, I've become immune to the predictability of them, the symmetry. Carter is pretty in a distinctive way: His eyes are big, and lined with the darkest, thickest lashes. His jaw is sharp. With the thick frames of his glasses, his is an oblivious type of beauty. He needs a haircut. When he smiles, I see that his teeth are white but not perfectly straight. It makes him seem immediately friendly. And his imperfections are surprising in a sea of Invisalign, Botox, and self-tanners. He looks . . . *real.*

Now, before you think I'm putting too much thought into this, let me remind you that I am no longer in my twenties, and when you meet men at my age you immediately place them on one of three lists, just to make life easier for everyone: datable, not datable, or gay. Datable basically means you wear your bra when they're around, and you don't talk about bodily functions or pimples. Not datable or gay: anything goes.

"You're ahead of me there. I never even had a plus one," he says. "I was threatened into coming by our illustrious hosts. How do you know them?"

"I used to work with Steph at Alterman."

Something passes over Carter's face—a flicker of recognition, maybe?—but before I can question it, Steph walks out juggling an armful of plates. Carter and I both struggle to make room for them amid the Red Bull.

"What's up with the bar selection?" I ask her, gesturing to the table. "Are you expecting frat boys later?"

"Oh my God, can you imagine?" Her question comes out breathy—nearly orgasmic—and I stare blankly at her. "Everything else is over there." She lifts her chin, gesturing to another table in the living room that I now see is covered with wine, beer, and all the usual spirits.

I slump my shoulders in mock defeat. "But that's in *married* territory."

"We don't have tickets to that side of the room," Carter adds.

Steph looks like she's about to roll her eyes at us but then freezes, and her mouth drops open. "You guys match."

Carter and I exchange a knowing look. "We talked earlier," he says. "Made sure to coordinate it for maximum awkward."

She slaps his arm. "Shut up! Mikey and I *knew* the two of you would really hit it off. Did you know that we're *all* in talent management? I mean, *guys*. The two of you are like a match made in heaven, right?"

Just before she heads back in the direction of the kitchen, Steph scrunches her nose at us as if we are a cute set of porcelain figures on a shelf and she's tilted us *just so* toward each other.

When Carter turns to me, we stare at each other for a wordless, stunned beat.

"Those assholes set us up," he whispers.

"It appears so." I glare back in Steph's direction. "Don't they know that sort of thing never works?"

"It's like that movie with Seth Rogen and Katherine Heigl where they have that disastrous date." He pauses with his can partway to his lips. "Or wait . . . am I remembering that wrong?"

A sensation like Pop Rocks goes off in my chest—I know which movie he's talking about. "You mean *Knocked Up*?" He nods, and I roll on: "It's not a date, actually. They meet at a club after she—Katherine Heigl—gets a promotion. She meets Seth Rogen at an actual club here in LA called Plan B, and they get drunk and have unprotected sex. She realizes she's pregnant eight weeks later and *then* they have the awkward date where she tells him."

When I finally come up for air, I see him watching me, eyebrows raised over the top of his Red Bull. "That was an impressive summary for a movie that came out over ten years ago."

I give him a little shimmy. "It's my other gift."

His eyes shine. "I have to be honest, Stephanie should know better. You are incredibly pretty, and obviously blessed with at least two enviable gifts, but sight unseen, nothing sounds worse than dating a fellow agent."

God, I agree. Dating someone in my business would be a disaster: the hours are terrible, the phone calls are constant, and the blood pressure—and the sex life—suffer.

So I'm glad he's said it, glad he's just thrown it out there. It's like we're on the same team and suddenly there is zero pressure: Team *They're Cute But It Could Never Work*.

"And," he adds, "I just realized that you're the beloved Evelyn Abbey. It's all falling into place now."

I'm caught off guard for a second and not sure how to react. Hollywood is an industry of almost forty thousand people, but its circles are small. If he's heard of me—and my track record—it could be great . . . or not. I feel uneasy not knowing which.

"So you're an agent?" I ask. "How have we never met?"

"I'm in TV-Literary." *Small circles.* I relax a little. "But Michael Christopher and Steph talk about you all the time."

"You call Mike 'Michael Christopher'?" I ask. "That's really cute. I'm getting Winnie the Pooh vibes."

"We went to grade school together," Carter explains, "and old habits die hard. He tries to pretend he's cool being married and having a three-year-old kid who makes him wear tiaras, but deep down I know it makes him crazy that I'm still single and there are no pictures of me on Instagram wearing my kid's sparkly lip gloss."

I laugh. "Well, if it makes you feel better, this is going so much better than the last time Steph tried to set me up."

Carter has the magical ability to sharply lift one eyebrow, and it makes a chemical reaction in me go off like a bomb. "She does this to you a lot?"

"Last time," I explain, "she set me up with her chubby twenty-two-year-old cousin, Wyatt."

"That's thoughtful. She must really like Wyatt."

I let this compliment slide warmly over me. "I'm thirty-three, so . . ."

Carter's laugh is soft, but his entire face smiles when he does it. "He couldn't handle you, I take it." "Newly graduated from UCLA, poor Wyatt hadn't been out on a date in a few months." I smile. "Or . . . ever."

I'm unsure what to do with the straightforward honesty of his attention as he listens. I'm used to being the person who dissolves into the background, by necessity. Most of my life—most of my socializing—is centered around work. And there I make myself seen when I need to raise the red flag or go to bat for my clients, but otherwise my job is best done from backstage. It's only when I'm here, standing with a man who is watching me like I'm the only thing in the room, that I realize how long it's been since anyone has looked at me this way.

A thought occurs to me: although he grew up with Mike back east, if Carter's in TV-Lit, he's probably local. Daryl might even know him. "Where do you work?"

Carter smiles, as if he realizes that what he's about to say is a tiny social stink bomb dropped between us. "CTM."

CT Management is our biggest rival. Inside of me there are warring impulses: an urge to fist-pump because he's local, offset by an instinctive spike of competitiveness.

If he notices my silence, he rolls past it. "I moved out here two years ago, and I'm saying this as someone who grew up surrounded by subways and a million other ways to get where you need to be," he says. "But here? God. I live in Beverly Hills—never thought I'd say that—and it's still a nightmare getting anywhere."

"You East Coasters are so spoiled with your"—I make finger quotes—"*subways* and *efficient taxi system*."

Carter's laugh is a quiet, whiskery chuckle. "It's true. I'm a Long Island boy at heart. But now, I'm going Hollywood."

"Just make sure you don't go *full-on* Hollywood."

"I'm not even sure I know what it means to go 'full-on Hollywood.' Is that when you look at the five-hundred-dollar shoes at Saks and think, 'I should probably get those'? Because we had that in Manhattan."

"Worse," I say. "It's when you recognize the five-hundred-dollar shoes on someone else's feet and know where they probably bought them. And then you judge the person wearing them a little because those loafers are no longer the town's number one underappreciated, overpriced designer and you know they were on sale last week so they didn't pay full price."

"Wow. You *are* Eve-il."

"Oh, that's not me." I hold up my hands and then point to my simple yellow flats peeking out beneath my robe. "I'll have you know these shoes are from Old Navy, sir. Purchased on clearance. But I've lived here my entire life. Every day it's a struggle to not get pulled down into the game."

" 'The game'?"

"Talent agents in Hollywood?" I say. "You *know* it's a game."

"Right, right." He nods, and I realize that with that one subtle gesture, he's already *playing*. And if my instinct is right, he's good at it, too. He's wide open until the subject of work comes up, and then a filter slides into place.

Interesting.

I take a sip of my drink, looking out at the party around us. Together, Carter and I form this tiny island in the dining room; it's almost as if the rest of the guests have been instructed to leave us alone.

"So you're at P&D," he says.

"I am." I look at him, trying to read him like I do every new person I meet so I can figure out how to best interact, and I think: *He's unflappable.* "Under Brad Kingman."

Carter doesn't react, and if my guess is correct, it's because he already knew this about me.

"Is it true he's notoriously picky about food and only eats raw, unprocessed, no sugar . . ." Carter grins as he cheekily tilts his can of Red Bull to his lips. "Obviously I am very health conscious, myself."

I laugh. "It's true—all of it."

"It can't be as extreme as everyone says."

"One time," I begin, "I put a home-and-garden magazine on his desk, thinking he could take the dog-food-bar sample stuck to the cover home to his pampered Great Dane. I walked by later and *he* was eating it. Like, he's so used to bland, tasteless food that he ate an organic dog-food bar and didn't realize it wasn't for people."

Carter looks horrified. "Did you say anything?"

"Um, *no*," I say, unable to keep from laughing. "But in my own defense, he'd just told me I looked a little *fluffy* in my new dress. So maybe he deserved it."

As soon as the last word is out of my mouth, I wish I could take it back.

Agents are notoriously gossipy. In some ways, sharing confidences to make inroads is part of the business. But it's never been a very large part of *my* business. I keep it level. I keep it up front. I get things done. And as much as I felt justified letting my boss eat dog food, I don't get bogged down in sharing stories of bad behavior, drunken antics on tabletops at bars, or which intern is banging which partner. Unless I'm with Daryl or Amelia—in which case, the gloves come off. And in general, I like to run in like-minded circles. Reputation is everything.

Carter leans in. "That's a pretty terrible thing to say to you, though."

And dammit—by whispering this reassurance, he's managed to play both the professional *and* the reassuring angle. Good agents can read people, instinctively put them at ease and get them talking, or remain discreet in every situation. Great agents can seamlessly do all three.

We all tend to keep our cards pretty close to our chests and not let on what we're really thinking. Our guards are up, our walls are high, and our bullshit meters are tuned to the most sensitive setting possible.

It occurs to me, looking at him a little more closely, that Carter definitely keeps his cards close to his chest, yeah. But he also seems to have a really good hand.

chapter two

Michael Christopher finds me Saturday morning, paper open on the table, coffeemaker sputtering quietly in the background.

"Glad you didn't try to drive home." His voice is broken-glass scratchy, and when I look up, I grin at the sight of him in a blue velvet bathrobe hanging haphazardly open over a faded T-shirt and a pair of striped boxers. Atop his head, his hair reaches a campfire peak.

"Morning, Mr. Hefner."

He swears roundly when his foot locates a handful of Legos buried in the fluffy kitchen rug.

"Language." I've heard Stephanie give him this understated reminder at least a dozen times.

Michael growls, bending to inspect the damage. "You don't know pain until you've had one of these fuckers embedded into the arch of your foot." Satisfied he isn't bleeding, he hobbles the rest of the way to the cupboard, pulls down a white ceramic coffee mug with Morgan's tiny handprints stamped on the side, and pours himself some coffee. "Why are you always up so early?"

"I don't know. My internal clock refuses to give up being a New Yorker."

"Your internal clock is an idiot."

"I know." I laugh. "Nice robe, by the way."

He pours cream into his mug and slips the carton back into the refrigerator. The fridge in the apartment we shared in college was covered in pizza coupons and phone numbers; this one has a giant drawing of Big Bird and reminders about play dates.

Michael drops into the seat across from me and takes a sip of his coffee. "It was a gift from Steph for Father's Day."

"Well, congratulations. You're officially your dad."

Leaning over the table, Michael inhales the steam rising from his coffee. "I can't do smartass yet, Carter. My head is killing me and I'm still trying to figure out why I was wearing Steph's underwear when I woke up."

"Nope. No. No." I shake my head, hoping to dislodge this particular mental image before it burns itself into my brain.

Standing, I head for the ibuprofen I know is kept in the cupboard next to the sink—the medicine cabinet, they call it. It's filled with prescriptions and Band-Aids and every over-the-counter medication you could ever need. There's a bottle of iodine in there, for God's sake.

Adults have iodine. *My mom* has iodine. I'm twenty-eight years old and couldn't tell you with absolute certainty what a bottle of iodine is even *for.*

It's at these moments that I see the stark contrast between our lives. Michael and Steph have a three-bedroom house on a quiet residential street. They have a mailbox with *Evans* whimsically hand-painted across the side, and a growth chart on the back of a closet door. *They have a kid.* I have a small one-bedroom apartment and a cactus I'm proud to have kept alive for six months.

When did he move past me on the Adult Achievement Scale?

Maybe it was getting married or braving the real estate adventure that did it, or maybe it was becoming a dad. Either way, I could never ask, because as responsible as he and Steph have become, they both still consider themselves barely out of adolescence, and any mention to the contrary would lead to their insisting we crash a kegger or find the nearest rave. And I, ironically, am definitely too old for that.

With three brown Advil and a glass of water in hand, I return to the table and set it all in front of him.

He mumbles his thanks and takes both the drugs and the glass, draining the water in one long drink. "I am rough this morning."

"How are you surprised?" I sit back down. "You had Red Bull and three different types of marijuana products at your party. I haven't seen booze and weed in the same place since senior year."

He looks up, mildly offended. "It was a great party."

"It was, but it was also a costume party in late September."

"Halloween is a busy time for Morgan," he explains. "There are play dates and costume parades and fall carnivals to contend with. That kid is busier than I am. Steph and I had to move our party up."

I go quiet, hoping the echo of his words sinks in a bit, but he still seems to be falling in love with his coffee.

Finally, I break: "I think the female wearing the most actual clothing was your wife dressed as Miley Cyrus."

Michael Christopher gets a tiny glint in his eye. "I don't know about that. Evie seemed to be showing about as much skin as you were. You adorable Hogwartsers, you."

Here we go.

I bend, taking another sip of my coffee.

In my peripheral vision, I see him try to pull off a casual shrug. "Steph thought you guys might hit it off."

"I'm taking at least five of your remaining cool points for letting your wife set me up with someone."

"You didn't seem to mind last night."

I set down my cup and do my best to ignore the small surge in my pulse. It's true that I had more chemistry with Evie in the three hours we were together than I'd had with all my dates in the past year combined.

"I didn't mind, really," I tell him. "She's hot, she's funny, and that laugh? Amazing."

He pauses, and I feel him lean in a little across the table. "I'm about to do that thing where I get excited at the prospect of you hooking up with someone we know and us hanging out together as couples. I need a cool couple to hang out with, Carter. Everyone here wants to talk about how going gluten-free has changed their life, or how much they've put into their particular SEP IRA."

"Let's not get too far ahead of ourselves. I like her enough, but . . . come on." I lean my elbows on the table. "You live with Steph, you see the hours she works. Imagine Steph dating Steph. No way. It'd be a nightmare and we'd end up hating each other."

"Why does logic always have to crush all my dreams?" He takes a moment to look behind him to the open doorway before quietly adding, "Never tell my wife I suggested this, but you could just hook up? Have a little fun, see where it goes?"

"I don't know if that's a good idea. We traded numbers, at least." I stand to put my cup in the sink. "She was fun to talk to and the connection might come in handy at some point if I can move into features."

"This could still work out for me if one of you got fired," he says with a grin.

"Not exactly where I was going with that, but I like your twisted brand of optimism."

We look up at the same time at the sound of bass thumping and a car driving too fast down the quiet, sleeping street.

Michael stands and stares out the window overlooking the driveway. "Didn't you tell me Jonah drives a black Range Rover?"

"Jonah? As in *my brother* Jonah?" I ask, moving to join him.

Sure enough, we watch as a shiny black Range Rover makes a skidding turn into Michael Christopher's narrow driveway. The engine abruptly cuts off and the sudden silence makes my ears ring.

I'm already dreading this confrontation. I haven't seen or spoken to my younger brother in months. I have no idea what he's doing here now. We watch as the driver-side door opens and a pair of denim-clad legs emerge.

"Well, he looks . . . different," Michael says, brows raised.

"You haven't seen him since he was eighteen; of course he looks different." I push off the counter and head toward the front door.

In fact, most people we grew up with haven't seen Jonah since he left home right after graduation. He was the artsy kid, the one with the camera around his neck who took photos of power lines and brick walls and depressing candid shots of people who seemed incapable of smiling. It was one of these photos that won him a scholarship to some elite arts academy senior year, but while everyone else was making plans for college, Jonah took his camera and a duffel bag and moved to LA. Just like that. Once here, he got the right guy high at a party and was hired on the spot for a black-and-white candid shoot of one of rock and roll's biggest guitar legends. The musician died tragically only days later, and overnight Jonah went from starving artist to the cover photographer for a record-selling issue of *Rolling Stone* and the "it" boy, with more jobs and women and money than he knew what to do with.

My mom never stops talking about him.

It's strange to be the older brother and still feel like the one who's so far behind.

"I'm talking about the tattoos and the earrings," Michael is saying, following me down the hall. "He looks like the purposefully 'cool guy' from a boy band."

I fling open the front door just as Jonah begins stomping up the front steps. "Do you have any idea what time it is?" I whisper-yell, stepping out onto the porch and inwardly cringing because I sound exactly like our mother.

Jonah drops a cigarette onto Michael's porch, stubs it out with the pointy toe of a boot, and then has the nerve to seem confused. "Huh?"

"Steph and Morgan are in bed," I explain slowly. "It's Saturday morning in a quiet neighborhood." I take in his jeans and T-shirt, the black leather jacket and days' worth of stubble. "*Most people* are still in bed and you come tearing down the street like you've got your own personal house party going on in that thing."

"Okay, *Dad*." He shoulders past me into the house, giving Michael Christopher the once-over before laughing, a little unkindly. "So this is what married with kids looks like? *Rugged*."

Michael opens his mouth to reply before the insult seems to register and he gives Jonah a *what the fuck* face. Unfortunately, Jonah misses it because he's already moving past him toward the kitchen.

"Nice place."

I follow my brother and watch as he pours himself a cup of coffee. "Help yourself, Jones."

He turns, leaning back against the counter and lifting his cup to his lips. "Mom sent me about two hundred texts asking if I knew where you were." He sips, swallowing loudly. "Guess she doesn't know we've only seen each other once since you moved here."

"You've been home one time in four years," I remind him. "So spare me the family bonding lecture."

"Yes, I'm busy, but I'd make time for my family. Thank God Mom sent me this address or who knows how long before I found out you're basically homeless and sleeping on your college roommate's couch."

"Actually, we have a guest room," Michael Christopher offers unhelpfully.

"I'm not *homeless*, dumbass," I tell Jonah. "I just crashed here last night."

Michael claps us both on the shoulders with an awkward laugh. "Moving on: How's work, Jones? I saw that blurb about you in *People* last year. Fucking *People*. Amazing, man."

My brother pulls out a chair, turns it around, and straddles it. Like an asshole. "It was okay," he says. "Now *Vogue* . . . *that* was badass."

I study him for a few seconds. "Jones, you look like you haven't showered in a week."

He grins over the top of his mug. "Fucking crazy night."

Michael Christopher spins his own chair around and straddles it, just like Jonah. "We had a pretty crazy night ourselves, didn't we, Carter?"

"It was . . . pret-ty crazy," I agree, heavy on the sarcasm. They might have had Red Bull and pot, but there was also a sangria bar, a tampon bouquet in the bathroom, and a pumping room cordoned off for nursing mothers.

"Yeah, this place was off the *hook*," Michael says, undeterred. "Went pretty late, too. Well . . . I mean, it was over by eleven because Morgan gets cranky if she doesn't get enough sleep and a lot of the people here had sitters they had to get home to. But until then? *In-sane*."

Jonah nods like he can relate, and to his credit he doesn't give Michael a hard time.

"Carter even hit it off with someone," Michael says. I groan as soon as the words are out of his mouth.

"A girl?" Jonah grins.

I scowl at him. "A woman, yeah."

Jonah laughs into his coffee. "Sorry," he says. "I mean *woman*."

I give Michael a look that I hope is terrifying.

"What's her name, MC?" Jonah asks. "Do I know her?"

"No," I interject. Who knows if I'm right, but it's a desperate wish tossed out to the universe.

"Evie," MC says eagerly. "She's hot, smart, *great* body. She used to work with Steph over at Alter—"

I cut him off. "Michael. Zip it."

Jonah claps his hands together and I startle. "Man, Mom is going to *love* this."

"Don't talk to Mom about my dating life, and I won't mention to her the rotating buffet of barely-legals in your bed."

He counters my low blow with an even lower one. "You're right. I wouldn't want to get her hopes up. You remember how hard she took it when you screwed things up with Gwen."

I think I hear Michael Christopher wince from across the room.

"Oh my God," I groan, cupping my forehead.

Gwen Talbot was the first girl I fell in love with, and my mom adored her. Where most mothers might try to convince their twenty-four-year-old son he was too young to get serious, let alone engaged, I could practically see Mom naming her grandchildren whenever I brought Gwen home. But Gwen and I were never on the same page. She wanted a quiet life in Long Island with a house and kids. I was working for an agent and living in a crappy apartment in the city so I could go to every show and meet every influential person in theater. The pay was terrible and the hours were even worse, and we ended our engagement after a year. I don't think Mom has recovered.

Jonah loves to push this particular bruise and looks pleased as he sits there and continues to drink his coffee. I work on remembering why it'd be a bad idea to punch him in the throat. Jonah with his Range Rover and money and dragon tattoos. Jonah is an asshole.

"Gwen was a whore," MC finally says, breaking the loaded silence. "And I don't mean that in a loose-with-her-sexual-morals sort of way, because I totally approve of that and girls should be able to have sex with whomever they want and not be judged. Just, the way she acted when you guys ended things. What a dick."

I nod in thanks to Michael, because yeah, Gwen *was* a dick, and then I turn back to my brother. "Just keep your mouth closed. Seriously, why are you here?"

"Mom called a bunch of times and said you weren't answering your phone. Then she said to check in with MC because if you were dead in a ditch somewhere he'd probably know where."

"I . . . wait, what?" MC says, looking insulted.

Jonah drains his mug and stands, letting his chair slide nois-
ily against the floor. He leaves both the cup and the chair where
they are. "And since you're not, I can go. Later, big brother."

And like that he's gone.

● ● ●

As if she's been camped in the hall plotting an ambush, my assistant sees me the minute I step out of the elevator on Monday
morning.

"You're here!" she chirps.

"Becca, what are you doing? It's barely eight a.m."

Undeterred, she starts toward my office, notebook in hand,
and unless I plan on turning back into the elevator—which isn't
the worst idea I've ever had—there's really no choice but to follow.

"I wanted to make sure I caught you before anyone else did,"
she says over her shoulder. "One of Blake's clients has been asking
about you."

"Who?"

"Pretty One with Biceps."

Becca rarely calls anyone by their given name. In TV-
Literary, we represent an assortment of writers and creators, but
very few actors. Most of those land in features. Emil Shepard is
one of ours, however, and it takes a moment for me to process
what she's said. If Emil wants to move from Blake's client list to
mine, that would make him the third in the last two months
alone, and my first big actor.

Understatement: Blake isn't going to be happy about this.

"Emil was asking about *me*?"

"He called three times over the weekend," she says, tugging
on my arm to get me moving again.

"Does Blake know?"

Becca tears off a piece of paper covered in lines of almost indecipherable cursive and hands it to me. "I haven't heard any tables being flipped, so I'm assuming the answer is no. You need to call Emil this morning if you're interested, before anyone else catches wind of it. You know what a nightmare that kind of thing can be, and if Emil's moving, he's moving. You're not poaching."

Her reassurance is nice, but it's still a messy situation. I want to eventually move into features, but taking talent from colleagues isn't the ideal way to get there. I can't even think about what this could mean.

Becca rattles off my schedule: meetings at nine and nine thirty, another at ten over Skype, a staff meeting immediately after, and a possible new author over lunch. I'd always thought that if I had a type, Becca would be it. She's smart and sarcastic, with red hair and blue eyes and a body that's on the curvy side. We met by chance in a coffee shop one day right after I moved here, and I'd liked her immediately. In fact, I'd liked her so much I was about to ask her out when she exclaimed she was about to be late for a job interview. That interview, it turned out, was with me. I'm thankful every day that she glanced down at her watch *before* I asked her to dinner.

But despite our less-than-conventional beginning, things have never been weird between the two of us, or anything other than professional. Becca is amazing at her job, and in reality knows more about what goes on here than any of the partners do. Which also means she'd make a fantastic agent in her own right; she swears she doesn't have the particular muscle for it, though.

We've reached my office by the time she gets to the bottom of her very long list. "Carter?" she asks, noting that my attention has strayed to a spot in the distance. "Did you get all that?"

I glance back down and scan the paper in my hand, pointedly not looking at the piles of mail and various *Call me when you're in!* Post-its stuck to my computer monitor. "Most of it, I think," I tell her. "But it's possible I haven't had enough caffeine and I'm not functioning on all four cylinders yet. Give me an hour and check in again."

"I don't know what you did to deserve me," she says, stepping around my desk and lifting a steaming paper cup from just beside my keyboard.

"You are a goddess." The smell alone sets off some Pavlovian response and I already feel more alert. "I didn't leave myself enough time to grab another on my way in. I'm buying you lunch today."

She points to the twelve o'clock on my paper. "No, you'll be buying Alan Porter lunch. Possible new client. Remember?"

My posture slumps. "Right."

She grips me by the shoulders and leads me to my desk. "Today is packed, but you might as well get it over with." I drop into my chair and watch as she walks to the window and yanks open the blinds. "Happy Monday."

chapter three

"Evie, I need to see you for a minute."

I look up to see Brad's shadow already disappearing from my doorway.

"Sure thing," I say to my empty office, pushing back from my desk.

The sounds of phones and the clicking of keys greet me as I walk down the gray-carpeted hall. The layout is long and narrow, with smaller individual offices bordering the exterior walls, and larger offices or executives on each end. The assistants don't sit outside their particular agent's office, where it would be convenient to grab them should the need arise. No, they—along with the interns—sit in an inner ring of long tables creating a shared workspace. That way everything feels like a team effort, rather than individuals cast adrift without support. That's how *Brad* feels about the arrangement, at least. To everyone who actually has to work, it's a giant pain in the ass.

My relationship with Brad Kingman has always been delicate. For starters, though he didn't know me at the time, Brad was an agent at my first real, postcollege job, almost ten years ago. He wasn't always the nicest guy and had a reputation for some shady practices, including client poaching. Not illegal, but definitely not encouraged, either. He would keep track of actors just coming off a failure and quietly suggest to them that their agent should shoulder some of the blame, that more should have been done to protect the actor. He would find a client he was interested in representing and stop by a shoot while they were on set, explaining that he was there visiting another client and then acting surprised to hear that *their* agent had never been on set before. Brad was a master of planting seeds that in the end did most of the dirty work for him. He did this repeatedly on the set of a movie called *Uprising* and, funnily enough, ended up signing the lead actor a mere two months after shooting wrapped. Only one month after that, he was put in charge of Features at P&D.

While that's not how *I* do business—and I would never admit this to anyone—I did learn a few tricks from him, the most important of which is: don't forget for even one second that the moment you leave your house and step out in Hollywood, people are paying attention.

Brad only learned we had worked at the same agency years later, after I'd been hired at P&D. And I'm sure it's because he knows I would have heard a few inside stories—or learned a little too much about how he does things—that he keeps me close. Not as a confidante or friend, but close enough to hold under his thumb.

"Go on in," his assistant, Kylie, tells me.

Kylie seems smart and reasonably good at her job, plus she puts up with Brad all day, every day. Her bullshit tolerance must be off the chart.

Brad Kingman looks a little like the miracle baby produced by Hugh Jackman and Christopher Walken. Good skin, stark blue eyes, and severe bone structure. Sitting here in this office, surrounded by awards and celebrity photos and framed by a sweeping view of the Hollywood Hills, he's the portrait of success.

He reaches for a paper clip and his custom-tailored shirt stretches across the type of chest and arms you can only get from a lot of time at the gym. A green smoothie sits on the corner of his desk, and despite my annoyance at being here, I inwardly smile. That kale sludge is his version of junk food; no wonder he didn't notice the dog-food bar.

"Have a seat," he says, and I do, waiting while he takes the next few minutes to finish scribbling something in a black ledger before securing the entire booklet with a thick leather band. Not like he couldn't have done that *before* he called me in. "Listen, kiddo, I need you to throw in a team token."

I remind myself to count to three before I answer. *Team token* is one of my least favorite Bradisms. It's his stupid catchphrase for a favor. But if he makes it about being a team player, there's no way to pass without looking like the bad guy.

"For what?" I keep my expression neutral.

"I want you to give John a little help building his list back up."

I look up, confused. John Fineman is a very well-established colleague in Features. "Brad, he's been here longer than I have."

"I'm aware." Brad leans back in his chair. "But we all know he's lost two heavy hitters this year. Now he's in the middle of a divorce and a little distracted. Maybe throw him a pass once in a while. Something you hear, someone you have a hunch about. Keep him busy. Teamwork."

Keep him busy? A few years ago, John was paid the lion's share of a six-figure commission that I earned on my own, simply because the call was forwarded to his line when I was out of the office at a meeting. John called Kylie to let her know we'd signed the client on to the project, and she mistakenly started the paperwork assuming it was his.

He never corrected her.

When I raised hell, Brad's compromise was to give me a *little* more money in my bonus and a lecture about team tokens. And yes, John has lost two clients this year. But he lost them because he's a backstabbing jerk who got caught gossiping nastily about one client to another client, not because he's *a little distracted*. When I needed a few days to help my mom during Dad's knee surgery, Brad suggested I hand over some of my clients so I wouldn't feel "overwhelmed." He certainly wasn't offering to have someone assist me, not that I'd have accepted anyway.

"I'm fine helping if that's really what he needs," I start, tone cautious, "but—"

"Evie." Brad sighs, pushing away from his desk to stand with his back to the wall of spotless glass behind him. "You know I don't like to bring this up, but *you* needed a team around you when you dropped the ball on *Field Day*."

I stiffen. Here we go.

Field Day was one of the biggest box office flops of recent years, and I was the agent representing—and pushing for *huge* money for—the lead actor whose sign-on resulted in the entire project being greenlit. Think *Waterworld* and *Gigli* and you've got the right idea. It was so bad that both the film and my client won armloads of Razzies and became standard gossip rag fodder for the masses. I've actually heard someone use the phrase, "It totally *Field Day*'ed" as a metaphor when a film royally underperformed.

My in-house legacy, ladies and gents.

The worst part is that I was crushing it before that all happened. I was the top-performing agent at Alterman my last two years there, and I'm still in the top twenty percent at P&D. But with *Field Day*, my reputation—and confidence—took a major hit. I can't seem to shake the sense that it's the first thing everyone in the business thinks about when they meet me.

Brad seems to delight in the leverage it gives him postbomb. But, like any good underling, I never remind him how many times he praised the movie's potential as "like *Bull Durham* meets *Avengers*—sports hero gold."

As if on cue, Brad walks around his desk and props himself on the edge of it. "A bad decision like *Field Day* would've killed most agents, let alone one who hasn't proven herself yet. But did I let that happen?" he asks, pinning me with an expression that from an outsider's perspective would read a lot like genuine concern.

I swallow back a snide retort because he's right, Brad *did* come to my rescue. He stuck up for me when others thought I should be let go. But he'll never let me forget about it, either.

"No, you had my back," I say, not pointing out that I *had* proven myself by then. I'd been an agent nearly eight years at the time.

"That's right. Because your failures are *my* failures. And your wins . . . ?" He pauses, waiting expectantly.

"Are your wins," I finish for him.

"That's my girl." Those three words send a blazing shiver of rage down my spine, and he rounds the desk to sink back into his chair again. "Keep me updated and go ahead and close the door on your way out."

And I'm dismissed.

• • •

After my last meeting of the day, I hook up with Daryl and Amelia at Café Med for dinner. It has to still be at least seventy degrees where we sit on the patio, but Daryl is wrapped in a giant beige sweater and wearing sunglasses even though the sun set nearly an hour ago. Los Angeles, man.

Café Med is a cool little restaurant on Sunset Boulevard, which means it offers some of the best people-watching around. On the sidewalk just on the opposite side of the green railing, a woman walks by in a pair of three-inch platforms and a silk kimono. A car pulls up at the corner with an entire desert diorama built in its rear window. We're just as likely to see a celebrity walk by as we are to see a man in a tutu pushing a baby carriage full of aluminum cans.

"Heard you were in with Brad today," Amelia says to me, and then adds with a giant grin, "Bet that was fun!"

"He's always such a dick to you," Daryl says.

"I don't know," I hedge. "I think he probably has his own version of dick for everyone. He's smart. He knows all of our buttons."

We all look up as Steph dodges the hostess with a smile and jogs over to the table.

"Sorry I'm late." She hangs her purse on the back of the empty chair next to Daryl and takes a seat. "Longest client meeting ever."

"We haven't even ordered yet." I hand her a menu. "But wine is on the way."

"And the angels sing hallelujah," Steph mumbles, looking at the food options.

"Did you guys have a good time Friday night?" Daryl asks.

"I did," I say honestly.

"Does this mean I'm forgiven for missing it?" she asks.

Steph nods emphatically, but I pop a piece of bread in my mouth and tilt my head, chewing. "Still thinking about it."

Daryl pretends to take a bullet to the chest.

I open my mouth to tell both her and Amelia all about the party when I realize that if Steph is twenty-seven, and Mike is twenty-seven, and Carter is the same age they are . . . then Carter is six years younger than I am.

Six *years*.

As if she's read my mind, Steph puts her menu down and says, "Carter seemed to really like you."

I don't know why the age difference didn't occur to me at the party, but it seems to be a deal breaker, like a knee-jerk instinct. I've never really dated a significantly younger guy. And twenty-seven versus thirty-three feels pretty significant. We're not going to date, obviously, but if I happen to drop him a text and maybe think about him naked while doing so, does six years make me a cougar?

I thank the waiter when he puts my wine down in front of me, then turn to Steph. "Oyyyy, Steph. I just realized he's your age."

"Who's Carter?" Amelia asks. "I don't remember hearing anything about a Carter."

"He's a friend of Mike and Steph's," I tell them before sipping my wine. "He was fun. Daryl might know him, actually. He's in TV-Lit at CTM?"

"Carter Aaron? I've never worked with him but hear he's good."

"He is good," Steph says before looking back to me. "And 'fun'? He's *hot*, Evie. Carter is great-looking, and smart, and he's a genuinely good guy who might even be good enough for *you*."

I ignore this suggestion that I'm picky. "He's *young*," I say. "A fact you neglected to mention."

"He's twenty-eight!"

"*Oof*," I groan. Okay, so I'm only five years older than he is. "I was already in school when he was born."

"In *kindergarten*," Steph says.

"Those feel like important years." I remember being twenty-eight, and watching my guy friends then was like watching Muppets in adult male bodies try to navigate the world.

"Well, guys on the East Coast mature earlier," Steph reasons.

Amelia and I exchange a skeptical look. "Twenty-eight is everyone's fake age once they turn thirty," she says.

I nod. "And I'm three years *past* thirty."

"That just means you're in your sexual prime!" Daryl sings. "Come on, live a little." She does a little shimmy and leers in my direction, adding, "A younger guy."

I groan.

"Honestly, Evie," Steph says, "I feel like you're always looking for reasons why you can't date someone." These words seem to reverberate in my head, even as she continues, "He had fun. *You* had fun. Why not call him?"

"I do *not* look for reasons not to date someone." I frown, mildly offended.

"Actually," Daryl interjects, "you do. You're picky and impossible."

I give Daryl a dubious glance. "Says the *also*-single girl."

"Okay, now look." Amelia holds up her hand. "I get what you're saying about the age, but five years doesn't seem *that* bad. Would you give a second thought to dating a guy who was five years older than you are?"

"Stop being smart, Amelia," I mumble.

She laughs. "I think you should call him."

"Did you not hear the part where he's also an agent? A *younger* agent."

Amelia winces.

"This reminds me." Daryl finally slips off her sunglasses. "You never said what Brad wanted to talk to you about."

"Oh, he wants me to help John Fineman, to make sure he stays *busy*." I laugh. "In what universe does that make sense? John's the one who showed me around when I started at P&D."

I look out to the patio area, just to be sure nobody we know is around, then turn back to the girls. "You know when someone's up to something, but they're questioning everything everyone *else* is doing? That's how I feel about Brad lately."

"Like when someone's having an affair and suddenly suspicious of what their partner is doing," Daryl says, nodding.

"Maybe." I shrug. "Something's definitely up."

"I know he's been having a lot of earnings reports sent to his office," Amelia adds. "I don't know what it means, but it's unusual enough that some of the girls in Finance had to scramble."

"Why does that make me a little uneasy?" I ask, and reach for my glass. "I just don't trust Brad."

"See, this is exactly why you should call Carter," Steph says. "Stress relief via orgasms."

My friends are no help at all.

chapter four

carter

MC and I are the only people who are genuinely happy that I live in LA now. My brother, obviously, could not care less, and my parents . . . well, even two years on they're just to the left of violently opposed. It's fine for Jonah to live in Malibu because Jonah is young and chasing a dream and can do no wrong. But Carter moving to Beverly Hills? *Hellfire.*

I call my parents Monday night to verify for them that I'm not dead in a ditch somewhere.

"Well good," Dad says. "But you should go see your brother more. He's lonely."

"Jonah?" I laugh, flipping my grilled cheese in the pan. "Trust me, he's not."

"Go see him," Mom needles from the other extension. "He's just next door."

"Mom, he's in Malibu. It's like an hour away."

Dad coughs. "It's an hour from here to Brooklyn, but we make it to see your aunts every weekend, and you know what they have in Brooklyn? *Sweaters on trees*, Carter. I saw someone walking a goddamn peacock the last time I was there, and when I stopped for coffee? This weird little hipster place sold yarn, too. Coffee and yarn. Who the hell puts those things together?"

"Okay, so I'll put you in the *no* column for Thanksgiving in LA," I say, sliding my sandwich onto a plate. There are weirder things in LA than coffee and yarn.

There's a heavy, meaningful pause before Mom speaks next. "Jonah said you were sleeping at Michael Christopher's because you didn't have a place to live."

I rub my temples. Of course he did. "Jonah is a liar."

"You be nice," she chastises. "He also said you met a girl."

Taking a bite of my sandwich, I chew and swallow to give myself time to hide my irritation with my brother. "She's a friend of a friend, Mom. I met her at a party."

"You met this woman at a *party?*"

"A costume party, not a rave," I say. "She's a friend of Michael and Stephanie's, so I'm assuming she's not a Hollywood madam."

"You're making that assumption based on *Michael* liking her?" Mom asks.

This makes me laugh. "We spent a grand total of three hours together. It's not a thing. And I promise, she's okay."

"She lives in *Los Angeles*, Carter," Mom growls. "That's not okay with *me*. I don't understand why you couldn't find someone here. She's probably got fake boobs and that—that—poison they put inside their foreheads."

"Botox?" I guess.

"*That.*"

"All right, let's take it down a notch," I say. "Jonah lives in LA and I don't recall you ever giving him this much shit."

"One, watch your mouth. And two, I barely see your brother, so don't use him as a shining example." She sighs into the line. "Jonah has always been a dreamer. You're my responsible one. Call him."

"Okay, Mom. It might take some time to get our schedules worked out, but I'll call him."

"That's my sweet boy."

• • •

In this business, not hearing back from someone for seven days is nothing. We're all busy, with stacks of scripts and books and audition footage to go through, phone calls to return, and emails to read. Callbacks get shuffled around and ranked in order of priority.

A week is nothing.

I gently remind clients of this truth on a daily basis. I remind them that no news is good news. No news means they haven't heard *no*. But when it's your dream on the line, time takes on an entirely different meaning, and even the most patient person can lose it.

"But wouldn't they know right away if they loved it?"

"If they wanted me they'd have called by now, right?"

Being patient is a lot easier said than done. I should know, because despite what I told Michael Christopher about not getting involved with Evie, I haven't been able to stop thinking about her. By the time Thursday afternoon rolls around and I haven't heard from her, I'm devolving into a hot mess.

I think about what I said when I gave her my number Friday night: *"I know what we said about dating someone in this business, but I could really use more evil friends. The ball's in your court, and if you want to smack-talk our bosses or coworkers a little bit, or even just hang out and plot world domination with zero romantic expectations, you have my number."*

She'd laughed, ruffled my hair a little longer than was probably platonically appropriate, and then left.

What I *should* have said was "*I really like you. Could we exchange numbers and make plans to see each other naked?*"

My phone rings and I jump to answer, snatching it from where it vibrates across a stack of files.

"Hello?" I'm breathless.

"Hey." It's Michael Christopher. "How's your day?"

Standing, I walk around the side of my desk and push the door closed with my foot. "Pretty good. I haven't heard from her, in case that's why you're calling. Again."

He pauses. "Did you have that tie on Friday night?"

I drop back into my chair and grin. "Which tie would that be?"

"You *know* which tie. The crime against humanity."

I look down at my shirt and smooth the very same tie over my chest. He knows me pretty well, apparently. "Yes," I tell him. "This tie is my good luck charm. Bonus points for being Harry Potter appropriate."

He groans. "You're wearing it today, aren't you? It's so bad, Carter."

"Evie wouldn't not call because of a *tie*."

"Look, I'm a dude, and Stephanie still has to convince me that I can't wear sweatpants when we meet friends for dinner, so I'm not casting any stones here. But even *I*—a slovenly wreck of a man—know that that thing should be shot and put out of its misery. I feel like I'm being visually assaulted whenever you have it on."

"But not to be dramatic?" A cup of paper clips sits next to my monitor and I reach for one, absently straightening the end.

"I'm not saying it'd be the tie's fault," he continues. "What I am saying is that you should not be wearing something you wore while attending a sophomore-year Mathletes competition, Carter."

"*Winning* a Mathletes competition," I correct, tossing the paper clip in the direction of the trash can and raising my arm in victory when it hits the rim and falls inside. "Winning, not just attending. And for your information, I wore that same tie the day I had my scholarship interview, the day I took the SAT, and the night I got lucky with Samantha Rigby at freshman rush. Quality items get better with age, and that tie is one of them."

"You are the most superstitious person I know," he says.

"I'm a complicated man," I tell him. "But you're getting a little overly involved in this, I think. Did you really call just to hassle me?"

"That part was a bonus. I was sitting here at work, making plans with Steph for the weekend, when I realized the weekend means it's been almost a week and we aren't double-dating yet. Then I started thinking about that tie . . ."

I flip a pencil along my knuckles. "Michael."

"You know I'm just yanking your chain. You're my favorite third wheel."

"Very funny." My phone vibrates against my ear with an incoming text. My mom has called twice since we last spoke—to ask if I've reached out to Jonah yet, I'm sure—but I haven't called her back either time. It's terrible, I know this, and I know that if she's texting me right now, I have two choices: man up and call my brother, or learn how to make my own lasagna when I visit. I *really* don't want to do that because Mom is the best cook on the planet.

I pull the phone away to check, but it's not my mom's name on the screen. It's Evie's, and she's texted me a few times already.

"I need to call you back," I tell Michael, and quickly end the call.

Hi stranger.

Not to be a total creeper but, do you
know an agent named Elsa Tippett?

She's interviewing here.

We're having drinks tonight and Steph
mentioned she used to work with you.

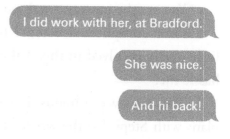

I did work with her, at Bradford.

She was nice.

And hi back!

A few minutes pass and I wonder if that's it, if that's all she had to say.

Elsa worked at Bradford for four years, overlapping with me for three of them before I moved to LA. Some of the grosser men called her the Bone Collector for her propensity to sleep around the office. For the record: I never slept with Elsa, nor did I ever call her by that name. But the idea of her and Evie talking about me makes a nauseating hum take up residence in my blood.

I turn back to the open script on my desk. I read. I check my phone. Nothing. Another minute ticks by. I'm halfway down the page and have no idea what any of it said. I glance at my phone again.

Should I elaborate on my connection to Elsa? Say something else?

Probably yes.

Should I ask her out? *Think, Carter.*

My phone buzzes again.

I emailed confirming tonight
and happened to mention your name.

Apparently she has a few Carter Aaron stories . . .

Oh Jesus.

/is intrigued

I have no Elsa stories. Others, however . . .

Heading out. I'll report back later.

An hour goes by with nothing from Evie, and I've just forgotten about it when her name pops up again on my phone.

Oh boy. Elsa LOVES you.

Oh, God.

This is like meeting a
Penthouse letter in person.

She joined the firm about a year after I did.

She may have . . . known some of the
men there. I am not one of those men.

Ugh I feel faintly queasy imagining what
yarns she is currently spinning.

Five minutes go by, then ten. Nothing. Crap.

Evil?

I'm watching TV almost two hours later when I finally get a response.

Okay drinks are over.

And yes her stories were really oversold.

Also lol @ Evil

Told you.

And my phone autocompletes it.

It's like it knows.

I was hoping for some dirt.

Apparently you're sweet, sexy and responsible.

Snore.

I want to point out you called me sexy.

Do you want to grab dinner next week?

Yes. Yes I do.

So of course I immediately text Michael Christopher.

ALL HAIL THE LUCKY TIE

No.

Yes.

NO!

YES!

We're having dinner.

YES

I'M GOING STREAKING

Noooooooooooooooooo

chapter five

"Are you nervous?"

I look up at Daryl from where I'm currently curled in half in the leg-press machine. "For what?" My eyes go wide in fear. "Are you adding more weight?"

She stares at me, unblinking, and then looks across the gym with a pointed sigh.

"Oh. Because of Carter?"

"Yes, because of Carter," she says, and follows it with this deep little growl. "I can't believe you have me sucked into this soap opera. I'm basically wandering the social Sahara by myself, but I could probably recite *your* text messages from memory. What am I doing with my life?"

"Sorry, I've been trying not to think about it," I say. "Like, if I pretend I'm hanging out with any old agent buddy it won't be as big a deal."

"I still can't believe you asked him out." She takes a drink from her water bottle. "You're usually so good about sticking to your guns, but you folded. You're so going to bang him."

I cover my ears. Don't get me wrong, I do want to bang him, but Carter and I have been texting back and forth over the last week, and with each exchange I actually *like* him just a little more. And this is why the nerves are really starting to sink in. It's all well and good to have this flirtation when he's on the other end of a screen. It's harder to mess up when I have minutes to craft perfect witty responses. But face-to-face I'm likely to mess it up somehow, right?

As much as I try to avoid this way of thinking, it's hard not to be cynical. Like every single woman my age, I've been fixed up, from the bar scene to the book club and everything in between; had plenty of spectacularly bad one-night stands; and test-driven my fair share of dating sites. Personally, I'd rather die alone in a house full of cats in tiny matching sweaters than ever attempt any of it again.

I try to ignore the pressure to be coupled up, but it's everywhere. Romance is the subject of movies and books and practically every song on the radio. There's my own biological clock, quietly yet persistently ticking away. My parents—who had me later in life—are nearing their seventies. They've long since retired from their own Hollywood careers, and when they aren't gardening or grooming their shih tzu, they're asking me about my dating life.

But of course there's that niggling voice suggesting I not care about any of it, that maybe I should give in and buy the cats instead. The problem is that I don't like them. I may be a terrible married person someday, but I know for sure I would be an even worse cat lady.

"Evie?"

"Sorry," I say, exhaling as I push the weight up, extending my legs. "I was just trying to figure out whether I could still be a crazy cat lady without the actual animals."

"Don't be weird," Daryl says. Helping me up, she reminds me, "It's just a date. If you hit it off, you tell me every filthy detail tomorrow. If it sucks, you go home and we plan how we're finally going to give up on this whole dating thing and just marry each other for the tax breaks."

"It'll be fine." I inhale, watching as she takes my place on the bench. "Anyway, how's your new assistant?"

Daryl lets out a loud laugh, looking up at me as she moves through her reps. "Eric? Let's just say I probably do more of his work than he does."

"Oh, no."

On top of all the other weirdness at work right now, Daryl's boss called her into his office on Monday to inform her that she's got a new assistant on her desk: Brad Kingman's nephew. Recently injured UCLA quarterback Eric Kingman is six foot three, gorgeous, and not the sharpest tool in the shed. It took him two days to realize that the people calling his desk and asking for Daryl did not, in fact, have the wrong number.

A little smile plucks at me. "It's not getting any better then?"

"I wouldn't say that, exactly." She sits up, shrugging as she stands from the machine. "The dryer in his apartment complex overheated and all his shirts shrank. So at least the view from my office door has greatly improved."

I grin as we both move to the treadmills. My assistant, Jess, is a godsend, and I would cut down anyone who tried to take her. "Hot or not, I'm not trading you."

Daryl shrugs. "He's sweet and makes me laugh, but come staffing season I will burn the place to the ground if he still hasn't learned how to answer a damn email."

I'm sure Daryl will be fine—she runs with the upper middle of the pack performance-wise, but she's undoubtedly beautiful, and charming enough that any agency would want to keep her around.

"You're so good at this, Evie," she says. "You're so good at handling the stress and the personalities." Blowing her cheeks out, Daryl releases a long breath. "Eric is probably never going to remember everything we went over this week. Hopefully Brad will eventually figure out that this isn't the kid for the job."

And *I* just hope Daryl isn't blamed when Eric messes something up. Because it's true that there are a million little things to remember, and when you try to make your brain roll through them like a list, they feel overwhelming. On top of that, the P&D organization itself seems to be made up of a constellation of eccentricities. Of tiny, nitpicky, really irritating eccentricities.

Like the way the legal department won't read emails or contracts that aren't in one of two specific fonts.

Or John Fineman's odd—and dramatic—disdain for scripts with female characters named Maria.

And the fact that Brad once outright fired an assistant whose heels clicked too loudly on the marble floors near the elevators.

Being an agent is about a lot of things—balancing egos, co-ordinating projects, managing expectations, and above all, making money—but one thing it is never about is how something makes us feel.

And as Daryl and I each retreat into our own heads and I put on my headphones, something slowly dawns on me. Perhaps one of the reasons I'm not in a relationship is that I live all of my life precisely like that: assuming that nothing is ever about how I feel.

•   •   •

Carter and I are meeting at Eveleigh, a rustic farm-to-table joint on Sunset in West Hollywood. It's perfectly situated between our two offices, as though we might simply leave work and stroll down the road for dinner. And although our texts have grown increasingly flirty, I wish it had occurred to me sooner that this might *really* just be a casual work-buddy dinner, because I have very clearly not come straight from work. Do I look too eager? Too high maintenance? I'm already concocting a credible explanation for why I might have worn a strapless black jersey dress and gold sandals to work, but when I hand my keys to the valet and look up under the vine-wrapped awning, I see Carter there, right in front of me in a dress shirt and freshly pressed trousers. He looks too crisp; there's no way he's just come from work, either.

In the time since I saw him last, I think I'd somehow convinced myself that he couldn't be as cute as I remembered. Which would be fine because I like his personality a lot. But he *is* that cute; he's even better-looking than I remembered, with dark shaggy hair and a sharp jaw, and this sweetly earnest gaze behind his glasses. And when he smiles, charisma just pours out of him and onto the sidewalk.

"Hey, Evil," he says, walking toward me.

It doesn't feel weird to reach up and hug him.

He wraps his arms all the way around me, and I shiver a little when I feel the solidness of his body against mine.

"It's so good to see you."

Don't think dirty thoughts. Don't think dirty thoughts. "You too," I say.

The embrace lingers, like we're old friends seeing each other after a long separation. It isn't weird, though—it's easy, just like before.

I know relationships are work. My mom reminds me of this all the time, and of the balance it takes for two people to combine their lives into one. But I've always felt like it shouldn't be work right away. Over time, yeah, I can see some effort needing to come into play when the honeymoon phase wears off and you can finally admit to yourself that it's really irritating when they leave their socks on the couch or how they slurp their milk while eating cereal. But initially, being with someone should feel like the best and most natural thing in the world.

I've never really felt that chemistry before, but I definitely feel it with Carter. My blood hums just being near him, and I can't stop grinning. He smells amazing and holds me so tight, squeezing a little more just before letting go.

Straightening, he gazes down at my face. "I think I forgot how pretty you are."

"Me too."

Wait, what did I just say?

"Aww," he says, laughing. "I like being called pretty."

Linking his fingers with mine, he turns and we check in at the hostess stand. His hand is big and secure—like a clamp around mine—and I can't stop focusing on the way it feels. So not a buddy dinner then.

Hand-holding might seem like a simple, innocent way to signify closeness and attraction, but my hand in Carter's feels anything but simple.

They say we have more nerve endings in our fingertips than we do in our lips, and as we snake our way through the dining area and to our table I swear I feel every millimeter of contact between us. When he lets go so we can sit, my entire body feels cold.

He swallows, and I'm mesmerized by his neck and the bobbing of his Adam's apple, the way his smile slowly creeps in from the side of his mouth.

"You're quiet," he says.

"I'm really glad to be here." It's not like me to be so forthcoming, but I can't help myself. My filter seems to have malfunctioned on the walk from the front of the restaurant to my chair.

"Me too," he says, and then turns his attention to the incoming waiter, who tells us the specials and takes our drink orders.

"I'll have a Red Bull and vodka," Carter says, and I snort. When the waiter makes a slight face but starts to write it down, Carter stops him. "Not really. Sorry. I'm kidding. Inside joke. Bad joke. I'll have whatever IPA you have on tap."

The waiter is unamused. "Stone or Lagunitas?"

"Lagunitas." Carter's tongue peeks out, touching his lower lip.

I can't stop looking at him.

The waiter turns to me.

"I'll have a glass of the Preston Barbera."

When the waiter leaves, Carter leans an elbow on the table. "You give good shoulder."

"I . . . what?"

He nods to my dress. "Your dress. Your shoulders." Clearing his throat, he adds quietly, "You just . . . look amazing."

I whisper, "Thanks," and take a long drink of ice water to cool down the boiling just beneath the surface of my skin. "So, what's the latest in Carterland?"

He grins at my subject change. "Work. Dodging calls from my parents. Texting a cute agent down the road. You know."

I blush, deflecting, "You're dodging your parents?"

"They want me to make more of an effort with my brother, but really it's just their continued disapproval that I moved here in the first place."

"Oh, no."

He waves this off. "Mom is positive I'm going to end up homeless and buying crystal meth from a guy living in a box on

Skid Row. I tried to tell her my apartment has a doorman and I don't even know where Skid Row is, but she remains unconvinced."

The waiter brings our drinks, bread, and a tiny notepad ready for our orders.

"My parents are both in Burbank now," I tell Carter once the waiter leaves again, "so I see them a few times a month, but I can imagine how much my mom would worry if I lived across the country."

"Yes, but my brother moved here when he was eighteen, and there was little to no meltdown."

I tear off a piece of bread. "I don't think I knew that."

"Jonah," he explains over his glass, "took his camera and his clothes and left. He went to a party one of his first weekends in town and ended up taking some photos that were featured in *Rolling Stone*."

"You're kidding me."

"Nope. From there it was *Elle*, then *People*. For some reason my parents think lightning only strikes once and I am destined to flop."

I want to remind him that all parents worry their children will struggle and that if there was ever a place where that happened a lot, it's Hollywood, but my mind snags on something he's said.

"Wait, is your brother Jonah Aaron?"

"He . . . is." His eyes go wide, his hand frozen where it was lifting a piece of bread to his lips. "Please tell me you haven't slept with him."

I cough out a laugh. "That would be a no. But for some reason I think my friend Amelia has." I take a sip of wine, thinking. "I think she met him at a *Vanity Fair* party or something."

Carter gives me a rueful half smile. "Maybe I should find her and apologize on behalf of my family." When I laugh again he seems to realize what he's said. "I mean no," he corrects, brows furrowed. "Sex with the Aaron men is prime. Best sex of your life. I should clarify that . . . Let's move on. Work is good?"

A laugh trips out of me, and I press my napkin to my lips. "It's really good. I'm putting together a package right now and it could be pretty big." There's something about Carter that diffuses my usual instinct to keep everything close, and it's a struggle to not spill every detail.

But if he notices how I've reeled myself in, he's polite enough not to let on, and instead knocks on the top of the table.

"Superstitious?" I ask, but he's kept from answering as the waiter arrives with our entrées.

Carter washes his first bite of steak down with his beer and then sets the glass back on the table. "In answer to your question, I would never say that I'm superstitious, because that would be bad luck. But it has been suggested to be one of my less charming traits."

I grin up at him, spearing a piece of broccoli.

"Mostly, I consider them *quirks*," he says. "It's possible I have a lucky tie. The old knock-on-wood one is a favorite. I throw spilled salt over my left shoulder. I've been known to frequent wishing wells, and I have to let the phone ring twice before answering."

"Those are so adorably minor," I say.

"You have some better ones?"

"I'm sure my friends would tell you I am quirks galore."

Carter leans back in his chair and motions for me to proceed.

"I've already illustrated my knack for recalling random movie details."

"I don't know if that counts—maybe more of an asset, considering your line of work. I'm going to need a bit quirkier from you, Evil."

I smile. "I can't eat at buffets—a snag when so many catered events are the serve-yourself variety. It's like I see that innocent serving spoon and all I can think about is how many unwashed hands have touched it. I always watch the twenty-four-hour *Christmas Story* marathon, and I'm an obsessive hand-creamer."

He stops with his fork halfway to his mouth. "That can't possibly mean what just popped into my head."

I move to gently kick him, but he traps my foot, keeping it there between his shoes.

"It means that when I'm on a call or sitting at my desk thinking about something, I tend to reach for my lotion, sort of instinctively. The longer the call, the more lotion I'll use, and by the end I can barely grip my phone."

"Okay, that's pretty great." Carter rubs his palms together, thinking. "I'm going to give you another one of mine so you don't feel all insecure about your germ phobia or cream-filled hands: I can barely inhale before I've had coffee. I know people say that all the time, but in my case I almost feel like it's a medical condition. I've brushed my teeth with shaving cream on more than one occasion and once relieved myself in my mom's favorite potted palm."

"I'm not sure you should share that last part," I whisper.

Carter wipes his mouth and sets his napkin on the table in front of him. "You've got a very mischievous smile there, Evil."

I point to my chest. "Me? You should see yours."

He leans forward. "It's because I like being around you. It's like the same buzzy feeling I get when one of my clients posts a grammatically correct tweet."

This makes me laugh because I can absolutely relate. "That's pretty buzzy."

He pulls his lower lip into his mouth and sucks it, watching me.

I don't remember Carter being this overwhelmingly sexual when we first met. Maybe it was because I wasn't showing shoulder, or because we were both dressed as preteens, but it's definitely overwhelming right now.

Carter sips his beer, looking out through the foliage of the indoor-outdoor space to the sidewalk. It's a busy neighborhood anytime, but it's cooled down a bit tonight and the streets seem full of people out walking, headed somewhere, headed nowhere.

"It's so warm here in the fall," he says, tilting his glass up to his mouth again. I watch him swallow, feeling this tight, creeping anxiety, because dammit, I like him. "It surprises me every time."

I might *really* like him.

"Our summer always comes late," I say. "June and July are pretty nice. The summer really hits in August through October."

He turns back to me and smiles. "I wonder if I'll ever get used to it."

"Was it a hard decision to leave New York?"

He shakes his head. "Not really. I'd thought about it for a few years, but always hesitated because it sort of felt like Jonah's territory."

"I could see that, I guess."

"But as my career progressed, LA became an obvious option." He spins his spoon on the table, absently staring down at it. "There's only so much for talent agents in New York—theater is huge, obviously, but . . . I don't know . . ." Taking a deep breath, he seems to grow more contemplative, until he exhales and turns his face up to me, smiling again. "I needed to do something different. I like TV-Lit but would like to be more film-based. Baby steps."

The degree to which he's genuine throws me again and again. Everything about him seems so up front and frank, but there's a complexity, too. No wonder he's good at this job.

"Have you ever considered leaving California?" he asks.

"Not really," I admit, scrunching my nose. "I'm too much of a movie fanatic to give it up."

"Where did you grow up?"

I hook my thumb behind me, as if he can see it from here. "Not LA proper. In San Dimas."

"Bill and Ted's!" he sings.

"That's what everyone says," I tell him, laughing. "And yes. It's a pretty small town. I was *such* a nerd in high school."

He gives a skeptical snort.

"Honestly," I assure him, "I was."

"You couldn't have been as nerdy as I was: the founder of my school's *Magic: The Gathering* club."

Nodding, I tell him, "I was president and sole member of the anime club at my school before anyone else liked it."

"Anime is cool."

"It wasn't then, trust me."

Carter leans in, clearly ready to bring out his big guns. "I didn't get a date in high school until senior year because I liked show tunes and the girls assumed I was gay. No guys asked me out, either, because they assumed I was stuck-up, not straight."

"My first concert was Hanson." I pause, watching him. "My worst fear is someone posting a video of me in isolation rocking my face off the entire time."

"Are you trying to scare me away?" He pulls out his phone

and spends about thirty seconds scrolling until he turns it for me to see. "Look at this mess."

Carter is probably fourteen in the picture. His nose is too big for his face. His hair looks like it was cut by a distracted parent. He's laughing, and his mouth seems completely filled with metal.

"I can top that." I pull out my phone and open it to my mother's Facebook page, easily finding her Throwback Thursday post to my tenth-grade school picture. This was before my Lasik, so I have glasses thicker than an ashtray and am wearing a tie because I was trying to pull off some ill-advised skater chic.

Carter's eyes narrow and he leans in to look closer. "What are you talking about, Evie? You're pretty here."

Wow. He is blind. "Carter."

"What?"

He looks up and something—no, everything—in me melts. When he blinks, the soft expression doesn't dissolve; it stays there, stronger now as he lets his gaze move across my face and to my mouth.

"What?" he says again, smiling now. "You know I'm hoping to kiss you later, no matter how many dorky pictures you show me."

My heart takes off, a beating drum in the wild jungle beneath my ribs. "I'm older than you," I blurt.

He just shrugs, like this was a completely normal thing to say. "So?"

"We're in the same business."

I watch him process this for a breath, and he chews on his lip before saying, "Maybe it's not ideal, but it's not worth staying away from you because of it."

My heart seems intent on climbing up into my throat. "I'm notoriously married to my job."

"That's super convenient because so am I. It'll be like we're cheating on our jobs with *each other*." He says this as if he's just discovered some brilliant loophole.

I'm aware of how I'm perched on my chair, and of the woman at the table next to us watching us without any subtlety. I'm aware of the car alarm going off somewhere down the street and the waiter clearing plates at the table behind me. I have the sense that Carter can see me reacting to all of these things but isn't fazed by it in the slightest.

"I'm pretty bad at this," I admit. "But I have a great romance backup plan that includes a pack of small animals in sweaters, with me as their leader."

His smile is warm and slow, and when it reaches his eyes, something inside my chest turns over in defeat. "That could be cool, too."

In the silence that follows, it seems like an enormous hole opens up in front of me and I decide to jump straight in. "Do you want to come back to my place after this?"

This surprises him, and his eyes widen slightly behind his glasses. "Yes."

•   •   •

Because it's Southern California and everyone drives everywhere—alone in their own car—Carter follows me back to my place. My building is in Beverly Grove, just southeast of Santa Monica Boulevard; the area has sprawling houses and wide lawns interspersed with larger remodeled art deco apartment buildings. LA is like that: suburb and city all swirled together.

I meet him at the front entrance and try to smile like this is no big deal, but it's an *enormous* deal. The last guy I had at my place was my dad. Before that, it was Mike when he came for dinner with Steph. Before that, I can hardly remember. Probably the cable guy.

I can tell we're both unsure what to say, and the energy between us buzzes. He has this sexual charisma that I'm not convinced I can handle. I can't stop replaying our hug at the front of the restaurant and how he felt against me, all long bones and firm muscle.

I'm sort of relieved that Carter isn't one for small talk in situations like this. Are we going to have sex? I *feel* like sex is imminent but would rather shove a hot poker in my ear than trust my instincts on this right now.

He could ask me about the weather, or about traffic, or earthquake statistics, or any number of the obvious California topics, but he just follows me into my place and pauses in the living room, looking around.

It's a nice place, and I'm proud of it, even though I'm hardly ever home for more than sleeping. The building is modern, and my apartment is an open floor plan that includes a large main room with living room, kitchen, and small nook by the window, where I have a table. There's a vase of flowers on top, and everything smells subtly of the peppermint candle near the stove. I can even see Carter's eyes widen at the enormous flat-screen I inherited from my dad when he upgraded to the obscene flat-screen.

"The guy across the alley is a juggler," I say, motioning to the window. "Apparently it's a clothing-optional hobby. I'm not going to lie: it's pretty great."

"I was already going to say this place was cool, but that might earn an upgrade to amazing," he says. "I can promise you that none of the apartments I looked at came with a naked juggler."

"It's usually in the morning . . ." The implication of my words—*sleepover!*—lingers between us as he steps closer, clearly moving past the Exploring Evie's Apartment phase of the evening and into just Exploring Evie.

Carter is only a step away from me and his hand comes out, curling around my hip. A few beats of silence pass.

"Are you thirsty?" I ask, jittery.

Traffic on the street blares past, and a dog barks obnoxiously in the building next door.

Carter shakes his head. "No, I'm okay."

"Okay." I chew my lip. "Hungry? Or need to use the restroom?"

He laughs. "No."

My hand is shaking when I take his and lead him down the hall.

"Evie?" He hooks his thumb back over his shoulder. "We can stay out here . . ."

I shake my head, and he follows me wordlessly down the hall into my bedroom.

He pulls up short just inside the door. "It's just that . . . I don't think we should . . ." He glances to the bed and then back to me. "Yet."

"That's okay," I agree in a nervous whisper. "I just want to be in here. My parents gave me all the furniture in the living room, and I don't want to be thinking about this the next time they're over here sitting on their old couch."

His eyes crinkle behind his glasses when he smiles at this. "You're a trip."

He says it like it's a good thing. Like it's a *great* thing. In my room we stare at each other for a few seconds. I keep waiting for the weirdness to descend, but it doesn't.

Carter lifts his hands, cups my face, and smiles at me.

Oh God, my heart is going to jackhammer its way out of my chest. I am definitely not planning a wedding to Daryl tonight.

"You okay?" he whispers, just an inch away from kissing me.

"Yeah."

He leans in, putting his lips against mine.

I can't—I honestly can't describe the way it feels to kiss him. I marvel at the smooth firmness of his lips and the contrasting sharp stubble on his upper lip and chin. I imagine it scraping the skin of my neck and down, down. I marvel at his hands, holding me right up against him, sliding around my back.

A current runs through me when his tongue touches mine; it's even stronger when he makes a quiet little groan and slides one hand down over my ass. I feel like a teenager the way I'm unable to get enough of his mouth, and just come at it from every angle, needing every kind of kiss he has: bigger and smaller, deeper and just these tiny little kisses like raindrops.

I feel like I've been kissing him forever, and also like I've never really been kissed before tonight. He's taller than me and I'm on my toes, stretching to get closer, like I need him inside me however I can.

Gently, his hands slide to my hips, guiding me back toward the bed and down.

He follows, helping us both toward the pillows, and I haven't felt this hunger in so long. The consuming kind of *want*, where kissing like this is nearly overstimulating but my body keeps pushing for more and more.

Carter is over me, and we're moving together and I feel him, hard between my legs. His bare hand cups the back of my bare leg and I bring my knee toward my chest, opening myself, wanting him closer. He lets out this small grunt before telling me we seem to be really good at this.

The way he moves, rocking just right against me, I know I'm already close because, God, it's been so long and it's so so good. We *are* good at this. And if almost-sex with our clothes on has me on the edge already, how would I survive naked Carter, Carter that has access to every part of me? I can feel that tension and warmth just there, but he pulls away. I start to tell him to come back, reaching for his hips, but his hand is there, warm and steady, up my leg, down inside my underwear, and he groans into a kiss when he feels me, slippery under his fingers.

I feel frantic, like I've been twisted in a wringer, and I have to clench my teeth so I don't cry out.

Instead, a shaky whine escapes, and it makes his breath catch. He pulls back to look at my face.

"You're wound so tight," he whispers before bending to kiss my neck. "How do I make you unravel?"

His hand is moving and his mouth slides from my neck to my jaw, and even when I arch away, eyes closed, I feel him follow me, his lips chasing my skin, telling me to come here, kiss him, tell him what I like. When I open my eyes, he's still watching me. He smiles, leaning in to kiss me again.

"This okay?" he says, eyes clear and earnest.

I nod. Relief is like a drug, warm, rushing through my limbs. *We're doing this.*

I work at his belt clumsily, no longer concerned with when and where we have sex, and his laugh is a tiny warm burst of air against my lips. I get that he's not laughing at me, he's laughing at *this*, at the frantic, fumbling *groping*.

I smooth my palm down his stomach and gasp at the feel of

him, the thrill of making him hard like this, the rush from the power of it. He moves into my touch and I slide my leg over his hip and like this we shift together, letting our hips do the work, letting our mouths move in this easy, hungry tandem.

I've forgotten the fevered powerlessness of letting someone else touch me, the desperate hope that they'll get me there. But very soon I realize that he will, and he does, his hand steady against me. I try to keep my eyes open as it builds, but he watches me with such a singular intensity that I close them so it's just the sensation of his fingers on my clit and his cock in my hand . . . and I dissolve.

His sounds propel me on, quiet grunts, and he's moving faster, so hard against my palm, fucking, and then he comes with a helpless groan: living and vital in my grip, his relief so warm against my skin.

He laughs again, stilling my hips with the hand he's used to touch me; it's wet, and the intimacy of that—the knowledge that he knows how I feel and just made me come—makes me ache all over again.

We fall quiet in the darkness.

Carter's mouth finds mine and he kisses me with that telling, satisfied laziness.

"Still okay?" he asks in a deep, scratchy rumble.

"Yeah. You?"

"I'm great, are you kidding? I didn't have to do that by myself later tonight."

I start to laugh but he immediately consumes the sound of it, his mouth coming back over mine.

"I think I made a mess on your comforter, though."

I pull away, feeling down between us. "My bed is like, 'What *is* this substance?'"

He laughs hoarsely into my neck, and just when I start to worry whether I've just sounded too . . . *single*, he says, "Yeah, me too."

"You're insanely hot. I don't believe you haven't been with someone recently."

"And you're gorgeous. The lack of opportunity isn't why we're single."

I nod, looking up at his face. "It's been suggested that I'm picky. And maybe a little work-obsessed."

He laughs again at this, bending to kiss me. "I just think we both need something else to look forward to every day."

chapter six

Saturday night, Michael Christopher and I have been put in charge of food prep, which is just code for me doing the cooking and Michael keeping Morgan from pulling out every pot and pan in the house. He's at the table and she is happily pelting him in the face with Cheerios.

Steph comes in, carrying with her the scent of freshly cut grass, and a rush of cool air slips in through the door behind her. Although it's the weekend, she'd gone into work when a huge up-and-coming actor landed himself in jail. It reminds me of what Evie said about being married to her job, and I know this kind of thing—the late nights and missed dinners—is exactly what she meant.

She looks at us, impressed with the dinner spread, and sits down. "Wow." She doesn't even have to ask to know how it all materialized in front of her. "Well done, Carter."

"It's nice to cook in an actual kitchen with actual cookware."

Steph gives me a sympathetic smile while MC glares at me, envious.

"So how've you been?" Steph asks.

"Busy. Emil Shepard is moving to my list and it's creating a little paperwork headache in-house."

She winces. "Oh God. Is Blake losing his mind?"

"You'd think so. But honestly, he barely blinked." I shrug and spear a piece of chicken for my plate. "Maybe he's getting laid. Old Blake would have ripped off my legs and beaten me with them."

"There's something in the air. It has been such a shit show of a day." Steph cringes, glancing to Morgan. "Oops! Earmuffs, baby!"

We all wait in tense silence, wondering whether Morgan is going to gleefully sing out the words *shit show!* It's happened before with *dammit, motherfucker,* and *asshole.*

This time, she refrains.

Relieved, Steph turns back to me. "How was your date?"

MC perks up. I take a bite of my dinner and chew while I think, hoping my face doesn't betray me. My heart jolts noticeably when I think about last night. I haven't had this kind of physical reaction to a woman in years.

"It was great," I say. "She's just . . . she's fu—" I glance at Morgan midsentence. "Fu-reaking great."

"Great," Steph agrees slowly, with a smile to match her tone. She watches me like I'm going to elaborate, but in reality what more can I say? I want things with Evie to go somewhere, and I really think that they can. It's why I told her I didn't want us to have sex yet, even though I really, really wanted to.

"She was similarly bare bones on details." Stephanie stabs her chicken with a fork. "You're both brats."

"Am I supposed to tell you about our first kiss during study hall?"

She shoots up, eyes glimmering. "You guys kissed!"

"*All right,* crazy." Michael puts his hand on her forearm. "Let's not scare the nice boy away. They'll tell us what they want us to know when they want us to know it. I mean, at the very least they'll remember who brought them together when they're deciding who's best man at their wedding."

"Is this what happens when you're married with kids?" I grin at each of them in turn. "You have nothing to do but pair everyone off?"

On cue, they both lean in, voices erupting in unison.

"We haven't slowed down."

"We have a crazy social life!"

Morgan, who clearly finds the synchronized outburst cause for celebration, blows bubbles in her milk until it's foaming over the sides.

"No, no," I say, "full of youth. Of course. But you're also sort of . . . settled."

" 'Settled'?" Steph scoffs. "Please. *We*"—she points between the two of them—"are crazy. We can party with the best of them. Trust me."

"You still hit the clubs sometimes?" I give them an encouraging nod.

"Of course we do." She points to her arm and after a bewildered moment, I realize she's wordlessly reminding me that she has a *flower tattoo*, and that people with tattoos are obviously likely to be found at *clubs*. "There's this place called Foxtail that's so cool. You should definitely take Evie there."

"Or he could take her to Orchid, right, Steph?"

"That place is pretty good," she agrees. "Craft cocktails, right? Or there's that other one." She snaps her fingers as if this will help her recall the name.

"Areola," Michael finishes for her. "Now that place"—he whistles—"that place is insaaane," he says, dragging the word out into about four syllables.

Steph is nodding.

I have to ask: "There's a club called *Areola*?"

"Oh yeah, it's like—the hippest place in LA," she says. "Oh." She deflates a little. "No, babe, I think it's not Areola, that's a nipple, right? I think it's Ariela?"

"I mean, that's a pretty big difference," I note with a serious nod.

"Ariela," Michael agrees, laughing as he avoids my gaze.

"Have you two gone?"

"Us? Come on," MC says with a tight cough like *of course we have.* "We—well—no. We *wanted* to, but they don't even open until like nine? I think, babe? Is it nine?" Steph nods as she attempts to extract crushed garbanzo beans from Morgan's hair. "And that's . . . that's really late. I mean, not for *us*, but you know, for Morgan."

"She doesn't sleep well with a sitter, or *God* we'd be all over that place." Steph does a grinding little dance in her chair. "It would be off the hook."

"Off the hook," he agrees. "Causing some trouble is what we'd be doing."

"Areola," I say, grinning. "Amazing."

* * *

My phone chimes on the seat next to me as I make a left onto Santa Monica Boulevard. I ignore it, letting another Monday-morning commuter in front of me and waiting for the light to turn green so we can all move another twelve feet before it changes again. It will never stop bewildering me that a four-and-a-half-mile trip takes almost an hour.

I'm just about to reach for the dial on the radio when my phone chimes again . . . and again . . . and again. I glance over at it, the screen facedown on the seat, and mentally calculate the rest of my drive. In California it's illegal to use a cell phone while driving, so it's against the law to read or reply to any text messages. I'm about to tell myself I can wait when it goes off again.

And again.

When the light turns red, I slip my phone onto my lap and unlock the screen to reveal a slew of missed calls and messages from Becca.

My passcode isn't working and I can't get in the building.

Security says he can't let me in.

Ok Tarah and Kyle can't get in either.

What's going on?

I can't get into my email???

CARTER

911 EMERGENCY FIRE WHATEVER.

CALL ME NOW

I dial, listening to the phone ring through my Bluetooth.

"Carter."

"Hey." I accelerate, moving through the intersection. My heart is doing a weird dance in my chest. "What's going on?"

"No idea." Someone says something in the background, and Becca gives a quiet "Okay." Louder, she says to me, "Check your email. We have a meeting at a building in West Hollywood. I'll see you there."

And then she's gone. Bewildered, at the next red light I open my email program and find a two-line company-wide memo from CTM containing an address and instructions to be there by nine thirty.

Beyond that, nothing. Instead of heading straight, I turn right onto La Cienega.

.   .   .

Parked in an underground lot, I emerge and stare up at the glass-and-steel building. It looks like any other sleek new office structure; no identifying names or logos mark the front courtyard.

The only thing I can imagine is that we're moving offices, or that something horrible has happened to our own building . . . but I've heard nothing on the news. And Becca—calm, collected, and immediately responsive ninety-nine percent of the time—hasn't answered my follow-up call.

I'm hit in the face with a blast of refrigerated air as soon as I step inside, and combined with the adrenaline pulsing through my veins, it awakens something instinctively New Yorker in me.

It's settling, oddly.

Turning down a marble hall, I check my phone a final time before slipping it into my pocket. A circular reception area is just ahead, topped by a set of large screens with the words *Price &* *Dickle*, and the logos and movie posters of some of the actors they represent, moving in and out of focus.

My pulse trills in my throat.

P&D recently moved. Is this where they're located?

Off to the side is a smaller, temporary table with a paper sign that reads *CTM sign-in* taped to the top, a beautiful blonde sitting behind it, and two uniformed security guards hovering nearby.

Are we moving offices into the same building as P&D? The whole scene is odd enough to make me slow my steps; a red flare has just been shot up into the sky.

Warily, I approach the table and catch the attention of the blonde wearing a headset. Through my nerves, I attempt my best smile. "Hi, this is going to sound crazy, but—"

She's all business: "You're with CTM?"

I nod.

She looks down at her list. "Name?"

"Aaron," I say, giving her my last name, then quickly clarifying, "*Carter* Aaron."

She hums, flipping through a few pages. "Here we are, Aaron Carter." She hands me a clipboard with several pieces of paper trapped there. "Did you know you have the same name as a Backstreet Boy?"

"Actually, you're thinking of Nick Carter," I say. "Aaron Carter is his younger brother. My name is Carter *Aaron*, not Aaron Carter . . ."

I can tell she's already lost interest as she looks up at me beneath a set of gravity-defying false lashes. And who could blame her? I should not know the name of a Backstreet Boy's younger brother. Except I do, because it's something I've had to explain at least a dozen times in my life.

I push on, covertly glancing down at her list. There are a few names I recognize. Cameron from Literary, Sally from Foreign Rights, and a handful of others.

"Can you tell me why I'm here?" I ask.

"Fill out those forms," she says, nodding to the clipboard in my hand, "then head to the second floor. Oh, and sign in, here."

She hands me a badge with my name written across the front, and I reluctantly fill in the log. With a bland smile, she points me in the direction of the elevators. A guard swipes his badge to let me past the security gate, and once inside the elevator, I press the button for the second floor.

Pulling my phone back out, I send a quick message to Evie.

> I think I'm in your building?

> Something weird is going on.

> Call me?

After a moment, a vibrant elevator chime tells me I'm on the next floor, and when the doors open I'm met by a smiling middle-aged woman and another set of matching security guards.

Okay . . .

I'm instructed to have a seat in the lobby, and, after peppering the woman with questions, I'm assured that someone will be along shortly to explain everything. The space is bright and expansive, with a number of plush chairs in small clusters that line a long bank of windows overlooking Beverly Boulevard.

There are already a handful of people milling about; I recognize only a few. Nobody seems to have any idea what's going on. The lobby slowly fills and yet somehow manages to remain almost eerily quiet. Someone will walk in, invariably make some sort of squeak on the floor or some other noise that draws everyone's attention, and then nothing. It feels a lot like we're all thirteen years old and waiting around to be called into the principal's office.

"Carter."

I turn to see Kurt Elwood from Features walking toward me, hands in his hair and the usual grim expression on his face.

"I thought I saw your name downstairs." I take in his appearance. "You okay, man?" He's a little on the green side and there's a hint of perspiration dotting his upper lip.

He pulls a roll of antacids from his pocket and pops one in his mouth, grimacing as he chews. "You know what this looks like to me?"

I follow his gaze and survey the room. Everyone looks confused, but nobody seems on the verge of outright panic. "No?"

"Like a company-wide layoff. Get us out of the building, away from our computers, where we can't access our files."

"What?" I say, a bit taken aback by his suggestion, and look around the room again. I've just assumed we're *moving*. We've been hiring like crazy; layoffs have been as far from my mind as they could be.

"You don't think they'd do something like that?" he asks. "Features aren't paying the bills anymore. People aren't going to the movies like they used to. Pirating is up, profits are down. Not even you guys in TV are safe—P&D are packaging monsters." He stares at me. "What? You think they'd hand us all parting gifts and send us on our way? No, they separate us from everyone else to keep the drama to a minimum. Why do you think not everyone's here?" He pulls another Tums from the foil wrapping and looks at it before putting it between his lips and biting down. "The signs have been there for weeks."

I'm torn between wanting to look away from the chalky pink antacid coloring his teeth and wanting to hear more. Every odd, unexplained event plays through my head, and I wonder if there could be some truth to his words. Emil Shepard has been less than thrilled with CTM for a while now. If he somehow got wind of this, he could move to me and when I was let go he'd have the option to transfer to someone else, or leave altogether.

Only a few boats rocked and he's free. If Blake knew about this, it would explain his surprising nonreaction to everything with Emil so far.

Kurt breaks into my thoughts. "Jesus Christ, I am forty-two years old. Nobody wants a middle-aged, mediocre agent these days. They want sharks. They want agents as good-looking as the actors. I can't compete with that! Oh my God," he groans, "I just bought a boat!"

"Okay, let's take a breath." I hope I sound calmer than I feel. "We don't even know what's happening yet. Let's not jump to any conclusions. Why would they bring us to P&D if they're laying us off? Why not just hold us in our own lobby?"

I try to steer him away from the rest of the group and he laughs, clapping me on the back of the shoulder.

"Young, hopeful, naive Carter. Maybe you should take one of these," he says, turning my hand over and placing the last of the Tums in my palm. "You mark my words: we'll all be out of a job by lunch."

chapter seven

evie

With my phone to my ear, I cross the parking garage and search for my badge in the bottom of my purse. I'm running late and this call has gone on longer than I expected, but if I can make everything work, it'll be worth it.

"So then let's talk seriously for a minute," I say into the line, badge finally in hand. "I have no problem getting Tyler out to see you, but you've got to promise me it's to sit in front of a director. He's not back until November and aside from all the work stuff he'll have scheduled, he'll want a little reconnecting time with his wife and kid. Tell me there's an actual meeting and I'll get it on the books."

I pass through the glass doors and head straight for the elevators.

"Okay," I say into the phone, swiping my badge at the security bars in the lobby. "Take a look at your schedule. I'll have Jess follow up this afternoon." My assistant usually silently sits in on every call, but this morning she's oddly MIA.

The security gate doesn't open, and I slide my card through the reader again. Nothing lights up, nothing dings. "We'll talk soon. Thanks, Nev."

With my phone tucked back into my purse, I walk across the

lobby to the main security post, warily eyeing the makeshift table off to the side, where two security guards stand stoically.

I lean across the broad marble counter and look at the familiar guard sitting there. "Hey, Jake, what's with the table over there?"

Jake looks up and back over my shoulder toward the elevators. "Ms. Abbey, is your card not working?"

I hand it over, shaking my head.

His wire-frame glasses glint in the light as he glances down at something on his monitor before standing. "Your card's been locked. I need to send you up to the second floor."

"Locked?" And second floor? That's the P&D lobby and the conference center. No one really *works* there.

"That's all I can really say, Ms. Abbey, but you aren't the only one. Let's get you upstairs." He rounds the desk, signaling to another guard that he'll be right back.

"This doesn't make any sense," I say, and pull out my phone again. "Let me call Amelia, she'll know what's going on."

"I believe Ms. Baker is already here," he says, and swipes his badge before following me to the elevators and pressing the button for the second floor. "Don't worry, I'm sure everything is going to be just fine."

Inside the elevator, I nearly throw my phone against the wall when I realize the ringer has been on silent all morning. There are messages from Daryl and Carter, and one from Steph. A rare all-caps text from Jess sits at the top of the list: EVIE WHAT IS GOING ON?

My hands are shaking as I leave my text app without reading the rest and open my phone's browser to check *Variety*, knowing that whatever happens in this town, *Variety*—or Twitter—usually gets wind of it first. Of course, there's next to no reception inside the elevator and my browser app is only beginning to load as the doors open with a loud ding.

There's the sound of a voice echoing in the sudden silence and I look down the wide hall to see an entire lobby of people turn to look at me.

A woman near the front smiles in my direction. "Please, have a seat. We were just getting started."

The normally sparse lobby has been filled with chairs; about two-thirds of them are occupied. Mumbling a quiet apology, I tuck my phone away and speed-walk across the room to the first empty spot I see.

"Good morning again," the woman says, her smile bright—if a little forced. Her hair is long and red and hangs in thick waves to the middle of her back. I have no idea who she is, but my first thought is that she reminds me of a news anchor. She's perfectly groomed and looks exactly like the person you'd expect to tell you that everything is going to be all right . . . or whether you should run.

"As I'm sure most of you have gathered, it has been *quite* a morning," she says. "My name is Lisa and I work in HR for the New York office of CTM."

Wait. She works for *who*?

I'm about to raise my hand and ask what in the actual hell is going on when a few rows up I spot a head turned to face me with a familiar set of green eyes.

Carter.

When I saw his name in my text scroll, I optimistically assumed he was seeing if I had time for a make-out session in the car over lunch. But he's *here*, in this hushed den of bewilderment? I try to put this all together, but my thoughts are like a record skipping uselessly upstairs: *CTM's HR rep in the P&D lobby.*

Carter's eyes go wide to communicate his own confusion before he turns back toward the front.

What the fuck is going on?

I slump in my seat, staring at the back of his head before I look around at the rows of chairs in front of and behind me, searching for more faces I recognize. Donald from Accounting; Rose, who works with me in Features; and a handful of others. I see a mass of dark curls rising high above the other heads—thank all that is holy: Jess is here. Finally, I see Daryl in the back row.

She throws her hands up as if to say *finally*, and it's clear from her expression that she doesn't know what's going on, either. She points to her phone just as the sound of footsteps draws both of our attention back to the front.

Lisa hands a stack of files to a man now standing beside her. "You're all either wondering what in the world is going on, or maybe you've heard already, but CTM and Price & Dickle have merged."

She's saying something else but it takes my brain a few seconds to process the words in order. When it does, the sound in my head is a little like tires screeching to a halt.

CTM has merged with Price & Dickle.

We are one agency.

We are one agency with a huge amount of overlap.

My stomach seems to have dissolved away, leaving a hollow space beneath my ribs.

I look to Daryl, who seems to be reaching the same conclusion I have, and then around the room. A few heads nod, but not many. Most faces have gone ashen.

"And if you *hadn't* heard," she continues, making eye contact with a few of us, "don't worry. It was only announced about half an hour ago."

Half an hour ago.

I think about all the strangeness in the office over the past few weeks, knowing that this type of thing doesn't just happen overnight. Those few people at the top, in the know, can strategize, position themselves. The big question is how long they had to prepare. The bigger question is who *they* are. Who knew?

I think I might be sick.

"To be completely frank, we aren't sure what the merge looks like quite yet," Lisa says. "Some of the dust needs to settle before we know what shape we'll take and how the new structure will work. But as the news will likely break widely soon, we wanted to gather you here to communicate information all together."

A few people shift in their seats. A guy next to me is scrolling through his Twitter feed, presumably looking for information.

"As many of you know," Lisa continues, "both P&D and CTM have corporate offices in New York as well as LA. P&D is the acquiring company and will be bringing staff from both offices here to consolidate, as well as transferring some local staff to New York." My jaw drops open when she says this, and I barely hear what comes next. "These are details you'll discuss with your direct managers in your department. But the bottom line—and the good news—is that if you're in this room, it's very likely that you still have a job at one office or the other."

. . . very likely that you still have a job at one office or the other.

I mean . . . that's *something* at least. *Right?*

Most of the room has slumped somewhat in relief. I glance over at Carter. From what I can tell from the back, he's just sitting there, unmoving.

"Sorry, can you clarify?" he asks in a garbled whisper. He has to clear his throat before adding, "Some of us will be transferred to New York and some will remain here? And when will this be decided?"

At this Lisa turns to him and smiles like he's asked something as benign as whether the vending machines in the staff lounge will be stocked with Coke or Pepsi. "Who stays—and who is transferred—is being left up to your individual departments."

The way she says it, with an almost journalistic indifference, doesn't help the panic hijacking my motor system. I slip my fingers between my knees to keep them from shaking where anyone can see. It feels like a rug has just been pulled out from beneath me.

A murmur of voices—verging on angry—begins to build within the room.

"Honestly, I would love to be able to tell you all more," Lisa says above the fray, "but as you can see, we're still getting details on this ourselves."

In my peripheral vision, I can see Carter's shoulders curl in, his head bow. He looks like I feel: like he wants to drop his head between his legs and look for something to throw up in.

I lock eyes with Daryl and wonder if we're both thinking the same thing: We work for the acquiring company. We have some sort of advantage here, right?

Tonight I am going to stress-eat a box of cookies like the world has never seen.

• • •

We're dismissed shortly after, given a stack of papers, and told where to report for more information. It's likely everyone in this room had a packed schedule filled with *actual* work—I know I did—but that's all been changed into a schedule of determining whether we get to continue *doing* that actual work. Now we all wait while the people in charge try to figure out what the hell is going on.

Carter is already speaking privately with Lisa; I move straight to Daryl.

"Where's Amelia?" she says, and I realize—that's right. I haven't seen her.

"I don't know." I search the room again. Amelia has worked in HR longer than either Daryl or I have been here. They wouldn't let her go. Would they? "Wait," I say, remembering. "On my way in, Jake said she was already here."

"I'm texting her." Daryl's fingers fly over her phone. "She wouldn't just not tell us—" She pauses and I see exactly where her train of thought is going.

"If she knew, she wouldn't have been able to tell us," I say, and Daryl's shoulders sag.

"What a mess." She toys with the elastic at the end of her braid, eyes scanning the room. "I'll be right back. Eric's over there and I am going to see if he knows anything. I doubt it, but his uncle is the damn boss, after all."

She moves to leave and then stops, turning back to whisper, "Unless this means Brad is out?"

"Oh my God. Is that . . ." I look around us before leaning in. "Is that even possible?" I am unable to hide the tiny spark of hope that creeps into my voice.

"I mean, why not? I wouldn't have guessed any of this in a million years. I'd say all bets are off. Back in a sec."

As soon as she's gone, Carter pulls me aside. My pulse accelerates again.

"What the hell is happening?" His hand lingers around my

upper arm, grip tight, and for a couple of psychotic seconds, this entire thing seems oddly comical.

"No idea," I say. "I'd been on a call all morning and then couldn't get into the elevators. As you saw from my less-than-subtle entrance, I just got here. My friend Amelia works in HR and we're trying to see if she knows anything, but . . . I doubt she'd be able to say."

"This is nuts. Merging means *downsizing*."

"I know." I feel fairly secure in my position here at P&D, but in this moment, even with all the wins in my résumé, the opening score to *Field Day* blares like a trumpet in the back of my mind.

The air conditioning in the lobby seems to be set to ultra-mega-freezing and I shiver, crossing my arms over my chest, trying to stay warm.

"I'd give you my jacket if we weren't suddenly in the weirdest dating-coworker situation in the history of time," he says—and God, I hadn't even considered that.

Our phones vibrate at the same moment.

"Well, look at that. I have an email from Price & Dickle," he says.

"Same."

"Is it too early for a drink?"

. . .

With a new keycard in hand, I head upstairs to my office, only to be greeted by an eerie silence.

Gone is the cacophony of printers and voices answering phones. Instead, calls are left to voicemail, because what would the people answering them say anyway?

We've all been told to come back tomorrow for the transition—

the CTM folks who weren't laid off were denied all access to their files and computers—but those of us from P&D with offices in the building came upstairs. What the hell else would we do?

Despite Carter's very sound instincts, it really is way too early to start drinking. Not that anybody seems to be doing any *actual* work: Turns out, P&D employees are locked out of our computers, too. Everyone is gathered in clumps at different desks, talking in hushed whispers and looking around, on edge.

And who can blame them? Questions hang like thought bubbles suspended above heads, and the people who should be around to answer them are nowhere in sight. *Who has a job today? Who will still have one tomorrow?*

I think back on some of the larger acquisitions I've read about over the years. The worst kind of merge is one where it happens quickly, before management can hammer out all the details and create a clear plan for combining departments and dealing with overlap. But here, I've been noticing oddities for a couple of weeks, which I hope means that it's been in the works for a while and there's a plan in place.

I look around, and there are a lot of long faces in the common areas. Most agencies are bottom-heavy, with tons of support staff, because so much of what gets done involves phone calls, emails, shuffling papers, and coordinating schedules. This new, combined agency is going to be doubly bottom-heavy, and the staff out here—barely out of their starving student days—knows it. I suppose they were all meant to go home for the day, but being here lends some sense of control, some hope they can influence decisions. Besides, who wants to be the one caught away from their desk when those kinds of decisions are being made?

I head down the hall without speaking to anyone, torn between banging on Brad's door to get answers and crawling under my desk. Lucky for him, he's nowhere to be found: his office is dark, desk empty.

In the blissful silence of my own office, I decide to keep the lights off, collapsing into my chair for the first time today. A part of me wonders if I can manage to hide here until it's time to go home, maybe even come in tomorrow to find this has all been one giant practical joke.

Not likely. Through my interior windows I see Daryl's blond head as she weaves her way through the tables toward me, with Amelia—thank God—right behind.

"Hiding out? Good thinking," Daryl says, peeking through the crack in the door before closing it behind them. She groans, dropping onto my small office sofa with one leg curled underneath her. "Eric was a bust. He doesn't know anything, either. His greatest curiosity was whether the vending machine was still plugged in so he could get some chili cheese Fritos. Spoiler alert: he could."

Amelia moves to sit at her side, closing her eyes as she settles back against the cushions. She looks exhausted.

"You doing okay?" I ask her.

Wincing, she admits, "I wish I had more to tell you guys. A few of us got phone calls at around ten last night, saying we needed to get in as early as possible this morning. I got in at five. I didn't tell you guys because blah blah confidentiality."

Kicking her shoes off, she stretches her legs out in front of her. "Anyway, I don't know a whole lot more than you. Apparently P&D has been looking at CTM for some time but the partners didn't want to sell. They must've changed their minds. I assume it was kept hush-hush because of what happened at Fairmount, when the top agents got wind and everyone jumped ship before the deal could be finalized." She lifts her chin to me. "Maybe you were onto something after all, Nancy Drew."

"So, if we're here we still have jobs?" I ask, my head spinning. "Do they have any of that figured out yet?"

She shakes her head. "I'm sure they do, but I haven't seen the department org charts yet. Tomorrow is when all the details are supposed to drop."

Ugh, this is a nightmare.

"Here's the *Variety* article," Daryl says, looking up from her iPad and tilting it so we can all see.

> In a surprising move Monday morning, top talent agency Price & Dickle, along with private equity backer William Trainer Group, acquired the competing agency Creative Talent and Media. The new company will retain the P&D name, and according to CEO Jared Helmsworth will be a full-service agency. In his statement, Helmsworth said, "With offices in New York, Los Angeles and London, this partnership will provide our clients access to the smartest and most creative minds in the business, with more opportunities to strike deals in digital content, TV, film, books, sports, licensing and speaking engagements." The acquisition price remains undisclosed. It is likely that in the coming days, the restructured agency will be forced to lay off hundreds of supporting staff, as well as agents, but when *Variety* reached out to a company spokesman for comment, we were told, "Any speculation at this time would be premature." More to come.

We sit back and marinate in our uneasy silence.

"I mean, it's not like there was really any new information in there," Daryl says finally. "So why do I feel worse?"

Amelia closes her eyes. "This is exactly why my mother told me to marry rich."

"I don't think you have anything to worry about. You practically run your department." Turning to Daryl, I ask, "How long do you have left on your contract?"

"A year and a half." She gives a real smile for the first time in an hour. "Let them buy me out, I could use some time off. What about you?"

Every agency does things a little differently, but at P&D we're salaried with a bonus structure, and contracted for a certain number of years. This could not have come at a worse time. "Five months," I say.

A lead ball of dread settles in my stomach.

I can tell that my friends never quite perfected their game faces because their expressions make my nausea roll more intensely. I would be very easy—and very inexpensive—to lay off.

Amelia quickly recovers. "Evie, you don't have anything to worry about. It's not the best timing, but you'll be fine. You kick ass here."

"But Brad?" I remind them. "He'd be overjoyed to have a reason to toss another vagina overboard."

"At least, a vagina he doesn't get to play in," Daryl interjects.

I laugh, but it fades into a wary groan. "Or maybe he'll just lord this over my head for the next five months and not renew my contract." I slip farther into my chair. "Oh! Not to mention the whole Carter thing." I rub my hand over my face. "I finally meet a guy I like—a guy who's straight and doesn't live with his mom—and he was downstairs, in that meeting."

"What?" Daryl's eyes go wide.

I nod. "He was at CTM, remember? And it looks like he made the first cut. He works with us now."

Amelia is staring at me in amused shock, but Daryl quickly recovers. "Okay, first of all, let's all breathe. *Breeeeeathe.* Second, the Carter thing will work itself out. Let's see—"

Daryl stops, and I know exactly what she was going to say: *Let's see if you even have a job tomorrow to worry about.*

"Let's see how everything plays out," she finishes instead. "And third? We don't even know whether *Brad* still works here. Nobody knows where he is. Kylie is MIA, too. If he's not here, your agency record—minus a few tiny bumps along the way—stands on its own. Don't count yourself out yet. I have a good feeling about this."

God. Please let her be right.

• • •

I can only assume Carter likewise polished off a bottle of wine by himself last night and that's why I didn't hear from him.

At least that's what I keep telling myself.

Suffice it to say, I am not the best version of Evie on Tuesday morning. My mom, who reads *Variety* and *Deadline* religiously, called about seven thousand times yesterday. I finally answer her call when I'm picking up my morning coffee at Verve, after maybe two hours of restless sleep.

"Evie, baby," she says. "I'm on my way over."

"Mom, no. I'm not home right now."

"I'll meet you. Tell me where."

I sigh, sitting down at a small table in the corner. I don't even need to ask what she's thinking to know exactly how her mind works. "I don't want you to come do my hair."

My mom has done hair in this town for almost thirty-five years, her crowning achievement being the episodes of *Dynasty* in 1984 for which she was personally responsible for Joan Collins's wigs. According to my mom, there is no problem a good blowout can't solve.

"It will make you feel better," she says, and I can hear the familiar theme song to *Good Morning America* playing in the background. To my mom, nothing fixes a bad day faster than fresh hair, a scalp massage, and the confidence of stiff hairspray. "I could give you a little trim? Your hair's gotten so long and you know it has a tendency to look a little raggedy at the ends."

"It's going to be fine. I don't need a haircut. Cut Dad's hair. I love you. I've got to get in to work."

Even if I have no idea what that work might entail . . .

My phone rings again as I walk out of Verve, coffee in hand. I have to look twice for confirmation when I see the name illuminated on the screen.

Carter.

"Hello?"

"Hey," he says, and if I'm not mistaken, he, too, is mildly hungover and in desperate need of caffeine. "How are you?"

I want to laugh at his tone. It sounds a little like I feel: calm layered over a hurricane. "I'm good. A little . . . tired."

"Tell me about it," he says, voice rough. "I wanted to give you a heads-up that I'll be at P&D this morning. I guess everything's already been moved over, the computers, the files. Apparently, they did it all in the middle of the night after informing us of the merge, and informing the first cut of the . . . cuts."

"Wow, that sounds . . . harsh."

"Anyway," he says, "I just wanted to let you know. I realize this is weird, to say the least."

My heart gives a little jolt in my chest. Carter is such a nice guy. It makes all of this even more twisty.

"Well, at least I'll get to see you today, then," I tell him.

"How's everyone handling it on your end? Steph said the crew at Alterman went into panic mode thinking they'd get sucked into this."

"I talked to Michael Christopher last night and joked that I might need to move into his guest room if my position gets cut," he says, and I want to reach through the phone and hug him. P&D is pretty small, and notoriously cutthroat. "You hear anything on your end?"

"Not really. There was a company-wide email last night, but it was basically a rehash of what we already knew."

He sighs. "That's what I figured."

"What about you? You doing okay?"

"I've been better." He lets out a tight laugh. "I mean, I'm assuming I still have a job? Unlike my assistant. Which is why she wasn't at the meeting yesterday."

"Oh my God, Carter. I'm sorry."

"Thanks," he says. "Honestly, Becca was amazing. I'd be lost without her on a normal day. I have no idea how I'll navigate through all this."

I feel a little sick for him, knowing how I'd feel if I lost Jess, especially right now.

"On a brighter note," he adds, "looks like I'll finally be meeting the illustrious Brad Kingman."

A metaphorical trapdoor has just opened under my feet. "I'm sorry, what did you say?"

"Brad Kingman."

"He heads up my department—Features, not TV-Literary."

"I know," Carter says, and I can hear the shrug in his voice. "But that's what it said when they told me where to go this morning. My meeting is with Brad."

chapter eight

At five to ten, my desk phone rings. I keep my eyes on the monitor in front of me and exhale in relief when, after a second ring, it goes silent. *Good*, I think, finishing an email. *I don't want to talk to anyone today anyway.*

There's a knock less than a minute later, and I look up to see Jess standing in the doorway.

She nods toward the unanswered phone. "Despite the dark window"—she motions to the pane of glass next to my door—"I knew you were in here."

"I'm sorry," I tell her guiltily. "Would you think less of me if I told you I was scared?"

She laughs as she steps inside, closing the door behind her. "Now that we have computer access, most people are on Linked-In or Googling *How to Survive a Merger.*"

I press send before looking back up. "Though I don't know what we're all hiding for. Nobody's even seen Brad, and yesterday was such a confusing shit show, I should feel confident that today can't top it."

Jess clears her throat and I narrow my eyes at her, wary.

"What?"

"Well, the reason I called . . ." She winces a little. The gold studs in her ears twinkle back at me beneath the fluorescent lights as she grips the back of the chair she's leaning on. "He's here. When you didn't answer he called me. He wants to see you."

"Brad?"

"Brad."

I slump in my chair. "Well, fudge."

"He's been calling people in all morning and it looks like it's your turn. Or you know, 'Up to bat!' as he would say."

I groan. So he *is* staying.

· · ·

Everyone looks up as I walk past on my way to Brad's office. If he's been calling people in all morning, who knows what they've seen? Relief? Tantrums? Tears? Anything is possible.

I rarely question my appearance anymore—a gift that seems to have arrived with the transition into my thirties—but with all eyes on me, I feel like an awkward model on a catwalk. I really should have worn my padded bra.

In my peripheral vision, a few heads turn, their attention lingering on something at the other end of the hall. I follow their gaze.

Carter.

His suit is charcoal gray and looks like it was made for him by magical tailor elves. It hugs his shoulders, tapers at his waist, frames his body perfectly. I tug at the hem of my shift dress, suddenly feeling frumpy.

His long legs close the distance between us in just a few strides. "Hey."

I try to keep my gaze in the safe zone: on his tie. It's blue with tiny green flecks and I already know that if I look up, I'll see the way it brings out the color in his eyes.

Yup . . . it does.

"Hi." I am hyperaware of all eyes on us. I mean, why wouldn't they be watching this train wreck? I would. Not that they know I had his penis in my hand a few days ago, and now we apparently work together, but it's probably written all over my face—

Or maybe they aren't watching because of me at all. Maybe they're watching us because Carter is a new, gorgeous guy in the department.

I feel an odd mix of possessiveness and unease.

"I'm just on my way to Brad's office." I'm eager to put some space between us and the office full of onlookers. "How did it go with you?"

"I don't know yet," he says. "Our eight a.m. was delayed. I'm on my way there now. Kylie was just taking me."

And it's only now that I notice Brad's assistant, Kylie, standing a few paces away, nonchalantly checking out Carter's ass. When she catches my eye, she steps closer. Carter smiles down at her. She smiles back, a hint of pink blooming on her neck and cheeks.

A direct hit. An eerie sense of foreboding prods at my brain.

Kylie clears her throat and walks ahead of us, stopping outside the door to Brad's corner office.

"You can go on in." She gives Carter a smile that lingers just past too long and verges on weird. Or maybe it's only weird because I'm here, staring like she's committing some grave offense by looking at him. "He's expecting you both."

"I'm sorry, Kylie," I say, "did you say he's expecting us both? As in . . . together?"

"That's right."

"Do you know why?" My brain cycles back to the image of my hands in Carter's pants. His come on my——

I shake my head. Brad would have no way of knowing any of that, but it's the only connection I can make.

"Nope." She looks at each of us in turn. "Is there a problem?"

"No problem at all." Carter motions for me to lead the way. "Thanks, Kylie."

"Any time." She offers him an encouraging thumbs-up before whispering, "You'll do great!"

You have got to be kidding me.

With an awkward cough, Carter glances down to the floor as I pass, and we both step into Brad's office.

Brad Kingman has that air about him—you know the one, where it's clear he thinks he's a little better, a lot smarter, and leagues more connected in this town than you are. He also does that thing all the best intimidating people do where he stares directly at you when he's speaking. When you talk—if you're important enough for him to actually listen—he'll make you feel like the most fascinating person in the world. But be ready: If you call, you'd better know what you want to say. If you come to his office, get it out—and quickly. He doesn't do polite small talk and doesn't schmooze.

But when Carter steps through the door, it's like a Brad Kingman I've never seen before stands to greet him.

"Carter," he says, grinning widely. He rounds the desk, reaching out to offer a hand. "It's good to meet you, son."

Son?

Carter's posture tweaks initially as he's taken aback, but he recovers quickly. "It's good to meet you, too," he says, shoulders straight, chin up, and grip strong as he shakes Brad's proffered hand. He looks calm.

Good, he's done his homework.

Brad claps him on the back and motions for him to take a seat before turning his attention to me. "Evie. It's been quite a madhouse around here, hasn't it?"

He pulls out a chair for me and I give him a smile in return. "It sure has."

Circling back around his expansive walnut desk, Brad takes a moment to look at each of us in turn. "Have you met?"

I glance at Carter, offering a wan smile. "Yeah, we know each other."

"See, this is what I'm talking about," Brad says, "*this* is a team. Carter, I want you to know that Evie here has become my right-hand kid. Any questions you have, anything you need, Evie is the girl to talk to. Understand?"

I feel my cheeks warm under the simultaneous compliment and condescension of *right-hand kid* and *the girl to talk to*.

"Absolutely," Carter says, glancing at me a little uneasily. "She's been nothing but helpful so far."

Brad raps the knuckles of one hand against the desk and leans back in his chair. "That's good to hear. Now, if I had to guess what's cycling through your heads this morning, I suspect there's a bit of confusion about what's going on—am I right?"

"Pretty much," Carter says with a small laugh.

"I get that. I do get that." Brad straightens, hands folded in front of him. "Evie here will tell you that I am all about playing as a team, Carter. And here at Price & Dickle we are only as strong as our weakest player. Isn't that right, Evie?"

I say through clenched teeth, "That's right, Brad."

"Which means we need every player to be able to knock it out of the park. I brought the two of you in here together for a couple reasons. The first is that between the three of us, I think you two are the best we've got. I've heard a lot about you, Carter. It's why I snagged you from TV-Lit—you belong in Features. You two can bring our department back into the game."

He pulls two files from the bottom of a stack and opens the first.

"You started as a finance clerk at a boutique agency in New York?" he asks, and Carter nods. "And what did you learn from that?"

Carter shifts in his seat, glancing at me before returning his attention to Brad. I didn't know this.

Obviously, there's going to be quite a bit I don't know. So this is a first: getting to know a potential boyfriend through a thinly veiled grilling session in our boss's office.

"Well, of course I heard a lot of gossip," Carter admits, smiling easily. "There are agents who act like anyone not involved in a negotiation isn't really there. Because of that, I overheard conversations I probably shouldn't have."

To my own ear it sounds like he's underselling for some reason, still keeping his cards close. If I'm right, Brad knows it, too.

"That's it?" Brad asks.

Carter hesitates for a moment. "It's a good way to learn how people handle pressure, observing it from the outside. You learn to catalog everyone's reaction, anticipate who will do what when the shit hits the fan."

Brad smiles, and because I know Brad, I can tell he's amused by Carter's casual swearing. By contrast, he would wince and chastise me for doing the same. I feel queasy. I knew Carter was charming but secretly hoped it had something to do with my wanting to bang him. Apparently not, because he's playing Brad perfectly, too.

"Start at the bottom and take what you learn to the top," Brad says, nodding.

Carter grins, and charisma seeps into the room. "Something like that."

Brad scribbles down a couple of notes and turns to me. "Now, Evie here, she could talk a grenade out of exploding. That's a skill you want to learn, Carter. Lots of people can be decent agents, but it takes a special one to spot talent, and an even better one to keep it. There's been a stumble or two . . ." He pauses meaningfully. "But for the most part, she's proven she belongs with the big boys. Hell, she's trained some of the best agents in this town."

I bite my tongue. It's unlike Brad to hand out praise so baldly, and I brace myself, waiting for the other shoe to drop.

"Now, like I said, I think you two are the best we have, but I'll be honest. I don't know if we can *keep* you both—"

"*What?*" we both say in unison.

Brad holds up his hands, motioning for us to let him finish. "Your compensation is comparable—which is why I have you both in here—and I don't know if P&D will have the room to renew both contracts. At least not here in LA."

We stare ahead, stunned. I can feel my face going red, my stomach twisting into knots. I'm five years older than Carter and have been doing this job in one form or another since I was nineteen. Judging from what I've seen, Carter is probably a great agent, but he's only lived in LA for two years and is new to features. Like, *today* new. In what universe is our compensation comparable? Because he's a man? Who knew a penis was worth so much?

"Brad—" Carter begins, expression grim. I clench my fists at my sides and force myself to take a deep breath.

"It's not definite that one of you will be shifted over," Brad says, "but I'll be honest: it's likely. We're all going to have to do the work and see what fits best for the new, combined Features team."

"I don't understand," I say. "P&D is one of the most successful agencies in the country. How can it not keep us both?" I glance to Carter and back again. "Brad, look at my numbers, I outperform—"

"Minus your little speed bump with *Field Day*," he says with a superior nod, and I straighten in my chair. Fuck him for bringing that up right now. "Listen, kiddo, the simple fact is that the movie business is down. Expenses are up. Cuts are made in this type of situation, and that's just the way it is. You two aren't the only ones this is affecting."

I glance at Carter. He's staring directly at Brad. "When you said, 'Not here in LA,'" Carter begins carefully, "are you saying that if one of our contracts isn't renewed, there's a chance that individual would be offered a position in New York?"

Brad nods. "For sure there is a position in LA, and a spot in New York is always a possibility. Ideally there would be two positions here, but it's too early to speculate on that. On any of it, really."

We both sit there, silent. I stare at a glossy whorl of walnut that stands out in the section of wood grain just in front of me. It's the size of my fist but takes up only the smallest fraction of the surface of Brad's enormous executive desk. I wish I could press my finger to it, swirl, and flush this entire exchange down the toilet.

"What I want both of you to do for the short term," Brad says, pulling my eyes back to his face, "is to put this situation out of your heads. You each have a contract that P&D will see through, and then we'll examine it again. Evie, you've got five months left on your current contract. Carter, you're due to re-sign in six. At the time of renewal it's possible there will only be room for one. But you're not competing. Not exactly."

The words *not exactly* fall like bricks dropped from twenty feet up.

"Meet with some of the agents, the support staff—on both sides," Brad continues with practiced obliviousness. "Talk to the team we have here visiting from New York. Get a sense for how your lists are going to react and how you can retain them—we'll be talking about that a little later in the week." He turns to me. "Evie, I don't think retentions will be as big an issue for you, since your clients were already P&D—so what I would love is for you to show Carter around, show him how we do things. Maybe introduce him to some of your colleagues and contacts."

I feel sick. Just like with John Fineman, Brad is having me pass along some of my hard-earned connections to a coworker. But not just any coworker: to *Carter*, my new almost-boyfriend, with whom I'm *not exactly* competing for a job.

"Of course," I say, because what else can I do?

"Carter," Brad says, turning, "you have enough charisma to take over this entire town, and I think you'll do it. Listen to Evie, learn the ropes; she knows what she's talking about." He looks between us. "At least for the time being," he says, leaning back in his chair again, "I think you will make an amazing team. Try to see it that way."

He smiles, leans forward with his hands steepled beneath his chin, and gives us the patented icy blue stare.

Brad Kingman has excused us.

• • •

Out in the hallway Carter and I each study the floor, the wall, the table desks in the distance. The number of things we could say about the situation seems infinite. But oddly, as much as I've enjoyed his company and his kisses and his penis, Carter is the last person I want to talk to about this right now.

I can tell he's tense. I can tell we're *both* tense, but I need to process a little bit in my own head before I help him process it, too.

He lets out a quiet whistle. "This is unreal."

"I agree." I have to pull my eyes away from the tension in his jaw.

"When I heard we'd merged, my biggest fear was just that it would be hard to work with my new girlfriend."

My heart swoops low in my chest when he says this.

"But now, it's like . . ." He shakes his head, running a hand through his thick hair. "I *need* this job. I moved here for this job."

"My entire life is here," I remind him. "I've worked for P&D for five years. I realize the situation really sucks for you, but I've built connections here. I've built a *career* here."

You have enough charisma to take over this entire town, and I think you'll do it.

Brad's words to Carter bounce around the inside of my skull, and I squeeze my hands into fists at my sides. Brad wants Carter to take over the entire town; where exactly does that leave me?

Carter glances over to me, and for a flash I can see annoyance in his green eyes. But he quickly tucks it away.

"This is probably not the time to talk about it." He closes his eyes, taking a couple of deep breaths. "Look. This is the worst thing that could have happened between us, and I realize that." He puts a warm hand on my forearm. "But we're going to figure it out, don't worry."

For some reason his reassurance bothers me even more. It's true this isn't a great situation for either of us, but I don't need him to patronize me and tell me that everything will be okay when he knows exactly as much as I do. And I especially don't need him to try to reassure me after he's just told me how much he needs to be the one to keep his job.

We drift apart without more conversation, moving in opposite directions away from Brad's office: I head to get a drink of water from the break room while Carter walks toward the restrooms.

I know I should eat the Luna bar I put in my purse this morning, but my stomach seems to have closed up shop for the day.

*   *   *

In order to help with the transition, P&D brought in a few team members from New York. And just like Brad suggested, early that afternoon I have a one-on-one with a senior agent I've met on several occasions, a woman I deeply admire. Her name is Joanne Simms, and she's a shark. She started in Features and has moved over to the television side, but she knows *everyone*. At first blush, she's the sweetest human you could possibly meet. But in negotiations the gloves come off. She's my Kathy Bates in *Fried Green Tomatoes*. If you're in her parking spot, she will ram her car into your car without a second thought. And then maybe set it on fire.

Her temporary office is in the corner and has a beautiful view of downtown and the mountains beyond. This office was recently occupied by Tom Hetchum, head of Legal at P&D. Tom is no longer with us.

Joanne beckons me in, and while she finishes up a call, I stand near the window, trying to calm my racing heart. I love the view of LA from this side of the building. It reminds me how many people there are here, how many opportunities, how much space there is for everyone in the sprawling mass of buildings. I'm not an optimist, but I'm not exactly a pessimist, either. I'm a wait-and-see-when-you-have-more-info-ist. My opinions spend ninety percent of their time in a holding pattern before swooping in like a hawk.

And right now my opinions need Joanne to get off the phone and tell me this is all bullshit and everything will be fine.

In the end, she doesn't tell me that. But there's a hopeful vibe to the meeting, anyway. Joanne is hilarious, she loves her job, she loves what she does. And she's a woman who never lets the old boys' game get in her way. She is exactly what I want to be.

We talk about her list, about the kind of list I have and where I'd like to see it go. We talk about the clients I'll likely inherit from the agents who were let go, and how to manage my current clients' panic along with the panic of those actors passed off to someone new. We have a conversation that feels a lot like long-term planning, and although I won't get to work with Joanne much because she's in New York and in television, just knowing she'll be around for a while is reassuring.

At the end of the meeting I feel a million times better about my place here, and I generally feel like Carter and I can find a way to make this work. At the very least, I feel confident that I'm needed—and that upper management at P&D knows that.

The hallways are quiet as I leave Joanne's office, and I have a moment of peace to myself to sit and think about this morning. I saw Carter heading into John Fineman's office earlier, and instinctively I want to wait for him. I feel so much better after talking to Joanne, and I want to infuse a conversation with Carter with some of that hopefulness. But when I see him emerge, I immediately sense his meeting did not go as well. His position is admittedly more precarious than mine, and I *do* really like him. I don't want him moving to New York any more than I want to move there myself.

"How did it go with John?" I ask.

He smiles a little drily. "I think that was the most talking I've ever done in a one-on-one meeting before."

I laugh. "John is not known for his conversation skills. I sat next to him at a company Christmas dinner and let's just say it's amazing he does any deals. He's not known for being very . . . sociable." I feel a little like I'm marking my territory here, emphasizing my familiarity with people he's only just meeting. I know I should pull back and be more of a team player—Carter *is* the new guy, after all. So I go for encouragement: "I'm sure you were great. I bet everyone loves you."

Carter studies me for a few breaths, and I get the distinct impression that he knows exactly what I'm doing. "It looks like things went well with Joanne."

I nod, smiling. "When are you meeting with her?"

"Later this week."

"Do you want to grab some lunch?" I ask. "I could fill you in on what's what here. Who's sleeping with who and where the good coffee is hidden."

He looks away, unsmiling as he squints at a point in the distance down the hall. "I think I'm just going to grab a sandwich and catch up on all the emails I need to deal with," he says. "I've got a million things to handle right now. Maybe some other time?"

I know people. I can easily spot the careful stepping back. "Okay."

I watch as he pinches the bridge of his nose.

And then he looks up and gives me a pained smile. "I'll see you later?"

He turns to head down the hall and his posture immediately changes. His shoulders are straight, and his ass looks amazing in his dark dress pants. Heads turn. A few interns lean in and discuss him when he's walked past, their expressions eager, admiring. It's as if the star quarterback has just strolled down the hall. My high from my meeting with Joanne deflates as I see exactly what they see: confidence, charisma . . .

Competition.

chapter nine

"How can you not like brussels sprouts?" Amelia asks Daryl, holding the fork in front of our friend's scrunched-up face. We're doing an emergency happy hour, with food instead of drinks. I am not a consistent stress-drinker, but I am a fantastic stress-eater.

Daryl gently pushes away her hand. "Because they taste like ass in my mouth?"

"I'm up for ass in my mouth," I say. "I'll take her share."

Amelia studies me for a moment before dropping them onto my plate. "Careful who you say that to."

"Speaking of: We should have invited Carter," Daryl says. "He's cute and probably freaking out just as much as we are right now."

Daryl's department was hit a little differently than was Features. They still have cuts, but it's far cheaper to keep Daryl than to buy her out. She's safe for at least another year.

I shake my head, quickly swallowing an enormous bite. "He didn't *want* to."

So far I've only given them the bullet points:

- Hiding in my office, worrying I was going to be fired.
- Meeting with Brad.

- Thinking I might not be fired.

- Surprise! There might only be a job here for one of you.

- And by one of you, we mean you or this new guy you want to bang.

"Didn't you . . . *ya know* . . ." Daryl makes a crude sexual hand gesture, adding, "like, only a few nights ago?"

"Use your big-girl words, Daryl," Amelia says.

"Third base," I confirm. "And it was a holy experience. *Orgasmus maximus*. My bedspread and I were hoping for a repeat."

"So, how is it going to play out?" Amelia asks. "You can't work together and sleep together?"

"Or maybe you won't work together at all and can still sleep together?" Daryl counters.

"Great, except for that part about one of us being an unemployed hobo. Homelessness tends to be a real mood killer." I pop a pita chip in my mouth and chew, thinking. "We have a meeting to go over our new client lists on Thursday. And after that, I suppose we'll operate as though we're both working there forever, knowing that one of our contracts probably won't be renewed. New York was brought up, but . . . I don't know."

Daryl blanches. "You'd *move*?"

"Hell no. But P&D has huge resources. I don't want to burn any bridges until I have to."

"And Carter has huge resources, too?" At the meaningful tilt to Daryl's words, Amelia high-fives her.

My phone lights up on the table, and we all look down to see Carter's name.

"Oh *shit*," Daryl whispers. "It's like he *knows* . . ."

I stare at it as it rings, and rings.

Amelia sighs. "Will you answer that damn phone?"

I lift it, swiping my thumb across the screen. "Hey, Carter."

"Hey."

Standing, I walk to a quiet corner of the restaurant, near the windows.

"How are you holding up?" he asks.

I laugh, tracing my finger along the windowsill. "I'm working my way through the Post and Beam appetizer menu, so I'm doing okay."

Carter laughs now, too, and I realize when he does how awkward and unmirthful both of us have sounded. "Look, I was still sort of in reaction mode when you asked me about lunch and was probably a bit shorter than I meant to be. I know it's crazy, but I don't want this to get in the way of what was starting with us, you know?"

I nod but struggle to think of what to say in response. It's so complicated now.

"I know," I say finally. "You give good make-out."

"So do you." He's quiet for a few breaths. "Do you think we're competing for this job?"

"Brad sure made it sound that way. I don't know that we *need* to, though. I think we can figure out how to both be indispensable."

"Let's just make sure we communicate," he says. "If we stay open with each other, we'll be fine, right?"

I squeak out a limply enthusiastic "Sure!" and after a few more small words we agree to talk tomorrow.

It feels like we're standing on the deck of the *Titanic* as it goes down, saying, *It's gonna bob back up any second now.*

Date: Wed, Oct 14 at 5:03 AM
From: Bradley Kingman
To: Aimee Miller; Dudley Thompson; John Fineman;
Timothy Brown; Andrew Murphy; Carter Aaron;
Evelyn Abbey; Rose McCollough; Ashton Garcia
Subject: Dan Printz
Flagged: HIGHLY CONFIDENTIAL

Team,
I received word last night that Dan Printz is
leaving his current representation at Lorimac.
Anyone think they can snare him, let me know
and I'll set up a meeting. This is a $5M/
year potential client for us. Evie handled his
screenwriting credit over at Alterman a few
years back, so I'm leaning that way. Jump in
with any objections by 9 am.

Date: Wed, Oct 14 at 5:07 AM
From: Carter Aaron <caaron@PriceDicklepartners.com>
To: Bradley Kingman
CC: Aimee Miller; Dudley Thompson; John Fineman;
Timothy Brown; Andrew Murphy; Evelyn Abbey; Rose
McCollough; Ashton Garcia
Subject: Re: Dan Printz

Let me take a shot at this one, Brad. We have a
mutual friend in New York.

-C.

Date: Wed, Oct 14 at 5:08 AM
From: Evelyn Abbey
To: Bradley Kingman
Subject: Re: Dan Printz

I'm happy to keep working with Dan. He and I
had a great relationship and I'm confident I
could get him to move over.

Thanks,
Evie

Date: Wed, Oct 14 at 5:08 AM
From: Evelyn Abbey
To: Bradley Kingman
CC: Carter Aaron
Subject: Re: Dan Printz

Carter and I must have replied at the
same time. Looks like we're both happy to
take him onto our list. Perhaps this is a
good opportunity for a team representation
strategy. Let's discuss today?

Evie

Date: Wed, Oct 14 at 5:43 AM
From: Bradley Kingman
To: Aimee Miller; Dudley Thompson; John Fineman;
Timothy Brown; Andrew Murphy; Carter Aaron;
Evelyn Abbey; Rose McCollough; Ashton Garcia
Subject: Dan Printz

Early bird gets the worm, and good timing,
Carter. Joanne just called. Dan will be named
People's Sexiest Man Alive—not announced yet.
Would be a huge get for us. Carter, Kylie will
set up a one-on-one meeting for you and Dan
this week. Great job.

Brad

chapter ten

Thursday afternoon Michael Christopher sits at a table in the courtyard outside P&D. The sun is shining overhead, the sky is blue without a single cloud in sight, and he waits, eating his peanut butter and jelly sandwich while I pace.

Labeling the current situation "tense" would be like calling Usain Bolt "fast." Although most of the higher-ups seem thrilled with the merge because it makes P&D this enormous conglomerate monster, the rest of us are a flock of anxious birds, eyeing one another as if we're all plotting to not only take each other's jobs but also eat each other's children.

The situation with Evie isn't any better. We went from this budding thing, to sharing one of the hottest nights I've ever had, to clipped conversations as we pass in the hall at work. After our conversation on Tuesday night, I figured we would band together and talk this through, but she's been so busy with meetings, I barely saw her yesterday. All week, really.

And as much as I'd like to hope we're starting on equal footing with Brad, I know that isn't the reality. I don't think I'm wrong in my sense that he really liked me, and in my read that there's some old animosity between them, but she's also worked for him for years. Not to mention that she has the benefit of all her local contacts. I also get the sense that she's aligning with a

group of select colleagues and setting up an artillery in this position, hoping to be invaluable . . .

But didn't we agree we could work together?

"Can you sit down and eat something?" Michael says. "I'm
going to need a Dramamine if I keep watching you."

I push my hands into my pockets and make my way to the
bench beside him. He pulls something from a brown paper bag
and slides it and a Ziploc full of potato chips across to me. "Eat."

I look down. Grape jelly, diagonal cut. "You made me
lunch?"

He shrugs and takes another bite. "I knew you were preoccupied."

"Thanks."

"I'm guessing there's been no update?"

I'd gone straight from work to Michael and Steph's on Tuesday night, and in what had to resemble some sort of manic episode, I'd told them everything I knew about the merge, including
the meeting where Brad dropped a bomb on us. Neither of them
knew what to say, and I couldn't exactly blame them. Hello,
shitty situation with no good solution. So, after I called Evie, I
decided to stay at their place for a *Buffy* marathon and somehow
managed to eat an entire coconut cream pie.

"No update," I tell him, setting my food down and leaning
my elbows on the table.

"I do know that Brad doesn't like Evie," Michael says, "and
yet he keeps her around like it's some kind of game."

That sounds about right. "He had the nerve to bring up *Field
Day* right there in front of me. Sort of a dick move." I groan,
pressing my forehead to the table. "I really liked her, Michael.
No, present tense: I *like* her. There is no angle where this doesn't
suck."

"I know, man." He reaches over to give my shoulder a reassuring squeeze.

I sit up again, looking out over the grass and the cars moving along the street in the distance. Michael is quiet for a moment and slowly taps his fingers against his thigh.

"There's really only one thing you can do," he finally says. "You're going to have to get rid of her."

"Get *rid* of her?"

He nods, taking a huge bite of sandwich. "Make her look incompetent."

I gape at him. "What kind of asinine plan is that? I like her!"

He blinks, watching me as he chews.

"Besides," I continue, "Brad might've tried to throw her under the bus a little, but he also made sure I knew what I was up against. No one is going to think she's incompetent."

He stares blankly at me, which only makes me explode. "Not to mention, she's your friend, too, jackass!"

He pops a chip in his mouth with a satisfied grin. "Christ, I know you so well. You're such a Boy Scout, Aaron. I just wanted to make sure we were on the same page."

I stare at him. "Thank God you brought me lunch, because otherwise you're quickly veering out of helpful territory."

He laughs, wiping his mouth with a pink paper napkin. "Look, you like Evie, she likes you. You're both problem solvers, and if anyone can find a way to coexist, it's you two. Show these guys they're wrong and that they need you both. Isn't that what agents do anyways? Talk people into things they're not sure they want?"

"That is literally the opposite of what agents do. Do you ever listen to your wife when she talks about work?"

"Whatever. Do whatever it is that you guys do. Save your job, get the girl."

I ball up my bag of chips and throw it at him. "You're an idiot."

"Keeps people guessing."

I stand, picking up my trash and walking to the bin, tossing it all inside. *Save your job, get the girl.* He might be an idiot, but the thing is, a part of me can't help but wonder if maybe this time he's right.

· · ·

After lunch I head back inside, bidding a tragic farewell to both Michael Christopher and the perfect sunny day. I'm still learning my way around a new office, memorizing names and positions, getting a read on who I need to keep close and who I need to keep closer.

The building smells of fresh paint and carpet cleaner, and relative to CTM's funky 1970s vibe, everything here feels new new new. My steps are accompanied by the steady hum of voices, the ringing of phones, and the clicking of keyboards. In New York, we could always hear the traffic, even twelve floors up. It was the ever-present backing track to each conversation, the sound we fell asleep to every night. It grew so familiar that aside from the occasional horn or siren, it'd be easy to forget there were cars outside the building at all. At CTM, we were just beside a fire station, and the sound of the siren turning on and wailing out of the gate became so familiar, we never even remarked upon it when we'd stop talking midsentence in the conference room, waiting for quiet to return.

Here, it's quieter—and yet it *feels* louder. The lack of street noise inside the fancy, double-paned windows makes every other interior noise stand out. And as I walk into my office, I'm reminded again that the view couldn't be more different, too.

She's not there now, but Evie's office is just across the hall. I've noticed she likes to meet with clients at the little couch and chair just inside the door, and if I bend to reach the garbage can—coincidentally, not on purpose, of course—I can just see her legs through the glass, the way she crosses them, the way she—

The new assistant on my desk, Justin, knocks on my door before peeking in. I inherited him from a P&D agent who was cut loose, and he's a bit like a rescue dog brought home from the shelter. If he's still here, he's obviously considered good, but we're working out a rhythm. He's excitable, seems like the kind of guy who would use emojis in lieu of words in texts, and uses *we* when referencing anything on my to-do list.

We have a call with Patricia from Fox at eleven.

We have a one o'clock lunch with Peter in Legal.

We'll just make a note here that we need to talk to Brad about this.

He's also not Becca. I took a long shot and asked if there was any way to retain her; there wasn't. Apparently mergers don't work that way.

Becca used to argue with me, and she was right ninety-eight percent of the time. Becca would snap in my face when I wasn't paying attention and yell at me for leaving my empty coffee cups around. Becca would fix my grammar on Post-it notes. Becca, and her loopy script I could never decipher. I miss Becca.

"You're back," Justin says as he walks into my office. Like most of the interns and assistants here, he's barely old enough to drink and looks like he just stepped out of a Topman ad.

"Hey. Yeah." With my hands on my hips, I survey the newly unpacked office. It feels so empty.

"Good lunch?"

"Just met a friend."

"We've had a few people stop by." He looks down at his notes. "Angela from Literary. Esther from Legal. Aimee from—" He stops, eyes narrowing. "There are a lot of women on this list."

"Listen," I say, and walk to the door. Satisfied that nobody is within earshot, I close it quietly behind me. "Do you know where Evie is?"

"Evelyn . . . Ms. Abbey?" he asks formally, and I nod.

Justin jogs out of the room and comes back about twenty seconds later. "Jess says she had a lunch meeting and isn't back yet."

"Jess?"

"Her assistant."

"Right." I feel twisted inside and want to sit down with Evie sooner rather than later. We're meeting with Brad to review our client lists this afternoon, and I would prefer we go into that with a united front rather than under a cloud of miscommunication and awkward silence. "Do me a favor and let me know when she's back, okay?"

"We have that meeting with Joanne in about five minutes," he reminds me.

I give him a few seconds to hear the echo of that sentence, but he doesn't seem to regret his odd assistant-speak. "Thanks, Justin," I say. "I'm headed down there now. Just send me a text if you see Evie."

Justin's eyes widen at the prospect of being given a specific task, and it makes me feel bad for him for a beat. Mergers are terrible enough, but with a boss who doesn't quite have his sea legs yet? Torture.

"Absolutely," he says eagerly. "I'll keep an eye out and text you the minute I see her back! Have a good meeting." He turns to leave and then stops by the door. "Oh, and if you don't catch Ms. Abbey before, remember the two of you have a meeting with Brad at two."

As if I could forget.

*   *   *

I go into my meeting with Joanne trying to feel optimistic. Under normal circumstances, I would be floating on confidence. I know I'm outgoing and a good coworker. Everyone I've spoken to at P&D has been welcoming, excited, and enthusiastic about what I can offer this new combined firm.

I know that Joanne had been based in the LA office but transitioned to television in New York a few years ago. The rumor is she moved because Brad didn't play well with female others, and having seen him firsthand with Evie, I'm inclined to agree. Given that Joanne is just as senior as he is, I wonder whether it was his decision she be moved or hers. Hollywood is a world of big dogs and small pens.

Unfortunately, my feeling of optimism doesn't last. This was a basic get-to-know-you, where all Joanne has to go on is what she sees in my portfolio, what she's found on the web, or what she's heard from Brad. But Joanne clearly *knows* Evie. Clearly *likes* Evie. Where I might have felt I had some sort of edge with Brad—in the dudebro sense, which I don't really prefer anyway—that edge is clearly absent here. Joanne impresses upon me how lucky I am to be working with Evie, how great and well respected she is, how much I can learn from her.

Basically, there's a whole lot of *Evie is awesome* happening today, and it's only one o'clock.

With my stomach feeling like it's bottomed out somewhere

near my knees, I get a text from Justin on my way to the meeting with Brad, telling me that Evie came in, dropped her things off, and is already in the conference room, waiting.

Shit, so much for strategizing first. It's becoming clear that Evie has one hell of an upper hand. Not only is she smart and beautiful and fucking great at her job, but she's got the executives singing her praises. I definitely have my work cut out for me.

Rounding the corner, I spot her as soon as I walk in.

It doesn't matter how many times I see her, I'm always surprised by how gorgeous she is, like I forget somehow when we're apart. Her dark hair is piled on top of her head, and she's in a fitted sweater vest with a long-sleeved shirt underneath. She's wearing a skirt and as I slip into the seat next to her, it takes superhuman strength not to let my eyes—or hands—follow the length of her legs below the table. I can imagine how she'd look spread out on top of it, maybe pressed against that wall of windo—

Focus, Carter. Eyes on the prize.

Other than the occasional quick hello in the hallway as we pass, we haven't spoken since our brief phone call Tuesday night. I mean, obviously that's a little weird, given that less than a week ago I had my hand in her underwear and was already planning on when I could enjoy that again.

Brad hasn't joined us yet, so we're all alone in here, but just in case, I keep my voice low: "I was wondering if you wanted to go out tonight. Get dinner? Strategize?"

She finishes what she was writing and looks over to me. I envy her mask of calm as she quickly glances around. I'm close, but not too close. Definitely not encroaching on her space, but maybe giving her the hint that I'd still really, really like to.

"Dinner?" she repeats. I can tell her pulse has picked up. Her eyes dilate as we continue to stare at each other. "You want to have dinner."

It's like dropping a match in a puddle of gasoline, and even though I know I shouldn't, I want to lean in, press my mouth to her neck.

"Yeah. If you're not busy."

I swallow, working to keep my eyes on hers and not let them wander down to her mouth. Looking at her mouth could lead to *remembering* her mouth, which could lead to further imaginings of her mouth, and that would be a very, very bad idea.

Evie pulls out her phone and checks her calendar, her brows drawn together while she scrolls. "I have a meeting at five. What do you mean by strategize? Strategize what?"

Strategize you on top of me?

Brad picks this exact moment to walk into the room. He takes a seat and shuffles a few papers in front of him before looking up at us. "Evie, Carter, how are you doing? Playing nice?"

I can only wonder if Evie's reaction is the same as mine—an internal *What the fuck?*

"Sure," we both say, and I feel her foot nudge me slightly beneath the table. And yes, *this* is exactly what we need. Us against them. A united front. I bite back my smile. We can do this, I have no doubt.

Kylie walks in, setting a stack of files down in front of Brad, and he slips his glasses on as he opens the first one.

"Okay, great," he says absently, and I know we could have said, *We're doing pretty shitty, Brad. You've put us both on edge. A week ago we were cruising down the road toward a stellar bang, but now we're trying to seek out each other's weaknesses and exploit them,* and he would have had the same reaction. Brad really is a dick. I'm glad Evie gave him that dog-food bar.

"We're going to talk about clients today," he says, flipping the tops of a few pages down as he riffles through client sheets. "There will probably be a few more, but right now we're just here for the big ones." He looks up at me. "Carter, you're going to work on Dan Printz, correct?"

I nod. "I've already reached out to his team. We're playing phone tag."

I feel Evie shift beside me, and there's something in her posture . . . some stiffness that wasn't there only a few seconds ago. Her foot is no longer pressed to mine, and out of the corner of my eye I see her slowly fold her hands across her middle.

Is she . . . is she pissed that I stepped up to try for Dan Printz?

My chest seems to sink in as the sequence of emails unscrolls in my memory. Evie emailed, throwing her hat in the ring as well, and Brad handed him over to me. At the time, it was only one string of emails in the hysterical post-merge blur of my inbox, but now it occurs to me Evie probably saw my email as completely underhanded.

Oh shit. *Was* it? Wouldn't she have done the same?

I blink into focus, catching what Brad is already saying. ". . . assume you have people who will transition here from CTM, including Emil and a few others, so for the time being I want to start you slowly, focus on reassuring everyone that it's business as usual. But adding Dan would be a big coup." He sorts through a few papers and then glances up at me, and I nod, letting him know I've heard him. He looks back down again. "The first new player on your list of P&D clients will be Jett Payne. Jett starred in a few indies and was added to MTV's biggest series a few years ago. His character was killed off in the finale when he was offered a larger part with a network show, and, in my opinion, he's primed to blow up. Your TV experience will come in handy, but talk to Joanne about him. She's helped folks transition back and forth there."

He slides the file across to me and I scan it, jotting down a few notes.

Dan is a heavy hitter in features, Jett is an up-and-comer. So far, so good.

"Next for you, Carter, is Jamie Huang, reality show darling." It's impossible to miss the mocking in his tone, but outwardly, I ignore it. Reality television is one of the largest markets in the eighteen-to-twenty-nine demographic, and Jamie's show consistently runs in the top five. She has a huge social media presence, and while that means nothing if people don't show up and *buy* the thing you're selling, from what I've gathered, her fans do. A friend of mine met her briefly and mentioned that she was eager to move into film.

"Jamie's manager is Allie . . ." He searches his notes. "Allie Brynn. She's good—Jamie has had a fast rise and a wild online following, but she's as dumb as a bag of sand." Evie clears her throat—meaningfully—but Brad doesn't seem to notice. "Allie keeps her in line, and her main job is to get Jamie to do whatever you want her to do."

"Got it," I say, noting Allie's name. I've worked with managers extensively in the past. For the most part, they make my job easier.

"Alex Young is one of our biggest clients, Carter, and I think he'd do well on your list," Brad continues, and I feel my heart speed up. Alex is a singer-songwriter whose breakout album debuted at number two in the UK, and he's poised to become a massive US star.

My palms are sweating.

"I'm giving him to you because of your theater and music

background in New York. You'll be working in collaboration with the music team here and I'll get that over to you, but people are poking around him for features. Personally, I think there's no rush there and you can be picky. You'll have fewer clients than Evie at first, but I think Alex is going to be right up your alley."

I take a moment to glance from Alex's file to Evie, and she looks impressed. *We can do this*, I think. We have complementary strengths, and we can sell Brad on the idea of us as a team. A wild little part of me daydreams that we could become something like our own specialized subdepartment if we mesh really well.

"Have your assistant get me your current list—only the folks who are sticking around after this merge—and we'll update and go from there," Brad says, and I nod, reaching for my phone and firing off a message to Justin.

"Evie," Brad says, and she straightens in her chair. "I know you've got a pretty heavy list already and are working on contracts for Adam Elliott and Sarah Hill. That's amazing." He shakes his head and seems to add somewhat begrudgingly, "Well. I'm thrilled."

Great. Both Adam and Sarah are A-listers, already chest-deep in the industry. Brad glances back to Evie's folder, open in front of him. "The first one I'm going to give to you is Marian Isaac."

I hate the way my first response to this is to want to laugh, because although Marian will bring in a ton of money, it'll be no picnic for Evie. Marian is a model turned A-list actress who's known for being a nightmare. She's demanding, she's often rude to interviewers and fans, and some of her screaming matches with her last director are legendary. I'm not surprised some other agent used the merge as an excuse to trade her off.

Evie nods, expression largely unreadable, but I'll admit she doesn't look particularly surprised. *Evie could talk a grenade out of exploding*, Brad had said. This is exactly what he meant.

"She was recently dropped from Lorimac," Evie says.

"That's right." Brad laughs. "She made them three million dollars last year and they still dropped her like a hot potato."

"Who was handling her before?" she asks.

"Chad." Brad gives a sardonic grin. "He was happy to pass her off."

"Oh, I'm sure he was." Evie laughs knowingly, and something itches inside me to enter this banter so I don't continue to feel like the newbie.

It's just that I have no idea who Chad is.

Brad leans in, giving her a confident nod. "I have zero doubt that you're the one to handle her."

This feels like a sharp stab.

And I'm growing uneasy, because aside from her current list, he's given her a big name, with the probability of signing two more, and all three of these clients are huge commissions.

Why the hell was I starting to feel bad about jumping in and taking Dan Printz?

Brad settles in again, looking back to his stack of folders. "Next up, Keaton Avery. I'm sure you remember that little tiff he had with the paparazzi last year, so I want to make sure image repair is at the front of your mind."

Her pen slows on the pad in front of her, but she doesn't question or object. Keaton was in an Oscar-nominated film last year and is poised to become the new art-house darling.

Fuck.

"Trent Vanh," Brad says. "Just wrapped filming on the final season of *Burn Brightly*." I lean back in my chair, feeling feverish.

Trent won an Emmy last year. "He's hoping to transition to film, so we'll need to land him something big, and fast."

Brad pulls out the final folder in the Evie stack. I feel my blood pressure rise about ten points and wonder what else he could possibly have.

"Last we have Seamus Aston, YouTuber."

And *goddammit*. My hands curl into fists in my lap. Evie sits up, leaning her elbows on the table.

"Incidentally, Seamus and Jamie starred together in the new Scott film, so the two of you will have promo for that to coordinate. Seamus had seventeen million subscribers on his channel, along with pretty much every millennial endorsement you can imagine, and was just cast in what some are predicting to be the biggest film of next year. But," Brad says, and leans back in his chair, "he is an *epic* asshole."

You would know, I think.

As if on cue, Evie reaches for her handbag at her feet and pulls out a small tube of hand cream. Despite how tense things are, I know what she's doing and have to stifle a smile as I watch her squeeze a dollop into the center of her palm and start vigorously rubbing her hands together.

"Not a problem," she says.

This pulls a grin out of Brad. "That's what I like to hear, kiddo. Glad you're taking our talk to heart. *Team player*."

Evie's reputation is as an agent who keeps her cool and can handle divas, but there's something else lurking here. Brad is being so nice to her about it, like he's helping her to the top of a mountain. He's intending to either let her plant the flag or shove her off the sharp ledge on the other side.

"I know the scales seem a bit tipped right now," he says to me. "But Evie knows this town and the people in it, and like

I've said before, it's one thing to land talent—it's another to keep it."

"Got it," I say.

Yes, Evie has more contacts, experience with features, and several more years in the business than I do, but that doesn't necessarily make her the better agent. Logically, I know that what Brad is saying makes sense. But there's a part of me that can't help but bristle.

We end the meeting and begin gathering up our things. My optimism has dissolved. Yes, we can work as a team, and yes, we have complementary skills. But do I want it to appear that I'm learning from her, and benefitting from her experience? I'm trying to talk myself down, but my pulse is racing and I can barely look in her direction.

I stall to let Brad and Evie leave the room first, but I'm not surprised to find Evie waiting in the hall when I make it outside. She stops me with a look, leaning back against the wall. She's got a head start in this race and seems to know it.

"So, that was interesting." She folds her arms over her chest.

"That's one word for it."

"About that strategizing," she says, looking away. "Like I said, I have an appointment at five, but we could still get together afterward. It might be nice to download all of this."

Fuck.

My heart is a hammer against my breastbone; my stomach is a pit of guilt. "You know, I forgot that I told Michael I'd watch Morgan tonight. She has swimming and I said I'd walk her down to the pool and stay until he's free to pick her up."

"Oh," she says, and she knows I'm lying. She *knows*. "Another time."

"Of course."

Evie is a master of the calm mask, but I can see the tightness around her eyes. "You happy with your list?" And the tiny amused tilt to her voice tells me she wouldn't be if she were me.

"Yeah," I say. "Combined with what I'm bringing, I'll be busy. You?"

"Thrilled," she says, and grins. "Glad you jumped in on the Dan Printz thing after all. I don't know how I'd find time for him *and* Adam, Sarah, Seamus . . ."

I pause, trying to hold back my first reaction: to call her out on her passive-aggressive shit. I fail. "So you *were* pissed about my email to Brad about Dan?"

"I wasn't pissed," she says evenly; she was totally pissed. "It's just funny that only a few hours before, you were calling me to say we should keep our lines of communication open. Then you swoop in to grab a client Brad was thinking of giving to me."

Is she serious with this?

Neither of us likes this situation. Each of us sees the other clearly—at least I think we do. I would still give my small finger to bang her until the sun comes up, but in this moment, when Evie is staring at me like I'm an opponent on the other side of the field, I decide I have to close one door to keep another open. I can't do both things right now. And if I can't get the girl, at least I can keep the job.

"I *did* keep our line of communication open," I tell her. "I CC'd you on the email, didn't I? It was all in plain sight. There was no 'swooping' about it."

There's a moment of awkward silence before she turns and walks down the hall. I continue to watch long after she's rounded the corner and probably disappeared inside her office.

Justin steps up beside me. "How'd it go in there?" he asks, motioning to the conference room.

I clap my hand on his shoulder and give him my best smile. "Great," I say. "In fact, it looks like we have a lot of research to do. Tell me, what do you know about YouTube?"

A plan begins to form in my head as he prattles on excitedly, and even though it makes me feel a little underhanded, it takes hold. I need this job. I need to figure out a way to make this work for me. Brad may think Evie's the right one for the position, but that's only because he hasn't seen what I can do.

If I have to do a little homework and learn everything there is to learn—and more—about my client list *and* hers, that's exactly what I'm going to do.

There is no way I'm losing to Evil.

chapter eleven

Date: Fri, Oct 30 at 4:12 PM
From: Kylie Salisbury
To: Carter Aaron; Evelyn Abbey
Subject: Department Retreat

Hi Evie, Carter,
Brad has asked that the two of you be in charge
of the annual department retreat up in Big
Bear. It is back on the calendar for January
14–16. As Evie knows, I've organized it the
last two years, so let me know when is a good
time for the three of us to sit down and go
over the format, activities, and any other
relevant details.

Best,
Kylie

I've read the email about seven times and still am not sure I understand it. I walk into Daryl's office and have her confirm I've read it correctly. I call Amelia in to have her verify that I am not, in fact, reading this wrong.

Wasn't this canceled? Is it back on—but this time with *senior agents* in charge of the itinerary? Am I having a stroke?

Apparently, I'm not. On top of everything else on our plates,

Carter and I have been given an assistant's task: organize the departmental retreat.

Brad is a piece of work.

Since this isn't coming from Brad himself, I have no way of knowing the subtext, but I'm sure there is one. It's possible Kylie dropped the ball somewhere, but it's *more* possible that this is Brad's first twist in the P&D Hunger Games.

I lean against Daryl's door, rubbing my face.

"This means I'm going to have to talk to him," I say. Two weeks ago this wouldn't have seemed like such a bad thing because (let's be honest) I wanted to talk my way into his pants. But after Carter's pouty blow-off—*Let's have dinner, oh wait, you got a better list than I did, no dinner for you!*—I'm beginning to think the best strategy is just to never, ever interact with him at the office again.

Which . . . surprisingly, wouldn't be that hard. With new clients and new coworkers on top of my normal schedule, I've been completely swamped. In the past week and a half, I've arrived at work by eight and stayed long after the office is empty, had nine lunch meetings, eleven meetings after work over drinks, and wall-to-wall clients during work hours. I've barely seen Carter. Except for when I watch him leave his office and find a way to enjoy the view from behind all the way down the hall . . .

I have a short break between a lunch meeting and an off-site and hope I can catch him for a few minutes. Because the odds of me wrestling him out of anger or lust are roughly equivalent, I decide to call in Daryl's IOU for ditching me at Steph's party and make her act as chaperone, possibly witness.

I am the best of friends.

We stop outside his office door, and I lift my fist, giving a single tentative knock.

Normally, Carter isn't really a closed-door kind of guy. From what I've seen so far, he's always in the hall talking to people, or has two or three other agents in his office. I get that it's just a way we do business differently—I tend to be to the point, friendly but brief, whereas he chats and wanders. *Everyone* likes Carter. I know he's been crazy busy this week, too, but he always seems to have a moment to say hi to someone, to stop and socialize for a spell.

I realize this makes our styles complementary, and I get a warm little pull in my stomach.

Wouldn't it be nice if we could collaborate?

Wouldn't it be nice if he didn't immediately turn into a threatened, competitive jackass?

"Stop it," Daryl says, and I look over to her.

"Stop what?"

"You're fidgeting. You're supposed to be a badass here. Badasses don't fidget. And don't give me that face; this is exactly why you brought me."

"Okay, right right." I close my eyes, summoning my inner badass. "I'm Uma Thurman in *Kill Bill*. Linda Hamilton in *Terminator 2*. Sigourney Weaver in *Aliens*—because let's be honest, that's *really* where she came into her own. Fascinating that it's the sequels where those two really—"

"Will you focus?"

When he calls out, "Come in," I'm a little taken aback at the way his voice sounds—deep and quiet, not at all his normal easygoing tone. It reminds me of how he sounded against me, on my bed, and I want to walk repeatedly into the nearest wall.

This whole situation would be about a million times easier if I didn't want to kiss him as much as I want to shove him.

Pushing open the door, I look up to find him sitting at his desk, hair messy, glasses crooked. He's oddly rumpled.

"Hey, Evie." His expression is hard to read. Surprised, maybe. Nervous? A little. Good.

Carter looks behind me to where Daryl has just walked right into my back.

"Thanks for the warning," she says, rubbing her nose. I should be more careful; she paid a lot of money for that nose.

"I don't think we've officially met," Carter says, and stands to walk around the desk, reaching out to shake Daryl's hand. "Carter Aaron. New guy."

"Daryl Jordan. Sagittarius."

"Aries," he says with a sly grin. "You know that makes us most compatible out of all the zodiac signs."

My God in heaven.

Daryl smiles, charmed. "Convenient, considering you're my new best friend for knowing that."

I turn to her, eyes wide. *Traitor.*

"I didn't peg you for an astrology buff," I say, not sure which of them I should glare at first. "Big horoscope reader, Carter?"

Your competitive moon is eclipsing my happy place sun, jack-hole.

"Not much these days, I'm afraid," he says, expression serious again. "My mom is really into astrology and used to read us our horoscopes every morning during breakfast. Whenever I hear someone mention it I get a little homesick."

Son of a—

"That might be the sweetest thing I've ever heard." Daryl swoons visibly. Bringing her was obviously a mistake. I wonder if anyone would notice if I gently shoved her out of the room.

"Unfortunately, I don't get to see her as often as I'd like, but I'm hoping soon. For the holidays, at least. Anyway." He straightens his glasses but doesn't bother to do anything about his hair.

Motioning for us to have a seat, he walks back around to his chair. "I've been buried in contracts. What's up?"

"I gather you've seen Kylie's email?" I ask.

He shakes his head and turns to his monitor.

"How are you liking it here?" Daryl asks. "Getting to know everyone?"

I hear the double click of his mouse and watch him quickly scan the email. "Yeah," he says slowly. "Just making friends, getting the lay of the land. Everyone was a little standoffish at first, but I think I've overcome it. Feels like a really good group."

Just like I did, he rereads the message a few times and then looks up at me. "Is this serious?"

Shrugging, I say, "I assume so."

"Brad doesn't think we have enough to do?"

"That, or he thinks Kylie did a shitty job in years past."

Carter looks up at me disapprovingly. "She's good, Evie."

Daryl pinches my arm, and seriously, *what the hell?* Weren't we just coming up with hypotheses about why we've been asked to do this?

Ignoring Daryl's attempt to keep me calm, I glare at him. "I'm sure she is, maybe retreats just aren't her thing?"

He laughs drily, shaking his head as he reads the email again. "You have such a chip on your shoulder about her."

This takes me a few breaths to process. In the two whole weeks he's been here, when has he ever witnessed me having a problem with Kylie? And why does he feel the need to defend her to *me?* My instinct is to pick up his stapler and launch it at his head. But a good agent keeps a lid on their temper unless it's really necessary to unleash the fury. A *great* agent doesn't have a temper, but can unleash the fury when necessary.

The difference is everything. I'm still working on being great.

"Okay, then," I say calmly, brushing off Daryl's grip. "I can tell you're overwhelmed with work. I'm happy to organize this alone, if you prefer."

Daryl shakes her head. "Evie, I don't think he's saying he—"

"I'm not *overwhelmed*," Carter cuts in.

"Of course you're not," I say meaningfully, and his cheeks go pink at the implication that he's got a light list.

I glance around his office. It's certainly more lived in than it was. His walls are covered with framed photos of landmarks on the East Coast, pictures of him with clients, his diploma, a framed copy of his first signed contract. There's a plant in the corner, and instead of a couch he has two chairs with colorful pillows, a giant ottoman in between. It looks cozy and warm, somewhere you'd sit and chat, make friends, maybe sign a contract or two.

Why does he have to be so damn smooth with everything?

I can tell he's not going to say anything now that I've just dropped a bomb of snark, and Daryl seems to have given up hope of running interference. "Anyway," I say as breezily as possible, "I just came down here to see if you wanted to go chat with Kylie really quick about the retreat."

Pushing back from his desk to stand, he wordlessly gestures for me to lead us onward.

•   •   •

At least we don't have to reinvent the wheel—Kylie doesn't really give us anything I didn't already know: It's a retreat for the Features department and support staff. We drink, we do team-building activities, we drink. We listen to Brad tell boring stories where he is the starring attraction, we drink. Basically, it's a giant drink fest with a few team-building games thrown in, which seems easy enough to organize—especially given that we'll have an events coordinator on-site. I'm now taking my peeved with a side of relieved.

I can't help but notice that Kylie directs nearly all of her attention to Carter while she recounts the activities she's put together the last two years. But . . . I can't blame her, either. I also quite enjoy looking at Carter. But since Carter has pointed out that I have *such a chip on my shoulder* about Kylie—I mean, what even—I work to look as unaffected by her obvious crush on him as possible. Under normal circumstances, I would ask questions and redirect her attention back to the two of us, but since this situation is completely *ab*normal, and as long as there is food and booze at this event no one is going to care about other specifics, I can't be bothered to get too worked up.

It all seems pretty straightforward, and we're about to walk back to our respective offices when Kylie stops us with a whispered, "*Guys.*"

We turn back to face her.

She looks almost apologetic and glances around us to make sure no one is listening. "That was all the regular stuff, but just remember: this is Brad's favorite weekend all year. Add to that the merge, and that people are paying attention to how he runs things, and he *really* expects it to be . . . like, a big deal. Okay?" Her wobbly smile tells us that she's relieved she's not in charge anymore, and it will be a bloodbath if we mess it up.

Carter must sense it, too, because he stops me on our way back down the hall. "Would you have any time to talk this out?" he says in a rush, looking the slightest bit queasy. "I know we're both busy, but she made it sound like this was pretty intense, and I've never been to one of Brad's retreats. I can clear my afternoon if I need to. If you can, of course."

I'm already shaking my head. "I'm heading out early to catch someone on set. I'll finish up around seven or so." I pause, then wonder if I'm going to regret what I say next. "We could meet after? Unless you have something to do."

"After is perfect. I'll clear my schedule and meet you wherever you are."

For a moment I think about having him just meet me at my place, but then I realize what a giant mistake that would be. "How about BOA, seven thirty?" I suggest instead.

He's already putting it into his phone. "Seven thirty. I'll get us a reservation and see you there. Thanks, Evie."

●   ●   ●

Carter is seated when I arrive, and the hostess walks me to the table. He's changed out of his work clothes and now has on a white button-down shirt and soft, dark jeans. The effect on me is immediate; because he looks like any other guy out on the street, it's both easier and harder to be with him right now. Easier because I don't feel the need to try to match his charisma like I do every day at the office. Harder because he looks so much like the Potential Boyfriend version of Carter. It sucks that the dynamic between us is so strained now.

I sit, unfolding my napkin and placing it on my lap.

We both thank the waiter when he fills our water glasses.

To my surprise, Carter declines any sort of cocktail . . . so I do, too.

The waiter lists the specials and says he'll be back once we've had time to look over the menu. The silence stretches between us. The contrast between this dinner and our first together is pretty stark. And the longer we're quiet, the harder it is to find a single word to say.

I could really use that cocktail.

The sun is setting through the windows and I look out at the street, marveling at how quiet this intersection gets when the offices shut down for the night.

I glance over to see him watching me, and he quickly looks away, back down to scan the menu. His eyes are so bright behind the glasses. I think I forgot how green they are, how perfect his mouth is.

"So," he says, and I realize it's my turn to be caught staring. "So."

His attention is so steady. I wish I had a Carter Thought Decoder Ring. His lips tilt up into a knowing half smile. "How're things?"

I burst out laughing and his smile grows, morphing into the real deal, the goofy, crooked smile, not the flashy work one.

"We probably should have ordered drinks," he says.

I am so relieved that his easy frankness is back that I nearly want to launch myself across the table.

"Yeah, like a hundred." Nervously, I straighten my spoon and knife beside each other on the table. "Carter," I start, "I'm really glad we did this. I wish we could start over in some ways."

He nods, swallowing a sip of his water. "Me too. Though maybe not *all* of it. Some of it wasn't too bad."

My face heats at his meaningful smile. "Agree. And the work situation sucks, but I think we can work better together."

Relief seems to wash over him and he reaches across the table to take my hand. "I agree. We haven't been great."

"I really do think they could have positions for both of us here. The more I look, the more I realize there's a lot of deadweight in the Features department . . . but it isn't *us*."

"Obviously I haven't been there as long," he says with a nod in my direction, and I appreciate the small acknowledgment, "but yeah, I agree." He leans forward. "Our strengths are so complementary. Rose and Ashton might be better suited for New York. They love to do the theater stuff; it's just there isn't that much of it out here. Maybe they would want to be transferred if given the choice?"

"Exactly."

It loosens something for us to agree on this one tiny point. I feel a fondness seeping back in and his smile is even easier now. The waiter stops at our table to take our orders, and we let go of each other's hand, but once he's gone, we immediately look back to each other.

"There's so much good in all of this," he says quietly. "I like Features, I like you. I hate the situation, but I sort of like being at P&D."

"I'm glad. And I like you, too."

"I had a really good time that night," he says, and he leans in, taking my hand again. "I don't think I ever got to tell you that."

This makes me laugh, and his eyes widen in surprise and amusement at the sound of it. "I had an inkling."

He clears his throat. "I'm sorry if it felt underhanded that I volunteered to take Dan."

"It's fine," I tell him. "I like Dan, and we've worked well together in the past, but your list needs it more."

His eyebrow twitches and I realize how unfiltered that came out. What is it about Carter that brings out my competitive side so immediately?

"I really didn't mean that to sound rude," I say, wanting him to believe me. "I'm just being honest. I think you can sign him, easily. With Dan, you just need to call him up and ask him what he's looking for."

He lets go of my hand to take a quick sip of water, shaking his head. With the loss of contact, the intimacy of the vibe at the table is immediately flipped on its head. "Dan will talk about it when he's ready," he says. "I know a bit about how he works. He wants to feel like he's in control, and calling him will just make me seem pushy."

Carter has amazing instincts, but right now he's wrong. He just is. Dan likes being chased a little. I've worked with him and I know: he doesn't like to be the one making calls, he wants to be the one choosing whether or not to answer.

"I just really think—"

"Christ, Evie, just let me do my job, okay?" he snaps.

I open my mouth, and a few garbled sounds come out before I mumble a quiet "Sure, of course."

I can see immediately that he regrets his tone. But it's too late. The tension is back with a vengeance.

Our food comes, and we bend to our plates, eating in silence.

Carter puts his fork down after a few bites, leaning in. "Evie . . ."

"No, seriously, it's okay." I put on my best smile, because I really don't want him to feel micromanaged by me. This is an impossible situation: If I help him, I could lose a job. If he doesn't fight for a better list, he could. And there is basically no way we can solve this with kissing, no matter how much I'd like to. "You're right. I was being pushy. You do your thing."

Carter nods, and I decide to move on. "Now, let's talk about that retreat."

• • •

Dinner turned out as well as could be hoped. We have a solid plan for the event in January, and we each have a list of piddly homework items we need to find time for before we meet up again. As we walk out, one comment leads to another and Carter is telling me a story about how Michael got Steph a kinky cast-making kit for their anniversary so they could craft a mold of his penis and build her a toy for whenever she travels. Instead, she thought he was subtly telling her he had cancer and had found a way for her to remember him when he was gone.

I laugh so hard Carter wraps his hand around my forearm and keeps it there for a moment to make sure I'm steady. I hate how funny he is, and I hate how much I want him to keep touching me. I hate this entire situation.

We pull apart and keep walking away from Sunset, up Doheny. It's warm, but not with the cloying death haze of early October. I look over at him as he takes a deep, calming breath.

"It's nice out, isn't it?" I say.

He looks up at the sky. "I wonder whether I'll ever live somewhere where I can see all the stars."

"That's what vacations are for."

He grins. "Vacation? *Was ist das?*"

This makes me laugh. "I know. I guess we can't really expect much of that this year."

He gives me a smile that's both sweet and a little sad, and then shakes himself out of it. Pointing up the hill, he says, "I live just a few blocks up."

I look over his shoulder and off in that direction. His apartment is that way.

His bed.

I've never been to his place. I mean, of course I haven't: we had a relationship for a *weekend*, if that. Even though it feels like a much bigger event in my romantic life than it actually was. I can't decide if that's internally meaningful in a rallying *Don't give up* way, or in a pathetic *This is the sad state of your romantic land-scape* way.

Regardless, he hasn't said this as a lead-up to asking whether I want to walk up there with him, because we both know there's no way that can happen, even if we both clearly grapple with the un-said: Under other circumstances we would totally be banging there tonight. And given what I know—

1. We're both stressed out of our minds

2. Carter is fun and fun*ny*

3. Carter has a great penis

—the sex would undoubtedly be stellar.

But instead, we exchange a lingering hug and part ways on the sidewalk. Watching him disappear up the tree-shrouded hill, I can't decide if tonight was a step forward or sideways. Should I be grateful for sideways? Carter sparks these enormous emotions in me—most of them good, and then I resent the situation all over again—but then he gets defensive and weird, and I basically want to strangle him. All we can do is try to make the best of things. I like Carter, but simply put: neither of us is doing this job because we like coming in second. Signing Adam Elliott and Sarah Hill was a huge coup for me, and Carter's got to be feeling the pressure. Of course he wants to land Dan. Maybe I should try to show a little more empathy and eventually, we might even find a way to be friends.

As if the universe finds this all completely hilarious, just as I climb into my car my phone chimes with an email from a VIP sender. It's from Dave Cyrus, my entertainment contact at the *Hollywood Vine.*

Date: Fri, Oct 30 at 9:42 PM

From: Dave Cyrus

To: Evelyn Abbey

Subject: Dan Printz

Evie,

Reaching out to hear if Dan is headed onto your
list. That's the buzz, at least. Likely to
run with something either way, but if you know
something, I'd like to wait for the scoop and
run a Hot Buzz feature when he signs on. Let me
know.

Dave

With a groan, I let my head fall back against the headrest,
closing my eyes. This is huge. Dave has heard from somewhere
that Dan is signing with me. A Hot Buzz feature means print edition of the monthly magazine—with the best circulation of any
trade journal in the industry—as well as a huge spread in the online edition. It would be great promo for Dan, and an amazing
carrot to dangle to get him to join P&D.

I am ninety-eight percent positive I could call Dan right
now, find out what he's thinking he's going to do, and convince
him to join my list.

But I can't.

Because I am not a backstabbing monster.

Date: Fri, Oct 30 at 9:47 PM
From: Evelyn Abbey
To: Dave Cyrus
Subject: Re: Dan Printz

Dave, it kills me to have to say this, but
a colleague is angling to sign Dan, and I
couldn't in good conscience use this to snag
him. It would be a huge, huge favor to me if
you would extend the same offer to him. His
name is Carter Aaron. He's new to P&D and we
were lucky enough to land him in the merge—he's
spectacular. I would owe you big time.
His email is caaron@PriceDicklepartners.com.

Evie

_____

Date: Fri, Oct 30 at 9:59 PM
From: Dave Cyrus
To: Evelyn Abbey
Subject: Re: Dan Printz

Are you going soft in your old age?
I'm teasing. Sure, I'll reach out to Carter.
Drop me a line when you want to grab a drink.

Dave

chapter twelve

Y ou have got to be kidding.

I stare at my phone, mouth open and toothpaste running down my chin until the screen fades to black. After spitting into the sink, I bring up the email again. Unbelievable. Dave Cyrus wants to talk to me about Dan Printz.

I type out a quick reply telling him I'm definitely up for a chat and include all of my contact information. *Hollywood Vine* has the largest distribution of any Hollywood daily; going after Dan with this kind of thing in my back pocket could almost guarantee landing him. Landing him *and* getting this kind of press is exactly what I need right out of the gate. It could literally change everything.

Evie was right; it's time to make my move.

I've done every bit of research I can on Dan Printz. I know he wants to feel like he's the one calling the shots, despite surrounding himself with an entourage of school friends who influence almost every one of his decisions—a constant battle and, I'm guessing, a cause of some of the drama he's rumored to be having with his current agent. He regrets his biggest role to date, portraying a time-traveling vigilante, but is smart enough to never, ever allude to that during interviews. I know who he's dated, what kind of music he likes, and that he still can't distinguish between *your* and *you're* on Twitter. Last year he slept with his costar's now-ex-wife, and when he was twenty he spent a week at a Vegas brothel. However, he's never late, always respectful in interviews, and never a problem on set.

Some of that might seem unimportant, but I don't make money if my clients aren't busy working—an impossible task if the actor in question is a nightmare and nobody wants to be around them.

It's Saturday, but I'm still the new guy in town, which means that, while the office might technically be closed, there's no such thing as a day off—not even if it's Halloween. Especially given Dave's email. I need to get on this Dan Printz thing now.

A glance at my watch shows it's just after nine, and I'll have plenty of time to get in a quick call to Dan before brunch with a VP of development at Paramount. Normally I'd have Justin set up a phone call, but this doesn't feel like it can wait. The line rings once before being answered by a gruff voice.

"Dan Printz's phone," it says.

"This is Carter Aaron—"

"Aaron, hey. This is Caleb, Dan's manager."

"Caleb, I remember you. We met in New York. We had drinks at that little place—"

"—in Brooklyn, right! I remember. I kicked your ass at pool that night."

"You did, you little hustler. Still not sure I'll ever be man enough for a rematch."

"That's right," he's saying. I can hear him clapping on the other end of the phone and I know I've hit my mark. Caleb heavily influences a lot of Dan's decisions, and having him on my side is another point in my favor.

"Listen, Caleb, I was wondering if I could talk to Dan."

"He's on set right now, reshoots and shit, but I'll tell him you called. I'm sure he'll be glad to hear it."

I silently fist-pump into the air.

"I appreciate it. Let him know I'm available all weekend, no need to wait till Monday."

"Sure thing. You stay out of pool halls," he says, laughing at his own joke.

I smile as the line disconnects.

• • •

Forty minutes to drive six miles on a Saturday? Someone help me.

There were just as many cars on the road in New York, but there we had buses and the subway; we could *walk*. Everything was interconnected and taking public transportation was nearly always easier than driving. Within the LA city limits there are 181 miles of freeway and over 6,000 miles of surface streets—I know, I Googled it—and yet I *still* sit in traffic wherever I go.

Which of course means I'm in traffic on Sunset when my phone rings through the Bluetooth. I jump, clamoring to answer and hoping it's the call from Dan I've been waiting for, only to see my mom's name flash on the screen.

I answer only because it's better than putting it off until later.

"Hi, Mom."

"How are you, baby? Are you in your car?"

"I am. I'm meeting someone for breakfast, and stuck in traffic. In fact, I don't know how long I'll be able to talk. I'm expecting a call and it's kind of important. I might have to switch over."

"On a Saturday?"

"On a Saturday," I say, knowing what comes next.

"You know you wouldn't be working Saturdays if you had a normal job."

I ignore this, reaching up to rub my forehead.

"Is the call from Jonah?" she asks.

I pause, confused for a beat. "No, why would he be calling me?"

She's silent in response, and too late I realize what she's thinking—*Because he's your brother and you live in the same city, not to mention I specifically told you to call him*—but instead she says, "I haven't heard from him in a week and he's not answering his phone. It goes straight to that obnoxious message."

This makes me smile, because his bare-bones voicemail greeting really *is* horrible: "*Yeah, it's Jonah. You know what to do.*" It does me good to know that it makes even our own doting mother want to punch him in the throat.

"I'm sure he'll call you back when he can," I tell her. "You're the one always reminding me how busy he is."

"This is different," she says, voice tight. "He's terrible about visiting, but he *always* answers my calls. I've called four times without hearing back from him, and now the phone's not ringing at all—it just goes straight to voicemail. Your father is so worried about him." In the background I hear my Dad shout, "No, Dinah, I'm not!"

I take a deep breath. "Mom, what do you want me to—"

"I want you to call him," she cuts in, "and if he doesn't answer, I want you to drive up there and make sure he's okay."

My preferred response to this would be to tell her— honestly—that I don't have time to go out to Malibu today. But the conversation plays out like a chess game in my head: She would follow it up with some version of how she didn't have time to carry me around for nine months, but she *did it any-*

way. Or how she didn't have time to do our laundry or make our meals or clean up some of the horrifying things she found in our bathroom, but she did that, too.

I go for a different tactic. "He might be out of town—"

"Carter."

"Okay, listen. I'll call now and merge the calls, that way you can yell at him yourself when he answers."

Traffic is stopped dead, so I glance down to my phone, switching the line and adding Jonah's number. Right to voice-mail.

"Okay, he didn't answer," I tell her when I switch back over, and let my head fall back against the seat. There is no way in hell I'll be able to get out to his place and back again in time for my meeting. If he's passed out in a drunken stupor, I am going to kill him. "Let me move some stuff around and I'll drive up there."

"Thank you, honey."

"No problem, Mom."

"Let me know as soon as you hear something, okay? And there's a gate, so I'll text you the code."

"Will do," I say, scrubbing a hand over my face.

•   •   •

I'm able to move my meeting to later in the day with only minimal trouble. Hours away, plenty of time.

Malibu is about thirty miles west of Beverly Hills; it takes an hour to get there. Most of the drive I'm making phone calls and deciding how I'm going to kill my brother if I show up and he's not already dead.

I point my car onto Latigo Canyon, a two-lane road through chaparral-covered hills and steep, wooded canyons, with a view of the ocean along every turn. The houses are huge and spread wide up here, most of them hidden from view by tall fences and towering trees.

On Jonah's street I stop to enter the security code into an illuminated keypad. An intricate metal gate opens up onto a long, winding driveway, and at the top of the hill sits the terra-cotta-tiled house. I'd forgotten how ostentatiously huge his place is. Two stories wrapped in white stucco, it has to be at least five thousand square feet. My apartment *and* my parking space could fit into his front room alone.

I spot the front of Jonah's black Range Rover around the corner in front of the garage. He'd really better be dead.

The ocean wind whips at my hair and my clothes as I climb out of my car. A wide walkway leads up to a set of stained-concrete stairs and a massive double door, and I knock twice, turning to look around while I wait. Now that I'm closer, the yard looks a little more unkempt than I'd expect. A set of urns filled with dying flowers border a lawn that could definitely stand to be cut. It's quiet, too. It's still early, but not *that* early. Last time I came, there was music playing from the back near the pool and signs of life everywhere. People coming and going and multiple cars. A yard crew, a pool man, a housekeeper. This time, I don't hear anything coming from inside the house.

It might just be my mom's overreaction gene rearing its head, but anxiety gnaws at me, unease prickling along my skin.

I'm heading back to my car to call . . . I don't know— *someone*—when the door opens behind me. The guy is shorter than Jonah, but fit and tanned in a way that one becomes from spending a lot of time outside. His shorts-only outfit is just one indicator of his cool casualness.

I have no idea who he is.

"Hey," the guy says, waving the floppy slice of pizza in his hand at me. "You got through the gate, so I'm assuming you're supposed to be up here."

"I assume so," I say, and look above the door somewhere for a house number, wondering if it's possible I'm in the wrong place. "I'm Carter. Is Jonah here?"

Recognition dawns and the guy's face lights up. "You're the brother! Man, you two look so much alike."

I push up my glasses, tamping down irritation. "Is he home?"

He looks back over his shoulder. "Think he's on the patio," he says, and then motions for me to step inside.

There's a lot of white in Jonah's house—white floors, white walls, white stairs—but not much else. In fact, there's not much furniture at all.

"I don't think I caught your name," I say as I follow the stranger through the enormous entryway—my last apartment *could* fit in here, as well as my current one, and most of Michael Christopher's house. We pass through the kitchen and head toward the back door. Pizza-and-Shorts Guy is about my age, with dark, wavy hair and a smile I sort of want to wipe off his face with the back of my hand. If I had to guess, I'd say "actor" by day, waiter by night.

Or . . . kept man?

Standing here in Jonah's eerily empty house with this stranger, I realize that I don't know my brother that well at all.

"I'm Nick," he says, and stops in front of the back door. "Jonah is out there."

And sure enough, there he is, sitting in a chaise longue in jeans and a leather jacket, next to the giant swimming pool.

"Thanks," I say, stepping outside.

The view is spectacular, and again, I can see why Jonah bought this place. He's high enough up that the horizon stretches out over the hills to reach the ocean from what feels like one side of the world to the other. Palm trees tower overhead and there's just so much *space*.

But even finally seeing my missing brother, the feeling that things are a little off only grows. The pool is a dull, clear brown and a few stray leaves skip across the ground, spinning lazily on the surface of the water. Pots are empty; the patio has seen better days.

"Hey," I say when Jonah doesn't seem to notice I'm there. "You know it's like seventy degrees outside, right?"

He looks over and watches me through his sunglasses. "What are you doing here?"

"Mom sent me. Said you haven't been answering her calls."

He looks forward again. "Yeah, don't know where my phone is."

I take a seat on the chair next to him. "Don't you need it? For . . . I don't know, work?"

He reaches for a beer bottle perched on a glass table by his side and takes a long drink. It's not even eleven yet. I decide to try a different approach.

"Who was that?" I ask. "Inside."

"Nick," he says, and takes another drink.

"I got his name. I mean, does he live here?"

"Yeah."

I lean forward, resting my elbows on my thighs. "Is he . . . is he the boyfriend?"

"Whose boyfriend?" he asks, squinting into the sun.

"Well . . . yours."

Jonah turns his body to fully face me and gives me a look over the top of his sunglasses.

"Dude, I don't care who you sleep with," I say, shrugging. "It's not like we talk all that much anymore. Besides, you cut the elastic off all my underwear when I drank your orange juice, threw away my clothes when I left them in the dryer too long, and look like you want to murder anyone who wears shoes inside. The first conclusion I'm supposed to draw is that you have a roommate? You're a nightmare to live with. That Nick is your boyfriend seems the more likely explanation."

He sits back again. "People do change, you know. I'm not *that* hard to live with."

"Sort of. People might be influenced by things, but they don't change who they fundamentally *are*."

"So you're saying that fundamentally, I'm a dick."

I think about it for a moment. "Yeah."

This makes him laugh. "And you're an asshole."

"Why did you get a roommate?" I ask, but looking around, I'm beginning to think I get it. "Is everything okay?"

"Are we about to have a big brother–baby brother talk?" he asks.

"I would surely get some Mom points for it. I guarantee she's in New York right now telling the neighbors you've been sold into some sort of sex ring because you aren't answering the phone. Are you going to let her know you're okay?"

He shrugs, and I push my hands between my knees to keep from smacking the back of his head.

"Are you in trouble? Like . . . you bought a fucking mansion in Malibu. Money can't be the issue."

"Do you have any idea how much it costs to live here?"

"I can barely afford my apartment, so, yeah"—I gesture broadly—"the scope of this is beyond me."

"I probably couldn't afford your apartment, either, right now." He takes off his sunglasses and tosses them on the table. "Dude, it's fucking expensive to be me. I live up here and have parties and have to be seen with the right people and wear the right things. I'd get in a little over my head, but it was always okay because I'd just do another layout or magazine cover, you know? It was fine because there was always more work."

" 'Was'?"

Jonah leans his head against the back of his chair and exhales a long, tired breath. "I did a job for this designer—high fashion—and he wasn't happy. I mean, normally I'm cool with some people not liking my work, it's art and open to interpretation, but this . . . I sort of lost my cool. There was another shoot, but I couldn't seem to get the lighting right. I did some touch-up work to correct the shadows and it made the rounds of every women's magazine and gossip site, all talking about how I'd doctored the photos to slim down the model and done a shit job of it. Some fashion bloggers tore the shoot and *me* to pieces and . . . let's just say things have been a little tight."

"So you did a less-than-stellar shoot and your shitty diva attitude got you into trouble," I clarify.

With a dead-eyed look he grabs his sunglasses and puts them back on. "It'll be fine."

I pull out my phone and for the first time Google my brother. It takes a little scrolling, but he's right: on some of the trashier gossip sites there are archived articles with phrases like *has-been* and *washed up* and *fashion feature poison*. In this moment I'm eternally grateful my mom wouldn't know how to Google if her life depended on it.

"It doesn't *look* fine," I say.

Jonah stands to walk into the house.

"How much debt are we talking here?" I ask, following him through the door.

He stops at a trash can, drops the empty bottle, and moves to the fridge to get another beer, which is about the only thing I see inside. Walking around a corner to make sure we're alone, he closes a tall set of double doors, enclosing us in his massive white kitchen. "The credit cards alone?" he says, pulling at the label on his bottle. "I'm guessing about a hundred."

"*Thousand?*" My pulse takes off with a lurch.

"Then there's the house," he continues, "and the Rover. I already got rid of the other cars."

"Jesus Christ." I sink onto a kitchen stool. "Mom is—"

"Not going to find out." His voice is deep with warning. "It's none of your business and it sure as hell isn't hers."

"She'll want to help," I start to say, but I can already read the answer in his expression. She can't help. Mom and Dad live a simple life on a small budget. The scale of this is beyond *their* comprehension, too. If I didn't routinely see the money floating around California and my industry, it would be well beyond mine as well.

I sit back and think for a moment. Jonah has made a name for himself for a reason, and even though I think he should go back to the kind of photos he used to do—hell, our mom has had one of his earlier photographs, a black-and-white shot of a fence silhouetted by the setting sun, hanging over her fireplace since he was seventeen—it's clearly not what he's built a career on.

"We'll figure something out," I tell him.

He nods but doesn't look up from the floor, and inexplicably, my heart twists with protectiveness.

People fucking love a comeback story. I can do this.

"Bring me your portfolio. I've got some calls to make."

● ● ●

It takes a few hours and a lot of arguing from Jonah, but I think I've come up with a solution.

"What are you doing the seventeenth?" I ask him. I have no idea how I'll get Evie to agree to something like this, but I'll have to figure that out later.

"Working on my tan," he says with a shrug. "Just like yesterday and the day before that."

"In your leather jacket?"

He rocks back on the rear legs of one of his massive dining room chairs, staring at the ceiling.

I lean over and kick him to redirect his attention. "Evie and I have a shoot next week, and—"

"Evie?" he asks, grinning.

"Dude. Shut up. Listen. I have a really good friend from New York who's a creative director at *Vanity Fair*. He owes me a favor, so I'm pretty sure he'll do this for me. I hope."

"For a feature film?" Jonah asks, and I nod. He considers it before wrinkling his nose like he's smelled something bad. "Who is it?"

"Jamie Huang and Seamus—" I stop. "Are you seriously asking this? I'm trying to help you by putting my own ass on the line and—" I suddenly realize I have no idea what time it is. "Shit, where's my phone?" I find it under a stack of photographs and let out a tight "Fuck!" when I see the time. "I've got to go."

Jonah has the nerve to look upset. "What? Where?"

"I have a meeting I moved so I could come out and look for your dead body, and now I'm going to be late." I shove my phone in my pocket and find my keys on the dining room table, beneath another giant portfolio. "Get whatever you need ready and be there by nine on Friday the seventeenth. I'll have my assistant text you the address."

·   ·   ·

After a somewhat late night Saturday spent Uncle-Carter-trick-or-treating with Morgan and a Sunday recovering and researching, I get an email from Evie asking for some time in the morning to talk about the retreat. The mere idea sends a sharp spike of dread through my chest, not to mention the change to the photo shoot I have to tell her about now. There's no way she'll easily agree to it. Hell, I'm not even sure I would if the tables were turned. I'd ask myself what I was thinking setting the whole thing up in the first place, but the truth is, I wasn't. Never in my life have I been so frazzled.

We exchange a few short emails and agree on a time, and though it would be easier—not to mention quicker—for her to just text me, I get the feeling that after the odd intimacy-retreat of our dinner on Friday, she's trying to put some walls back up.

·   ·   ·

The phone call from my friend at *Vanity Fair* comes in just as I'm getting out of my car the next morning, so I'm running a few minutes late. Pulling a folder from my messenger bag—it's full of information and ideas I've gathered for the retreat—I pray to the gods of happy-flings-turned-rivals that this is enough to soften Evie up and get her to sign off on Jonah as our photographer.

Upstairs, Jess points me in the direction of the conference room. All the way down the hall, I can see Evie through the glass, her head bent so that her hair obstructs her face while she scribbles something in her notebook. Her skin is this insane combination of flawless and rosy that I've seen makeup artists try to mimic for years. Her brown eyes have thick lashes and a knowing gleam. Evie has that way about her, as if she's not often noticed in a crowd—maybe intentionally—but to me, she's like a beacon. Small but mighty. Unassuming but poised. I really wish I could fucking see her without it feeling like I've had the wind knocked out of me. It would make feigning indifference so much easier.

She has some sort of smoothie in front of her, and it matches the little jewels on a barrette in her hair.

Ugh, I am in deep.

"Sorry I'm a few minutes late." I take the seat across from her. "Some stuff came up."

"Stuff?" she asks, pushing the straw around in her drink.

"Work stuff," I clarify, and I hate the way my words come out like I'm explaining myself to her, laced with guilt. "Anyway, Kylie sent me some things from the planner they used last year. I printed them up and added a few new ideas I thought might work."

I place the packets on the table in front of her, avoiding her eyes and hoping she goes for the subject change. I'm sure she's wondering why I'm suddenly so helpful and Johnny-on-the-spot about this retreat.

I can feel her watching me, narrowed eyes tracking my movements as she picks up the papers I've given her and holds them warily. She still hasn't said anything and when she looks down to the printouts, I busy myself straightening the rest of my papers, making sure she has a pen, and generally behaving as though I'm being a lot more helpful than I am.

"Oh, right," I say casually, "I should mention before we get started: I need to switch the photographer for the *VF* shoot next week."

She turns her face up to me. Her brows come together in confusion. "Why?"

I debate whether I should lie and realize it's safer to just be honest. "I thought we might hire Jonah."

"As in your *brother*, Jonah?"

"Right." Scratching my eyebrow, I tell her, "He's going through a bit of a rough patch, and I told him I'd try to get him on this job."

She sets down the packet. "You think they're going to be able to switch it out last minute?"

I lean in, relieved her first reaction wasn't rage. I try on a smile I hope feels like the expressive version of triumphant jazz hands. "They already did."

Only when her eyes go wide do I fully register what I've just said.

Oh. Oh, fuck.

"You did it without talking to me?" she asks slowly.

Shaking my head, I say, "I dropped my friend a line yesterday to see if it would even be possible, but he called and said it was a go before I got in this morning."

Evie studies me for a few quiet beats. "I think it's a conflict of interest. I think Brad would agree."

There's the edge of a threat in her tone, and I twist the cardboard band around my coffee cup while I think of how to respond. "I'll talk to him."

"I'm not sure I understand what led to this," she says, confusion lacing her words. "You told me the two of you don't get along. This is Jamie and Seamus's first big shoot. Do you really want to—"

"How well Jonah and I get along isn't the point. He's the right guy for the job."

"Then why didn't you suggest him last week?"

"Because I assumed he was busy."

"Why would you assume that?" she asks, shaking her head a little. "He's been gossip fodder for *months*."

Heat rises in my neck with the humiliation that Evie knew all of this about Jonah and I didn't. "I think we both know that what people say about us isn't always reflective of our ability to do our job."

She nibbles her lower lip thoughtfully but doesn't say anything else. Evie: calm, as ever.

"It's not even that I mind your brother doing the shoot," she says at length. "He's still a big name, even with all the controversy." She pauses, studying me some more. "But did you think it would go over well with me for you to just roll over any input I have in this? You represent Jamie. I represent Seamus. This is a big shoot for *Trick*, and these are things you and I need to be incredibly thoughtful about."

I do a series of nods to be agreeable, though probably one too many. "If you don't mind that he's doing it, and agree that he's a big name, why are you getting so pissed about this?"

I want to make a fist and punch myself in the mouth as soon as the words are out. Evie is acting anything but *pissed* right now. I need to stop letting my temper shoot out so abruptly with her; this combination of attraction and competition makes me completely insane.

I see the angry flush rise in her cheeks—and the effect on me is a confusing rush of desire—but again, she stays calm, gathering her things and pushing back from the table.

"You're right," she says. "What's done is done. I'll have Jess email you the wardrobe notes for Seamus's end of the shoot, as well as my thoughts on the information you've given me today for the retreat." She closes the folder around her printouts and stands. "Justin can send Jess anything you need me to review."

"We're going to talk through our assistants now?" I ask, looking up at her.

"It seems like the best idea, for a number of reasons." She walks around the table and leaves the room.

chapter thirteen

"Evie, you're going to break this machine," Daryl laments, putting her hand on my quad to slow down my leg extensions. "What is *with* you?"

I offer up a breathless: "Carter."

Standing from the machine, I grab my water and take a few deep drinks. Sweat pours off me, and everything burns. I am a beast this morning, but it feels amazing. I realize it's either kill myself here at the gym, or go to work and punch someone in the solar plexus.

I should probably be mortified about getting up and walking out of our meeting yesterday, but screw him and his perfect forearms and cute crooked smile and diva brother.

I'm so tired of wanting to shove him into the wall and then shove my hand down his pants.

I am so over all of it.

"Not to poke the bear," she says, "because I can see you're just a little on edge today, but to be clear: we don't like Carter anymore, right?"

"No, we do *not* like Carter anymore." I use a towel to wipe the sweat from my forehead. "And I'd appreciate if you could remember that next time you're supposed to be my wingwoman. You told me to be a badass and then melted as soon as he turned on the charm. Remember when you wanted to get back at Brant and I went to your cousin's wedding as your lesbian fiancée? I kissed you—*with tongue*. That was *me* being Team Daryl."

She laughs. "I'm sorry, you're right. But to be fair, you really should have given me an adorable warning, because . . . well, shit, Evie," she says. "He's completely fuckable."

"Not helping!"

"I know I shouldn't be enjoying this so much, but look how much he riles you up. I knew you were bossy, but who knew you had such a power-play fetish?"

"A *what*?" I stumble after her over to the free weights.

"You heard me."

"Do I even want to know?" Amelia asks, racking her weights and looking between us.

I shake my head, watching as she moves to the squat frame.

Daryl leans against the metal bar, watching me. "Evie's in denial, trying to convince herself that she hates Carter."

"Ohhhh. I like Carter," Amelia bends her back, lowering for a dead lift. Coming back up, she says, "He came in to sign some tax forms. I didn't think the rest of the HR women were going to let him leave, and that's saying something. That one is a charmer."

"You realize he's my nemesis, right?" I say.

When she finishes her reps, Amelia guides me into position for my squats, with the bar against my shoulders and behind my neck. "Your 'nemesis.' You are so cute."

"Are you poisoned by his charm, too?"

She smiles at me. "Shut up and squat." She startles as if she's just remembered something. "Oh! You will never believe who Brad just signed."

I stop, locking the bar into place and meeting her eyes in the mirror. "If you say Gabe Vestes I'm going to scream."

"That's right. The same Gabe you mentioned having lunch with Brad right before the merge went public. I don't know exactly who's doing what, but something tells me Brad has his hands in a couple cookie jars."

"I *knew* something was off about that. Brad got caught calling him a no-talent hack when I was still at Alterman; it didn't make sense that they'd suddenly decided to mend their fences." I step away from the squat frame and turn to face them both. "Likely Brad knew about the merger beforehand—and if he knew which of the CTM agents were getting the boot, he'd know to swoop in and make friends with Gabe again."

"Just another shady move," Amelia says.

"Why do you think he took Kylie off retreat planning?" Daryl asks, sitting on the bench next to us.

Amelia considers this. "Maybe he's keeping her busy in other ways." She grins at us. "Maybe they're having an affair."

I shiver, repulsed. "I'd like to think Kylie has a little more sense than that."

See, Carter? I don't think the absolute worst of her after all.

"And better taste." Amelia looks at her watch. "I have a payroll meeting I can't be late for."

A smart woman would leave a workout like the one I've just had and go get something healthy for breakfast. An egg-white omelet, maybe. Or something whole grain. A smoothie.

Apparently, I am not a smart woman. I go straight to Sidecar Doughnuts and order three butter-and-salts and a giant latte. But I *am* smart enough to leave two of the doughnuts on my desk, bringing only one to the team breakfast meeting scheduled for eight a.m. in the conference room.

Coffee: check. Sugar and carbs: check.

Adjusted attitude: in progress.

My stomach—and attitude—plummet when I walk in and find Carter already there. I was really hoping I'd have at least a few minutes more to rally. He glances up, does a slight double take, and attempts a smile that looks a lot like a sneer before looking back down at his phone.

After yesterday, I don't even know how to handle myself in a room alone with him. My heart is pounding, my lady parts on high alert, and my free hand gets all tight-fisty and punchy at my side. Confusing as hell. Plus, I'm suddenly very aware of the doughnut I'm holding, and the fact that Carter is having nothing but sparkling water for a breakfast meeting. Water. I hate him.

He's flanked by two empty chairs, but I ignore them, pointedly taking a seat on the other side of the table. Battle lines drawn.

I can hear the buzzing hum of the overhead lights. Carter's pen makes an exaggerated *scritch-scritch* sound in a notebook as he pulls his attention away from his phone long enough to seemingly jot down a flurry of ideas. I'd bet solid money he's really just scribbling down the alphabet or a manifesto about all the ways he plans to be underhanded in the coming months.

The room fills as the rest of the department slowly filters in. Breakfast meetings are the worst; no human alive is in a hurry to spend an hour first thing in the morning with Brad.

We all look toward the door at the sound of our boss's booming voice and see Kylie jogging in her four-inch stiletto heels to keep up behind him. With barely a glance at me, Brad looks down at my doughnut and wordlessly swipes it directly from the tabletop into the trash can just beside my feet.

I hear a strangled gasp come out of my mouth. "Wh-wh—?"

"Come on, Evie," Brad says as he pulls out his chair. He looks up and catches my horrified expression. "What? Are you depressed? Trust me, you don't need that."

I have no idea what to say to this. A storm seems to build in my chest and I can feel my face turning red. "Except that was my *breakfast*."

He doesn't answer, just sits down and quietly tells Kylie to get the laptop set up. I think I hear Rose mumble something about a son of a bitch, but otherwise there's only stunned silence from the rest of the table around me.

"We're having some food brought in," Kylie squeaks. "So . . . you'll get something then. Like fruit and organic bars and stuff."

I don't want fruit or an organic bar—I want the *motherfucking doughnut* I brought in.

No, what I really want is to lift my coffee and toss it at Brad, right in Mr. Congeniality's face.

But I can't do that, either.

Looking down to regroup, I see that two buttons on my top are open, revealing my pink bra beneath. I gasp, quickly fastening them closed again.

I know this hasn't recently happened. I know that it's been like this since I first walked into the room because I realize in hindsight that I felt the draft on my chest for the last few minutes. Carter is *right here*, across from me; we were the only two people in the room. It explains his double take and sneaky little smile, and it also explains why I'm going to kill him later.

My pulse is a booming drum in my ear. I stare at the side of Carter's face so hard I hope his cheekbones begin to ache under the force of it.

As the woman from catering comes in pushing a cart laden with fruit and fat-free, taste-free bran muffins, I think of my delicious doughnut and wonder what everyone would do if I just reached into the trash can, brushed it off, and went to town. I'm so hungry I'm tempted to try. Instead, I abandon hope of sugar and delicious carbs since, by the looks of it, we're all about to be subjected to Brad's fifty-year-old-man breakfast. Great.

Of course, everyone is too polite to go get anything to eat until Brad does first. And he seems to be in no immediate hurry.

My stomach gnaws at itself like a starving wolf . . . so, fuck it.

I stand and walk to the food, bypassing the muffin-bricks to pile a bunch of berries on a small paper plate. When I return to the table, Brad is eyeing me like I've just broken a cardinal rule. Rose's smirk is aimed at her hands folded on the table. Rose and I don't always have the same sense of humor, but I know that if we make eye contact right now, she will lose her shit.

"Let's get started." Brad taps a few papers in front of him and leans back in his chair, glancing at Rose. "How did it go with Tom on Monday?"

"Good," she tells him. "Paramount contract's signed. Everything's moving along."

He nods, pleased. "Carter, what's going on for the *Vanity Fair* shoot?"

Carter slides his eyes to me. "All set."

"Who's doing the photography again?"

Hesitating, Carter pretends to need to look at his notes before he says, "Ah, it's Jonah. Jonah Aaron."

"No relation?" Brad asks distractedly. Assuming.

"Relation. Brother."

Brad looks up and considers Carter frankly for a few seconds. "The photographer is your brother?"

And this is it—this is when Carter will finally get what's

coming to him. I didn't overreact. This entire situation is bullshit. And the best part is that *I* won't need to do a thing because Brad will do it for me.

Doughnut incident forgiven, I settle into my seat, wishing I had some popcorn instead of berries for the show.

Carter's face slowly blooms red. "That's right. My younger brother. I assure you he's fully qualified."

Brad's expression remains unreadable and I think I can hear Carter sweating. I could kiss Brad for this. Come to think of it, I think I missed Bosses' Day. I make a mental note to send Brad a card.

"You might have even seen some of his work in *Rolling Stone*," Carter continues. "I can get you a list of references if you'd like."

Silence. You could hear a pin drop and I gleefully swing my eyes to Brad, waiting for the explosion. Here it comes . . . any minute now . . .

But it doesn't. Instead, a smile worthy of the Grinch slowly spreads across Brad's face, until I can see every one of his perfectly capped teeth.

"Now that is what I've been talking about!" he says, and slaps a hand on the table.

Son of a bitch.

"Carter rallying the troops and giving us an inside edge." Brad all but leaps across the table to give Carter a bro-pal high five. "I'll tell you something, I am not surprised. Everyone watch this guy," he says, pointing around the table. "This is how you get shit done."

I sink down in my chair, furious. We already *had* a photographer, so I'm not sure what, specifically, Brad thinks has gotten "done." Carter shouldn't have made the switch without asking me, and he knows it. That Brad is now giving him a verbal hand job is infuriating. It sets Carter apart in a way Brad never has before at these meetings. There is an unspoken pecking order in agenting, defined primarily by who brings in the most publicity and money—and this year, that is likely to be me.

But there are other factors, too. Such as: having a penis. Apparently that's a big one.

There's some awkward shuffling around the table—either people don't like being told to emulate the newest newbie around town, or they agree with me that hiring your brother for a cover shoot is a screaming mile past Sketchy Town—but I make a point of not looking up, refusing to make eye contact. Taking a calming breath, I lift my coffee to my lips, truly enjoying it as I imagine it scalding Carter's lap instead of my tongue. I glance down when my phone buzzes with a text.

> Can you make sure to follow up with
> Seamus about the start time next week?

I blink, staring at the screen. Brad has moved on from his gushing over Carter, and now Ashton's voice is a nasal lull in the background.

> Did you send this to the wrong person?

> Is this Evelyn Abbey?

> Why would I forget to follow up with my own client?

> I was just making sure.

> Just contact Jess with the list of information you need.

Beside me, he snorts out a dickish little laugh and shakes his head, sliding his phone onto the tabletop.

Livid, I type one more thought.

> You could have given me a heads up that my shirt was unbuttoned.

Your shirt was unbuttoned?

> You're sitting right across from me.

> It would be impossible for you to not have noticed.

Well, I didn't ;-)

Holy shit. Did Carter just type the bird-flip of smiley faces? *Did Carter just give me the smiley-finger?*

My heart is pounding so hard, I can barely hear what Ashton is saying. I'm sure I look like a mouth-breathing wrestler, but my thoughts won't budge away from how much I despise Carter this very second.

I'm not entirely sure what this feeling is, because I've never had it before . . . but I think it's unmitigated rage.

I think my brain has just declared war on Carter Aaron.

•   •   •

In my office, I descend upon my other two doughnuts with a kind of desperate, two-handed, open-mouthed vigor. Coffee and berries long gone, these doughnuts are my entire life now.

But because the universe is a cat, and I am but a fuzzy ball of string, Carter walks in right when I take down half of one doughnut in a single bite.

"Hey, Evil," he says, eyes on his phone. "Jonah needs to start at eleven next Friday. Does that work?" He looks up and startles at the sight of my face, both cheeks bulging with food. "I'll . . . give you a second to answer."

And then he just stands there, watching me chew behind my hand, his eyebrows raised in amusement. When the chewing takes me longer than either of us would have liked, he adds, "You must have been starving" with a mocking half smile.

Swallowing, I say, "You may have noticed Brad knocking my breakfast into the trash."

He eyes the sugar crumbs littering the bag on my desk. "Good thing you had spares."

I make a point of walking to my door and dramatically motioning to where Jess is sitting in front of her computer, next to the other assistants.

Carter follows me and looks out. "Yeah?"

"*That* is my assistant, Jess. Talk to her about scheduling."

He peeks out again, offering Jess a wave and an adorable smile. "How's your mom's cat doing?" he calls out.

Her face lights up. "Good! First couple nights were rough, but the stitches come out next week. Thanks for asking!" Her eyes swing to me, and she looks like a deer caught in headlights. You have got to be kidding.

"So can we?" he says.

I turn my head to see him looking down at me. He is entirely too close. I'll never be able to get any real leverage kicking him in the balls at this angle. Straightening, I take a step back. "Can we what?"

"Can we start shooting at eleven instead of noon next week?" He says it slowly, as if the problem is me and my comprehension, and not the fact that he's a plotting weasel. "Jonah has 'a thing' at three."

I should be difficult and insist he go through Jess with this, but apparently the Team Evie ship has sailed. "God, you're a pain in the ass. Let me check my calendar." I move to sit down behind my desk, saying pointedly, "I sure appreciate being involved in the coordination."

He sighs. "It wasn't like that, Evie."

"It wasn't?" I turn on my computer, typing in my password with shaking hands. I hope he doesn't notice; the last thing I want is for Carter to see how much this gets to me.

He pushes his hands into his pockets. "Look, if Brad had an issue with Jonah doing the shoot, then okay, we could discuss how to adjust the plan. But he didn't."

Carter clearly knows as well as I do that Brad approved of this for reasons completely unfathomable to either of us. Even a nearsighted dog in the room would know that what Carter did was outright nepotism. "Are you using Brad Kingman as your litmus test for honorable behavior?"

"I just want to have a job," he says. "My mistake was in not getting an okay from you up front, I get that. Can we move on?"

Staring at him in the answering quiet, I finally say, "Do I really have a choice?"

I must have made my point, because for the first time since I've known Carter, he doesn't have a comeback.

"Next week . . . Friday?" I ask, back to business. Carter nods. "Eleven should work. I told Seamus to get there at eight thirty for makeup anyway to make sure he gets there on time."

Carter's eyes go wide. "That was pretty smart."

"Try not to look so surprised."

This makes him laugh, but he doesn't bother to correct me.

Just as Carter is about to turn and leave, Rose ducks into my office, closing the door behind her.

"Do you want me to go, or . . . ?" Carter asks her.

"You're fine. You can stay, I want both of your opinions."

Oh, great. Here comes the gossip.

I glance up at Carter, unsure as to whether he's been subjected to her yet. He's got his blank face on, which means he probably already knows exactly how indiscreet Rose can be. I constantly fear that any legitimate work conversation with her will devolve into gossip and name-dropping. It's not that I am necessarily against gossip and name-dropping, but it has to be done in the right way, with the right people. *Discreet* people, for Christ's sake, who do it only with the right combination of irony and credibility.

But instead of slowly building an intriguing story of flirting, or client drama, or sexual harassment, Rose drops an incredibly personal grievance right in the middle of my office: "Ashton's bonus was about seven *thousand* dollars bigger than mine."

My eyes widen.

Carter takes a small step back, as if he's trying to blend into the background.

"How do you know that?" I ask. We talk about money all day with clients, but rarely do we share our own income with colleagues. And, I'm guessing, it's for precisely this reason. Nothing is ever as clear and fair as we expect it to be.

"We were talking yesterday about our projected year-end totals, you know, with the merge? Everyone's head seems to be on the chopping block. So we went back to our desks, and our bonus statements were there. I guess because we were already talking money, he was comfortable enough to tell me what he got."

"Were his signings and bookings bigger than—" I begin, but she cuts me off, shaking her head.

"The same," she says. "We were almost dead even." She looks over to Carter. "Bullshit, right?"

"Unacceptable," I say. "You need to ask Brad. Or go straight to Accounting and have them check the numbers."

Rose gasps. "I can't do that!"

"Then you're out seven grand." I shrug.

"This sucks!" she growls.

"Talk to Brad," Carter gently urges. Naive Carter. As if Brad doesn't already know.

She looks up at him, miserable. "He won't care."

I lift my hands in front of me, exasperated. "Honestly, Rose, if you're only going to complain here—where I have no power to help you at all—the money must not be the reason you're in this job."

She looks down to the floor, nodding for a few seconds. "I know. I know, it's just so frustrating."

"I get it, sweets, but you've got to be your own advocate. No one else is going to be that for you."

With a small smile of thanks, she turns and leaves.

Carter steps away from the wall. "Wow, Evie. That was a bit of tough love."

I look up at his face, at the wide green eyes behind his glasses, his clean-shaven jaw and mussy hair. It's a good thing he's so pretty, because the attitude is not making any friends today. "You could have added anything you wanted to."

He considers this for a few seconds and then shrugs. "Is she sure that's really the case? I've never had any sort of pay disparity." He seems to realize what he's just said. "I mean, obviously. I know that sort of thing happens, but . . ." He winces, backpedaling. "That sucks for her. Hopefully she'll get it fixed."

He can't be serious.

"This isn't some rare case of a mathematical error in finance, Carter. This sort of thing happens *every day*. It's happened to me."

"Really? It's just, you seem so in command all the time, I have a hard time imagining anyone taking something that's yours."

He moves another step closer, leaning back against my desk, facing me. It's so close, it's almost like we're friendly, or flirting, but obviously we aren't.

"It happens in this business all the time," I say quietly. "You just don't see it. It doesn't affect you."

"It should."

I nod. "I agree."

"So what do you think we should do?"

I don't miss the way he looks at my lips for a tiny beat, and it suddenly feels like we're not talking about pay disparity anymore.

"I don't know," I whisper.

But I definitely feel like making out with Carter right now would help lead us in the right direction.

His eyes seem to roam all over my face, and then lower; he leans in . . .

For the span of two . . . three . . . four frantic heartbeats, I think he's going to kiss me.

"Your shirt seems intent on staying open today," he whispers, nodding.

Startled, I follow his eyes, and sure enough my top two buttons have popped open again, leaving a good deal of cleavage perfectly visible to both of us.

"Oh." I look up at him, feeling my cheeks heat.

I start to smile at him, but instead of leaning closer to kiss me like I still think he's going to, he leans back, offering an unreadable expression before he turns and leaves my office.

chapter fourteen

carter

THAT WAS CLOSE.

If this isn't about a bank robbery

I don't think I want to hear it.

MC, I nearly put my face in Evie's boobs in her office.

Okay, no, I want to hear this.

She's so badass and straightforward.

Which is sexy and intimidating all at once, and her shirt keeps popping open.

And then I went to tell her and it was like . . . impossible to want to leave without kissing.

Dude.

Just keep reminding me she's Lucifer.

I mean, not really she isn't.

She's the nicest person.

It seemed like she wanted to kiss me.

Or bite your face?

In a good way.

In a bad way.

Whose side are you on?

The side where the two of you get married and she gives birth to a fully formed toddler who draws on your bedspread with toothpaste.

Dick.

Bye.

chapter fifteen

evie

If I thought I was angry with Carter before, now there's humiliation thrown into the mix. Over the next couple of days, I spend entirely too much time looping back through those few seconds he'd leaned in and looked at me like I wasn't the enemy. I must have appeared to melt in my chair.

With any other romantic failure, there's the regret, and the replaying of the good times and bad times. Maybe there's even the occasional awkward run-in around town because, as huge as LA is, it *feels* tiny. But it's a different matter altogether to work alongside a romantic failure. To pass him in the hall, to see him at meetings, to be forced into a tiny space to plan company retreats together . . .

I get to the small conference room first and take a seat on the couch at the far end, near the windows. It gives me the benefit of being able to see Carter walking all the way down the hall and toward me—not the worst view in the world—escorting the planner from Corporate Fun!

She's put together in a bland, anonymous way, but Carter—because he's the devil—exudes sex. Hands in his pockets; lazy, confident stride; crooked smile. Is it more noticeable now because I'm not getting any? Probably. Or is it just how he *is*? His dark dress pants fit him perfectly, sitting low on his slim hips and hugging his quads. I swear I can see the outline of his cock along his thigh. His dress shirt today is a subtle blue-and-white-check pattern and seems like it was poured on him, it looks so good. When he smiles more broadly at something the planner says, his entire face lights up and somehow, he looks sweet again.

I'm ruined, I can see that now. I look bleakly out at the next few years of my life, working here or somewhere else and unable to get over my hate-crush on Carter Aaron. Or even worse, watching him with someone else. I'm doomed.

I stand when they enter, smoothing my skirt before shaking hands with the woman—Libby Truman—who already seems enamored with Satan's Errand Boy and his stupid perfect face. As she holds on to his upper arm, she gushes about how funny he was on the walk down here.

On the walk down the *hall.* Thirty seconds, tops. How amazing, no doubt.

We sit, do the perfunctory explanation of what we need— and honestly, I feel like we could have had this meeting over the phone. We require someone to plan some games for the group of fifty or so people over two days. We require activities that won't (a) make us all cringe or (b) trigger our grossly competitive natures. We require alcohol. That's it; it's pretty simple.

But whenever possible, people like to come to the P&D offices for meetings. It's for the exact reason I can see Libby occasionally looking out through the glass walls of the room: she's hoping to spot a celebrity.

Unfortunately for her, she sees only Justin, who peeks his head in about five minutes into things.

"Jett Payne is here; he's waiting for us upstairs. Also, Kylie wanted me to let you know that she overordered for the break room Keurig, and you're free to take a box or two home."

Carter stands with a smile. "Thanks, Justin."

My jaw drops.

"You double booked?" I ask him, wearing a tight *fuck you* smile of my own.

"I guess I did. Sorry about that," he says, as if it were purely accidental and he's not meticulous about his calendar. He stands, reaching forward to shake Libby's hand. "Great to meet you, Libby. Evie can handle the rest of the discussion. And make sure she validates your parking. Looking forward to what you two have planned!"

Libby, a little breathless, overexclaims, "It will be great!"

●   ●   ●

About an hour later I wrap up the meeting with Libby—still fuming—and head back to my office while checking the rest of today's schedule on my phone.

I have forty-five minutes to get across town to meet Sarah Hill for a hair appointment. We just landed Sarah a part in an adaptation of a runaway bestselling teen novel, and the studio insists her hair be a specific shade of blue for the role. It's in her contract that her agent and the producer be present for quality control. What it means, essentially, is four hours in a salon, trying to stay alert enough to be able to tell the subtle difference between fifteen different shades of blue hair.

Passing Carter's office, I stop dead in my tracks, seeing that he's already put two boxes of K-Cups in the middle of his desk.

When I was a teenager, my father was strict; it was the opposite of Daryl's family, who basically let her run around with whoever she wanted. I wasn't allowed to date until I was sixteen, and even then there were rules. I could date as much as I wanted, but I couldn't have a *boyfriend*, which meant no consecutive dates with the same guy. I'm sure the intent there was that I didn't get too serious with any one guy, because serious leads to sex. Their plan worked, mostly: by eleventh grade, I hadn't had sex yet. Had never really even come close.

And then I met Kai Paialua. I managed to sneak as much time with him as I could, away from my parents' watchful eyes. The night of the Homecoming game our senior year, we found ourselves in a bedroom at a party. Somewhere in another room Santana was playing on repeat, his sexy guitar riffs egging action along, and . . . I wanted to have sex with Kai. I was pretty damn close, too—his pants were around his ankles and he was checking to see if the condom he'd carried in his wallet since sophomore year had expired—and I knew I was at a crossroads. Go one way and that was it, we'd have sex and there would be no turning back. *Or* pull my skirt down from around my armpits and my hymen would live another day.

Needless to say, I never saw my virginity again.

Loitering in the hall outside Carter's office, staring at those damn K-Cups on his desk, I feel that same potent blend of thrill and dread. If I follow through with the plan forming in my head, I won't be innocent anymore.

And so, five minutes later, the K-Cups are all swapped out, the pods inside no longer matching what it says on the boxes. And I'm on my way to the salon, nobody the wiser.

Same great flavor . . . now in decaf!

• • •

Friday may go on record as being the best day of my life, because it's the day that Carter Aaron can't keep track of a single thought at work.

It's a little like watching a lion with a limp: it's just not something you see very often, making it incredibly hard to look away. He wasn't kidding when he said he can't function without coffee. Apparently, he walked into the women's room and stared at the wall, obviously shocked that the urinals were gone, until Jess emerged from a stall and steered him in the right direction. He spluttered his way through a conference call with Smashbox Studios about the setup for the *Vanity Fair* photo shoot next Friday, and afterward stood in the hall, confused, before turning into his office and sitting down in front of the cup of decaf I'd stealthily placed on his desk.

I wonder if I'm turning into a horrible human being, really, because I am completely alive watching all of this. Who does this kind of backhanded crap? Well, aside from everyone in this business.

Except . . . *I've* never stooped this low, and as soon as I really start to think about how far I've strayed from my own ideals, my guilt begins to eat at me.

I dial Steph's number, thankful when she answers on the first ring. "I'm a terrible human," I say in lieu of a greeting.

"Is this for anything specific or just in general?" she asks.

I think about it. "A little of both, I think."

"Do you want to tell me about it or should I have plausible deniability?"

I can hear voices and the sound of glasses and cutlery clinking in the background, so I assume she's meeting someone and doesn't have much time.

"Are you busy? I can stop by and confess tonight."

"Just waiting on a casting agent," she says. "And by the way, you'll never guess what my assistant told me this morning."

I lean to the right, where I can see Carter at his desk, staring blankly at a pencil. I bite back a laugh. "What?"

"She slept with Carter's brother last night."

This gets my attention.

"No," I say, straightening. "*Your* assistant?"

"Yep."

"Jesus, this town is small. Where did this happen?"

"At some party. They didn't exactly do a lot of talking, and she only put two and two together this morning."

Honestly, if I weren't busy hating Carter Aaron, I would be texting him immediately to share this so we could laugh together.

Unable to resist, I lean over again and peek into his office. Today just keeps giving. "And?"

"And . . . from what I gather, it was a ringing endorsement for the Aaron family. A fact you'd have personal knowledge of if you two would get your heads out of your asses."

I groan. "Do not remind me. Speaking of his brother, we have a shoot with him next week. Now I'm going to be thinking of him banging Anna."

Steph laughs into the line. "Tell him she says hi!"

"Yeah, I don't think so."

"Okay, well then tell Carter his suit is hanging in my bathroom. He needs it for Friday."

"His suit?"

"He took Morgan trick-or-treating so we could go out, and she threw up all over him. I'd yell at him for letting her eat an entire bag of candy, but I got a grown-up party and hotel sex, so . . ."

"No, Mistress Overshare, not today. Don't tell me about your sex life, and definitely don't tell me cute things about Carter. He's a monster."

"Keep telling yourself that. Okay, I see my person walking in. Love you and stop being a terrible human."

Why does the universe do this to me? I'm riding high on inefficient, undercaffeinated Carter when the world has to remind me that he might not be entirely awful. I think it's safe to say that I've messed up, and maybe Steph's right: I *am* a terrible human.

The anxiety gnaws at me a little during a lunch meeting with Adam Elliott, and when I'm with America's favorite aging hottie I can't be distracted, not even a little.

Carter isn't in his office when I return, so I can't confess, can't even give him the fully caffeinated cup of joe I got him on the way back from lunch. I open my email and absently reach for the bottle of moisturizer on my desk. But instead of reading, and instead of cultivating the lingering guilt, my mind goes back to Carter forgetting Brad's name this morning when they passed in the hall. That one was pretty great.

I rub my hands together and smooth a little on my elbows and my face, and a little more on my legs as I recall Jess telling me how Carter got off on the wrong floor earlier, and sat down at Evan Curtis's desk up in Legal.

I've repeated the process two more times before the guilt returns and I realize what I need to do: I need to replace the coffee and 'fess up. Karma is a bitch I do not need coming after me.

I'm just reaching for the phone to ring Jess and confess, to ask if she'll help me switch it all back, when a call comes in that I've been waiting for.

Forty-five minutes of actress flattering later, a knock sounds at my door.

"Come in," I say, eyes still on my computer screen as the bottom of the door whispers across the carpet.

"Hey, did you see that email about the aud—*holy hell!*" Jess gasps, and I look up to meet her wide eyes.

"What? *What?*"

She shakes her head, a hand coming over her mouth. "Evie, oh my God. I'll be right back."

She rushes out of the room, returning a moment later with Daryl at her heels and closing the door behind them.

"What's going on?" I ask. "Why are you two looking at me like that?"

Daryl can barely keep it together. "What did you do, Garfield?"

"I—*what?*" I reach for the compact I keep in the bottom drawer, and I immediately see it. My hands, mostly my palms and up to my wrists, are orange. "Oh my God."

"You look like a construction cone," Daryl says, and she finally loses it, barely managing to add, "You're making me crave buffalo wings."

"Oh my God, would you *shut it?*" In fumbling with the mirror, I manage to nearly hurl it across the room.

My *face* is orange, too. Not just orange but shimmery. I look like a sparkly Circus Peanut.

Daryl moves to stand next to me. "What did you *use?*"

"I didn't—!"

I stop, reaching for the lotion bottle I used earlier.

No.

Unscrewing the cap, I bring it up to my nose and sniff.

No.

Instead of the subtle vanilla scent I'm used to, I now notice a faint chemical smell.

"Nooooo," I growl, my voice low and savage. "I'm going to *kill* him."

"He put sunless tanner in your lotion bottle?" Daryl whispers, sounding horrified . . . but also a little impressed.

Jess runs out and runs right back in again. Coming around

the desk, she kneels on the floor next to me, pulling a makeup wipe from a little plastic package. "I'm now afraid for him." She reaches for my arm and starts to scrub. "Okay, a lot of it is coming off. It's just bronzer."

Daryl laughs. "Give it eight hours."

"Oh, Evie, what *happened*?" a deep, mocking voice says, and we all look up to see a smiling Carter leaning against the doorframe. Jess practically falls backward in her attempt to flee.

"*You* did this!"

"You want to start pointing fingers, Chef Decaf?"

I giggle in spite of myself. "Pardon?"

Pushing off the doorway, he steps closer. Daryl and Jess, wisely, clear the room. "I ran home at lunch to make some of my own coffee, because the cups here just weren't cutting it. But sure enough, the ones *at home* are decaf, too. In the grocery store parking lot I couldn't remember where I parked my car and nearly got arrested trying to get into a different silver Audi."

I feel a surge of pride rush through my blood. "You did?"

He grins, shaking his head at me. "I did. Not cool."

Holding out an arm for him to inspect, I say, "You don't get to come in here and play the victim card, sir."

"I wouldn't dare." He steps closer, so close that I can feel the warmth of his skin against mine. The playfully contentious mood slips away and I can practically feel the sweep of his attention as he moves his gaze briefly to my lips.

As if he might kiss me again.

No way. I think we both know that that won't ever happen.

"I *liked* you," he whispers.

An ache worms itself between my ribs when he says this, and my response comes out more raw than I'd planned: "I liked you, too."

He stares at me, unblinking. "Evie—"

"I'm just glad I figured out who you really are before we got in too deep."

. . .

From deep in a pile of bubbles in Steph's bathtub I address everyone and my innermost core at once. "I'm going to bury him."

We're all here, crowded into Michael and Steph's small bathroom: Daryl, Amelia, Jess, Steph, and, of course, me. Naked and slightly less orange.

"That's great, honey," Daryl says, handing me another loofah around the shower curtain. "Just not tonight."

"You have to admit that was pretty fucking clever," Amelia says. "To figure out how to use your lotion fetish against you?"

I look sullenly at the murky water around me. Makeup kept most of the bronzer from absorbing into my face, and it washed off pretty easily. But my palms and elbows absorbed more of the color, and both remain a faded, sickly shade of orange.

"It's not a fetish. More of a nervous tic. And he didn't figure anything out, I *told* him about the lotion thing. He took something I shared and used it against me. Dirty traitor."

"Yeah, let's not let that halo slip too far there, Evie. You did strike first," Amelia reminds me. "His decaffeinated self walked into a wall in front of my office."

I peek my head around the shower curtain. "He did?" I say gleefully, wishing I'd been there to see it.

My smile straightens as she stares at me with a single stern eyebrow raised.

"Come on," I whine, breaking under the pressure, "it was coffee. I struck first with *coffee*. Besides, he pulled Dan Printz away from me, swapped out the *Vanity Fair* photographer for his *brother* without consulting me, and ditched our joint meeting with the chatty retreat coordinator. I wanted him to know I wasn't going to roll over."

"So all he did was up the stakes," Amelia says calmly. "And if I know anything about you, you're already plotting retaliation."

"You're damn right I am. Jess?" I say. "I'm going to need you to do some unsavory things."

She looks over at me from where she's sitting on the bathroom counter. "Am I going to be doing anything illegal?"

"Ummmm . . . not sure yet."

She rolls her eyes. "Will you at least take the fall if I get busted?"

"Absolutely."

"I'd like to go on record as saying I think this is a bad idea, but fine, I'm in."

"You know, as Carter's friend, I feel I should step in here," Steph says.

I tilt my head. "Perhaps you'd like to see the inside of your bathtub?"

She holds her hands up to stop me from moving. "No, no. Not necessary." She looks over her shoulder toward the sound of the doorbell. "I'll be right back."

Slipping back behind the curtain, I pick up the bar of soap and lather the loofah again. "The shoot is next week—and he may have won this battle, but I'm winning the war."

"Before I forget," Jess says, "I was originally coming into your office today to ask if you'd seen the email from Accounting. They're doing an audit and I need copies of all your expense reports."

"Audit?" Daryl repeats.

"Yeah," Jess says, "it has something to do with the private equity firm that backed P&D in the merge. I guess outside money means a closer eye on things. They want everyone's records, even mine."

"Just reconciling the books post-merge," Amelia says. "Pretty normal stuff."

Footsteps carry down the hall and I peek out again to see Steph walking back into the bathroom with Daryl's assistant, Eric, right behind her.

"What are you *doing*?" I shout, clutching the shower curtain to my chest.

"I have my eyes closed," Eric says. "I needed to drop off these contracts for Daryl."

And as if to illustrate that he really does have his eyes closed, he runs into the doorjamb.

"Right here," Daryl says, maneuvering her way over to him. "Thanks for coming all the way out here, Eric."

"What are you all doing, anyway?" Eric peeks one eye open to glance around the room. "Secret meeting . . . in a bathroom?" He squeezes his eyes closed again when he catches sight of me in the tub, and offers me a small wave. "Oh hi, Ms. Abbey."

"Plotting revenge against one of your own," Daryl tells him with the cap of a pen between her teeth. She turns him, holding the papers up against his rather broad, muscled back so she can use him as a makeshift table. "You might be wondering why Evie is sitting in a nest of orange bubbles."

"I mean," he says quietly, "the question had crossed my mind, but Ms. Baker from HR is here so I figured this is a don't ask, don't tell situation."

Amelia nods. "Good instinct."

"Someone put bronzer in the lotion on Evie's desk," Daryl

says, and Eric is unable to hold in a single, loud burst of laughter. In a whisper, Daryl adds, "*Carter* did it."

Amelia slides her hand down her face.

"Daryl—don't reveal names to the civilian," I say, a little loudly.

"Relax," she says. "Eric is cool. Hell, he might even have some ideas." She turns him back around, handing him the stack of signed papers. "You might be pretty terrible with phones but you're a genius with computers." She smiles winningly up at him. "No offense."

"Could you create a program that automatically reconciles our expenses with invoices?" Jess quips drily from her perch on the counter.

Daryl waves her off. "Boring, Jess. We're talking *sabotage*."

He shrugs. "I could be Team Estrogen. What do you need? I could wipe Carter's credit score. Create a warrant for his arrest?"

My stomach gives a surprising lurch. "I don't actually want him to go to prison."

"I could hack into his email?" Eric suggests. "Maybe rearrange his calendar?"

My interest is momentarily piqued. "You can *do* all that?"

We're treated to a sexy little lift of his chin. "Sure. I can do pretty much anything."

A roomful of women watches Eric when he says this, *absolutely* taking his word for it.

Finally, Amelia covers her ears. "No way this won't end badly."

"She's right," I say. "I appreciate it, but I'm going to have to keep it more zany hijinks and less criminal mastermind."

Steph throws one of Morgan's ducky washcloths in my direction, and the group files out of the bathroom, leaving me to finish up and ponder revenge alone. Climbing out onto the bath mat, I look up, and through the steam on the mirror, I see something hanging on the door behind me.

Carter's suit.

I smile at my reflection. Zany hijinks it is. He does call me Evil, after all.

If I'm going to the dark side anyway, I might as well do it right.

chapter sixteen

It's been two days and I haven't been able to stop thinking about what Evie said to me.

"You're doing it again, aren't you?"

I lie: "No."

Michael Christopher looks up at me from across the table at Creme de la Crepe. "Yes, you are." He nods to Jonah. "Doesn't he always do this?"

Jonah nods.

I look between them. "What do I always do?"

"Obsess over something someone might have said, or the possibility that—heaven forbid—someone might not like you. You've been like this your entire life. Maybe that's why you've escalated this thing with Evie. She doesn't like you and so you make sure it's because of something you've done, rather than the possibility she might not like you as a person."

Ow. That hits me right where it hurts. "No, she was pretty clear: she used to like me, but was glad to find out who I really am before we got too involved. Essentially: I'm a prick."

"You're not a prick," Michael says, and waves a spoon in front of Morgan, trying to divert her attention away from basically every other moving thing in the restaurant. "You're just dumb."

"Don't lie to him, MC. He's a *total* prick," Jonah says, and I glare at him. Aside from a few texts to set things up for the photo shoot, Jonah and I haven't really talked since I found out about his little money situation. I invited him to join us for breakfast so I could go over the details for Friday and reiterate how important it is that he not fuck this up. So far all he's done is stare at his phone and make wisecracks at my expense.

It's nauseating to think how much I have riding on my brother here. Brad thinks I brought him in because I have some sort of master plan, which means that if Jonah screws up and the shoot is any flavor of diva, there's *no* way Brad won't find out. There would be no coming back from that. The new contract will be Evie's and I'll be on a plane back to my parents' house.

"He's *not* a prick," Steph says to Jonah. Apparently she caught this last bit from him as she was returning from the bathroom. "Why would you say that?" It's heartwarming to see both MC and Steph sticking up for me, but let's be real, I deserve at least some shit for the other day with Evie.

"You've been quiet today," I say to her. "Everything okay?"

"Yeah, just . . . you know. Work," she says, repeatedly stabbing her ice water with a straw.

She seems off, but when I look at what she's eating, who could blame her? Her husband is shoveling down the *Oh La La*—an enormous plate of waffles smothered in Nutella, strawberries, bananas, and mango—and she's having egg whites with sautéed spinach before she heads to yoga. *Yoga.* As if that's not bad enough, she'll essentially be doing it on an empty stomach.

I think I'm only now realizing how hard it must be to be a woman. Too thin or not thin enough. Do your job flawlessly, but don't show up any of the men. Speak up, but don't be bitchy. *Smile.* And then you have people like Brad totally playing into it.

I rub my finger along the side of my water glass, watching the condensation drip onto the napkin underneath it. I'm feeling like a dick for playing into it myself.

"Do you ever have one of those moments when something seems like a good idea, and then you realize later that you are in fact a total fucking moron?"

Michael doesn't miss a beat. "Every day."

Jonah looks up from his phone again, as if the topic of my failures is the only conversation worthy of his attention. "What did you do?"

I jab of piece of sausage with my fork. "Nothing. Never mind."

"Come on," he says. "In case you haven't noticed, my life is in the toilet right now. I'm a total fucking moron, give me something here."

His honesty catches me off guard. "It's just a series of really stupid things that snowballed," I tell them, "and now I'm legitimately afraid to go to work on Monday."

Steph coughs.

"Okay . . ." Jonah says.

"Let's see, where to start," I say. "I guess we could go with when our boss knocked Evie's breakfast into the trash because he's a sexist dick, and I just sat there and watched. Or when I let her sit through a meeting with two of her shirt buttons undone. Two very important buttons," I clarify.

"She didn't tell me about that," Steph says, and her expression is a little terrifying.

"How were the tits?" Jonah asks, bringing it all back to the important issues. "Nice?"

Before I can reach across and smack him, Steph does it, then turns to Michael. "Did you know about all this?"

"I . . . heard that . . . something . . . untoward had occurred," he says, choosing his words carefully. "I told him it was wrong. *Very* wrong." He gives me a stern expression that says he'll murder me in my sleep if I so much as hint at the truth.

Steph groans. "I knew about Jonah and the weird Dan Printz situation, and that you'd flaked out on the meeting with the retreat coordinator."

"I—"

"All of that is professional stuff between the two of you. But playing into Brad's sexism? That makes me angry at *you*, Carter. It's hard enough for a woman to be taken seriously in this business and seen as a person with a brain and not an object. Men get passes for acting like it's 1960 and every woman in the office is their secretary. Evie will have to be smarter, faster, and better at her job than you are, for possibly less money and a whole lot less recognition, all while appearing totally grateful for it."

I want to crawl under the table.

"That's exactly what I told him," Michael says, nodding feverishly. "That it undermines her credibility. Didn't I tell you that, Carter? If I had a shame bell I would follow him around. Very disappointed in you."

"I felt trapped," I say. "If I said something, would she have been more embarrassed? Plus she would know I was looking at her boobs."

"Which you were, I'm sure," Steph says.

"Well, yeah. Because they're *great*."

She reaches across and smacks me this time.

"I don't see the problem," Jonah says. "None of this sounds bad so far."

"That's not very reassuring," I say, and then look back at Steph. "Like I said, it escalated. I don't even know how it happened. One minute I was in line at the store getting caffeinated K-Cups for the office, and the next I look over and see this giant display of bronzer. To summarize, I'm pretty sure I'm going to end up in a ditch somewhere."

"Wait—is this the girl from the party?" Jonah asks around a mouthful of potatoes. *My* potatoes. "The one you couldn't close the deal with?"

I toss him an icy glance. "Why are you even here?"

"You *asked* me to come, dickbag. You wanted to lecture me about this stupid shoot. You do understand this is what I do, right?" He straightens—a sign he's getting riled up. "You think I've made it this far because I need you to show me how to do my job?"

Annoyance flares in my chest, but I do my best to push it down. I reacted almost exactly the same way when Evie told me it was time to move on Dan.

"Just remember, I made sure they could work with your schedule and the new shoot time is eleven," I tell him. "We're doing makeup at eight thirty. Be there at nine. *Don't be late.* And no attitude, either. I put my neck out for you on this. Not to mention Evie's."

"Fucking hell, I'll be there, Carter." My brother shoves his phone into his pocket and stands. "Why are you such a dick all the time?"

"Dick!" Morgan screams, and we watch Jonah storm out of the restaurant.

"On that note," Steph says, checking the time, "my class starts in ten." She kisses each of us on the head—Morgan twice—grabs her gym bag, and heads out.

Michael Christopher cuts up some more of his waffle into bite-size pieces and slides them onto his daughter's plate. But

Morgan, tired of sitting quietly, has climbed out of her seat and relocated to my lap. Michael watches us, his face slowly melting into a floppy expression of fondness. I know what he's thinking— he wants this for me. He wants us to meet for breakfast on Sundays and watch our kids play together; he wants our wives to be the best of friends. I don't need to be a genius to know he still wants me to find that with Evie. I'd be lying if I didn't say that I wanted it a little, too. I was never on the right page with Gwen, but something tells me I might have found it with Evie. We'd probably kill each other first, but who knows, that might have been part of the fun.

"You have your dad's face on," I tell him.

"I do *not* have my dad's face on."

"Yeah you do." I lift a hand, drawing a vague circle in the air. "You get all glassy-eyed and sentimental, like you're mentally embroidering our names on a quilt."

"All this talk of sabotage is going to make it really awkward for me to make the toast at your guys' wedding."

"I hate to break it to you, but I think that ship sailed about the same time I was refilling her lotion bottle on Friday afternoon."

Michael picks up his mug and looks at me over the top of it, smug. "I forgot Steph had a cat for a week when she was on a trip in college, and I'm still here. You never know. Besides, you seem strangely optimistic—dare I say, chipper—for a man who plans to die this week. One might even think you're enjoying this a little."

My face says no, but the jump in my pulse as he mirrors my earlier thoughts says otherwise. Evil would cut off my balls and hand them to me if she thought it would give her an edge. And while that's not particularly appealing, the idea that I have to constantly keep up is. Evie is smarter, and there's a rush of adrenaline in having to work to stay one step ahead.

If only I knew how to do that.

• • •

Mildly obsessing over my next move, I barely sleep Sunday night, and feel like a walking time bomb the next morning.

I'm not sure what I'm expecting. Burning bags of excrement on my porch? To be accosted by hired ninjas in the stairway? Both of these possibilities seem highly unlikely, and yet I look out the peephole before I leave, peek around the corner as I head to the stairs, even check beneath the hood of my car before I start it.

Get a grip, Carter.

I try to laugh off my nerves as I turn the key and the engine comes to life without exploding into a ball of fire. Maybe the best retaliation is no retaliation at all. Damn you, Evie.

Traffic is better than usual this morning, and with my second cup of coffee down by the time I get to work, I've regained a bit of my nerve.

Justin is out sick today, and I make small talk with a couple of the interns as I pass. Kylie looks frazzled about something, but I steer clear, stopping by the Keurig in the break room before officially starting my day.

It's regular. I check.

My door is still locked, a good sign. Evie's light is on, but her door is closed, and if I'm careful not to jangle my keys or make any unnecessary noise it's because I'm considerate, not scared.

Nothing has changed. My computer is where I left it; my stapler is still on the corner of my desk. The words *DIE CARTER DIE* aren't scribbled on the wall in poop or blood.

I'm calling it a win.

Still, I close the door quietly and tiptoe to my desk. I log into the network, wincing, but the computer seems normal, too. I pull up an address and answer a few emails, grab the papers I need, and then casually lean to the side, where I can usually get a view of Evie's legs. No dice.

I'm just about to head out when my phone rings.

"This is Carter."

"Hello?" I think the caller says. I fiddle with the volume.

"Hello," I repeat. "This is Carter Aaron. Hello?" The voice on the other end is so faint, I find myself squinting as I try to hear. "I'm sorry, I think we have a bad connection. Can you call back? Hello?"

The line disconnects, only to ring a moment later.

"Carter Aaron," I say.

"Carter, this is Caleb," I make out. Caleb Ferraz, Dan Printz's manager. We've been playing phone tag for two weeks now.

"Caleb, there's . . . Can you hear me? I think there's something wrong with my phone." I'm shouting. I look at the handset, shaking it before bringing it back to my ear. "Can you call my cell?"

"Can't," I think I make out. Followed by "Taking off." There are more words, but I'm not sure whether I'm hearing them or just making them up. "Dan . . . talk . . . trip . . . weeks."

Fuck.

"Caleb, send me a text when you can and I'll talk to you soon!"

I think he says good-bye, but I'm not even sure. I hang up and dial Michael Christopher's number. He answers and it's more of the same. I think he can hear me, but there's no way to tell because I can't hear him. I send him a text letting him know I'll explain later.

Grabbing the needed files, I head out, a little disappointed when I find that Evie's door is still closed. Why am I in a hurry to run into her? I'm sure she's furious, and the last thing I'll see before I die will be an orange-tinted Evie with her hands wrapped around my neck.

With Justin gone, I stop at Kylie's desk on my way out. She's talking to some guy from the mailroom and so I pull out my phone while I wait.

"Just make sure that anything with a PO box goes straight to Mr. Kingman, okay? He was very specific about that."

"Post office box. Got it," the kid says, typing a note into a little handheld machine. "Later, Ky."

Kylie peeks around the departing employee and smiles widely at me. "Carter! How are you?"

"I'm well, how are you?"

"Great! Want to grab lunch today?"

I make a show of looking disappointed, when in fact I'm a little relieved to have an excuse. "I'm meeting a client," I say, and her face falls into an attractive pout. Something tells me that look almost always works. "I was just leaving, but wanted to see if we could get someone to check my phone."

"Your phone?"

"Something's wrong with the volume," I tell her.

She follows me down the hall, picking up the handset and holding it up to her ear, pressing the volume buttons a few times before unscrewing the earpiece.

"Oh," she says, and I lean in, too. "There's a piece of tape in here. That's weird."

Carefully, she removes the offending item and puts the handset back together.

I stare at the curl of plastic in her outstretched palm. "Yeah. *Weird.*"

On her way out, she leans against the doorway instead. "Glad I could help. Don't be afraid to call if you, uh . . . need anything else," she says, pausing at the sound of Evie's opening door. "Or want to grab lunch sometime . . ."

Evie steps out into the hall and pauses behind where Kylie stands, now straighter in awareness.

With a little smile and a quiet "Hi, Evie," Kylie heads down the hall.

Leaning against her open doorway with a pair of—thank God—normal-colored arms folded across her chest, Evie smiles at me. "Didn't mean to interrupt. Close your door next time?"

Ignoring this, I tell her, "Funny story: my phone wasn't working and Kylie helped me figure out why. Seems someone put a piece of tape over the earpiece. Wonder who would have done that?"

"No idea," Evie says with a shrug. "I just got in. But if we're going by the number of people who are out to make you look bad, there's probably a few to choose from."

"What is that supposed to mean?" I ask, genuinely offended now, and following when she pushes away from her door and heads into the break room. "People *like* me. *You're* the one they're afraid of."

She pulls a mug down from the cupboard and pours herself a cup of coffee. "Okay, Carter."

"What do you mean—?" I stop in my tracks. "Don't do that."

She slowly pours cream into her cup and looks up at me. "Do what?"

"Pretend that none of this gets to you. Play some juvenile mind game."

"You're the one who followed me down here." Unaffected, she puts the cream away and heads for the door.

"Fine," I say.

"Fine."

Her evil laugh rings down the hallway.

chapter seventeen

evie

> Steph—Steph—taping Carter's phone was pretty great.

> So simple.

> Maybe my best idea ever.

Evie, did you do something to Carter's suit?

The one that was in the bathroom?

> What? I can't hear you.

> I'm going through Laurel Canyon.

We're texting, asshole.

Did you?

> Maybe a little

> In which case I'm going to change my previous answer and say that THIS was my best idea ever.

Sigh

Don't worry!

A little fun, totally harmless.

You realize this isn't normal behavior, right??

chapter eighteen

carter

Things have not been pretty at P&D. Monday was the stupid tape incident. Tuesday I snuck a pretty healthy splash of Dave's Ghost Pepper hot sauce into Evie's burrito, and quite enjoyed her angry, sexy little growl as she ran back to the break room and chugged down some half-and-half we keep in the fridge. She returned the favor on Wednesday by soaking my desk chair so my ass was visibly wet for the rest of my meetings.

She didn't come straight to the office Thursday, so I didn't get to enjoy how she might have looked with all the glitter I put in the vents of her car, but it was a chilly morning and I'm sure the glitter got pretty sticky when it blew out with all that nice warm air. Admittedly, after that I was so paranoid she'd booby-trapped my office that I could barely touch anything without wincing. She stopped by at the end of the day—still a little sparkly around the hairline—just in time to see me bite into what I thought was a candy apple from Kylie but was actually a candy onion from Evie.

I was thwarted in my desire to murder her by the news that Steve Gainor in Television was let go. Nothing like a dose of reality to put things in perspective.

We're supposed to be on set with Jonah by eight thirty on Friday, but my Evil paranoia has me there by eight, standing outside the locked studio, shivering. My jacket feels tight—my pants, too—and I can barely wrap my arms around my shoulders to keep warm.

Great. All the stress-eating is taking a toll.

About half of the crew arrives a few minutes after I do, including Jamie's manager, who—as soon as we get inside—begins arguing with the *Vanity Fair* creative director and one of Jonah's assistants about the lighting.

"Carter, hey," Allie says, excusing herself and crossing over to where craft services are just starting to set up behind me.

"Hey." Just like Brad mentioned when he initially placed Jamie on my list, Allie is what you would call a hands-on manager. Whereas some managers are just yes men, there to make their client happy and get a producer credit along the way, Allie is involved in almost every aspect of Jamie's career. My life will be a hell of a lot easier because of it. "Do we know what time to expect Jamie—?"

"She just got here," she says, nodding over to a doorway leading to the dressing rooms. "She's in her room with her trainer."

"Great."

"That's how we roll." Her eyes follow some of the caterers as they begin unloading. She taps one of them on the shoulder as she sets down a tray of cookies, and points to the rest wrapped in cellophane. "There are no raisins in any of these, right?"

The woman looks at a label on the bottom of a tray and then consults a well-worn clipboard. "Food allergy? I didn't see that on the order."

"Fussy actress," Allie corrects, and the caterer offers her an understanding smile.

"Let's see," the woman says, scanning the pages before stopping on an itemized list. "We have coffee and tea service, soda, fruit juices, ice water with assorted citrus, energy drinks, chocolate chip cookies, assorted Danishes, sports bars . . ." She rattles off a seemingly endless list, flipping through the papers again before smiling up at Allie. "The only raisins should be in the trail mix and it will be clearly labeled."

Allie gives her the thumbs-up and turns back to me. I snag a cookie from the tray and then pause, looking down at it. My suit is becoming increasingly uncomfortable, like Spanx. Have I put on that much weight? Absently, I touch my stomach.

"Jamie is fussy about raisins?"

Allie nods. "She's one of the most level-headed actresses I've worked with, but, Lord, is she particular about her food." I raise a brow and Allie waves me off. "Don't worry, she's not a diva or anything and would never hold up a shoot, she's just really, *really* particular."

"As in particular with a side of losing it?"

"Borderline?" she says, grinning. "But regardless, that's why I'm here." Her phone dings and she swipes across the screen. "Which is more than I can say for Seamus. I'll take care of Jamie; you just make sure he's on his best behavior today."

"Seamus is Evelyn Abbey's problem, not mine." I casually scan the room for Evil over Allie's shoulder, not sure if I feel more pleased or disappointed when I don't see her.

"Good luck to her, is all I have to say. He's so used to having his head filled with adoration on that YouTube channel of his that he can't take a simple *no.* I know it's a sign of the times, but he got his start on the same platform where my nine-year-old uploads her *What's in My Backpack* videos. Kids today want to be famous. You ask them, 'Famous for what?' and they don't care. Did you know that at Seamus's first YouTube photo shoot he wanted *his own toilet seat* and Kanye's *Graduation* album played on a continual loop—and when he didn't like the color scheme in one of the set designs, he said he'd be back when it was repainted?" Allie scans the area. "He will lose the plot one day, mark my words."

I nod, having heard all of this—and more. "If you feel that way, then why on earth did you encourage Jamie to take this part?"

She lowers her voice. "Because Jamie needs this role, and right now Seamus is hot. Let him pay six hundred dollars for a hipster reflexologist to blow marijuana smoke in his face and balance his fucking chakras—I don't care. But here? He'd better show up and do the work, not fly off the handle. Pretty early in his game to start showing his ass."

I laugh. "I'll be sure to give my colleague the heads-up. And keep those raisins away from Jamie."

"I will." Allie switches off her phone and slips it into her pocket. "Let me know when the photographer is here."

I give her a tight smile when I realize that means Jonah still hasn't materialized. "Will do."

I turn and almost run right into Evie.

Shit. "Oops, didn't see you eavesdropping behind me."

"Eavesdropping?" She pulls back to give me an amused smile. "Oh, Carter. You love hearing yourself talk enough for the both of us."

Like they have a mind of their own, my eyes quickly skirt down the length of her body and back up again. She's wearing a sleeveless button-down shirt dress, with the top two buttons open, exposing collarbone and just a hint of cleavage, and I'm left momentarily speechless by her shoulders *and* her boobs. When I meet her gaze, the corner of her mouth twitches and I know that I'm busted.

"I see all your buttons are accounted for today," I say.

"See? That wasn't so hard. You'll learn this workplace etiquette with more seasoning, sport."

I turn as she slips past me. "It was simply a battle between workplace etiquette and a complete lack of interest," I call after her. "Lack of interest won."

She stops, spinning slowly to face me, and I feel sweat prick at the back of my neck. My suit seems to shrink further. Instinctively, I tighten my fingers around the cookie in one hand and the phone in the other, feeling every one of my stupid texts with Michael Christopher flash before my eyes. I can't help but worry the sentiment in each is scrolling across my face, too.

I nearly put my face in Evie's boobs in her office.

Keep reminding me that she's Lucifer.

Right. Lucifer. *Remember, Carter: it's essentially her or you.*

"Did I touch a nerve?" I ask.

There's the slightest twitch in her jaw, one so slight it would probably go unnoticed by someone who hasn't memorized every inch of her face.

Her posture becomes less rigid, her expression suddenly softer. "How are you feeling today? You good?"

Confused by this change of tactic, I instinctively want to cover my crotch. Instead, I straighten, taking the smallest step back. "Why?"

"No reason," she says with a casual shrug. "You just look a little, I don't know . . . fluffier than normal."

There's a distinct emphasis on the word *fluffier*, and I feel naked and afraid as her eyes drop all the way down my body and back up, before she takes the cookie from me.

"Are you depressed?" she asks, tossing it into the trash. Smiling sweetly at me, she coos, "Carter, you don't need that."

It takes a minute for the pattern of her questions to register—

How are you feeling today? You good? Fluffier than normal . . . —and then I get it: Evie fucked with my suit.

I would strangle her right now if I had more range of motion inside this tiny jacket. But instead, as I watch her walk triumphantly down the hall, I pull my phone from my pocket, open the saved post in my browser, and hit submit.

One . . .

Two . . .

She pulls up short as her phone rings, retrieving it from her purse. "Evelyn Abbey speaking." A pause, and her forehead furrows. "What? No, I think there's been some mistake. I don't have a car for sale."

I rock back on my heels. My bad mood is a distant memory.

"*No,*" she says again. "I told you, I don't have—yes, that's my number, but I'm not selling a car. And definitely not at that price." Ending the call, she turns to leave, but the phone rings again.

"Hello? . . . No, there's been some sort of mix-up, someone else just . . . No, I don't have a car for sale. Can I ask where you saw this? Craigslist . . . and the *Times?*" She looks back at me from over her shoulder. "And what did the ad say?" A moment of silence. "Tesla Model S, one owner . . . *One thousand dollars or best offer?*" she shouts, and hangs up the phone, turning to me. "You did this!"

It's my turn to shrug. "Did what? I didn't know you were selling a car. Good for you—taking a chance on the LA public transit system!"

"That's it, Aaron," she growls, walking back to me and pointing a finger to my chest. "No more freebies, no more help. From now on, you're on your own."

"Narcissist much?"

She leans in close and I get a whiff of her. It slaps me some-where nostalgic, making me dizzy. "Just do your job today, okay?" she growls. "Watch that your brother doesn't screw this up, and make sure Jamie doesn't slow Seamus down."

•   •   •

Come nine thirty, Jonah is still nowhere to be found. By ten, I've almost worn a hole through the studio floor—and possibly the seams of these pants—when he comes strolling in.

Talking on his cell phone.

Carrying a takeout coffee cup and sporting dark sunglasses.

Evie, thankfully, is in Seamus's dressing room trying to calm the actor down.

"What the fuck, Jonah?" I say, crossing to him. The fabric between my thighs chafes audibly with each step. *Swish swish swish.* "Nice of you to stop by."

He looks up at me over the top of his lenses. "Chill out."

"Chill out," I repeat under my breath, turning away and pushing a hand through my hair. The seams of my jacket protest. "We moved things to accommodate *your* schedule."

"Would you relax?" he says, clearly agitated now. "My assis-tant has everything set up, and I've already gone through the shoot list with the creative director. I'll do a final check of the lights and we can get started. By eleven, exactly like we discussed. Just get out of my fucking space."

If my brother came with one set of instructions, they would say: *Does not play well with others.* In school he used to get into fights almost daily with kids who teased him about his ever-present camera. Now, as an adult, he just doesn't care what any-one thinks about him; as long as he's making money, he's fine. It's something I've never been able to understand. His assistant took care of it this time, but what Jonah fails to realize is that at some point, somewhere, someone will decide he's not worth the hassle. Now the crew are annoyed about being kept waiting, the talent have both returned to their dressing rooms in varying states of frustration, the editors are all typing wildly into their phones because the photographer *I* arranged has them already behind schedule, and Evie—aside from telling off people wanting to buy her car—has been wearing her best *I told you so* expression since the moment eight thirty came and went without any sign of my brother.

Thank God I posted that ad this morning. The delight in seeing Evie lose it is the only thing keeping me together.

I'm halfway down the hall on my way to Jamie's dressing room when the screaming starts.

"Who put raisins in these cookies!"

I knock on the partially open door and poke my head inside. "Is everything okay?"

By this point Jamie is dramatically retching into a garbage can and Allie is standing over her, rubbing her back.

"There was a *raisin* in the *cookie*," Allie says to me before turning back to Jamie. "Honey, let's take it down a notch before people start talking. If I have to get makeup back in here to clean you up, I'm going to lose my mind."

"Aren't these the ones from craft services?" I ask, picking one up to examine it before turning it over. "We looked at these earlier, I don't remember any—" I stop and stare down at the cookie in my hand. It looks like someone has pressed raisins into the underside of the cookie. Lots of them. Raisins that weren't there earlier this morning.

I swing my head around to face the door. "I'll be back."

I set down the cookie and head toward the door. "Allie, the

photographer is here. Can you get Jamie prepped to start soon? I'm sorry about all this, by the way."

"Carter, they're raisins, not amphetamines. She'll be fine."

I nod, offering Jamie another apologetic smile before I step out and close the door behind me. I am fuming.

Evie is with Seamus and his assistant in his dressing room. If I had any doubt that she was the one responsible, those hopes are dashed as soon as she sees my face. Her eyes light up, cheeks flush.

"Sorry to interrupt," I growl, poking my head through the doorway. "Evie? I need to talk to you."

"Sorry, Carter, we're just in the middle of something," she says, but pointedly looks down at the floor.

"Unfortunately, it's important. Excuse us for just a second, guys?" With a calm touch that surprises me, I reach for Evie's arm and gently lead her down a narrow hallway and into a sound-mixing room, empty but for some cables, a dim fluorescent light on in the corner, and equipment locked up along the far wall, my pants swishing the entire way.

"What's that sound?" she asks with a grin, but I ignore her.

My hand around her arm is shaking, I'm so furious.

Furious . . . and hot. I'm really hot. These pants are tight as hell.

"You are fucking unreal."

"What the hell are you doing?" she says. "We're minutes away from starting the light tests."

The door closes behind us, sealing us in the dim light, and Evie wrenches her arm out of my grip. "We don't have time for this."

"We can take five minutes to fucking talk."

"So talk."

"Is this where we are now? We'll just keep tearing little pieces out of each other?"

"Oh, I'm sorry," she says, hands to her hips, "I can't hear your man-baby words over the *seventy-five* phone calls from people wanting to buy my nonexistent Tesla."

"Did I do the lotion thing to get back at you for the coffee?" I begin. "Yeah. Do I regret it? Hell no. I can still hear the echo of your frustrated roar from the other end of the hall."

She takes a swaggering step closer. "That must be rough, being the consummate people-pleaser that you are. How depressing to need every single person's approval."

"That would be a first for you, right?" I ask, leaning in. "Caring what other people think?"

"Only because I don't need to be everyone's best friend to get the job done."

"Or *anyone's*, for that matter."

Her face is so close to mine, brown eyes flashing. "Are we really getting into this again?" she asks, shaking her head at me. "Carter, look at this from my side. No one ever told a guy he needs to be nicer at work to get ahead."

I open my mouth to respond, but snap it shut. Evie moves in even closer, close enough that she has to tilt her head to look up at me. We could be embracing. It takes every ounce of restraint I have to not glance down to her dress.

"I tried *nice*, Carter," she says, "and here I am, fighting to keep my job—a job I'm more qualified for, if we're being honest. You might be the one everyone likes, but I'm the one who gets the job done. So stay out of my way."

Her words bounce around the otherwise silent room, and I'm left a little stunned. The truth of what Steph said about being a woman in this business comes rushing back, and the weight of guilt settles deep in my stomach—which is laughable because the last thing Evie would want from me is pity.

"Fine," I say.

She clearly didn't expect this. "'Fine'?"

I nod. "Yeah." I take a couple of steps back so I'm leaning against a wall. I need air with her so close. "You *are* good at your job. We both are. From the start we agreed that wasn't the problem. Brad set up this bullshit competition, and we played right into it. Little did I know what a sexist shit show it would become, and I hate it. I do." I push off again, and move back to her. "But you're pretending the fucked-up system of toxic masculinity is the reason you're a dick to *me*, when really I think you just hate how things have changed between us."

When she doesn't respond, I lean in. "So here's the thing, Evie: if we put our heads down, and do our jobs, and stay out of each other's way, then we can just be colleagues."

She gives me an aggressive shrug. "Okay? Sounds good to me."

"Colleagues. That's *it*," I say, and her shoulders fall a little as she gets where I'm going with this. My heart is pounding so hard, I have to pull off my suit jacket so I don't feel like I'm going to hyperventilate. Evie watches me take it off and drop it next to us, eyes rapt as she looks back to my face.

"Passing in the hallway, small talk, work emails. Whatever this is," I say, waving between us, "would go away. You may not like the glitter explosion in your car, but at least you know I was thinking about you when I did it." I pause, swallowing. "At least now you know I can't *stop* thinking about you."

I can't believe I just said this. I can't believe I didn't really realize it before just now. Are we really this immature? Jesus Christ, I guess we are. With this admission, it feels like a tight cage around my chest has been unlocked, and I can let out a huge breath.

"Well," I say quietly, "there's my dramatic admission for the day."

I expect her victorious Evil cackle, or even awkward, stunned silence. So I'm surprised when she moves up against me and slides her hand into my hair, pulling me down, down to her mouth.

I am immediately, *completely* on board. She pulls my lower lip into her mouth, sucking and nipping just hard enough to tap a mallet to the gunpowder of my blood. My hips press forward against hers, and the sound she makes in response dumps fuel everywhere.

I am on fire.

We don't have time for this. She says it into my lips even as she stretches higher, pressing into me. Even when she reaches for my hand, urging me to touch her.

We don't have time for this.

Her hand is like a clamp around my wrist, dragging it down over her breast, beneath her dress, up her leg. Against my mouth, her lips feel like a holy experience—eager in a way that tells me I'm not the only one who thinks about this all the fucking time.

My hand finds the lace of her underwear, sliding under, and her little gasp telegraphs her thoughts immediately: *Touch me there, get me off, do it quickly.*

I laugh in thrill, amazed at how easy she is to remember. The shape of her, the way she moves against my hand. Only the second time I've touched her, but here we are, snapping back into focus. Her hand slides down over the front of my pants—which have become their own kind of torture device—and she giggles into my mouth.

"I'm sorry," she says between shallow breaths.

I don't care about my fucking suit. I don't even care when

her hand loses focus and slides back up my body, pulling my head against her. Her neck is warm and thrumming beneath my teeth. Half of me wants to bite her so she comes stumbling out of this room like a screaming sex telegraph, but the other half wants her to leave the room put back together—keeping this perfect little secret after she comes around my fingers with her hands digging into my shoulders and her mouth open in that quiet, soft cry.

After, I slow my touch but don't pull away. Evie's eyes are closed, her face tilted up to the ceiling. With my free arm around her, I'm practically holding her up, and this mighty force in my arms somehow feels so fragile.

But I like that about her. I like that when she's on alert, every tiny bit of her packs a punch.

"We didn't have time for this," she whispers again.

"Oh well."

She pulls her head up, looking at me with unfocused eyes, and grins. "Oh well."

Evie makes to move back, and I untangle my hand from her underwear, letting her go. She looks at the buttons of her dress, straightening things, running fingers through her hair. With reluctance, I bend, picking up my jacket.

"Thanks," she says, then bites her lip.

I laugh, and this breaks her grin free. "You're welcome."

What the fuck happens now?

She opens her mouth to speak, but a fist bangs on the door and I swear to God all four of our collective feet leave the ground with how much it terrifies us.

"*Carter!*"

I clasp a hand over my chest. It's only Jonah, but I think I've just lost three years of my life.

I lean over, opening the door. Light from the hallway spills into the dim room and I squint over at him. "What?"

He takes quick stock of the scene before him. "We're getting some green-screen shots before we move the set pieces into place." With a little grin, he adds, "Thought you two might want to come out."

"Is everything okay?" I ask.

"You think I'm a fucking idiot?"

I stare at him wordlessly.

Jonah rolls his eyes and then looks past me to Evie. "You must be the maddening *wo-man*."

"You must be the douchebag *bro-ther*."

He smiles, delighted. "Carter's love looks a lot like hate, doesn't it?"

Evie unleashes her amazing cackle and I reach forward and smack him. "How did you know we were in here?"

Jonah turns, laughing, and heads back down the hall. He calls over his shoulder, "That's where everyone goes in this studio to fuck."

chapter nineteen

Monday-morning meetings are going to be an issue.

Carter is sitting across from me, bent head-to-head with Aimee over a spreadsheet. I'm only now taking the time to notice that his hair has gotten a little shaggy in front, but he's kept it short on the sides and . . . well, I'm quite enjoying it. Today he's wearing a light blue shirt, and I don't know if it's intentional, but the top two buttons are undone, showing a nice hint of his pecs. Unfortunately, now I can't really blame him for the Evie Blouse Disaster of Late October, because there is no way I am telling him that I can see chest-below-collarbone for fear that he would remove it from my view. His sleeves are rolled up, exposing his forearms, and he's doing that fascinating trick where he flips a pen over the back of his hand.

Back and forth.

Back and forth.

He made me come with those fingers.

Back and forth.

My chest twists a little as I realize how hard I'm swooning, and how far that will take me. Because who knows what is going on between us? We sure haven't talked about what happened Friday.

After Jonah found us, we left the mixing room in silence. We walked down the hall and found that our presence was completely useless anyway: Jonah and the crew had the shoot under control, and we wrapped right on time.

After only a brief shared look of bewilderment, Carter went to his car, I went to mine, and we left separately. He didn't call, I didn't call, and we haven't made eye contact again. But, thankfully, we haven't melted back down into petty sabotage, either.

Oh, no.

I'm softening toward him again, which can mean only one thing: my defenses are down. It would probably be wise for me to make a list of all the ways he offends me on a personal and professional level.

1. He's too overtly sexy for the workplace.

2. ~~He clearly can't button his shirts.~~ Deleted b/c hypocritical.

3. He

I look up and stare blankly at the fingers flipping the pen back and forth across his hand.

I'll compile the rest of the list later.

I'm also—and I loathe saying it because I despise the cliché of two girls pitted against each other for the boy—slightly annoyed by Kylie. She's sitting at the end of the table near Brad's perch, waiting like all of us for the boss man to appear, but she isn't even trying to be subtle about staring at Carter. She may or may not be having an affair with Brad, but she definitely wants to bang Carter. I am zero percent on board with this plan, because just before I light his tight pants on fire, *I'd* like to actually have sex with him.

Maybe that'd get him out of my system.

"How was the *Vanity Fair* shoot?" Brad asks, strolling into the room, and both Carter and I jump.

"Great!" we exclaim in unison.

Brad narrows his eyes at us, and Carter grins. "It went off without a hitch."

I nod. "No bumps."

"Or grinds," Carter adds, and stifles a grin.

I stare at the table, trying to strangle down my laugh. The giddy thrill of having Carter acknowledge what we did on Friday makes me want to jump on the table and start channeling Missy Elliott.

Out of the corner of my eye, I see Brad sit up. "Yeah?"

"They got all the shots they needed," Carter says. "Everyone left happy."

"On the whole, I was very satisfied," I add.

Carter coughs, and the room falls into a heavy silence.

Brad's steely gaze narrows and he glances back and forth between me and Carter, who are very pointedly not looking at each other. "What am I missing?"

"Nothing," we say in unison again.

"I don't want to know any more," Brad says, turning to Ashton.

Everyone is awkwardly shifting in their seats, looking at each other in silent *What do you know about this?* communication. No one cares about the photo shoot; there's drama all the time at those things, but it's rarely between the agents. Now they're pigs sniffing for truffles. Our colleagues are either dying of curiosity or convinced they know something, but no one is oblivious. Not in this business.

I glance over at Kylie and catch her sullen pout directed at Carter. He seems to catch it at the same time, doing a tiny double take before busying himself with something on his phone.

But I don't miss the way he peeks up at me, eyes shining.

"Ashton," Brad says, "have you heard back from Joe Tierney over at Paramount?"

"He moved to DreamWorks last week," I say absently, tearing my attention from Carter.

Everyone goes silent.

It's an unspoken rule that any correcting of the boss is done way more subtly than that. Brad is top dog here. Brad is the first to know everything. That's the rule, did I forget about that?

"No. I don't think so," Brad says, pulling his glasses lower so he can peer at me over the rims. "He's there until March."

I wince, shaking my head, inwardly telling myself to shut the hell up. The last thing I need to give Brad is another reason to dislike me.

"He left early. Wiggled out of his contract." I try to lighten this with a little smile, but Brad just stares blankly at me for several silent seconds.

"Getting out of a contract. What an interesting idea." The room is as silent as a grave. "Thanks for the clarification," he says, slow-blinking back down to his notes and writing it down.

My good mood vanishes. What have I just done?

● ● ●

Despite the flirtation of the Monday meeting, for the rest of the week Carter and I really do put our heads down and bust our asses. It's the end of the year, when we're all scrambling to wrap up the last few contracts before Hollywood essentially shuts down for a month around Christmas. It seems as though every time I'm in the office, Carter is at an off-site. We don't even pass each other in the halls or parking deck.

To be honest, it's better this way. Having that random tension-release hookup on Friday doesn't really change anything, as Brad so aptly reminded me on Monday. Looking back, I missed the beginning of the shoot while I was getting pleasured by Carter, and lost some of my professional traction by being punny with him in front of the entire Features department. Not to mention this little game we've been playing. Thank God we both pulled our heads out of our asses before someone lost a client, or worse.

I've never put a guy before my career, although the impact of that decision sometimes needles my thoughts: if you always put career first, you will only have your career to put first. Unfortunately, in this case, it really is a choice of the job or the guy.

By Friday afternoon, everyone is in the rising phase of cocktail hour. Every November Brad hosts a tree-lighting party at his house; this year's party is tonight, which adds extra oomph to the office drinking. The atmosphere outside my door is cheerful if not yet booming. I can feel everyone's giddiness, the relief of being able to let their proverbial hair down. Unfortunately, I have about seven calls to return and three contracts to pore through before I can call it a day and join the pre-party.

With my door closed, I tap the space bar to wake up my computer and try not to groan out loud at the seventy-five new emails since I last checked, only an hour ago.

A quiet knock lands on my door, and Carter pokes his head in.

My heart takes off running, and a heavy ache builds beneath

my ribs, and just maybe between my legs, too. I missed him this week more than I wanted to admit.

"We're all out here, hanging . . ." he says, tilting his head back a little and then giving me a tentative smile.

I'd rather have him sit down and just . . . hang with *me*.

"Come in," I say, and he steps inside, nudging my door mostly closed behind him.

He looks around my office for a few quiet seconds. "How are you?"

"Good." I feel like he can probably see my heart punching me from the inside. "How are you?"

Carter nods. "I'm good. Are you going to come out and join us?"

"I was out with a client most of the afternoon and have a few things I need to do before I can call it a day."

"Do you want me to bring you a beer?"

As if to remind me what I'd be facing out there, Brad's voice booms down the hall, causing me to grimace. The last thing I want to do is be with Mr. Team Token when I'm already stressed and buried under a to-do list the size of California.

"I'm good," I say. "But thanks."

Carter sighs, glancing over to the door. "Okay." His jaw is tight, and even his frustrated profile looks amazing.

Wait. Why is he frustrated?

"'Okay'?" I repeat, mimicking his tone. "What's wrong?"

He looks back at me, and his expression softens a little. "Everyone else is out there. And you're in here."

"I'm working," I say gently. It's surprising in an awesome way that he wants me out there, but he seems more irritated than sweet about it. "I'm swamped."

This seems to frustrate him even more. "We're *all* swamped.

But maybe if you joined in these things, you wouldn't feel like such an outsider. I'm trying to *help* you, Evie. Jesus."

I try to focus on my monitor and feel a crushing bleakness in my chest when I hear him slip out of my office back into the revelry.

I'm tempted to follow, engage with honest anger for once, but am immediately choked by my own voice in my head, telling me to hold strong to that desire to be myself in this business. As soon as I give an inch, I'll lose a mile.

•   •   •

Brad's driveway is a quarter mile long and lined with tiny glittering lights. I've been here before. One year, his wife—an executive at Warner Bros.—threw a wrap party for a film starring one of my clients. That night, amid the champagne and hors d'oeuvres and live music, I watched Brad slip away with my actor's girlfriend.

Brad caught my eye as they wound up the staircase just off the downstairs guest bathroom and knew he was busted. I guess that's one of a hundred pieces of dirt I've got on him, though I never said anything to anyone.

Rule one: get neither invested nor involved in actors' or bosses' private lives.

The tires of my Prius crunch down the gravel, and I pull up in front, handing my keys off to the valet and thanking him with a smile.

Memories of parties and betrayals and the simple madness of personal relationships in this town all filter through my thoughts as I walk to the front doors, making the situation with Carter seem somehow so insignificant. We had the workplace equivalent of a couple of pillow fights and then tucked away our bratty sides and made out in a closet. Even when I do drama, I do it so *tamely*.

I think what worries me the most about it is that there's no sign of resolution anywhere. We're both on tenterhooks, with the clock ticking down to the end of our contracts. And while I know I'd be devastated if I lost this position, it's not as though I would be particularly happy if Carter lost, either. I might want to watch him suffer, but I don't want him to be miserable.

Because you like him, my brain teases in a sneering whisper. *Really, really like him.*

My brain is such an asshole.

Brad's wife, Maxine, greets me just inside the foyer, taking my coat and telling me where to find the alcohol and—with de-cidedly less emphasis—the food. I never try to meticulously time my arrival at these events, but glancing around I realize I'm one of the last to show up.

Looking for my lifelines, I immediately search for Amelia, who sometimes attends these gatherings. There are only about fifty people here, but the buzz of conversation makes it sound far larger. As usual, Maxine has arranged for live music, appetizers, and flutes of champagne on trays circulated by waitstaff. The main living area is expansive and faces a backyard with a view of the Hollywood Hills. Three sets of French doors are thrown open to the night, but heaters are placed just outside, keeping the mild chill at bay.

It's gorgeous, it really is, and at times like this I'm over-whelmed with how lucky I am to be able to dip in and out of the lavish aspects of this world. It is a world of privilege and excess, and whenever I register how easy we all have it, it makes me realize how petty I am to ever complain about a few asshole personalities. By and large the people in this room are good. This is a cutthroat business, but few of us are as terrible as our actions would lead one to believe. Insecurity and competition make us all monsters.

I should know.

There's no Amelia in sight, but I spot Carter with Brad across the room, near the open doors. Knowing he grew up in New York, I wonder what it's like for him here, in November, where we shiver when it dips below sixty-five and wear fur coats out to dinner. I also wonder what it's like to be celebrating with an almost entirely new team this year. The reorganization has been slow, but the first transition was deft, and the majority of the cuts were from CTM's side of the table.

He's changed into a sapphire-blue dress shirt rolled up to his elbows and exposing those forearms I alternately want to lick and amputate.

I hate to think that there is some fated connection there, but I can't deny that when he looks up and sees me walking toward him it makes my stomach flutter a little.

His expression betrays his happiness to see me, and then immediately pinches inward and he returns to the conversation with Brad. It hadn't even occurred to me to come over and interrupt Carter's one-on-one time with the boss . . . because I wasn't coming over there for Brad. I was coming for Carter. Of course, he has no way of knowing that.

But the hesitation in his face makes *me* hesitate, taking a detour toward the tray of wine headed in my direction. Swiping a glass, I say hello to a few colleagues and stand admiring the towering Christmas tree on the far end of the room.

Each ornament is gold, but there are enormous balls and tiny balls; horses, sleighs, and snowflakes. The tree seems to shimmer beneath the warm light of the room.

I can still hear Brad's voice, which is low but carries in an odd, booming way. "So, you think you're up for it?"

"Vegas and golfing?" Carter says. "I'm up for it any day of the week."

"Good man. With you on board, I think we've got the whole team."

A boys' golf trip to Vegas?

I roll my eyes and turn to make my way over there. Things are strained enough as it is, and I know I should tread lightly, but I can't let this one slide.

"Hey, guys!" I say.

"Evie!" Brad crows, leaning in to kiss my cheek in a way he would never dare do at the office.

Carter doesn't kiss my cheek, but he does offer a half smile. "Hey, Evie."

I smile at him, then turn to Brad. "Just overheard you—a department trip to Vegas? How cool!"

My game face is always on. I wish it weren't the case, but I can never, ever let my guard down. Of course Brad hasn't mentioned Vegas to me, and I would bet a large chunk of my salary that he hasn't mentioned it to Rose or Aimee, or any of the other female agents. The only vaginas they want on their trip are the ones two inches from their faces at the strip clubs.

"Right," Brad says, deflating just slightly but hiding it pretty well. He's good at the game, too, after all. "You coming?"

"When is it, again?" I smile at him, letting him save face and act like he's mentioned this to me.

"First week in March."

He shifts on his feet. No doubt he assumed that the female agents, who weren't invited to—or interested in—hungover golfing in Las Vegas, would be *fine* without an invitation. An added bonus? We'd be here to put out any emergency weekend fires. Those of us who are left, anyway . . . and I'm up for renewal in February.

Carter is March. Interesting.

"Should work for me." I smile over at Carter, whose expression tells me he's putting two and two together about the non-invites for the ladies.

I want to hug him for working to be more aware of Brad's sexist shit, but also give him a patronizing head pat and a sing-song *Of course Brad didn't invite any of "his girls," poodle.*

"Great!" Brad says, and flags down a passing waiter to bring him a scotch, neat. "You know, I meant to ask you the other day, but I have a friend who does a local podcast. *Yeah, Here Today.* Ever heard of it?"

I shake my head. "Can't say that I have."

"Well, he's doing a series on career road bumps and I was mentioning to him that you might be great as a guest."

Carter outwardly flinches. Embarrassment flashes across my skin and I'm hoping I can keep the blood from flooding my face by sheer will alone.

I force a tight smile. "I'm intrigued."

"Great, great," he says, reaching for the drink set in front of him. "I'll connect you two. You get knocked down but always manage to get yourself back up. That's what I like, sport. Good talking to you, Carter."

And with that, he pats us each on the shoulder in turn and moves on to the next conversation.

Carter's expression shines with irritation. He's doing that thing that makes me insane—the quiet studying, with those honest green eyes—and it feels so dangerous to be standing here with him, in this setting, which is somehow both work and social, and a little Us Against Them.

I can't resist him when he's like this. He looks gorgeous. His lips are slightly wet from his beer, eyes relaxing into that knowing glint, like he can read every thought I have and he finds each one amusing.

I wish I could be more like him, and I realize with a slug to my gut that *that's* what a lot of this is for me. I've always been good at my job, but Carter has an easiness about him that I'll never be able to emulate. He's simply . . . comfortable in his body, in his mind. I have to work so hard for every client, every deal, every second maintaining my level head. It's satisfying that I can make him insane sometimes, but it's short-lived.

Still . . . I seem to get to him, too, in a way that I haven't seen anyone else do.

I pull my lip between my teeth, thinking on this possibility that maybe Carter is a little hung up on me, too.

"You look like you're cycling through a lot of things right now," he says.

"Like what?"

He shrugs and steps a little closer. "Like whether you should kiss me or punch me."

The bald honesty of this makes my chest squeeze so tight, I have a moment of breathlessness. "It's a daily struggle."

This seems to delight him. "Really? I was kidding. Friday aside, I figured you were mostly up for the punching."

"It *is* heavily favored."

"If it makes you feel any better, I struggle similarly." He pauses, taking a sip of his beer. "Alas, kissing is usually favored."

I swallow, working to contain my outward reaction to this. My shoulders go up in this external tiny squeal and I lift my drink to my lips to mask it as a shiver from the chill.

"Should we talk about that?" he asks quietly.

I'm opening my mouth to tell him *yes, absolutely, but not here* when a floppy arm comes around me. I startle, and Rose appears at my side, bringing with her a heavy whiff of tequila.

"Evie!"

"Hey, Rose." I smile as she presses a wet kiss to my cheek.

Aimee comes up behind her, and I get the distinct impression she's been keeping an eye on Rose's booze intake. "Hey, guys," she says.

Rose leans in closer. "You're *amaaazing*." The word is drawn out into several syllables and brings out the lime smell just on the edge of the tequila.

I laugh at this, working to gently step out of her embrace. "Aww, thanks."

"No, I mean it. You're my girl hero."

I look up at Carter's face and bite back a laugh at the surprised amusement there. For once he doesn't seem annoyed to hear someone compliment me.

"Just your *girl* hero?" Carter asks, laughing.

"My *hero* he-ro . . ."

"Rose has had a really good party," Aimee says with a smile and a nod. "Rose, honey? Are you ready to head out yet? I can drop you on my way."

Rose waves her off and looks at Carter, giving him a very long, very drunken once-over. "Hey, Carter."

He laughs, cheeks a little pink. "Hey, Rose."

He slips one hand in his pocket and gazes back at my face. Something inside me pulls tight, a string being tied around my midsection, at the way his attention to me is a quiet statement about where his thoughts are . . . and who he's here for.

I get caught in that look, snagged by it.

"Evie," Rose stage-whispers into my ear, and I shiver from the wet condensation of her breath on my neck. "Any chance we'll get to be Eskimo sisters on this one?"

This question comes like a bucket of ice poured over my head, and I step away, fully out of her arm now, shaking my head. "I'm not sure that has anything to do with me."

I look up at Carter but can't tell whether he's heard. I want to take Rose's drink away, lead her to a couch where she can sit down and get some air, maybe sober up.

Turning, I collide directly with Brad's chest.

"I see Rose has her fifth margarita," he says with a laugh caught somewhere between reprimand and pride.

"Fourth," Rose says, and then adds, "But these are *strong*."

Without preamble, Brad lifts his chin to her, asking, "You gonna pick up the pace this quarter, Rosie?"

I feel my face heat at the patronizing *Rosie* and the work-performance question thrown so sharply down into the small circle of us standing here.

Rose flushes, too, and says, "Oh, yeah, Q3 was just an outlier for me." She looks away, glancing out the back doors, and sips her drink as we all drown in awkward silence.

"Well, not *so* much of an outlier," Brad says, bringing her back into it. "The rest of the team is crushing deals left and right. Ashton signed three majors this month. Carter got Jett Payne a recurring spot on a Netflix show and a starring role in a Ridley Scott movie. Evie here has Sarah Hill in this year's biggest teen craze. I think you're gonna need to figure out where you fit into the puzzle."

"*If* I do," Rose says, and never before have I wanted to escape a conversation more than this one. "Sometimes I look at someone like Evie and wonder if I'm cut out for this. I mean, I love it, okay? But . . ."

Carter and I meet eyes and quickly look away. This is painful for both of us. I want to tell Rose to stop. I want to tell her she's gone too far, this is a conversation for closed doors, with me or someone else who's sympathetic—not here. Seven days of the week—even on holidays—Brad is out to win. He's not going to worry about appearances and say something to ease her mind. He's a predator, and if you show him a trail of blood he will hunt you down until he's eating your entrails.

Graphic but true.

"Just depends," Brad says with menacing quiet, "whether you're more comfortable being a failure or a quitter."

I down my wine, knowing I'll regret drinking it so fast but also unable to stop myself because I need to do something other than stand here, listening to Brad give this poor, *nice* person her very negative year-end review in the middle of a party.

Snagging another glass from a passing tray, I turn and walk toward the Christmas tree, intent on admiring it and getting the hell away from the echo of that conversation.

But I can feel Carter on my heels, and he stops just behind me, staying quiet while we each take a few breaths.

"Wow," he says quietly, and I nod.

A few more seconds pass before he whispers, "Evie?"

"Yeah?"

"What are Eskimo sisters?"

The anticipatory horror on his face when I turn is like a hammer to a pane of glass for the tension in my chest, and I burst out laughing. "Two women who have slept with the same man."

If possible, the horror intensifies. "And this man would be . . . *me?*"

"I presume so, but I know *I* didn't become a sister."

His face straightens. "Only because of *circumstances*."

"I assume whenever two people don't sleep together, one way or another it's because of *circumstances*."

"Right," he says, easy again now, with the smile and the eyes and the collarbones. "But those circumstances are entirely different from the ones surrounding why I didn't sleep with Rose."

I glance back over to where Rose is still in a tense conversation with Brad, having been abandoned by the rest of us. I want to joke some more, keep it light here with Carter, but it's nearly impossible when the weight of the job seems to follow us everywhere. I've never been let go. I'm not even sure how to deal with that.

"You okay?"

I nod, numb. "Sometimes I just can't believe I do this for a living."

His brows pull together. "You don't love it?"

Instinct makes me tread carefully. Why is it that the one person I want to confide in the most is the one who could use it against me so easily? "I do love it. I love making these things happen, and connecting people. I love the clients and the art they make. It's the politics I hate. The team behind the curtain is starting to feel . . . terrible. I don't want to become that."

His hand is warm when it comes up and cups my shoulder.

The touch feels like the most intimate thing he could do right now—beyond even kissing me—because it makes me remember. I remember his mouth there. I remember that Carter likes my shoulders. I remember how his eyes seemed to ignite when he saw them bare, in the dress, that first date, and again on Friday.

It doesn't feel like an innocent touch, it feels like a message.

"You aren't like that, Evie."

But when I look up at his face, he smiles a little, and it carries a shadow of regret.

I know we're thinking the same thing: *But I've been like that with you.*

chapter twenty

Eighteen-hour workdays, no social life, and I'm boarding the plane for New York wondering if the fact that it's December twenty-first and the only Los Angeles holiday parties I managed to attend were work-related makes me an amazing career man or a terrible single dude.

Michael Christopher and Steph were hosting one—no costumes this time, sadly—but it conflicted with the Paramount party. Jonah invited me to his new apartment in West Hollywood, but the only evening I was free overlapped with his meeting a bankruptcy lawyer. We ended up exchanging small gifts over lunch at a food truck outside my building.

I've barely seen Evie, but we seem to have reached a sort of cease-fire. I guess hand jobs foster goodwill? Or maybe it was because I told her she had a poppy seed between her teeth before a Monday meeting, and she gave me a grateful *you're no longer Satan* look. Whatever the reason, things have softened between us, and I'm so goddamn grateful for it I nearly want to weep. I've never in my life been so busy at a job, so desperate to prove myself and make myself indispensable. But seeing her face as we pass in the hall or hearing her voice coming from her office has made the last three weeks more bearable.

It makes no sense, I realize that. Hers should be the voice

that reminds me that the clock is ticking, that the direct deposit notice I find in my inbox every two weeks isn't a sure thing. And still, hers is the presence that feels the most grounding, the most sane. It's terrifying to realize that no matter how this turns out, I probably won't have her as a colleague much longer. So I go into ostrich mode and just don't think about it.

•   •   •

Christmas is in two days and I'm shopping with family. The mall is packed, but there's this shared type of last-minute chaos that puts people in a good mood despite the number of bodies clogging the stores.

Doris and Dolores are my two favorite aunts. They're my dad's sisters—twins, of course—and although they might look identical, they couldn't be more different. For as long as I can remember, if Doris was hot, Dolores was cold. If Doris wanted burgers for dinner, Dolores wanted fish. If one wanted to watch a comedy, the other was absolutely in the mood for sci-fi.

"Why so quiet, Scooter?" Doris says, apparently still refusing to believe I am nearing thirty. She peers at me across the clothing rack through glasses so thick her blue eyes are magnified to three times their actual size. "What are you thinking about?"

Dolores picks through a table piled high with brightly colored polo shirts and looks up at her sister. "He's a boy. He's not thinking about anything."

I slide my eyes to her. "Easy, Dolores."

Holiday music plays on a loop overhead and Doris squints at me. "Look at him. He's percolating."

My mom lays a gentle hand on my shoulder. "You stressed about work, honey?"

As far as she knows, work is fine. I haven't told her that in the past two months her eldest son began bronzing women without their consent and dealing in contraband glitter and hot sauce. I haven't told her about my boss and how it's like working for a real-life Ron Burgundy. I certainly haven't told her that there's a small chance I could be transferred back here, because the sabotage I've seen from Evie would pale in comparison to what Mom would do to make that transfer happen. And I haven't mentioned that the girl I met at the party all those months ago is becoming my favorite person in the world and I'm feeling mildly lovesick.

"Just wondering," I say, pointing at the pile of shirts Dolores is upturning, "what kind of monster digs through clothes during Christmas shopping and pulls every single shirt from the pile, unfolding it?"

Dolores throws me the stink eye.

"Don't you know how long it takes to fold all of those, Double D?" I started calling my aunts this long before I knew—or appreciated—what it meant. They've always found it hilarious, but after twenty-plus years of hearing it, my mom no longer finds humor in Double D: The Twins. She gives my aunts a reproachful look for encouraging me by laughing. I adjust the bags in my hands and follow her as she moves to another table.

"*Honey,*" she says. "Tell me what's bothering you. Are you in some kind of trouble? You know, I saw this episode of *Law & Order* where it talked about the underbelly of Hollywood." She lowers her voice on that last part, the tiny bells on her earrings jingling as she sorts through shirts. "Anyway, they exposed it all. About the prostitutes and gangs, the *drug dealers.*" She looks at me with wide eyes. "You're not near that, are you?"

"No, Mom. I think the underbelly is on the other side of LA. The side Jonah is on."

This time the reproachful look is all mine.

"Mom, I'm fine. Was just thinking about him, actually. Wondering if he's going to be all alone on Christmas."

I am an excellent manipulator, and if there's one thing I've learned growing up in this family, it's that the way to change the tide of any conversation is to steer it directly toward Jonah.

Mom frowns, and even though I'm sure she knows exactly what I'm doing, her desire to defend her can-do-no-wrong son wins out. "You know how busy he is," she says to me, but also toward Dolores and Doris, who've stopped to listen. "He said he'd be fine. He has friends. I'm sure he has some important job he's wrapped up in, it being the holidays and all."

I nod, remaining silent on the topic of Jonah's schedule. Old Carter would have spilled all the details about my brother's fall from grace, his money troubles, his current adventures in bankruptcy, because—at least for a few minutes—it would mean I'm the good one. But this strange guarded sensation in my chest feels something like protectiveness.

Toward *Jonah*. I think . . . I might be starting to like him?

"He does have a lot on his plate," I say.

My mom puts down a particularly hideous shirt and pins me with narrowed eyes. "This is usually the point where you call him something colorful and tell me how many days it's been since he last visited."

"Maybe I'm being a grown-up."

"Maybe you're full of it," she counters. And there it is, there's that little spark I love. I sometimes wonder how much Mom knows about the particulars of Jonah's life. They obviously talk because he told her about Evie, but he rarely comes home, and getting my parents onto a metallic death tube piloted by alcoholics (their words) is unlikely.

I'm twenty-eight years old and moved out of my parents' house when I was nineteen, but I still miss my mom sometimes, my dad, the rest of my crazy family. I'm really not sure how Jonah does it. Then again, maybe that's *exactly* how. If he came home, she'd probably figure out what a mess he is right now. Maybe he'd rather be the perfect Jonah they all remember than the one he actually is.

"LA is just . . . a lot," I say finally, lamely.

It must communicate what I mean it to, because Mom nods, refolds the terrible shirt. "Just be sure you don't become *a lot*, too."

I sit in the backseat next to Doris on our way back to the house. Ten minutes into the drive, she's asleep, which doesn't make for the best conversation but does allow me to scroll through my texts and maybe mope a bit without anyone reading over my shoulder.

I'm not going to lie: it's a little depressing to open my text window with Evie and realize how much time has passed since things were so good between us. I start to reread some of our exchanges, wondering if it's possible I made then-Evie out to be funnier, smarter, or sexier than she really was.

I didn't. The Evie in these texts is just like I remembered, and basically just like the one I see every day—maybe with just a touch more fire.

• • •

My phone rings as I'm carrying packages into the house, and I double take when I see the name on the screen.

Zach Barker is one of my stage-to-film clients. He was offered a last-minute role in an action movie when one of the supporting cast had to be replaced. Despite the fact that he and his wife, Avya, were living in New York and expecting a second child, he was needed on set right away. It wasn't an ideal situation, but the last I heard, Avya decided to stay behind and wait for their son to finish up the fall semester before joining Zach in California around the time the baby is due.

"Zach, hey," I say into the receiver, looking up to see snow beginning to fall. "You back in New York?"

"I'm still in LA. Avya and Josh are there. That's why I'm calling."

My heart speeds up and my mind races with thoughts of impending disaster. "Tell me what's going on."

"Jason broke his ankle," he says, and I wince.

Jason Dover, the lead.

"Okay, what does this mean?" I ask, walking to the edge of the driveway.

"We're almost done, so they think they can shoot the remaining scenes around him and use a double for the rest, but they had to rearrange the shooting schedule and I won't be home until tomorrow."

"Do you want me to call someone, or . . . what can I do?"

"I need to call in a favor from Friend Carter, not Agent Carter."

"Yeah, whatever you need."

He laughs. "You might regret that in a second."

"Let's hear it."

"I was supposed to make it back yesterday, in time to go with Avya to birthing class tonight."

"To *what?*" I bark out a laugh and a cloud of condensation hangs in the air in front of me. My mom's little garden is frozen over, forgotten vines covered in ice and snow. A group of teens huddle together on the corner a few houses down, the end of a joint glowing in the fading daylight.

"Yeah . . ." Zach says, trailing off before laughing again. "I told you."

I squeeze my eyes closed, pinching the bridge of my nose. "No, no, it's cool."

"You are such a liar."

"Are you sure *Avya's* fine with this?" Avya and I knew each other before she started dating Zach, but I don't want her to be uncomfortable.

"She's the one who suggested you."

I open my eyes, staring up at the foggy, snowy sky. I love the day-to-day interactions with my clients. This is just . . . an odd one.

How could I possibly say no? Birthing class it is.

•   •   •

If you were to have asked me what I thought I might be doing tonight, there are a lot of answers I could have given you: Xbox with my cousins, wrapping presents with Double D, rereading Evil's old texts again and again until I eat a box of ice cream sandwiches solo and blame it on my dad somehow.

The possibility of ending up with someone else's wife in a room full of pregnant women and their partners would not have occurred to me.

Yet here I am.

I meet Avya out front and we hug, exchanging a few pleasantries and a comment or two about the weather. It's a little awkward at first because I don't know where to look or what to say—or really even how to hug a very, *very* pregnant woman.

Per usual, Avya breaks the ice. "Ready to go talk about my vaginal birth?" she says, yoga mat rolled up under one arm.

I don't even know what to say to this. With a smile, I open the door, motion for her to lead, and follow her inside.

As far as birthing classes go, this one doesn't seem too bad. It's in a large open space and feels a lot like hanging out in sweatpants in a friend's living room. It's a plus if you're trying to keep things natural, I guess.

Natural seems to be an ongoing theme: managing pain as best you can through natural methods, but not placing judgment on yourself or anyone else if a situation arises where you change your mind. An aside: if modern science ever figures out a way for men to experience the miracle of birth, put me down for a No. If the No option is full, I'll take drugs. Lots of them.

Our teacher's name is Meredith. She's knowledgeable and soft-spoken and walks from couple to couple adjusting posture and widening a stance, or moving a foot here and there. We go through a series of stretches, the first with all of us on our hands and knees, gently rocking our hips back and forth in some sort of air hump, and I am *so* glad in this moment that Avya and I never had sex before Zach came along.

"That's good," Meredith says, looking out over the class. "Arch that back, swing those hips in a figure eight. Feel the motion. Back and forth, back and forth. Enjoy that movement, because who knows when you'll feel it again after this, am I right?"

Avya catches my eye over her shoulder for a beat before we dissolve into laughter.

"God, Evie will not believe this," I say, helping Avya into the next position.

"Evie, Evie," she repeats slowly. "Don't think Zach's mentioned that name before."

"She's an agent back in LA."

"Same agency?"

"Yeah. Sort of. It's a long story."

"You're dating an agent you work with? My life is so boring right now—thank *God* I made Zach ask you to come."

"Not *dating*." Even I hear the *ew, girls* implied by my tone.

"Snooze," Avya complains, bending forward, her long black hair hiding her face. "Then why would she particularly care about this class? Entertain me, Carter."

"She was with P&D before the merge," I say, and Avya nods. "Anyway, she goes with the wife and child of one of her clients to a sensory class in Beverly Hills."

"Let me guess: they paid the equivalent of one month's rent on a one-bedroom in Queens to have their kids play in some totally basic thing, like pudding or bedsheets."

"Pasta, actually. How'd you know?"

"I went to something similar when Joshua was little, but with parachutes."

"Parachutes?"

"We adopted Joshua from his birth mother when he was a newborn," she explains, "so I missed the whole birthing thing with him. Hence this class." She gives me another smile over her shoulder. "We laid all the babies down in a big circle, and all the mommies lifted this giant, circus-tent-looking parachute over them, fanning it up and down. It sounds great in theory, but the babies were just way too young to enjoy it. You're basically yanking this parachute out of their faces and scaring the shit out of them. Half are crying, a few are trying to get away, and the rest are too scared to move."

"Oh my God," I say, biting my lip and looking around for the instructor. The last thing I need is to get a client's wife kicked out of her birthing class. "I'm sorry, that's not funny."

"Oh, it's *totally* funny. As parents we put our kids through the strangest things because we think it's giving them some sort of advantage."

The instructor has the mothers-to-be move into a squat that looks a lot like they're sitting on a toilet, and explains the benefits of this position, including what it's doing to the perineum, and some other things I can't focus on.

"How's the perineum?" I say. "Good?"

Avya shakes her head like she can't believe we're doing this. "Relaxed. Thanks. Now, more about this Evie."

I sigh, then just let it all out. "Simply put, Evelyn Abbey is my former almost-girlfriend-turned-archnemesis-turned-tentative-ally whom I would now very much like to permanently seduce."

The glee on Avya's face tells me I should continue. "It's a long, complicated story involving first dates followed by corporate greed, competing for a single position, and sabotage."

"Okay, that is decidedly not as fun as I imagined."

"The thing is, she's smart and gorgeous and funny and amazing at her job, and it was infuriating. We were essentially told they could only keep one of us, and it made us into maniacs. I'd be listening to her in a meeting, totally mesmerized, then I would snap back to the conversation and want to let the air out of her tires for distracting me from my goal."

"And your goal was . . ."

"Total annihilation, of course."

We move to the next seated position, with Avya in front of me and between my legs, her back against my chest.

"And now?" she asks.

"Now she seems like the best person there."

"Have you two . . ." she starts, letting the question hang in the space between us while she practices her breathing exercises.

"I mean . . . almost? There was some under-the-clothes touching to completion, if you know what I'm saying."

She snickers. "And it was good?"

Fuck. "Yeah."

"I'm assuming you'd definitely like to do it again."

"Shouldn't you be focusing on something wholesome?" I ask.

"How can I be expected to focus when there's all this forbidden love and pining going on?"

"You can focus because at this point I fear there's a better chance of me *touching to completion* with any one of these ladies"—I say, motioning to the pregnant women around us—"than there is with Evie."

"Why? Because of the job? That feels like a detail to me."

"It's a pretty *big* detail, though. We're both married to our jobs. Jobs that may not even be around in three months. Not to mention we have this retreat thing in Big Bear coming up. I want to be around her, but we always fight. I really don't want us to end up stabbing each other. She's too bossy for prison and I have a hard time saying no."

"Okay, so big question here," Avya says. "Would you be with her if there were no job or anything else on the line?"

"That's a pretty fucking big *if*, Avya."

"You didn't answer the question, *Carter.*"

"Would I be with Evie if there was nothing else in the way? Probably." I scratch my jaw, wincing at this cop-out. "No, not 'probably.' For sure I would."

"So fix it."

"Oh my God, why didn't I think of that?"

"Carter, women are not that complicated," Avya says, half turning and smiling back at me. "Smarter? Yes. Complicated? Not really. We want progress, not perfection."

.   .   .

That night at my parents' house, I think about what Avya said.

Progress, not perfection.

I don't have to be perfect; I don't necessarily even have to fix everything with Evie, but I can at least own up to the things I did that even I'm not okay with. I can try to be a little less terrible.

Reaching across the bed, I find my phone where it's charging on the table. I scroll through the conversations until I find the one labeled *Evil* and open it.

I do the time zone math in my head; just after ten here, just after seven there. Definitely not too late.

> Hey.

I hold my breath, staring at the phone and hoping to see the little dots indicating she's typing. Just when I let out a long exhale and start to put my phone down, the bubble pops up. My heart bounces into my throat.

Hey, you.

Here goes. Time to get it all out there.

> I feel like I need to go back a bit.

> Starting with: I should have called you to talk about Dan Printz first.

I should have told you your shirt was unbuttoned. I should have ASKED you about Jonah doing the shoot.

Have you been visited by
the Ghost of Christmas Past?

Something like that.

Well, thanks.

No problem.

I can't apologize for the glitter though.

The glitter was pretty great.

And honestly, I'm sorry, too.

But not for the onion.

You're forgiven.

The onion was terrible/genius.

The mixing room, however, was enjoyable.

Will she appreciate my understating the obvious? Will she agree? Another minute goes by. My heart is basically inside my mouth, in my eyes, pounding my head off. Finally, my phone vibrates again.

You can say that again.

I exhale and roll into my pillow. *Thank God.*

Are you in New York?

> Yeah. What are you up to?

I had dinner with Daryl and have to finish up my expense reports before I go to Burbank tomorrow.

> Expense reports over the holiday?

> Hiss.

I know, but I think I'm the only one they're waiting on to finish up the audit.

What is it they think they're going to find? The vodka I expensed after dealing with Brad?

> I bet that's a whole lot of vodka.

Well, by the case makes it cheaper at least.

You'll see Michael and Steph while you're there?

> They usually stay with Steph's parents, so yeah.

> Is it weird that I'm excited to get together with them out here?

> Like, we live in the same city.

> It makes no sense.

It's because you miss partying at Areola.

I put my hand over my mouth to stifle a laugh, having forgotten I'd told her about that. Are we flirting? Is that what that is? She's bringing up our past conversations and I'm being . . . what?—charmed by it? *Think of something clever, Carter.*

Noted.

Nailed it.

Can you do me a dumb favor?

I live for dumb favors.

If you do something outdoorsy, can you take a picture of the snow?

That's not really that dumb.

I'm disappointed.

California Christmas not doing it for you?

Maybe . . .

How's this, I'll make a snow angel and even write your name next to it.

As long as it's not in yellow.

In yellow?

You'll get there.

Wait for it . . .

Oh. OH.

Bazinga.

You're broken.

I think you like it.

Goodnight, Carter.

Night, Evie.

chapter twenty-one

evie

My first morning back to work after the holidays, I am a mess of nerves. It's impossible to keep my calm, reasonable voice in my head because it's basically closed up shop for the winter.

Carter walks into work in what my stalker tendencies tell me is a new outfit, and looks . . . breathtaking. His pants are charcoal gray and slim cut, stopping just at his ankles and exposing a little flash of some exuberant socks. Are guys taking over the ankle flirtation game? I am here for it. His shirt is a cool purple print, and in general he just looks way too hip, even for an office full of Hollywood power players.

I'm standing in the doorway to the break room, watching his path from the elevators in total awe, but my world trips when he stops at my office and tentatively peeks in.

Obviously, I'm not there. I call out to him, my heart dropping somewhere in the vicinity of my vagina when he turns toward my voice and smiles.

Man. I am in deep.

"I brought you something." He walks toward me and holds out a cellophane-wrapped package. The tape is barely holding together and the ribbon looks like it was used as a handle. "Cookies. From my mom."

"You brought me cookies all the way from New York?" I ask, handling the small package carefully.

Whether he intended it or not, Carter seems to realize the implication of this.

"I . . . There were a lot of extras?" He gives me an adorable self-deprecating smile. "I made it weird, didn't I?"

My heart is thrumming, my skin is all flushed, and the vision of grabbing him by the collar and kissing him is flashing like a Vegas billboard in my head.

"No, it's sweet." I gingerly pull apart the wrapper. The scent of chocolate and butter fills the air.

"Carter," Kylie says, winded as she jogs up. "I'm glad I found you."

He turns to her. "I just got in. What's up?"

"Brad wanted to know if you had a chance to look over the scripts he sent you."

"Oh, not yet," he says, clearly caught off guard. "I only saw the email last night."

Kylie laughs easily. "He wanted me to follow up. I was like, 'Brad, there were five of them! Give him time!'"

Carter laughs easily now, too, but my own smile is totally forced. A gallon of ice water could not have changed the tone of this conversation any quicker.

It's not that Brad doesn't forward along a script to an agent when he has someone in mind from said agent's list. It's just that he doesn't send *five* out, to *one* agent.

I'm trying to keep calm, but is this the golf weekend thing all over again? "Brad sent you some scripts?" I ask.

"Yeah, for one he wants to give the screenwriter some feedback and asked for my thoughts."

"I see." I put the plate of cookies down on a nearby table.

"Brad also wants Carter to help him decide how to best distribute to the team," Kylie adds helpfully.

I bite my lower lip to keep my jaw from falling open. So now I need to position myself with Carter in order to have him send work my clients' way?

When I'm sure I can ask it without yelling, I say, "Just Carter?"

"Yes, just Carter," Kylie says, shrugging a little helplessly.

We've finally arrived here. I can't even say I'm surprised.

"I *do* have some experience in this," he says, with a gentle lean to his voice. "In New York I did some playwright work. For what it's worth, I also have a decent eye for pairing talent with roles . . ."

I nod, forcing another smile. Why do Carter and I do so much better when we're not in the same room? After the texts, I was so excited to see him, and now I'm confused all over again about who he is. It's like fate keeps telling us there's just no way to make it work.

He glances quickly over to Kylie, who is watching us with flat curiosity.

"Well," I say, swallowing my pride, "let me know if you need some help, okay?"

Carter nods, but I don't stick around to see if he'll say anything else.

I'm so worked up I can barely concentrate. The worst part of being this mad is that I'm no longer rational. I hear Carter talking on his phone with his door open and I want to hurl a stapler at him for being loud enough for me to hear. I hear Brad thanking Kylie for the coffee she's handed him in the hall, and I want to yell, "If she was a male assistant, would you expect him to bring you coffee every goddamn hour?"

And I'm so angry that when my phone buzzes with a text

from Carter, I can't even read it. I flip my phone facedown when a second comes in, a third, a fourth, and dive into the process of answering emails, returning calls, and making deals. In essence, the anger fuels me—and if I don't have five hot scripts in my inbox, at least I have a motherfucking productive day.

Only when I'm home later—way past nine, and with a fishbowl-size glass of wine in my hand—do I read what he wrote.

> It's time for us to cut the shit.

> I don't know what kind of game Brad is playing.

> But I get that I'm coming out favored in part because I'm a guy. And that's fucked up.

> I like you. I liked us.

> I don't know how to manage this weird competition. I need you to tell me how I can fix this.

The problem with deciding to cut the shit is that it's easier said than done. I could reply to his texts, addressing everything, but in a lot of ways that feels like cheating. We *know* we can text. We know we can get along outside of work. What we can't seem to do, yet, is interact like rational humans when we're together at the office, and given that approximately ninety-eight percent of my life revolves around my job, I can't just accept the text-and-out-of-work approach to our relationship.

So I reply with a simple I feel the same about all of this. Let's talk more in person—that's where we always get stuck, and try to get to bed early.

. . .

Life has to go on, and because we all took time off to be with family for the holidays, there are a million things to handle. We each have endless producers to follow up with, staffing season to plan, directors and actors to call and cajole, schedules to massage.

It all makes me want to sledgehammer Brad for thinking mid-January was a good time for the department retreat, and my nerves climb higher in my throat with each day that passes without my speaking a word to Carter. I feel Brad's New York Decision looming like a dark thundercloud.

It's only about a two-hour drive from LA to Big Bear, but because we'd all planned to drive ourselves, and everyone works until the last second, we end up leaving at the worst possible time—four in the afternoon on a Friday. And yet, when I come outside, everyone is happily piling into a handful of limos parked out front.

A swank ride up to the retreat: a surprise from Brad.

"Limos!" Rose cries, and eight-year-old me can totally relate to the excitement of this, though thirty-three-year-old me remains cynical.

"Gotta treat my people well, don't I?" Brad says magnanimously, and claps me on the back. "I have high hopes that this retreat is the best one yet. Don't let me down, kiddo!"

"And Carter!" Carter adds with a nervous laugh, but Brad doesn't hear him.

Carter and I exchange brief looks, and despite the unspoken *everything* between us, I know we're both thinking the same thing: Brad wouldn't increase the budget for the lunch we planned, so we had to do a lame sandwich bar, yet he can be the big guy and bring everyone to the retreat in limos?

Jess grabs me as we're about to head out, dropping a small stack of files in my arms. "The invoices for this little adventure," she says, slightly out of breath. "Sorry that took so long, but the mailroom said they were labeled to go to Brad and I basically had to wrestle them away." She opens the one on top. "There are a bunch of vendors here I didn't book, so have a look to make sure it's all there, and we can talk when you're back."

"Thanks, Jess," I say, and take a deep, cleansing breath. I can do this, I remind myself. "I wish you were coming with us."

"Ha. Not to hurt your feelings, but *hell no*. Good luck and"—she looks meaningfully over my shoulder to where Carter is climbing into one of the cars—"have fun."

Right. *Fun.*

Amelia and Daryl stand near the sidewalk, waving and smiling their *Good luck, you'll need it* smiles. I give them my best *I wish you were suffering along with me, assholes* smile in return before climbing into the limo.

As nice as it would be to talk and smooth out some last-minute details during the drive up, Carter and I end up sitting on opposite ends of our car. Andrew and Carter exchange glances as their eyes wander over the minibar, calculating how long we need to sit here before they can pop into the champagne. According to Andrew, that duration is approximately the time it takes us to pull away from the front of the building.

I for one am giving that decision hallelujah hands and a *hell yes*, because we need this entire crew to have as good a time as possible, and that means getting everyone day drunk, *immediately*.

With a glass of bubbly headed my way and my inability to do any work in the car for fear of getting carsick, I can only join in the shenanigans.

Timothy shit-talks Ed Ruiz from Alterman for a little while—apparently he did some shady things to pull a potential client out from under Timothy—and I silently enjoy the hell out of the story he's telling, because Ed is a complete fuckwit.

"Didn't you work with him?" Andrew asks me.

"Yeah, but not much directly."

And that's all I'm going to give. I won't share the time that he vomited on my shoes in a cab on our way back from a work dinner, or that he slept with Ken Alterman's assistant and got so obsessed with her that he kept her underwear in a drawer in his desk, or that he once reassured an actor on his list that it was totally fine that he "accidentally" had sex with a seventeen-year-old and that Ed would be happy to hide any evidence.

Gossip is fun—don't get me wrong, I live for it—but I'm rarely the one letting on that I have anything exciting to share. So when Andrew starts telling us about how he saw a very huge A-list actress at a full-nudity sex club with a very important—and very old—male director, I tuck this story away in a little jewel box in my memory.

No one bothers to ask why the hell *Andrew* was there, mind you.

After everyone's spent their gossip currency, we still have over an hour left to drive, and we shift into the kind of silence that will result in at least three of us falling asleep with the champagne drowsies. I can see Kylie working up the nerve to move over toward Carter, and it is exactly like watching some elaborate bird mating ritual. She crouch-walks from her spot next to me at the back of the limo and sits next to Carter on the side bench, slowly scooting closer, leaning in like she wants to read over his shoulder. But . . . I mean . . . he's reading a *contract*, I can tell by the legal paper and prong fastener at the top. This isn't canoodling reading. This is legalese pouring off the page like a violent mud-slide.

Kylie does this weird catlike stretch and then slides her arm behind her a little so she's pressing her boob to his shoulder.

Carter startles, shifting away on instinct, and suddenly I am *living*.

"Hey," she says, looking at him like she's admiring herself in a hand mirror.

"Hey," he says, smiling briefly at her before returning to the papers on his lap.

"Excited for the trip?"

He nods. "Yeah. Should be good."

"Have you ever stayed at the Big Bear Lodge and Suites be-fore?"

"Nope."

"It's really nice," she tells him. "Big bar, big cozy lobby . . . big rooms."

And now I'm uncomfortable for them both, because Lord is she laying it on thick. He looks up and catches me eavesdrop-ping, so I look away but it's a horribly executed startle-blink and I have to pretend that I have something in my eye—which I don't, which we both know.

When I look back at Carter, he's still several inches away from Kylie, and he's still watching me, clearly wondering just how jealous I am right now. Carter's smile this time isn't cocky or teasing, it's happy. Just pure, quiet happy. Maybe cutting the shit in person won't be impossible after all.

•   •   •

For once, the reality lives up to the hype: the resort really *is* beau-tiful. Set near the top of one of the summits, the main building is an immense log-cabin-style lodge with several deluxe small cabins surrounding it. Towering ponderosa pines cluster around the grounds, and the air is so crisp it feels a little like I've never been outside before. The LA basin is notoriously smoggy, being trapped between the mountains and the marine layer, and although it's much better than it was when I was a kid, it still makes it easy to forget the sensation of truly fresh air.

I feel pretty optimistic as we emerge from the limos, squinting into the brilliant sun. The snowpack is light this year, but at least it's there. Even if everything else about this weekend sucks, it's beautiful and promises a lot of alcohol.

Brad stops us all outside the grand entrance, decorated with gold tassels and an impeccable red carpet leading from the curved driveway to the wide lobby. "Welcome to the P&D Features Seventh Annual Retreat."

We clap politely: the most awkward round of applause ever witnessed.

"Thank you for taking the time to join me this weekend," he continues. "I want to thank each of you for your commitment to the agency and your continued dedication. Needless to say, it's been an interesting year."

A small laugh moves through the group.

"Understatement of the decade, am I right?" he adds, looking at the assembled crowd of agents and staff. "But none of that matters, because this, right here? This is what it's all about: seeing my team around me, ready to really show the world how it's done. Now more than ever we need talent that can do it all—TV, film, media—and they need a team behind them that can do it all, too. That's why I have you all here together, where you can learn to cheer each other on and become unstoppable. How do we do that?"

"As a team," someone says, and Brad nods.

"That's right. Not two individual companies, but as a team." Brad stops to look around before waving me to the front of the group. "Now, come on up here, Evie. You've done a great job as event planner. Tell us what we can expect for the night. Dazzle us."

Carter looks to me, frowning.

"We have a welcome dinner in the lodge," I tell them, glancing at my watch, "in about forty-five minutes. That should give everyone time to drop off their things and get sorted. The real fun starts tomorrow at ten."

At my side, Brad nods enthusiastically. "Can't wait. Now, I can tell you guys are chomping at the bit to get rolling! Let's go check in, team."

Looking up, I meet Carter's eyes. His expression is grim, his mouth a slash of disapproval.

Brad claps me on the back, shooting me forward toward the doors of the lodge. "Lead the way, kiddo!"

Sweet hellacious hellfire, this weekend is going to be a doozy.

• • •

When we all split off with room keys in our hands, I could be a CIA agent the way I covertly watch which way Carter goes (and also maybe which direction Kylie goes, too, celebrating internally when they turn down opposite halls).

I wheel my small suitcase behind me to 207, a few doors away from Rose. Inside, it's gorgeous, with an enormous bed in the middle of a spacious room, and a breathtaking view of the lake beyond a wide balcony. I mentally high-five Kylie for securing such a great deal with this place and walk outside to get a better look at the view.

It's never cold enough for the lake to freeze over, and so deep blue water laps gently against frost-covered rocks at the shore. The trees are brilliant green speckled with white, and for just a moment—a tiny, perfect inhale—I am absolutely giddy to be here.

Knowing I have a few minutes, I step back inside and pull the files Jess gave me from my bag. Jess's recordkeeping is usually flawless, but when I glance over the retreat vendors she mentioned, I see what she meant: I don't recall most of them, either. I'm in the middle of sending her a note to verify some of the entries with Kylie when my phone buzzes on the table with a text to me—and only me—from Brad:

> Please arrive to the lodge restaurant early
> to ensure everything is in order.

I give myself exactly three deep *what the actual hell is up with Brad?* breaths before I find my purse and my key and head downstairs.

● ● ●

As it happens, dinner is lovely. Or at least it is after Brad thanks everyone again for coming and asks me to get in front of the group and explain what we can expect on tonight's menu. I move from my seat, but the tension in my spine over being treated like his assistant—or an event coordinator—is slowly ratcheting tighter.

"I'm happy to explain the menu," Carter interrupts, beginning to stand.

Brad shakes his head. "Let Evie do it."

I hear Brad's message loud and clear aimed at me: *You're* my puppet. *You'll* do this if you want a job come Monday.

Slowly, Carter sits down, his face red. I give him a little nod and smile, grateful for his attempt at least, and rattle off the basics. Salad. Meat. Potatoes. Green beans. It's really nothing in need of explanation. Carter was smart to insist we go with *traditional* on our rather limited budget, knowing that they probably prepare it pretty nicely up at the lodge. We'd also selected a white wine and a red wine, and we run out of both before we're done with the salad course.

Thank God for the cash bar, I guess?

Forks and knives scrape and screech across porcelain as everyone chows down. We are at a small handful of long tables in the center of a cavernous private room, but I can't really accept blame for the oddity of this, since it was on Brad's list of demands that we take our meal here, together. Like a *team*.

A fire roars in a stone fireplace so enormous I could probably stand inside, and there are seven waiters milling timidly around the room, hoping they can be helpful in some way but unwilling to ask too often. It's the Brad Kingman Effect. You don't even have to know who he is to be mildly afraid of him.

Carter is at my left during dinner and it's strange to be in a room full of people and sounds and yet still be so aware of him. His arm brushes against mine as he cuts his steak, as he reaches for his wine, as he adjusts his napkin below the table. Is he *trying* to touch me? The more wine I have, the more my brain screams *YES!* to this question, and I start trying to reciprocate a little, leaning closer, resting my left arm lightly on the table so he has easier access.

Subtle stuff. I am a seduction ninja.

I'm so focused on what Carter's doing and saying and how amazing he smells that I'm somewhat startled when a few of the waiters start clearing plates, and I look down to realize I've barely touched mine.

The party transitions to the outdoor patio, where heat lamps glow from each corner and strings of paper lanterns frame a view of the lake just beyond.

Brad rarely lets go enough to really get drunk at these things, but when he does he's one of those intoxicated people who seems to have a volume knob attached to his drinking arm. By the time ten o'clock rolls around, most of the group is pretty tanked, but Brad isn't just tanked, it's like he's hooked up to some PA system.

Don't get me wrong; fewer people have better stories in this business than Brad Kingman, and sober, he's as sealed as a two-hundred-year-old grave, so we're all—even the ones who hate him—pretty enthralled. Tonight he is really on a roll.

Some highlights:

His wife paid for college by stripping. (I'm sure Maxine, *the studio executive*, would be thrilled he's shared this.)

He watched one of the most famous actors in the history of film (five Academy Awards, to be exact) "do some blow off a hooker's ass in Vegas."

The first time he met one of the industry's most powerful producers, said producer was so high he fell asleep in his salad, woke up, and pretended nothing had happened. He finished the meeting with shredded carrots in his hair and a smear of French dressing along the entire left side of his face. The movie they were discussing went on to win four Academy Awards and two Golden Globes, and made nearly a billion worldwide.

After some more stories, it's midnight, the outdoor bar has

closed, and my wineglass is empty. A passing server offers to find me a refill, but it's a perfect excuse to mosey to the bar inside, where it's quiet and warm, and get a few minutes to myself.

The bartender comes over and leans on the bar expectantly. "What'll it be, gorgeous?"

"Whatever your best red wine is," I tell him, reading his name tag. Woody. "I was drinking the pinot outside, but I think they ran out a while ago."

Woody smiles, revealing a top row of perfectly white, even teeth . . . with one front tooth completely missing. It's such an odd paradox, I am instantly *fascinated*. Was it pulled? If so, *why*? How could one tooth be so bad when the others are perfect?

These are the things that take up brain space that should be used to come up with snappy comebacks when Brad calls me kiddo or sport and insists that being a team player means I pass someone else my commission.

"I'll give you the Ravenswood zin then," he says, rapping his knuckles against the bar. "Not much to choose from, but that one is pretty decent."

Woody leaves to go grab a bottle, and I lean more heavily against the bar, wondering for a beat if I could just lay my head down here and take a little nap.

Oh, wine makes me sleepy.

And amorous, apparently, because tonight Carter is looking pretty—

"How's it going over here?"

Straightening, I look over my shoulder as the man himself approaches and pulls out the barstool next to me.

It's a struggle to keep my tipsy attention focused on his face and not stare at the smooth, exposed collarbone. "I'm wiped. And tipsy. I just want to head to bed."

"Me too." Glancing to the doors he's just come in through, he adds, "But I fear they're just getting started."

I find myself leaning into him, laughing into the shoulder of his jacket. God, he smells good. "Crazy kids. I guess we can't just disappear. Being the hosts and all."

He laughs. "How the fuck did we manage to get this gig?"

"No idea."

He looks down, running the tip of his index finger back and forth over a pattern in the wood bar top. "Brad is still treating you like his assistant."

"I know." I bite my lip, looking to the side.

"Evie," he says, "I'm so sorry. I contributed by ignoring it. I don't want to do that anymore."

His words make my windpipe feel tight, make my thoughts turn defensive.

Everything's fine.

You're just new to this, Carter.

I've dealt with Brad for years, I know his game.

Cut the shit, Evie.

Letting out a tiny steam whistle of vulnerability, I admit, "It always makes me mad, but now it's making me anxious. I have this strange itch in the back of my brain, this persistent worry that he's really trying to push me out."

He nods. "I see it. I see it, and I don't know what to do."

My chest, it aches. "I hate feeling helpless."

I didn't expect *this* to be our crescendo moment. In the movies, these admissions either soften someone up or harden them further, but they rarely come out as quietly as I've said it and still make a huge impact.

But somehow, this one does.

Carter leans down and slides his hand along my jaw, and then bends, kissing me in a way I've been dreaming about almost nonstop since that night in my apartment. It's different from the frantic kisses in the mixing room, rough and hurried. Those felt like secret, semiviolent betrayals of our better instincts.

But this. This is a stream of tiny tastes and pecks, little pieces of dialogue. They go from *I'm sorry* to *what are we doing* to *how do we do this deeper and all night* and I don't even notice when Woody has to place my drink on the bar because Carter has my back pressed to it.

I *do* notice when Carter pulls away to hand him a twenty.

My hand comes up, pressing to my mouth as if holding the sensation there. "You don't have to pay for my wine."

"I'm invested in getting this tab settled so we can leave."

"I thought we couldn't leave our party."

"Fuck this party."

The giggle that escapes me is high, and girlish, and very excited at the prospect of us leaving, together.

"What did you say?" I ask, mock scandalized.

"You heard me."

Drunken roars reach us from outside, and are followed by the unmistakable splashing of water.

"Skinny-dipping!" Kylie yells, and in the background rises a chorus of male cheers.

Carter is still looking at my mouth. "Hi."

"Hi."

His smile droops. "I have two full-size beds in my room."

My eyes shine, my smile goes wide. "Well, that's just fine. Because I have a king."

. . .

We trip through the doorway, laughing and breathless over having raced into the gift shop for condoms and throwing way too much money at the bewildered teenager working the night shift. I feel like I'm full of tiny bubbles or brilliant stars: inside, everything is alive.

Somehow, despite how many months it's been and all the games we've played between us, awkwardness never descends. It's us alone, smiling into kisses, pulling off clothes with the comfort of a couple long together and the excitement of two virgins. I swear his body is unreal and I can't stop touching it, memorizing it like my hands are scanning it into some memory database. I give my brain permission to overwrite anything it wants—take away my ability to ride a bike or crochet; the planes and dips of Carter's abdomen are way more important.

"Is this too fast?" he asks, barely pausing as he flings my bra behind him somewhere.

I laugh. "Hell no."

He leads us both farther into the room and then I'm lying down, the sheets cool along the back of my body and Carter pressed along the front.

He kisses a path down my neck. "Can we be friends now?"

The feel of his lips against my skin makes it hard to form words, but I swallow and do my best to focus. "Is that what you want?" I ask, a question that might be taken more seriously if his belt weren't hanging open, the metal buckle clinking in the space between us. "Friends?"

"Yes," he says, teeth scraping along my collarbone. "And no." He pulls back to look at me. "Does that make sense?"

"I think so." I finish unbuttoning his pants and push the fabric down his hips, smiling when the cold air leaves a trail of goose bumps across his skin. He kicks them the rest of the way off and then it's naked legs against naked legs, bare torso against bare torso.

He says something else, but the shape of his words is lost against my shoulder and then my breast as he moves lower. I arch my back when he takes my nipple into his mouth, and the sound I make surprises me.

Fuck. Why did we waste so much time?

I have the brief thought that we need to be quiet, that eventually Rose will be only two doors down or someone we know might be in the room right next door, but I can't even hear the shrieks of the skinny-dippers anymore, and the lake is *right there*.

We're in a fortress.

Carter's mouth is everywhere: he worships my breasts, sucking each nipple in turn while rolling the other between his fingers. His eyes are wild as he looks up my body, holding my gaze as he moves lower and lower still, pulling off my panties and finally settling between my legs. He leans forward, tentative at first and then greedy like I'm the sweetest thing he's ever tasted. I feel his breath and his sounds and he presses each into my skin and I want him to push them deeper so that I feel them vibrating up my spine, radiating out along my ribs. I feel empty; I might actually say this out loud because his fingers come alongside his kisses and then deep into me.

The world outside seems to stop. The idea of a retreat going on out there feels almost comically surreal. Everything collapses down to the insistent press of his tongue. Heat curls like ribbons around my spine and I pull his hair, arch my body into his touch, and try to tell him that I'm close, so so close.

"Carter," I gasp, grabbing at him again and oh God I'm coming . . . coming . . . so loud and fuck, I no longer understand why we ever left this place. No job is worth losing *this*.

There's a flash of cool air against my skin and then Carter is there, kissing me like I'm oxygen. His lips taste of me and, impossibly, it makes me want him more.

He reaches for the box on the bedside table, fumbling and opening it blindly while he kisses me with his eyes sweetly closed.

I can't close my eyes for even a second, though. I'm unwilling to miss the details I know I'll play over and over inside my head tomorrow. The curve of his shoulder, the way his arm flexes as he reaches between us, rolling the condom on before lining himself up against me.

Relief wipes his face blank for a heartbeat as he presses inside. But then my mind is erased. I can't think of a single thing except the feel of him moving forward. I would be hard-pressed to remember my own name.

I look up at him, focusing on his neck and his throat, where his head is tipped back, how his Adam's apple moves when he swallows.

He covers me completely, elbows planted above my shoulders as he looks between us, mouth open and breath escaping in sharp little stabs. He moves and he moves, fingers of one hand sliding down, biting into my hips, torso stretched above me as he pushes himself harder and faster and fuck, it's so good I wonder if I could keep him right here all weekend.

Our bodies slide together, skin damp with sweat and already flushed from exertion. My muscles tense and release, my leg slipping from his hip, and he reaches for the back of my knee, almost bending me in half with the force he uses to press back inside my body.

I don't recognize my own voice as it comes out sharp and surprised, bouncing back to us in the quiet room. The sound makes him harder, makes him wilder and frantic, and when I finally melt beneath him—pleasure so strong it takes me by surprise, drawing my legs open, my knees alongside his ribs—he grows fevered: hips and arms working, hands pulling me up onto him, pushing himself deep. I cling to him, panting hot into his shoulder as he says my name and yes and please and then we're coming both of us together, barely able to catch our breath. I wonder if I'll ever catch my breath again.

• • •

With his face pressed to my neck, Carter groans in his relief, back shaking beneath my hands.

He tries to move and hisses before bringing his mouth to the shell of my ear. "Holy shit."

I make some garbled sound of agreement, unable to complete the connection between my brain and words.

"I think I just found religion."

I giggle. I don't want him to move an inch. My legs come around his, twisting and twining, and he indulges me in breathless kisses delivered through smiles. My legs are smooth, his are covered in soft hair, and the sensation of them sliding together, the heat of him heavy and already hard again between our bodies, rekindles something inside me, triggering a desperate need for more.

When he pulls back, just barely, his eyes seem nearly backlit. "Be right back."

"Don't go."

He laughs, kissing the tip of my nose. "I should get rid of this."

Oh. Condom.

With a tiny groan of protest, I let him pull back and climb from the bed. He pads across the room. He is a study in shadow and geometry: straight lines frame the muscle along his spine, triangular planes at his shoulders, the hard curve of his backside.

I watch his shoulders as he works with his back to me, grabs a tissue from a box on the dresser, and drops the trash into the bin.

In the dim light I see the way he hesitates, taking a deep breath.

Carter straightens and turns. The front of my body is cold with the loss of him over me and it's compounded by the tremor of anxiety that he'll step away, clear his head, come to his senses.

"Are you sore?"

If anything, I feel hungrier. My voice is hoarse: "No."

He squints, seeming to study me from across the room. "Are you freaking out?"

It still feels like I can't catch my breath, and it hits me in this bewildering burst what we've just done and how much I want him back in bed with me. "Not in the way you mean."

He takes one step closer and stops, looking down at me.

"Are *you* freaking out?" I ask.

"A little." He reaches up, scratches the back of his neck while my stomach dissolves away inside my body. But then he adds, "I need to . . ."

More hesitation. My lungs are incinerated.

"I've thought about this a lot," he says, "about you. I'm in love with you, Evie. You're finally here with me. I don't want to sleep."

I sit up, aware that he can see me better with the moonlight coming in the window behind him. The sheet falls away, and I climb onto my knees.

I hear his breath catch somewhere high in his throat, but I don't have to tell him to come back to bed, that it's okay, that we're a done deal. He closes the distance between us, smooth skin sliding over mine as he pulls me down, pulls me under again.

chapter twenty-two

I wake to scratchy sheets, an unfamiliar ceiling, and the kind of artificial darkness that only comes from heavy curtains. There's movement at my side and for one horror-filled moment I remember Kylie, with her overglossed lips and no concept of personal space, and my heart nearly stops, starting again only when I see Evie sleeping next to me.

An electric shock rolls through my body when I think of how we got here, how kissing felt like drowning and never wanting to come back up.

Evie looks soft like this. Maybe *soft* isn't exactly the right word, but there's a stillness I've not seen in her before, like her walls are down and I could touch her skin and move straight past it to her bones.

She's so close—we're almost nose to nose—and I can make out every eyelash, count each tiny freckle. She's also naked, which I'm pretty happy about, but then I worry how she'll react when she wakes up and sees that I'm naked, too.

Are we still friends today?

Did she hear me say that I was in love with her?

A part of me wants to be more scared than I am. It would be easier if we came to our senses and chalked this up to a good time and crazy lapse in judgment. But my brain and body are a united front on this *in love with Evie* thing. The sheet is low on her back, her dark hair is tangled across the pillow. I think we had sex four times last night. I stretch my legs, clench my stomach. It *feels* like we had sex twenty times last night.

I reach out and run a finger over the hand tucked under her chin and up the length of her arm, and she starts to stir.

I suddenly realize I have no idea what I'm going to say and close my eyes, steadying my breaths so she thinks I'm still asleep. A few moments of silence pass before curiosity gets the best of me. I feel ridiculous; I'm a grown man pretending to sleep to avoid a grown-up conversation. A smile begins to tug at my mouth and I chance a peek, both of us bursting into laughter when we find the other doing the same thing.

With a hand on my face she pushes me away. "You're an idiot."

Warmth pools in my chest. "*I'm* the idiot? Have you seen your hair?" I reach to smooth it down and she laughs, trying to escape.

"Have you seen yours?" she asks with a grin.

I pause, serious for a moment. "Still freaking out?"

She plays with her lip and hesitates before answering. "A little. Are you?"

I tell her the truth: "A little."

"Do you want to stop this . . . whatever this is?"

I lean forward and press a kiss to the corner of her mouth before meeting her eyes. "No . . ."

"Okay," she says, her gaze falling to my lips. "Do you want to avoid discussing it and have sex again?"

I move until I'm hovering over her, marveling at how much of her body I can cover with mine. I look down between us, to where her legs bracket my hips. I rock forward, experimentally, and feel the way I easily slip across her skin, smooth and already wet.

She groans softly and I know that sound. I remember the way it echoed around the room.

Her hands move along my sides, nails dragging up my ribs and across my nipples to my shoulders. With a hand on the back of my neck she pulls me down and then there's nothing between us at all, not even air.

For a moment I think we could come from this, two bodies moving against each other at just the right speed, in just the right spot, like we did that night in her apartment. But that's not what I want.

Evie must be on the same page because her arm is already stretched to the side, fingers fumbling with the strip of gift shop condoms I tossed there at some point during the night.

My eyes nearly cross when she rolls the latex over me, and I give her a reproachful look, batting her hand away. There's no waiting after that. The sheet comes up and over our heads, a tent of white. My heart is racing and she rolls us over to straddle my hips, taking me inside and moving in tiny little starts and stops until she figures it out, gets where she really needs to be.

Her palms press into my chest as she shifts forward and back, over and over, and it feels so good I put my hands on her hips to distract myself, line up my thumbs with the gentle contours of her navel. I thrust up and into her, harder and then harder still, and her mouth falls open, the headboard tapping near the wall, the springs creaking beneath us. Her eyes are closed, mouth partially open, and I wonder why we waited so fucking long for this, how we managed to let everything else get in the way, because *this*—fuck—nothing compares to this.

She rolls her hips again, a tight little circle, and swears, her fingers moving between her legs in a practiced motion.

"You gonna fuck me?" I ask her in a whisper, mouth watering at the way her nipples harden further.

Her response is wordless, a soft little gasp that gets lost against my own sounds when she comes down harder, takes more of me inside. All I can do is watch her, nodding in time with her movements and feeling the muscles in my stomach tighten, the pressure build.

Her hair is damp against her forehead and where it curls along the curve of her breast and I think she's almost there, too, her movements getting choppy, rhythm frantic.

"Yeah?" I say, placing my fingers next to hers and circling.

"Tha—" she starts to say back when there's a pounding at her door, followed by a frantic scratching.

Our eyes meet, bodies immediately frozen, neither of us breathing. "Oh my God! Did I dead-bolt the door last night?" she whisper-hisses. "Housekeeping could—"

But it's not housekeeping, it's about a million times worse, because following another knock, and some more scratching, is Brad's voice.

Brad, our boss, on the other side of the door.

"Evie?" he calls, and knocks again.

I've never moved so fast in my life. It's a flurry of arms and legs, sheets and pillows. Evie jumps into a T-shirt and a pair of sweats at a speed that couldn't possibly be human. Meanwhile I'm naked, wearing a condom, and still pretty *hard* when she starts herding me in the direction of the closet.

"One second!" she calls, and then whispers, "I'll get rid of him. Stay in here and don't move." Her face is flushed, cheeks rosy with a light sheen of sweat, and there's no way he won't know what she's been doing.

I hold up my hand to object and she closes the door, shutting me inside. *Shit.*

I can't see anything but a strip of light down the center, and okay, that's mildly terrifying, but I'm an optimist so I'm going to see it less as *this is where Brad could see me standing naked and still wearing a condom,* and more as *this is where all the oxygen is coming in.*

They say when one sense is taken away, all the rest of them are heightened. It must be true because not only can I smell Evie's perfume when she sprays it lightly in the bedroom—good call, by the way—but I can hear her footsteps as she crosses to the door, then the sound of the lock disengaging, and can almost sense the moment that Brad is there, less than four feet from where I'm hiding.

"Brad, hi." Evie clears her throat. "Sorry, I was getting dressed. It's—" There's a pause and I imagine her checking her watch and giving him her best passive-aggressive smile. "Wow, it's not even seven. What can I do for you?"

There's some sort of scuffle and then Brad is yelling. "Bear, get back out here."

"You brought your dog?" Evie says, and I stifle a groan. Brad has a Great Dane that is basically the size of a horse, and if he's managed to escape from Brad and into the room, who knows what he'll find. Namely, me. I'm briefly overwhelmed with the mental image of him easily barreling through these cheap veneer doors and dragging my naked ass out into the room.

"Maxine drove him up last night. *Bear,*" he yells again, but it sounds half-assed at best. "He'll be fine," he says more quietly to

Evie, "just sniffing around. Now, I wanted to ask you about the schedule today. What have you planned?"

I can vaguely hear Evie rattling off the itinerary, and while I want to be furious at the way he's talking to her, there's a more pressing matter. Bear has obviously figured out that something about this closet isn't on the up-and-up, and he's sniffing around, his nose and dark eyes clogging up my oxygen crack.

I'm silently trying to will Bear away when he finds something more interesting and wanders off. Without the cloud of dog breath and sounds of his panting echoing around the closet, I can finally make out parts of the conversation again.

"And I guess I'm not really sure why you're asking me?" Evie is saying. "The event planner put most of the schedule together; we just okayed it all and picked between the steak and the fish. I have to be honest"—a pause—"Brad, what is he doing? He's in the trash."

"Bear, get out of there!" Brad shouts, and claps his hands. "What are you eating?" By the tinkling of his collar, I think Bear has run back to Brad, and he continues.

"I also wanted to talk to you about your assistant," he says.

"Jess?"

"Why are you having her email Kylie about vendors? Kylie doesn't have time for things like that, and frankly, neither do you."

"I was having her verify some of the—"

"You seem to forget I'm the coach here and I set the plays. Send all the invoices and receipts to Kylie to handle, where I'm assuming they were headed in the first place. I put you in charge of this event and that's what you should be worrying about. Not—"

"Carter," she interrupts, and I stop breathing. Whatever flagging erection I still had is no longer an issue.

"You put me *and Carter* in charge of this event, and yet I'm the only one you seem to be holding accountable. And you do realize none of this is anywhere in my job description."

There's a long pause and I'm afraid to move, afraid to blink, wondering whether my hammering pulse is actually audible outside the closet.

"Did you not hear anything I said last night, Evie?" Brad says, voice cool. "About working together? About us all coming together as a team?"

"I heard every word."

"Then maybe you should do yourself a favor and think on what that means. You don't have another strike left."

"What have any of my strikes *been*?" she asks, patience clearly thin. "*Field Day* was two years ago now, and there were about fifteen producers also on the hook. I've brought in more money than any other agent this year, male or female."

"Playing the girl card, I see," he says. "You know how I feel about that."

He lets the sentence hang there, and a few moments later I hear a snap, the sound of a dog running past, and then the door closing, the chain sliding into place.

Evie throws open the closet and a blast of fresh, cold air rushes into my face.

"Thank God," I say, my hand pressed to my chest as I attempt to slow my heart. "What the hell was that all about? What is his problem?"

Her jaw is tight as she looks past me, staring at the closed door. "I'll tell you, for a moment I blacked out and fantasized about pushing him off the balcony. Just a little shove and he would bounce like a tennis ball."

"Wow." I straighten. "I don't know what it says about me, but I am more than a little into your evil side."

"He is the worst," she whispers, "the *worst*." Walking toward the bed, she grabs a pillow and hurls it at the wall. "Lucky for both of us we weren't anywhere near it," she says. "I carry way too much guilt to be a very good killer."

"I mean, technically it would be gravity that'd kill him, so you just have to be a relatively good pusher."

She throws another pillow. "Why did he come to my room? Did he go to yours first?"

I sigh. "I suspect we both know the answer to that. I promise I would have said something if I hadn't been naked and—"

I motion to where the condom has probably permanently dried to my dick.

She winces, and I slip into the bathroom, taking a moment to clean myself up.

"Of course he let his horse-dog in to destroy my hotel room," she says from the bedroom. "Next he'll want me t—" She goes silent, then lets out a horrified "*Oh my God.*"

I lean out of the bathroom, looking across the room to where Evie is staring wide-eyed at something on the floor. "What's wrong?"

She looks up at me. "How many times did we have sex last night?"

"Ah, there it is." I laugh, giving her a winning smile. "Just sinking in for you now that you slept with the enemy?"

"No," she says, pointing down. "Bear got into the trash over here. I'm trying to figure out how many condoms he ate."

• • •

Are we dog killers?

I mean . . . I'm pretty sure we're not. I Googled it, and if Morgan can swallow a souvenir pressed penny the size of her entire windpipe and have it come out the other end just fine, Bear will be okay, too.

I think.

Evie is slightly less convinced and makes me clear my browser history so that if something goes awry it can't be used against us as evidence. I have some time until our first team-building activity, and I go to my room to shower before pulling out my laptop to check email. There's one from the creative director from the *Vanity Fair* shoot, and I'm initially afraid to open it.

I needn't be, because despite Jonah's diva entrance and Evie and I nearly losing our minds being idiots to each other before groping in the dark mixing room, the photos are great. So great, in fact, that they want to book Jonah for another shoot. My brother might be a giant asshat half of the time, but he clearly has the talent to back it up.

It's still early, but I take a chance and call him. He picks up after four rings. I hear the sound of a lawnmower somewhere in the distance, so I assume he must be up and outside.

A good sign.

"Listen," I say, buzzing with genuine excitement. "Have you checked your email? There are proofs from *Vanity Fair*, and they look great. Also, they want you to do another job."

Nothing but silence greets me on the other end of the line. I pull the phone away to make sure it hasn't disconnected.

"Did you hear me, Jones? They want you back."

"I saw," he says, but falls quiet again.

"You saw? That's it? Dude, this is exactly what we wanted. What *you* wanted—to *work*. To continue to live in the lifestyle to which you have so richly become accustomed."

"I'm just not sure that's what I want," he says. "Doing features shoots."

I gape for a few breaths, staring unseeing at the wall of my hotel room. "But isn't that the way you pay back your bills?"

"Yeah, but . . . I went to this gallery the other day, run by the friend of a friend, and some of the stuff was pretty good. Not fashion or anything, but like, abstracts and portraits."

"You're saying you want to go back to the kind of work you did in school?" I ask, confused. Wasn't the reason Jonah came out to Hollywood in the first place to be a star? I can't help but see doing small art shows as a step down on the particular ladder he chose.

"Do you remember the photo that won me the scholarship?" he asks, and I know exactly which one he means because it still hangs in our parents' house.

"The power lines," I say. "That's what you want to do?"

"A little here and there? Like if I could do a few shoots to pay the bills but the other stuff on the side. Maybe get a show or something."

I sit back in my chair. This has to be the most un-LA thing my brother has said since he was eighteen.

"What do you think?" he presses.

I come back to the conversation and realize I still haven't said anything. "Yeah, Jones. If you think that's what will make you happy then you should totally do it. And if you can do both and still make some money, well, that's even better. I guess what I'm saying is that you have that option, with *Vanity Fair*."

"Yeah."

"You'll figure it out." My phone clicks and I look down at the screen. Caleb, Dan's manager. "Listen, Jonah, I have another call and it's sort of important. Can I call you back?"

"No worries." I think he's going to hang up, but he speaks again: "Oh, and Carter?" He pauses. "Thanks."

Then he's gone.

I don't have time to reflect on this newfound vulnerability displayed by my douchenozzle brother, so I switch over and stand to pace the room. "Caleb, hi."

"Hey," he says, "I have Dan here. You free?"

"Absolutely."

There's some shuffling as the phone is passed around, and then Dan is there. "Carter, finally we connect."

"Dan, how's it going, man?"

"Good. Just finished reading a script and it's terrible." He laughs. "They're all pretty terrible, if I'm being honest."

I think of the last thing I saw Dan in—a giant action movie that takes place on a tanker stranded at sea; before that he played a cop trying to bring down a band of drug dealers—and wonder if the scripts he's being sent are all just carbon copies of what he's already done. I jot down a note to find out.

"What is it exactly you're looking for?" I ask, mentally filing through the stack of great scripts Brad recently sent me.

"What I'm looking for is an agent who sees what I am, but also what I can be. Jared Leto won an Oscar for *Dallas Buyers Club* but also gets to play the Joker."

"He gets to be a rock star, too," I say, and Dan laughs at this. "Pretty sweet gig if you can get it."

"Exactly," he agrees. "Nobody's telling him he can't pull off the Joker. He wanted it and he just did it."

"He's also got the talent to back it up," I say, leading him.

"You think I don't?"

"I wouldn't be having this conversation if I thought that," I tell him. "At least as an actor. I have to be honest, though, Dan. You'd be a shit rock star."

He laughs again. "That's what I need. An agent who gets me

the parts I need but also the parts I want. And one who steers me away from the things that won't work."

"It doesn't help anyone for me to kiss your ass," I tell him. "Neither of us gets paid that way."

"You think you're that guy?"

"I'm positive I'm that guy. You are a career, not just a role."

"Let's do this then," he says. "I need to get back on set, but Caleb can take care of the details. Let's make some movies, man!"

"And win some awards," I say in response and can hear his quiet "Hell yeah" as he passes the phone to Caleb.

I finish up the call, and when I hang up, I'm not quite sure if I imagined the entire thing.

There's some official stuff to be done, but I'm Dan Printz's new agent.

Me.

I push my hands into my hair and pace the room again before moving to pick up my phone, ready to call Evie with the good news when I stop, dropping it back to the bed.

There is absolutely no way I can tell Evie this today. She thinks Brad is trying to push her out, and after hearing their little altercation this morning, I agree. Not only did I pick up Dan from her in a semishady way, but I'm confident I can do things for him precisely because I have access to a stack of hot scripts that Evie never got to read.

I pick up my phone again, feeling the weight of it in my palm and wondering if there's some sort of twenty-four-hour grace period I get on delivering a possibly devastating blow to my new girlfriend's career.

I open the calendar app and send Justin a note to block out an hour on Tuesday, after I've had a chance to confirm the details with Dan. Best not to rush it. I'll finish out the weekend, get us back to LA, and then talk to Evie about it as soon as possible.

• • •

There's basically one goal for any team-building weekend: make a bunch of grown, moderately successful adults behave like idiots for a forty-eight-hour period all in the name of corporate bonding. This weekend is no different.

It's not that the games themselves are silly—they're actually a lot of fun—it's just hard to immediately spot the real-world utility. I mean, how can fighting off a zombie in a locked conference room ever help me tell my coworker in a calm and rational manner that I'm upset he ate my lunch?

Aptly, the first game is called Zombie Escape. A "zombie" is tethered to the center of the room and gradually given more floor space. The other team members are meant to solve various puzzles before the zombie is freed entirely. The best moment in this particular game comes when Evie's team sacrifices Ashton to get another three minutes.

The event planner, Libby, gives them kudos for real-world problem solving, but reminds them it wasn't exactly in the spirit of the game. But let me be clear: I would have done the same thing if the situation were real. Ashton is an ass.

Next up is Office Trivia. We're divided into new teams and earn points by answering questions correctly. The questions start out easy enough, and are meant to test our observation and recollection skills: On what floor is the shared bathroom? What color is the couch in Evie's office?

See? Simple.

But when the exercise devolves into a scene right out of Cards Against Humanity, with questions like "What most accurately fits the description of: *An hour of fun, perfect for lunch breaks*" and half the group shouts, "Rose!" it's time to pack it in.

The correct answer was break-room yoga, by the way.

It's hard to keep from watching Evie during all this, making my way over to her team and coming up with excuses to touch her. By the time lunch is over and everyone meets for a nature walk around the lake, if you'd dusted Evie for my fingerprints, she would've looked like a powdered doughnut.

The temperature is just above freezing, and we good little Californians pile on our bought-specifically-for-this-trip winter clothing and start the walk. I run to catch up with my girl—*my girl!*—and then tug on her hand so we're both lingering at the back of the group.

Evie's cheeks are pink from the cold, and I move in as close as I can without looking like I'm up to something.

"What's this all about?" she says, grinning as she watches the distance between us and the others grow.

I slip one hand out of my pocket and twist my pinkie around hers. "Just wanted to hold your hand."

"You're such a puppy," she says, but she squeezes my finger anyway.

Speaking of puppies . . . Bear runs around, ducking and dodging through the group as we walk along the lake. At one point he gingerly steps into the shallows and begins crouching.

"Oh God," I murmur, gently elbowing Evie.

She turns to follow my attention and lets out a quiet gasp.

His back legs shake, his spine is awkwardly curved, and if I had to guess, I would say Bear is feeling some intestinal distress.

"Bear!" Brad yells, and everyone looks awkwardly away from the pooping dog. "What in the hell are you doing? Get out of that water, it's freezing!"

Bear will not be moved. He carefully steps a little farther in, crouches a little more, whines, and looks back at us all.

Evie glances up at me, and then we both turn to watch in horror as Brad continues to yell and Bear continues to . . . well, bear down. Everyone is standing at the water's edge and it's like a slow-motion car accident. Nobody can seem to look away.

I let go of Evie's hand and make my way to the front of the group, on the verge of confessing and suggesting we run Bear to the nearest emergency vet, when the problem seems to solve itself. Bear barks happily and straightens, bounding back into the snow.

"Well, that was anticlimactic," Kylie says. "I thought he was having puppies or something." Every head in the group turns to look at her with the same confused expression when someone speaks up.

"Oh my God. Brad," Rose says. "I think Bear has worms."

We all look, because honestly, at this point what else can we do? Four pale yellow things are floating at the very surface of the water.

And I wince, turning toward Evie just in time to hear someone say, "Are those . . . wait, are those *condoms?*"

*   *   *

It is safe to say that I have never been more excited for a trip to end than I am right now. The retreat itself was fine—great if you count it was two nights and eight condoms (only seven of those used to completion)—but to say I was distracted would be a gross understatement. This weekend has felt like some kind of test, but aside from the Condom Incident, as we've decided to call it, and Brad and Evie's little altercation in her room, it feels like an overwhelming success.

Everyone is packed and having a final cup of coffee Sunday morning before the cars arrive to drive us back. The fire is roaring, a row of suitcases waits in a neat line near the doorway, and I'm counting down the minutes until Evie and I are alone again. I want to be alone so I can tell her about Dan, yes, but also to talk over and digest everything that's happened between us and to make a plan for how to deal with Brad, together.

Evie is on the phone with the drivers, and I'm near the fireplace, watching her as inconspicuously as I can manage. Brad and Kylie are talking in a corner nearby; I can hear bits and pieces of their conversation, not that I'm really paying much attention. I'm just ready to get out of here.

"I don't know," Kylie says. "I told them specifically that all of that was supposed to go straight to you." Brad nods. "I'm not sure where the miscommunication happened. I told them, Brad."

"I know you did," he says, and there's softness in his tone that suddenly has my attention. "People have too much time on their hands; I'll take care of it."

I don't realize that I'm staring until Brad looks over Kylie's shoulder and his eyes lock with mine. *Shit.*

He sends Kylie away, telling her to make sure everyone is accounted for, and moves to stand at my side.

"Carter," he says, eyebrows pulled in tight as he glances around the rest of the bar. "You weren't here last year, but did you think the retreat was a success?"

"Absolutely," I tell him. "Evie deserves every bit of the credit."

He leans against the fireplace and reaches for a few mints in a bowl there before popping one into his mouth. "You don't have to cover for her, you know. If she wasn't pulling her weight," he says, "you can tell me." He places an encouraging hand on my shoulder. "I know that you like her, Carter, and I do, too. Evie is a great girl. But she also has a reputation in this business."

"You mean *Field Day*."

"Exactly. And I'd hate to see you get caught up in anything that could jeopardize your trajectory. Especially considering I'd like to talk sometime this week about renewing your contract."

I straighten and take a step back. "With all due respect, Evie is one of the—"

I'm cut off by a round of cheers and applause inside the lobby. The cars have arrived, and a smiling Evie is now walking toward us.

"Time to go," she says, smile faltering as she looks between us. "Everything okay over here?"

Brad smiles that fucking smile of his. "We were just talking about how the weekend went."

"Yeah? I think it was pretty great." She gives us both a sweetly proud grin.

"It was amazing," I say. "I was just telling Brad here that I know we did this together, but you really impressed me: leading this, with everything else on your plate."

Her face lights up. "Thank you." She looks from me to Brad for some kind of confirmation.

Of course, it doesn't come. "Looks like it's time to head out," he says flatly. "I'll see you both tomorrow morning. Enjoy the rest of your day."

Evie's face falls, and I know that her fears were just confirmed. For whatever reason, Brad was hoping she would screw up.

Suddenly it occurs to me that it isn't just about Evie being a woman, or any hundred other possible forms of bigotry.

I mean, it *is* partly that. Evie's not crazy regarding all the double standards. But Brad isn't trying to get rid of *every* woman in the firm, even if he treats them all like shit. So his grudge isn't just that.

No. Evie has something on Brad.

The question I have, when I look over at her, is whether she even realizes it.

chapter twenty-three

evie

I consider myself to be an especially intuitive person, but even a newborn would pick up on the tension between me and Brad. Monday morning check-in goes by without a single word about the retreat. Brad doesn't even acknowledge me in the hallway as we pass. And Kylie's sweet *I still really like you!* smiles every time she sees me communicate more than Brad's stony silence. It's not unheard of to have tense relationships at work, even—maybe especially—with bosses, but given that I've done everything he's asked of me and then some, his behavior is bewildering.

As much as I love being an agent, and as much as I love having the reach of P&D and its resources at my fingertips, I have to admit that it's getting hard to give a shit about any of this.

Carter and I banged all of Friday and Saturday night, Saturday morning, of course, and back at my place the rest of the weekend on Sunday. That's pretty much all I can think about right now. Being sex drunk is certainly better than being work stressed, and I'm like a cartoon with a halo of spinning stars, but instead of being hit with an anvil over the head, I've been hit in the vagina with Carter's magical penis.

•　•　•

On Tuesday morning, Rose announces that she's leaving the business, moving back to Iowa, and opening a bookstore. Pretty much everyone's reaction to this is an internal, drawn-out *Okaaaay?*, which is less because doing so is a complete one-eighty from her job now and more because none of us could have guessed that Rose reads books, like ever.

She announces this in the middle of the wide outer hallway, in front of about sixteen assistants and interns working at the common area. It's followed by a chorus of simultaneous gasps—the interns love Rose because she tells them every bit of dirt she knows.

Rose presses a shaking hand to her chest. "I know," she says. "It hurts me, too. I'll miss you guys *so much*."

From across the hall, I can sense Carter's attention on my face. Our eyes snag, and we struggle to not break out into enormous grins.

This means one less agent in LA.

This means Brad could possibly keep us both.

I break my gaze from his when my phone buzzes in my palm with a call from a producer at Sony. I answer, turning and speed-walking to my office.

"Evie," the voice says. "It's Frank Nelson."

"Frank, nice to hear from you."

"Look, I'm on my way to a meeting but wanted to check in quickly. I have a script I'd really like you to consider for Trent Vanh. This one is a huge Michael Bay production, and we've already got Keira Knightley signed on. Trent's our lead, if he wants it."

My heart isn't galloping, it's swallowing itself whole with every clenching beat.

"I'd love to take a look," I say as calmly as I can. "Send it on over with the offer details, and we'll go from there."

"Great."

The call ends. Easy. Fast. Timely.

Life-altering.

.   .   .

"Come in," Brad says from the other side of the heavy oak door.

I push in, hands still shaking. He looks up, unblinking.

"Evie."

"I've got great news," I tell him.

He bids me to continue by putting his glasses down and folding his hands in front of him.

"Frank Nelson just called and offered Trent the lead on the next Bay film."

Brad's reaction to this is a tiny flicker of an eyebrow, a twitch at the side of his mouth. Six months ago he would have rounded the desk and hugged me over this.

But now all I get is a "Good. Good."

"He's sending over the script—and the offer—today."

Brad nods and finally offers a tiny flash of a smile. "That's good." He inhales sharply, leaning back in his chair to study me. "Did you tell Carter?"

My brain comes to a halt, and I know my face has just been wiped clean of any expression. Instinct makes me continue with caution. Did he ask me this because he knows I'm sleeping with Carter? Or did he ask me this because Trent will soon be Carter's, and I'll be packing my bags?

"I came to tell you first," I say. "I'll tell him whenever I see him."

Brad smiles. "He's looking at some big deals, too, coming up. Did he tell you? He landed Dan Printz on Saturday."

I am Alice, tumbling through the looking glass. I am Louise, driving the car over the cliff.

"He did?"

He did?

He did?

Why didn't he tell me? I *wanted* this for him!

My face feels hot—God, I must be bright red. I need to get the fuck out of here.

Brad puts his glasses back on and his smile is genuine this time. "Go congratulate him. It's a great signing for us."

• • •

I have about seven thousand reactions to this, and they're all happening in my body at once. Confusion, surprise, anger, sadness, worry, guilt, happiness, and whatever the other several thousand are—I feel them, each one.

Locking myself in a bathroom stall, I sit down and put my head in my hands.

Think, Evie.

Work through it all.

Why didn't he tell me?

I know why: this situation is complicated and our relationship is only a few days out of Cutthroat Situation and into All the Sex.

Is Carter really *that guy*? Am I so emotion-blind that I can't even see when he's collecting a few fucks before taking my job? My brain screams and I press my fists to my temples.

I know going to Sexist Asshat Town is my knee-jerk reaction. The sad thing is that I'm right most of the time. But this is *Carter*. I've seen him at his best, and his worst. I *know* him, don't I?

I squeeze my eyes closed, forcing my internal debate team to step up to the podium.

Would I have told him yet? Maybe, but likely no. I would

want to see that signature page first. I would want to know for sure that Dan Printz was mine, because it doesn't matter how many Michael Bay movies Trent gets. Dan Printz is the future. He's the next Brad Pitt, the next Clooney. He's not a small star, he's a sun.

What does this mean for me?

With Rose out of the picture, who knows. But it likely means that I'm second to the golden boy, and that golden boy is my boyfriend. Am I okay with that?

•   •   •

Carter isn't in his office when I come out of my panic room, and so I pace my own office, replying to emails as my brain takes tiny breaths of air. It's only noon, and I know I have a to-do list a mile long, but I can't for the life of me remember anything on it.

I call Jess in, tell her to go through and prioritize my monstrous call sheet, and focus on that for as long as I can. Work is grounding. It's the sharpening of a knife, the trimming of a hedge. Everything feels orderly once I've passed the ball into someone else's court.

Jess leans against my doorframe. "Did you have a chance to go over those retreat invoices again?"

I wince. "Dammit! It's on my list to do today. Thank you for the remin—"

Carter's shoes squeak on the marble when he steps off the elevator, and I am up, out of my chair, and sprinting. Jess's laughter follows me down the hall.

I jog over to him, clutching his arms in my hands. "Carter."

"Hey, crazy eyes," he says, laughing. But then his expression straightens—like he knows I know—and he lifts his chin for us to head back in the direction of his office.

He closes the door behind him. "Evie—"

"I just talked to Brad," I say breathlessly. "Trent was offered a role in the next Bay production and he told me about Dan, and—"

"I was going to tell you," he says urgently, and the frantic set of his eyes makes my chest twist. "I just got back from lunch with him, and was coming—"

"I'm not mad," I say quietly, interrupting him. "I was. But I calmed myself down."

Carter sits down heavily in a chair.

"I knew you were courting him," I remind him. "And, to be honest in my own actions, I told Dave from the *Vine* to email you and make the contact."

His eyebrows pull close together, and he swallows. "You did? When?"

"Like, maybe your second week here?" I say, shrugging. "Dave assumed Dan was coming to my list. I just sent him your way instead."

He shakes his head, stunned. "You didn't have to do that."

"The merge had just happened and you'd been dealt one hell of a blow. I wanted to win, but I wanted an even playing field first. Or maybe I just underestimated what a threat you'd be. I don't know. But I'm glad you got Dan. I think you'll be a great fit. I'm not mad you didn't tell me. I promise."

He seems to flounder for a few seconds, and then says quietly, "I can't believe you did that."

This makes me laugh, and it surprises him because it's never a soft laugh. It's a bursting Evil laugh. "Like I said, I wanted to beat you fairly."

He lifts a single teasing brow at the assumption that I would beat him at all. My pulse does a little jump, and I guess Daryl was right. I *like* competing with him. Who knew? And oh my God, we're talking this out. We're interacting like adults, *in person*.

"Besides, I like you. Dummy."

His hands come forward, finding my hips and pulling me closer so that I'm standing between his legs.

"Just 'like'?"

"Maybe more."

He growls a little, leaning to kiss my stomach once through my dress, then again, a little lower. "How can I get *you* to sign with me?"

"Keep doing that." As he kisses, and apologizes again, and lets his hands slide around and to my ass, over my thighs—*remembering*—my fingers find his hair, and I close my eyes, tilting my face to the ceiling.

I don't care about this office. I don't care about this agency.

I care about my clients. I care about this man.

"Dan hasn't signed the contract yet, but he has given me the verbal commitment. He wants to work with me." Carter hesitates. "He wants me more in a manager role, as well as agent. You know that legally, I can't do both. Caleb wants to move back to New York. I'd have to figure out how that could work."

I nod, but he doesn't see it. My silence doesn't seem to bother him. He wraps his arms fully around me, squeezing as he presses his face to my hip. But then he seems to remember something and pulls back, looking up at me.

"If you weren't mad, why did you look so panicked when I came in?"

When I try to smile, it comes out a little broken, so I give up and shrug instead. "I just get the feeling I'm not going to be here very much longer."

He studies my face, quiet for a few seconds. "Something's going on with Brad. With you, I mean."

I laugh. "You think?"

"No, seriously." Carter sits back and looks past me to make sure his door is firmly closed. "I was thinking about this all weekend. Why does he have it in for *you*, specifically?"

A world of unknowns in that one question. I shrug.

"Do you have something on him?" he asks me.

"I have a lot of little bits of dirt," I say. "No steaming pile. Nothing I'd really share with anyone."

"And he knows that." He bends, rubbing his hand over his face. "It just doesn't make sense."

• • •

Because Carter is obviously the most amazing boyfriend of all time, he takes me out to breakfast for dinner. Over enormous stacks of pancakes at the Griddle Cafe, we talk about everything but work, interrupted frequently by Mike and Steph's giddy, emoji-stringed texts. We texted them a selfie of us earlier: me, cross-eyed and cheeks puffed as Carter planted a giant smooch on my cheek. He typed the words *Meet my girlfriend, Evil,* before he hit send in the group window.

I suppose that got the message across that we are doing the couple thing and no longer plotting each other's murder.

We talk about our families, because it feels like a real possibility that we'll meet them soon—and maybe that they'll meet each other. He talks about how he was engaged once, and how he loved that girl, but not in that bone-crushing way where you would give up anything. She wanted small and Carter wanted the stars. We talk about how maybe Steph was right and I do always manage to find fault in the men I date—*Too motivated! Not moti-*

vated enough!—and the relief I usually felt at putting them in the not-datable column. That way it was them, not me. We talk about Daryl and Amelia and how much they mean to me. How I've known Daryl for most of my life and how I love Amelia in almost the same way.

"Have they seen you since Friday?" he asks proudly. "Because if they saw you walking lately . . ." He mimes me stumbling bow-legged with two fingers teetering across the tabletop and I chuck a piece of scrambled egg at him.

He picks it off his plate and eats it.

I might really love him.

"Sorry," he says quickly, reaching across the table to take my hand. "Did that gross you out?"

"What? No."

"Then why do you suddenly look like you're going to vomit?"

"Because I love you."

He laughs, delighted. "How terrible."

"I just . . . don't go," I say in a burst.

"Go where?"

"Anywhere."

He stands, leaning across the table. His lips taste like syrup, his smile feels like home.

Beneath him, on the table, his phone begins to jump.

Carter pulls away, grinning at me and slowly sitting down in his seat before glancing at the caller ID. With a tiny *just a sec* finger, he answers.

"Dave, hey."

I watch Carter's face go from flesh-colored to zombie pale in about two seconds.

"What? No, it wasn't me. Absolutely not."

He listens, shaking his head.

"Fuck, no. It—he hasn't even *signed* yet." Nodding, he says, "Just verbal. And the announcement was supposed to be yours, just as soon as I had the paperwork wrapped up."

Finally, he looks up at me and whispers, "Open *Variety*. Now."

Scrambling for my phone, I open my app. It loads slowly, but by the time it does, Carter has finished his call and he takes my phone when I hand it to him.

I've already read the headline.

I have no idea what is happening, but Carter looks like he is about to throw up his pancakes all over the table, and it isn't because I professed my love.

It's because *Variety* has just announced that Dan Printz has signed with Carter.

"What is going on?" I whisper.

Carter shakes his head, reading and rereading what's written before handing the phone back to me with a quietly hissed "*Ssssshiiiiit*."

I scan the article and feel my stomach drop.

People's Sexiest Man Alive Leaves Lorimac

Dan Printz, actor in the upcoming action blockbuster *Global* and recently voted *People* magazine's Sexiest Man Alive, has signed with talent agent Carter Aaron.

Printz has emerged as one of the hottest actors in Hollywood following the box-office success of *Under a Stony Sky*, in which Printz portrays a brooding cyborg who saves a family from a corporation bent on killing their genius children. To date, the film has earned over $750 million internationally.

Printz previously was repped by Joel Meyer over at Lorimac,

who launched Printz's career in his debut, *Edge*, produced by Universal and directed by George Stan. Lorimac has been in talks with Sony and Fox to cast Printz in several upcoming big-budget films, but according to Printz's spokesperson, those will pass over to Carter Aaron, effective immediately.

Aaron, originally from New York, works for newly merged Price & Dickle.

I stare at the screen, uncomprehending.

"Why is this in *Variety?*" It's a stupid first question, but I get now why Dave called. *Dave* was supposed to get this scoop. Dave was going to give Carter a huge spread in the *Hollywood Vine* print edition in exchange.

"No idea." His voice is clipped and loud. Carter pulls out his wallet, hastily grabbing a couple of twenties and dropping them on the table. His hands are shaking.

I scramble to follow him as he stands and heads for the door. A few diners near us have stopped talking to watch us bolt.

"Why . . . ?" I have so many questions. Why is this out now? Why did *Variety* get the scoop? And why is Carter mentioned so obviously?

It doesn't seem like that's what's happening, but . . . Carter wouldn't do this, right? He knows better?

He *has* to know better. This is Agenting 101.

"Lorimac knew?" I ask.

Carter bursts from the restaurant. "No, I don't think so. I mean, Dan couldn't hire me until he'd fired Joel, but that happened last week and I got the distinct impression Joel was keeping it from Lorimac, positive Dan would come back. I don't like Joel, but this is no way for them to find out. *Fuck*." He does an angry little fist-punch toward the sky. "*Fuck!*"

Actors leaving agencies is a big deal. A *huge* deal. Especially talent like Dan; he'll take millions of dollars with him, and it will not only affect the agency's bottom line, it will bruise their reputation. This announcement is bad for Lorimac, yes, but it could be just as bad for P&D because it makes us look like shady assholes doing underhanded things to steal talent; none of this should have been made public until we were sure Lorimac knew and had time to prepare their own statement.

More to the point, it makes *Carter* look like a shady asshole, because he's mentioned specifically, with very little mention of P&D at all. It's written as if Carter is the force behind the deal, not the agency.

Tripping after him, I start to form another question. "Carter, why—"

He wheels on me, face red. "I don't fucking know, Evie, okay? *I don't fucking know!*"

I pull back, hands to my chest. "Okay! *Jesus.*"

Deflating, he hangs his head, reaching for me, pulling me to his chest. I'm still stunned, and come a little reluctantly.

"I'm sorry," he whispers, kissing my hair. "I'm sorry. I don't know. I don't fucking know what just happened. I told Dave he had the exclusive. I met Dan today and we shook on it, I even told him about the offer of announcing with Dave and the *Vine*—he was thrilled—but he hasn't seen a contract. I've never spoken to Ted Statsky at *Variety*—I have no idea how he got this."

Taking his hand, I pull him toward my car. "Let's go to the office and figure this out."

It's nearly eight by the time we get to the fifth floor, but all the lights are on, and I can hear Brad's voice barking from his office all the way down by the elevator bank.

Carter blanches, glancing at me before heading straight down there.

I follow, and although I'm only a few steps behind him, I stay in the hall. I have no role in this crisis but to be Carter's support and his colleague, making whatever damage control calls he needs.

Brad's voice is a terrifying thunder. "What the fuck is this, Aaron? What the fuck is going on? Have you seen this fucking *Variety* article?"

"I spoke to Dave," Carter says, managing to sound calm. "This wasn't me. This wasn't us. This was an outside leak."

"The fuck it was!" Brad yells. "You pissed all over this article. You wrote your fucking name in loopy fucking letters all over this love note to *Variety*. P&D is barely fucking mentioned here. Do you work here? Are you in my department?"

"Of course, Brad."

"Well, not according to this, you're not! We get a line at the bottom. No one fucking reads the last line!"

Carter wisely doesn't point out that everyone at Lorimac will read the last line.

"I'm supposed to meet my wife tonight at an event where she's getting an award," Brad yells, "but instead I'm *here*—trying to make sense of this fuckup. Jesus, Carter, this is a huge shit storm."

I know I shouldn't—I *know* I shouldn't—but I step in, feeling my heart grow into a solid ball of pissed-off. "It wasn't Carter, Brad. I've been with him since he came back from his lunch with Dan."

"'Lunch with Dan'?" Brad says, turning back to Carter. "So he did sign?"

"Legal is still writing up the contracts," Carter says, trying to calm Brad down. "Brad, it's Tuesday. He confirmed over the phone three days ago. He did a verbal and a handshake today. I know better than to run to *Variety*—or anyone—with a handshake . . ."

Carter's voice trails off, because Brad isn't listening to him anymore. He's staring at me, and with a cold rush down my body, I realize why.

My heart, my lungs, my stomach are packed into a tight ball of fury.

"Are you fucking *kidding* me?" I ask, struggling to stay calm.

"I told you this *today*," he says through gritted teeth. "I told you about Dan Printz *today*, Abbey, and this is what you do? You're so jealous you gotta go screw Dave, Dan, Carter, and P&D in one blow?"

Carter takes a step back like he's been punched. I am shaking. At my side, my hand forms a fist, and I have to consciously unclench it or else I know it will be flying toward Brad.

"Brad, there is *no* way—" Carter starts.

"You need to take a deep breath, Brad," I interrupt, anger making my voice nearly inaudible. "It wasn't Carter, and it *wasn't* me."

He lifts his chin in a *fuck you* gesture and scoffs. "This is low, even for you."

What the hell does that mean?

I turn, walking on shaking legs to the door. "You're out of your damn mind, Brad. Go home. Sleep it off. I'll accept your apology in the morning."

chapter twenty-four

carter

After leaving Brad's office, Evie walked calmly back to her own, disappeared inside for a moment, and then slammed the door so hard the pictures in the hallway rattled against the walls.

I knock on her door and peek in. Her head is down, but she looks up at my entrance, cheeks tear-streaked. "This is bullshit, Carter."

Stepping in, I close the door behind me. "Of course it is. It's unconscionable."

She presses the heels of her hands to her eyes.

"What can I do?" I ask.

"You have your own mess to clean up," she says, voice nasal from crying. "I just need to get my shit together so I can walk out of here and go home."

I always thought Evie and I were two complementary halves of a whole, different strengths, a perfect team. But now I realize that in most ways, we're the same. Of course she doesn't want to lick her wounds with witnesses around.

"Call me later?" I say.

She nods, wiping her face. "And tell me if you need me to do anything. I'll get over this crying shit in a minute and be back in action."

I kiss her clammy cheek. "I know you will."

On my way home, I make some calls. Dan doesn't answer his phone, Caleb either. I text Evie my address, then I pace, and pace, and pace until the doorman sends her up. Stepping out into the hall, I find her loaded up with bags of takeout.

"I have no idea why I brought food," she says, and hands me a bag of what smells like Indian. She inhales deeply. "That's not true. I'm going to eat it all."

I set it on the table and pull her to me, pressing a kiss to her temple. "Feeling better?"

She sinks into me, her cheek pressed to my chest and arms wrapped around my waist. "I feel gross. You?"

"Waiting to hear back from Dan or Caleb." I rest my chin on the top of her head. "Do you want to talk about what happened with Brad?" I ask. "Eat our feelings? Watch a movie? Fuck like teenagers who don't have to worry about things like jobs or food or rent?"

She looks up at me with a smile, the first one I've seen since the *Variety* article went live. "My default answer is always going to be food, but now that I'm having sex with someone besides myself, I might have to reorganize my priorities."

I take her hand and lead us both to the kitchen. "How about if we talk a little first, and then we can eat *while* we have sex?"

"If we could have the TV on at the same time I might never leave this apartment." She eyes me while I get down a couple of plates. "Are you sure you're ready for that kind of hunkered-in-for-sex commitment?"

Evie dishes up our food and I grab two beers from the fridge. I remember she doesn't love beer, and grab her a glass for water instead.

"I've never been to your place before." She looks around. "It's a lot cleaner than your office."

"I think outside of Michael Christopher and Steph, you might be the only person who's been here."

"You're kidding."

"Let's just say that up until recently my social life was decidedly less active."

She takes a deep breath and smiles, like it was exactly what she needed to hear. "Well, I like it."

"I have my own parking spot. Oh, and granite countertops." I rap my knuckle on the surface in front of me. "Stainless steel appliances, one bedroom, recently updated floors, and a six-setting showerhead in the modern-yet-sizable bathroom. I tell you all this not to brag, but as a warning that you may have to take over my lease if I lose my job."

Evie frowns, pushing her food around on her plate. "I don't think you're the one who needs to worry. Brad is having a hard time letting *Field Day* go."

"I gathered that," I say simply. "It just seems so . . ."

"Petty?" she finishes for me.

"Yeah. I mean, it's not like P&D lost money. Obviously we made our commission. So why is Brad so obsessed with it? That's what I don't get."

"I think it's because he knew he had something to use against me. It tanked Mark Marsh's career, so it's like this little IOU Brad can pull out whenever he needs to feel superior."

"That's a lame IOU," I say. "That's like giving someone a homemade book of Free Back Rub coupons."

She gives me an amused *you're crazy* smile. "It's not really anything like that."

"But everyone has flops. Between everyone on your list, how many movies do you think you've been involved in?"

She blows out a breath, looking past me out the window. "Over a hundred, easily."

"Exactly. Statistics tell us that at least one of those is going to be a bomb."

"So?"

"*So*," I say, reaching across to finish her half-eaten samosa, "that's why I think there's something else going on with Brad and you. It doesn't add up."

"I have no idea what else it could be," she says, shrugging helplessly. "*Field Day* is what he always mentions." She wipes her mouth with her napkin and pushes her plate away. "Whatever, it doesn't matter. All it will take is for Brad to hint that I had something to do with this *Variety* leak, and that'll be it. Nobody will hire me."

"But you're not even mentioned in the article," I say.

"It doesn't matter. It might have been your name, but Dave came to me first, and I sent him on to you. Everyone knows Dave and I go way back. No matter what happens, I look like I had an ulterior motive." She presses her hands to her eyes. "God, this sucks. And you come out looking like a snake. It's unreal."

"I know," I say, pulling her closer. "But what I still don't understand is who could have given *Variety* the story to begin with. I only told Brad."

"Dan is surrounded by idiots," she says. "His manager is a nice enough guy, but the rest of his little entourage are world-class mooches; I wouldn't put it past any of them to mention it in passing to someone whose skirt they were trying to get into. Maybe they told the wrong person."

"So what now?" I ask. "I can't get hold of Dan or Caleb.

Dave is MIA, and we have to wait until tomorrow to rip Brad a new one."

Evie stands, carries our plates to the sink, and then takes my hand. "Let's see. So far I've seen the kitchen, the granite countertops, the parking space, and the wood floors. Maybe you could show me that adjustable showerhead?"

"I don't have a TV in the shower, Evil. So if you're looking to multitask in there I'm afraid I can't help you."

I can hear every footstep, every thump of my pulse in my ears as I lead Evie down the hall.

I wasn't expecting anyone, and only now does it register that I should do the mental girlfriend-in-the-house checklist. I exhale when we walk in and find everything in order: freshly washed comforter and sheets and a pile of pillows tossed haphazardly on top. My mind pushes forward and suddenly all I can see is Evie in that bed, sheets twisted around her or gone completely, her legs tangled with mine.

We're on the same page—Evie's already pulled her sweater off and then tugs off the shirt underneath. We stand, grinning at each other across a few feet, painted in stripes of fluorescent streetlight as we peel off our clothes one piece at a time.

"I feel like we should have music for this," she says, grin widening.

"I could beatbox?"

"No." She pushes me down and climbs over my lap, straddling my hips. Her kisses are soft and sucking, a sweep of tongue, the sharp bite of teeth. There are about two working cells in my brain right now and it takes both of them to move to the side of the bed and feel along the edge of my nightstand for a drawer.

"Condom?" she says, and I pull away, dragging in a lungful of air while she trails kisses down my neck.

"Looking." I pull the drawer open, searching. My movements become more frantic and I nearly dump Evie onto the floor when I stretch as far as I can, finally wrapping a triumphant hand around the box.

I pull the top half of her body back onto the mattress, climbing over her and laughing into her neck. "Sorry."

She's cracking up under me, legs and arms wrapped all around my torso. When I pull back, even in the dark I can see the happiness written all over her face. We needed this chance to lose ourselves and check out for a little bit.

I hand her the condom and she studies it very intently for a few shaking breaths before reaching between us.

And then, in a breath, I'm there and she's pulling my head back down to her neck. I can't decide which part of her I want to touch first and so my greedy hands grip her ass, squeezing so I can fuck harder. I skim across her stomach, her hips, her nipples. She rolls and arches from underneath me, and moving with her pulls every other thought from my mind. My hands are in her hair, and my head is full of her sounds. I am mesmerized by the way my movements alter the rhythm of her breaths.

We manage to pop the sheets off all four corners.

"How's the tour of the apartment?" I ask her at one point, my hand behind her knee, her luminous brown eyes focused on my face above her.

I feel the way she laughs, her body gripping me, and I smile into the dark. This is absolutely the most fun I've ever had . . . well, ever. She pulls me down, drawing her legs up to my chest and our hips flush together, and I come out of nowhere, too lost in her to even be embarrassed.

Pulling out, I move down between her legs, and with her

hands in my hair and my name ringing around the room, all is forgiven.

• • •

Evie has an early appointment to talk to Trent about the Bay script, so she doesn't spend the night. Just after midnight, I pull away from her and dress. I walk her down to where she's parked, take her face in my hands, and kiss her until I'm begging her to come back up to my apartment.

"Just another hour," I say against her mouth. "Thirty minutes. *Ten*. I think we both know I'm good for at least that. How about from behind, just inside the door."

She sucks in a breath, and with her palms on my chest, she pushes and puts the tiniest bit of space between us. "You're dangerous. I have to go."

I spend most of the next three hours awake and staring at the ceiling, head spinning with everything that's happened today.

My thoughts bounce around, and I'm not even sure what to focus on: that Evie and I are happening, that it's so fucking good, that Brad has apparently lost his mind, that I'm Dan Printz's agent, the possibility that I've damaged any future relationship with Dave *and* the *Hollywood Vine*, or that someone—still unknown—leaked the damn story to *Variety* in the first place.

Jesus, take the wheel.

Exhausted but too keyed up to sleep, I start scrolling through the various apps on my phone.

Michael Christopher might pride himself on being twenty-seven going on nineteen, but virtually every photo he posts, anywhere, is of Morgan. Morgan at the park, Morgan in the bathtub, Morgan playing dress-up with Daddy. I save the one of him wearing a tiara because that is going on his birthday card.

There's a post from Becca with her thumb pointed down in front of a treadmill, followed by one of a doughnut and a thumb pointed directly up. I laugh into the darkness.

The time stamp on the post is less than fifteen minutes old—still pretty early—so I decide to try my luck and send her a text.

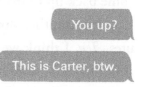

Is my eyeroll font coming through?

I know it's you.

You have a new job, you didn't die
and take your contact info with you.

I smile at my screen. God, I've missed her.

My phone rings almost immediately.

"Hey, everything okay?" she says before I've even had a chance to say hello. "It's, like, three in the morning. I know why I'm up, but why are you?"

"Was I a terrible boss?"

There's a pause and the unmistakable sound of her scoffing. "Are you drunk?"

I groan. "I wish."

"Okay, tell me what's happening."

"Just . . . a lot of stuff in my head, I think."

"I hate those nights where your brain suddenly fires and decides to question every decision you've made your entire life."

"That's pretty much it. How's the new job?"

"You know, same shit, different day. My new boss is an idiot. But then again so was my old boss, so points for consistency."

"Very funny," I say.

"So what's got your brain up, work stuff or life stuff?"

"A lot of both. I met someone."

"Shut up."

"Yeah. She's . . . she's really great. You'd like her. Maybe we can set something up and all have dinner."

"Wow, Carter. Introducing your new flame to your old assistant. That *is* serious."

I chuckle and say, "I don't think I realized exactly how serious until right now . . ."

"So did I just help you come to some sort of realization? Because my birthday is next month, and you still know my favorite shoe store."

I laugh. "I think you did."

"Okay, go to sleep or you'll be a monster tomorrow, and I'm not there to bring you coffee. Keep me posted, okay?"

"Yeah, thanks, Becca. I miss you, by the way."

"Miss you, too."

I end the call and fall asleep between one blink and the next.

•   •   •

I'm exhausted when my alarm goes off, but I get up and force myself to go for a run anyway.

It's cool enough for a jacket; the haze of the marine layer is still thick in the air and the sun isn't high enough to burn it all off yet. I take a different route today, where a long stretch of road hugs the base of the hill and the streets are lined with older apartment buildings and lots of trees. The traffic is heavy in this area, but it's still early enough that it's manageable.

I'm back at the apartment in record time, able to shower and change and still grab breakfast before heading out.

There are a few texts waiting, one from Michael and Stephanie about a long-awaited couples dinner this weekend and one from Evie, stressed out about taking her meeting instead of heading straight for the office where Brad could apologize and kiss her ass in front of everyone.

I'm a little worried that's not actually what's going to happen, but I do my best to distract her, suggesting she send *me* pictures of her ass and I'll describe how I plan on kissing it later, but she doesn't bite. I can almost feel her anxiety through the phone; I hate that she has to deal with all this. If *my* head is a mess over what's happening, I can't imagine how she must feel.

I've had three cups of coffee and am on a tear by the time I make it into work, having concocted an entire monologue to unleash in Brad's office. I march straight down the hallway, my carefully prepared words shifting carefully into place in my head, and stop short at Kylie's desk. The windows behind her are dark.

"Hey, Kylie. Is Brad in?" I ask, ignoring the sour bend to my stomach.

She shakes her head and offers me a small, practiced smile. This woman deals with Brad Kingman on a daily basis; something tells me she's mastered the art of apologizing for her boss. "He won't be in until later."

Fuck.

"Do you know when?" I ask, already anticipating the massacre that will take place if Evie catches him before I do.

Kylie taps out a few keystrokes and then looks back up at me. "About an hour or so. He has a meeting at eleven so he'll be here for that."

"Can you schedule me in?"

She winces and then frowns. "Nothing today. I can tell him you stopped by?"

"You know, I'll just keep an eye out," I tell her, and smile before heading back down the hall.

The tension is thick in the office. By now everyone has heard about the *Variety* article—and the fallout—and nobody really knows whether to offer congratulations or wince over how bad this could be for everyone involved. I don't even know myself.

Justin is at his desk when I get there. He hands me a stack of messages, but I wave off any discussion of what else we have going on today; I'm going to need him to get me on the phone with one person after another until I can get this straightened out.

Justin tries to connect me to Dave. Not surprisingly, it goes straight to his voicemail. Because I'm obviously not stressed enough, I log into my computer and check Google, and sure enough the story has been picked up everywhere.

"Hey, Justin?" I call out, and he pokes his head inside. "Can you let me know if you see Brad or Evie come in? Subtly though, okay?"

He nods. "Want me to close this for you?" he asks, standing in the doorway. I shake my head and he steps out, leaving me to my buzzy, anxious solitude.

The thing about having an office with sixteen assistants all corralled into one area is that it gets loud. It feels like the phones never stop ringing—and has everyone always stomped around here like a herd of horses? Add in the sound of typing, the occasional text alerts, a whole lot of water cooler conversation, and my total lack of focus, and I don't get anything done. Thank God that after only about an hour of this, there's a knock on my door.

It's Justin, peeking in and then glancing back over his shoulder, looking entirely too much like he's up to something.

"Mr. Kingman just got here. Want me to do anything?"

"No, I've got it. Thanks, though." I save my document and, hands sweating, step out.

Kylie sees me again and offers a sympathetic smile, one I can only assume means that Brad is in some kind of a mood.

"He's in there?" I say quietly, and she nods.

He looks up when I clear my throat, and pins me with a look that is only marginally more pleasant than the one he'd give Evie.

"What can I do for you, Aaron? I'm sure I don't have to explain how busy I am cleaning up all of this."

"That's what I want to talk to you about," I say, moving deeper into his office.

Brad takes his glasses off and sets them on the desk and then sits back, waiting for me to talk.

"I know that things look bad, and the timing of you telling Evie about Dan Printz and the article coming out looks suspicious, but I can guarantee she didn't have anything to do with it."

"Is that so?"

"Yes. The two of us have had our differences in the past, but she would never jeopardize her integrity, or that of anyone working here. She knows what's at stake—as do I—and respects you and the job, our clients and contacts too much."

"What the hell is going on, Carter?" Brad leans in, eyes narrowing. "Why are you in here telling me this? Are you white-knighting for the girl you're fucking? Is that it?" My heart claws its way up my chest. "Are we going to have a little talk about the birds and the bees right now?"

"No, Brad. I just wanted to clarify—"

Brad holds up a finger to stop me. "The only thing that needs clarifying is that you work for me. And right now I want you to get the hell back to your office and do exactly that—*work*. Just like I hired you to do. I don't want your drama in here. Evie fucked up, period, and it isn't the first time." He slides his hand horizontally above his desk. "Let her roll under the bus."

I think back to the day of the merge and how thankful I was that I still had a job. I remember the relief of thinking I was in the clear, and being in this very room when I realized that I wasn't. We did exactly what Brad had hoped we would do and went for each other's throats, in the hope that only one of us would be left standing. It's shocking to realize that the only one standing is me.

"Actually," I start, and the more I think on what I'm about to do, the more I know it's the right thing. "I don't think so. I'm done."

Brad sits back in his seat, surprised.

"Don't be an idiot, Carter. Think on it tonight. Don't be a hero and wake up regretting a decision you made with the wrong fucking head. Because whether you're here or not, she won't be."

• • •

My phone goes off on my way out of the office, but I ignore it. I don't bother to take anything, deciding there will be plenty of time, or I can have Justin send it to me . . . somewhere. My head is an absolute mess and I have zero idea what I'm going to do now, but at least it will be on my terms.

I take the stairs to the second level of the parking garage and unlock my car, sliding inside. My phone vibrates again and I go to reach for it, realizing it could be Evie.

It's not.

chapter twenty-five

"You can't put up with this anymore," Amelia says, well on her way to wearing a path in Daryl's new carpet. "I've sat by and let a lot of shit go because he's your boss and sometimes we all have to turn the other cheek, but this is it! You have to *do* something."

I close my eyes and lean my head against the back of one of Daryl's plush chairs. I read the script, took my meeting with Trent, met Sarah Hill for a lunch meeting, returned approximately seventy thousand phone calls, decided it would be best to avoid Brad entirely until I'd figured out what to do, and left the office at five for the first time in years, heading straight here.

Thankfully I have friends who will listen to me complain, rant on my behalf, and pour me lots of wine. It's only six o'clock and I'm on glass number three.

"What would you have me do?" I ask her. "I have fewer than forty-five days left on my contract. Brad is an asshole, but he's never done anything I could officially complain about. Reporting him now—after I'm about to be blamed for this enormous agency faux pas—would make me look like a crybaby who can't hang with the big boys. No way will I give him that kind of satisfaction."

Daryl groans into her glass. "I hate to say it, but she's right.

Brad isn't an idiot, and he's been very careful not to do anything she could specifically call him out on."

I nod, quickly swallowing a gulp of wine to add, "It's a hostile work environment, sure. But name me a place in Hollywood that isn't."

Amelia drops onto Daryl's fluffy white couch and gives one of the throw pillows a good shove. "We're three brilliant, successful women. There has to be something we can do."

"I have a grandpa who *knows people*," Daryl says without hesitation.

I cock an eyebrow at her. "Meaning?"

Daryl smiles innocently. "Murder?"

"Once again," Amelia says, motioning to Daryl, "too far."

There's a knock on the door, and realizing I haven't moved in a while, I offer to get it.

"I mean, at least I'd have three meals in prison and a little self-satisfaction?" I say, crossing the room. "A roof over my head?"

"You can barely watch *Orange Is the New Black* without getting queasy," Amelia reminds me. "Let's not go picking out your prison name just yet."

Opening the door, I'm surprised to find Eric on the other side with two steaming pizza boxes in his hands.

"Hey," I say, taking a step back so he can come in. "So do you just carry pizza around, or . . ."

"I ran into the pizza delivery guy in the stairway," he says, nodding hello to Amelia and making his way to the kitchen. "Thought I'd bring them up for you."

"That was sweet," Daryl says, taking down a stack of plates, motioning for us to help ourselves. "This is how my favorite porn films start."

I watch the two of them move back into the kitchen with renewed interest. They're bent together, whispering. Amelia catches
my eyes, mirroring my *Are they fucking?* expression. I look back
and forth between Daryl and Eric when they emerge.

"Are you two, um, working tonight?" I ask, picking up a slice
before taking a bite.

Daryl nods while she chews, but Eric answers, "Actually, I'm
glad you're here, Evie. I need your help."

I point a tipsy finger to my chest. "Mine?"

He nods, and Daryl explains, "Remember how Jess off-the-
cuff asked him to come up with a program that reconciles expenses with invoices?"

Squinting, I admit, "Sort of?"

She waves this off. "I liked the idea—and this audit was a
drag. So, Eric came up with the most ingenious program. It finds
and cross-references all my charges, and then reconciles them
with the right client, the relevant invoice, and the correct in-
house expense account."

I think about how much time this audit has taken and what
a miracle something like that would be. "Oh my God, that's
amazing."

"So I ran yours, too, to help Jess," Eric admits. "That's . . .
um, why I came over." He scratches his jaw. "See, something isn't
working right, because we found some charges on your expense
card that don't line up with any orders or invoices. I didn't want
to go through it at the office."

"What do you mean by 'don't line up'?" I sit up straighter.
My wine buzz is keeping my heart from taking off like a flock of
hysterical birds. "On *mine*? I haven't had time to sit at my desk
and go through it yet this week, but Jess also said something
about weird charges."

Eric pulls his laptop from his duffel and takes a seat at the bar. "Let's see," he says, opening the program. "Okay, here's one from September. There's a charge from a catering company—we actually saw it enough times that we tracked each one. The charge says you spent a hundred and twenty-three dollars for Debbie's Events—"

"But according to Jess's notes in your calendar," Daryl interrupts, "that day you were with a client for only an hour or two for voice-overs. There wasn't any catering on set because it wasn't *on* set. You met in the studio. What was that other one, Eric? The laundry?"

"Hollywood Linen," he answers, and I pause, that name poking at something in the back of my head.

"That's the one," Daryl says. "And with that one, it's not that the charges are for crazy amounts. Most of them are pretty small, like fifty dollars here, or a couple hundred at most, but they're recurring and add up. You probably would have never noticed if you didn't have to pull the reports for the audit."

"What was the name of that company again?" I ask, pushing away from the counter to search inside my laptop bag. Jess's retreat invoices are still in there.

The ones Brad told me to ignore and send directly to Kylie.

"Hollywood Linen?" he says.

"Yeah . . . right here." I find the line item and point to it on the most recent expense card statement. "That's here, too. There's a billing for linen service for the dining room, but we didn't use any at the retreat. The hotel included all of that in our block rate."

I sit on the couch, opening the folder and spreading the invoices on the coffee table in front of me. "Can you give me a few of the other names?"

"Sure," Eric says, clicking through his spreadsheet. "There's Ever Beauty . . ."

I search down my list, finding it and putting a red check mark out to the side. It's dated two days before the retreat. "Okay."

"Celebaby."

"That's a nanny service?" I ask, finger moving down the page.

"Yeah," Amelia says.

There it is. Another check, over the retreat weekend itself. Needless to say, no one brought their child to the department retreat.

"Roar PR."

"Okay," I say. Another red check.

What the hell?

"Glamband."

Amelia moves to stand over me, watching as I find the name and scratch out another checkmark. "Holy shit," she says, meeting my eyes. "That's a whole lot of coincidence."

"I bet if I started looking back through all my expenses, I'd find more," I say, looking to Eric for confirmation.

He's already nodding. "That would be my guess."

I stand up, chewing on my nail as I walk to the window. My head feels like a game of Tetris, small pieces everywhere and a clock ticking away while I scramble to make them all fit. I turn to face the group.

"So, these companies are billing P&D for a lot of services that aren't really happening?" I propose.

Eric shrugs, then nods. "I mean . . . yeah."

"You know *I'm* not doing this, right?" I ask, horrified.

Eric startles, like it would never have occurred to him that it was me, and Daryl and Amelia are vehemently shaking their heads.

My pulse seems to be thundering inside my skull. "Is this even a thing that a single person *could* do?"

"It would take a lot of work, but it's definitely possible," Eric says. "I do think it would have to be someone within the company, though. Someone who has access to the various expense accounts, and with enough power to keep people from looking too closely."

Carter's voice echoes in my thoughts.

Why does he have it in for you, specifically?

Do you have something on him?

It doesn't add up.

I let out a little gasp, and three sets of eyes meet mine.

I'm almost positive we're all thinking the exact same thing.

• • •

"Are we absolutely sure we don't want to call my grandpa?" Daryl says, lying next to me beneath a dirty old blanket in the bed of Eric Kingman's truck.

Amelia reaches across me and smacks her. "I swear to God, if you get us caught and I have to call my ex-husband to bail me out for breaking and entering, I will find your old nose and staple it back on."

Daryl lets out a horrified little squeak. "You monster!"

I bite back a laugh, and Daryl takes a deep, calming breath beside me. "Besides," she says, "we're with Eric, so I don't *technically* think what we're doing is considered breaking and entering, bu—"

"Shhhhh," Eric says through the open cab window as we reach the security gate.

"Evening, Mr. Kingman," the guard says.

The three of us stay completely still beneath the blanket, trying to make ourselves as small and invisible as humanly possible.

"Don't think your uncle is home tonight. But your aunt is up there."

"Thank you, Jerry. I'll have Aunt Maxine send down some of those cookies you love. You have a good night."

The truck starts moving again, slowly making its way up Brad Kingman's impossibly long drive.

We haven't lost our minds. It's just that we all know Brad well enough to know that if he's behind this, he wouldn't keep any of these fictional company files at *work*. I'm on the verge of losing my job, and in just a half hour at Daryl's apartment we totaled over fifty thousand dollars in money charged to *my* expense accounts alone. No wonder we're being audited! How many places has Brad skimmed from?

I am grateful to the wine because it's keeping at least half of my chill in place. Realizations keep falling onto each other like perfectly stacked dominoes. Primarily this: I was Brad's fall guy. No wonder he kept me on, assuming that if I ever found out about his little retirement plan, he's ensured that accusations against him are less credible if they come from a disgruntled has-been. Pinning me for screwing things up with Dave and Carter is one thing; there is no way in *hell* I'm going down for this level of outright fraud.

"We're clear," Eric says through the window, his voice tight and a little breathless. "You guys okay back there?"

We finally breathe. "This blanket smells like sewage, and my boss is stealing money under my expense accounts while he carefully frames me for a myriad of fuckups. But other than that, I think we're good. What about you? You okay?"

"Are you kidding me?" he sings into the cool night air. "This is awesome!"

"But are you sure you want to do this? I mean, you could just pull up, kick us out, and get the hell out of here," I say.

"Hell no. I hate the way Brad treats Maxine, and this shit is crazy! Can you feel that adrenaline?" He howls a little into the cab of the truck. "Let's take him down!"

"So Eric's definitely in," I whisper.

Amelia laughs at my side. "What tipped you off?"

The truck slows to a stop, and Eric unrolls the front windows before turning off the engine.

"All right. I'll go inside. None of the staff should be here, so I'll leave the front door open. His office is upstairs, fourth door on the right. You all remember the game plan?"

"Got it," Amelia says.

"Remember: give me two minutes and I'll get Maxine to take me into the kitchen for something to eat. I'm hoping I can get you guys at least fifteen minutes. That long enough?"

"It'll have to be," Amelia says.

The door opens and the truck shifts as Eric climbs out. "Okay," he says, taking a step before stopping again. "Should we like . . . synchronize our watches or something?"

"If we sang 'Swinging on a Star' to time ourselves we'd be just like Bruce Willis and Danny Aiello in *Hudson Hawk*."

Amelia glares at me in the dark. "Evie, usually I entertain these little movie tangents, but I'm going to need you to shut the fuck up."

"*Just go, Eric!*" Daryl whisper-yells.

"Right, right. Going."

The sound of Eric's feet on a gravel path carries through the dark, and he knocks on the door.

While we wait, Amelia taps my shoulder. "Does Carter know where you are?"

"Ha . . . no. I haven't talked to him since this morning. Right now we're dressed like cat burglars and hiding in the bed of our boss's nephew's truck. Probably best to leave this part out when I tell him about my day."

Voices carry from outside and we all straighten, straining to hear. The front door opens, and immediately we hear a woman exclaim, "Eric, honey! What a surprise!"

My heart is pounding in my head as I listen to their conversation dissipate and finally disappear.

"Okay," I whisper.

Pulling the blanket off of us and sitting up slowly, I look around, making sure we really are alone out here. I'm the first to climb out, keeping low to the ground and watching around us. Maxine's Mercedes is parked at the opposite end of the drive, but—thankfully—there's no sign of Brad's obnoxious yellow Ferrari anywhere.

Amelia is next, and she kneels on the ground by my side. As we both look around, Daryl falls out of the truck, rolling in the gravel.

"Smooth," Amelia whispers.

"Sorry," Daryl says. "I was kicked out of yoga."

It's strange being here without the Christmas lights and the valets, the holiday music and voices filtering out from inside the giant house. Instead there's just silence, the chirp of crickets in the bushes beyond. Then, as we get closer, the faint tinkling of laughter coming from the direction of the house, the door left conveniently ajar.

Thank you, Eric.

A tiny sliver of yellow light cuts a line across the porch, and we creep forward, peering through the crack and into the grand entryway. All clear.

Glancing at Amelia, I press a hand on the cool wood, wincing when the old hinge emits a tiny whine as it swings open. I wonder if Eric heard it, because his voice grows louder and more enthusiastic from the back of the house.

A wide staircase unscrolls in front of us. I motion for Amelia and Daryl to go on ahead, staying behind just long enough to close the door with a soft click. Our tennis shoes are almost silent on the steps as we climb, carefully peeking around the corner before turning right at the top of the stairs.

At my side, Amelia holds up four fingers and points to a door at the end of the hall. Nodding, I watch as she wraps her gloved hand around the knob and slowly turns.

It swings open.

Even here, Brad Kingman's office looks exactly the way you'd expect. His desk is huge and covered with books and piles of paper. In the light from the window we can see a bunch of golf memorabilia, and what has to be every award and accolade he's ever received—right down to newspaper clippings—proudly displayed. Framed photos line his bookcases, all sharing a single common characteristic: he's the star of each of them.

"Even his office is a pretentious dick," Daryl says, closing the door behind us. Turning on her small flashlight, she shines it around the walls. "Is that a safe?"

I follow her gaze and then run my own light along the desk, stopping when I come to a bank of filing cabinets. "Do you guys want to look for the file cabinet key and I'll start with his computer? I can try to work out his password."

Amelia agrees and begins to search. Together she and Daryl look under books and papers, in drawers, and behind every photo frame, while I wake up the computer, the password prompt lighting up the screen.

I start with Brad's name—first and last—then his wife's, and every combination in between. I try his birthday, the number of Oscars his clients have won, even combinations of his name with his golf handicap. (Yes, we've *all* had to hear stories of his country-club valor over the years.) No luck.

"I think I found something!" Daryl says, stretching to feel along the bottom of a drawer. Having struck out so far, I turn to watch, practically jumping with joy when she comes away with a small brass key in her hand.

"What kind of person tapes a key to the underside of a drawer in their own house?" she whispers, moving to the filing cabinet and sliding the key into the lock.

"Someone who's got a lot to hide," Amelia says.

We hold our breath as Daryl turns the key, and the lock clicks in the silence. "And doesn't think anyone has the balls to come looking," she adds.

"Thank fuck," Amelia says, flashlight in hand as she starts searching with renewed effort through files. "Anything that has to do with the names we found, tax ID numbers, web hosting companies, bank accounts, anything. If it looks shady, take a picture of it."

I turn back to the computer, determined to get in. I try a few more random words and phrases I associate with Brad, and when nothing comes up, I think back. Brad is too big of an egomaniac to ever pick a password at random, so it would have to mean something . . .

A thought flashes like a thunderstorm through my brain, and I type the words together:

B R A D U P R I S I N G

It's the film he worked on while I was an assistant—featuring the first client he flat-out stole.

Password accepted.

God, what a dick.

I search his hard drive for any of the companies that showed up in Eric's program. I open his Google drive and search there, too. It takes a few tries but then *bingo.*

A spreadsheet with names of companies and tax ID numbers, next to column after column of billed amounts. And he had the nerve to lecture me about being a team player. Jesus Christ.

"Oh my God!"

I turn toward the sound of Daryl's voice. She's looking out the window with wide, horrified eyes. A set of headlights are working their way up from the bottom of the winding drive.

"Sh-shit!" I say, jamming my thumb drive into the USB port with shaking hands. "Hurry! Did you get anything?"

"I have some invoices," Amelia answers, taking pictures of the invoices under her shirt to mute the flash. "This is a hot mess."

Amelia and Daryl rush around the room, straightening photos and smoothing the rug, righting papers, and rubbing their sleeves to clear fingerprints from anything they might have touched.

I glance out the window again and then quickly back to the screen. How many times have I had to watch this in a goddamn movie and thought, *Files transfer really fast, this is so unrealistic?*

My file transfer is only seventy-three percent complete. But my panic is total.

Headlights move across the room and Brad's yellow car pulls up alongside Eric's truck. *Come on come on come on.*

"Are you done? Evie." Daryl comes up and pulls on my arm, in the middle of a full-body freak-out behind me.

"Yeah, just . . . one sec."

"Evie, we have to go!" Amelia says, looking out the window and to the driveway below.

"It's at ninety-five . . . hurry upsss!" I hiss.

A car door closes outside. Voices carry from downstairs.

"Evie, come *on*!" Daryl says.

"It's almost there—dammit! How does a rich person have such a slow computer? What's he doing with all that money?"

"Eric!" We all freeze at the sound of Brad's voice in the entry-way below.

I look up to Daryl and Amelia, their faces illuminated in the light from the monitor, and for a horrifying second I realize that if I can see them, there's a chance that Brad could have seen them from outside, too.

My attention snaps to a little ding that says the files have transferred, and I close the drive, clicking out of all the windows as fast as I can.

Daryl moves to the door, opening it just enough to hear what's happening downstairs. "I think he's in the kitchen," she whispers, and we wait, just to be sure. When there's nothing else, I hold open the door and tiptoe into the hall.

There's a landing that looks down into the entryway, and when I peek over the rails, I see nothing but gleaming marble floors. No sign of Brad. The door is just at the bottom of the stairs and if we can get there, we're home free. I don't care if I have to walk back to my apartment.

Can we do this? I mouth, and while Amelia nods, Daryl is frantically shaking her head.

I've just taken my first step off the top landing when Eric's voice echoes through the house. "Wait, Uncle Brad, I wanted to show you my scar!" he essentially yells.

I almost fall in an attempt to scramble back, arms and legs

everywhere as we dart in different directions, each of us disappearing into a different room.

"Eric, what the hell is wrong with you?" Brad asks. "Are you taking drugs?"

"I'm . . . no . . . not drugs," Eric babbles, his eyes widening when, behind Brad and on the landing, he sees my head peeking out from one of the doorways. He pulls Brad to him in a tight embrace, and motions for me to run. "I've just missed you!"

I slip across the hall to the guest room over the garage, slamming into the window when Daryl and Amelia sprint in behind and slide across the wood floor, right into me. I let out a grunted *Oof.*

Voices fall quiet downstairs.

"Who's up there?" Brad asks.

"No one," Maxine says. "It's just us tonight."

My heart is a hammer, my chest feels like glass.

"I know I heard something," Brad says. "I'll run up—"

"But we were just going to have something to eat!" Eric says. "You have to be hungry. Have you lost weight?"

"Brad, we never get a chance to visit. Come have dinner with us."

There's a moment of silence before footsteps retreat along the marble hallway and I squeeze my eyes closed in prayer as I slide open the window.

"What are you doing?" Daryl hisses.

"We're going to have to climb out and shimmy down the trellis."

"I'm so confused by the term *shimmy* down the trellis. How is that even po—"

Amelia ignores her. "Are you out of your *goddamn mind?*" she whispers in my direction.

I look out the window. It's far, but I mean . . . it's not like *death* far. And we need to get the hell out of here, now.

"Come on," I say, throwing one leg over the windowsill. "Just do what I do."

Crawling out, I step on the roof of the garage—gingerly at first, making sure my footing is secure—and then shuffle over to the vine-lined trellis. My greatest fear is allayed when I tug at the flimsy structure and it holds securely to the wall.

"Come on," I urge again, returning to my downward climb when I see Daryl's leg come over the side of the window, her body emerging onto the roof. Amelia follows right after.

Back in the bed of the truck, we lie flat, staring at the sky and silent but for our jagged, heaving breaths. I'm calmed by the warmth of Amelia on my left and Daryl on my right. Their hands come down, twining with mine.

"Thanks, you guys," I whisper.

They squeeze my hands in unison as we struggle to catch our breath. Eventually, waiting for Eric to finish up his impromptu meal with his aunt and uncle, we manage to contain our maniacal laughter.

• • •

Carter shows up at my front door a little jittery, like he thought it might be a good idea to toss back an espresso at ten p.m.

Pushing past me, he heads straight for the kitchen and opens the cabinet with the plates. "Where do you keep the booze?"

"Erm," I say, following him, "above the stove, but don't get your hopes up. I think your options are Bacardi, Captain Morgan, triple sec, and . . ." I trail off as he pulls down a bottle of vodka I didn't know I had, grabs a glass, tosses some ice cubes in it, and pours himself a hefty shot.

His throat bobs distractingly as he swallows. I've only been home for about thirty minutes myself and want to tell him about our badass *9 to 5* adventure (Dolly Parton would be so proud!) and what we found, but he seems a little preoccupied.

"What's going on?" I ask, walking over and stretching to kiss his boozy mouth.

"I quit."

I pull back, shocked. "Pardon?"

"You heard me. I quit. I have no idea what comes tomorrow, but I told Brad that I was out."

"I . . . I. *Wow.*"

"I love you, but I didn't do it for you," he says, eyes wild. "I did it because I can't work there one more fucking second. Brad is scum."

"Well, yes," I say, stepping back and watching curiously as he reaches for the bottle again.

"I went to Brad to talk about how things went down with you and him."

I groan. "Carter, you don't have to fight my battles for me."

"I know this. If there's one thing I definitely know, it's that Evil Abbey can take care of herself. But . . . I had to say something. I couldn't *not.* The way he acted was completely unacceptable."

Well. He gets a kiss for this. It seems to calm him a little, too. I can't blame him for the vodka now; his adrenaline must be up to eleven.

"Anyway, he wasn't very receptive to the conversation—"

"I don't imagine."

"And it hit me," he says, shaking his head, "I *hate* it there. I love what I do—I love you—but I hate P&D. It's like trying to work in the middle of a dodgeball game."

This makes me laugh, and I pull him out of the kitchen and into the living room. He sits on the couch, and I follow him, straddling his lap.

"So we've made a fucking mess of things," he says, leaning to kiss my neck. "But I did hear from Dan today."

He pulls out his phone, showing me a string of texts from Dan Printz.

Hey man.

Sorry I haven't been around today.

I talked to Ted at Variety,
he said the announcement came
from some PR firm called Roar?

Who fucking knows.
Bottom line: I don't care what
the agency is, I just want to work
with you.

I have a press party I have to go to tonight
so give me a call in the morning.

Let's get some papers signed and
make some movies.

Roar PR. I freeze. "*Brad* was the one who spilled?"

Carter's eyes narrow. "What?"

I stretch across the couch, reaching for my laptop bag.

"Well . . . I had a bit of an adventure tonight." I slide the computer onto the coffee table, boot it up, open Jess's spreadsheet, and then turn the screen to face him.

"Okay?" he says, glancing from it to me again. "What's all this?"

"Have I got a story for you."

•   •   •

Former Price & Dickle talent agency executive Brad Kingman was arrested Tuesday in Los Angeles on charges of wire fraud, embezzlement, and identity theft.

According to prosecutors, Kingman set up a network of bogus companies, which he then used to submit fraudulent invoices to his agency for work that was never done. These bogus companies ranged from hair and makeup services to dog walkers and nanny agencies.

U.S. Attorney for the Southern District Emery Ridge said, "The FBI obtained emails and vendor contracts showing that Kingman used these stolen identities and tax ID numbers to submit fraudulent invoices and conceal his crimes. This isn't a matter of an employee taking a few extra dollars from petty cash. So far Kingman is accused of skimming upwards of two million dollars."

The print copy of the *Hollywood Vine* is laid out flat in front of us, and Daryl, Amelia, and Steph fall silent around the bar table. We're all here for the Super Bowl, and television sets overhead broadcast commercials that make the assembled mass fall into a reverent hush, but none of us are able to look anywhere but at the article in front of us.

"Two million dollars," Steph says quietly. "Guess it wasn't just expenses under your name."

"Just mine most recently—everyone else he used is gone."

"And now bye-bye, Brad," Daryl says.

The morning after our trip to Brad's home, Eric walked casually into Brad's empty office, drafted a new email to the FBI, and attached all the files I transferred to the thumb drive. The FBI would never know I had anything to do with this, but Brad would.

I've had dozens of pretty amazing orgasms with Carter, but I won't deny that one of the most euphoric feelings I've ever had was watching the FBI emerge onto our floor amid a deathly hush and move like a mob of righteous justice toward Brad's office.

They knocked on his door, ignoring Kylie's anxious yipping that he was busy. In fact, two agents quickly identified Kylie, pulled her aside, and took her into the conference room for questioning.

Brad opened the door, face stark, and looked right at me. I lifted my chin and smiled.

"Mr. Kingman, we have some questions." The voice of the lead agent carried easily down the hall. "If you don't mind coming with us, we can ask them in a more private setting."

I wanted Brad to refuse. I wanted them to question him right there, right in front of me. But it was also nice to watch him leave under the wide-eyed rubbernecking of everyone in the office. He moved, surrounded by the law, down the hall.

The elevator doors sealed around him, and then he was gone.

Bye, Brad.

I left P&D by choice that same day.

"So now I need to figure out what I'm going to do," I tell my friends, folding up the newspaper and tucking it back in my purse.

"You could come back to Alterman," Steph says with a hopeful smile.

"You could come work with *me*." The voice comes from behind me and we all turn. Carter has materialized, and looks . . . *stunning*. Flushed with some exuberant emotion, he's clearly just come from a meeting: neatly pressed suit, dress shirt open at the collar, tie loosened around his neck. I feel all of us exhale in a swoon in unison.

A swoonison.

"Or," he says, grinning as he walks toward us, "I could work with *you*." Pulling out the barstool beside me, he adds, "Or, I don't know, we could figure out how the hell to work together."

Carter sits down and pulls out a piece of paper folded into thirds. He carefully opens it, flattening it against the table for us to read. It's an agent contract between Dan Printz and Carter Aaron—just Dan, just Carter.

"I've secured twenty percent of fifteen million," he says with a casual grin. "If I did this on my own I could only take on one, maybe two more clients. It would help me out a lot if you could join me, show me the ropes?"

I stare at him, feeling my eyes fill, and he reaches up, pretending to be shocked by the presence of tears.

"Is that a yes? Are we going rogue?"

I surprise the hell out of my friends by launching myself into Carter's lap, but no one seems to mind. I think we all realize in this moment that I've worked my entire career so far for this—the opportunity of a lifetime.

chapter twenty-six

carter

As it turns out, you can't manage the career of the Next Big Thing from the kitchen of your tiny, one-bedroom Beverly Hills apartment.

It took approximately two weeks to come to this conclusion. Two weeks in which Evie and I shared the pantsless joy of not having an actual office to go to every morning or an actual boss checking in on us, and being able to have sex on the kitchen table whenever we want and not even have to close the door.

It was a beautiful time.

But eventually the pants had to go back on and we had to decide how we were going to do this. I had Dan and a handful of other clients but needed somewhere I could take meetings and . . . well, work.

Evie had toyed with the idea of going back to Alterman, but had already come to the conclusion that while she loved the people and the job, she could no longer stomach the games that seemed to inevitably dominate big-firm work. Luckily, Adam Elliott and Sarah Hill had signed on with Evie at P&D for project-by-project contracts only, and those two would follow her anywhere, it would seem.

And boom—we had an agency.

So going rogue meant we needed an office.

This is when I realized exactly how connected Evie was. Having already helped me find a great legal adviser, she found us a screaming deal on a handful of vacant offices . . . in a very nice building next to P&D.

●   ●   ●

There isn't any sort of official grand opening at Abbey & Aaron, but the Wi-Fi is connected on a Tuesday, and I get the password to the security system the day after that, which is good enough for us. We have the entire space repainted, line the lobby walls with Jonah's new black-and-white prints, and install the best Keurig machine money can buy. There isn't a need for a row of sixteen well-groomed and neatly arranged assistants, but there's more than enough need for Becca and Jess.

Becca and Evie spend thirty minutes on the phone—during which they immediately bond and become best friends forever through a rousing version of Carter Aaron's Top Ten Most Embarrassing Moments. Evie offers her a job and Becca—thank God—accepts. I am ecstatic. I will be surrounded by the two women who call me out the most, but I will never be disorganized or undercaffeinated again.

That first morning at the official office is fucking surreal. The sky looks exactly like it did my first day in LA—powder blue with just a trace of haze along the edge—and I make the familiar turn into the parking garage.

It's already warm as I climb out of my car just after eight and start the walk from the third-floor terrace of the garage to the lobby. Making a right turn instead of a left, I head into Building A, site of our new endeavor.

I make a quick check of my reflection in the door. Hair:

good. Tie: Ol' Lucky this time around, not some fancy new mistake. I burned that one.

It's mid-March, but I'm hit in the face with the same rush of refrigerated air as soon as I step inside. My blood feels carbonated; my stomach is tied in a hundred knots as I cross the marble floors.

In Building B—owned entirely by P&D—there are giant screens with scrolling head shots and posters for some of the larger clients the firm represents. But in Building A, it's more subdued. A simple gold plaque affixed to the wall lists the several offices housed inside the building, and there we are, Abbey & Aaron: Suite 303. Whereas P&D required floors and floors of staff and a step short of a retinal scan just to get into the elevator, it's pretty much just the two of us, a legal adviser we keep on payroll, Becca and Jess, and hopefully Steph, if we can ever convince her to come over with us.

I haven't seen Evie since I left her apartment this morning, and my fingers already itch with the need to touch her. We all met up yesterday for Morgan's birthday in Griffith Park, complete with food trucks and the biggest bouncy house I've ever seen.

Evie's favorite people hung with my favorite people, and seeing them all together—my future and my past—felt like stretching out a leg and putting my foot down on the right path. Michael Christopher is already planning my bachelor party. Which . . . isn't official or anything, but . . . you never know.

I followed Evie back to her apartment at the end of the night. Her kisses still tasted like sunshine and birthday cake, and she giggled while I checked every other inch of her to see whether the rest of her tasted like frosting, too. I left this morning just before five, feeling the best kind of exhausted, pressing kisses to her mouth and saying I'd see her at our office. Which is a really great thing I get to say now.

Becca is there when I step off the elevator; a strange sense of nostalgia and hope fills my chest.

"Here's your schedule," she says, handing me a few slips of paper from her desk. I can barely read any of them, but pocket them happily. "There's a phone call you'll want to get on right away. One of Jamie Huang's friends wants to talk to you, and Allie Brynn is about to have kittens in her excitement over it."

"Awesome," I say. "Is Evie here yet?"

"Conference room," she says, looking up at me through narrowed eyes. "It's so weird seeing you like this again, in your suit with that familiar, crazy caffeinated glaze to your eyes. It's pretty great. Or maybe I'm just jazzed to be in an office with an In-N-Out down the street."

I grin. "I am so fucking happy you're here."

"Same," she says, glancing down to her desk before handing me a small stack of mail. "Now get to work."

"Yes, ma'am."

It's quiet as I make my way to the conference room. The door's ajar, and I poke my head in when I knock and wait for Evie to look up.

She's sitting on a ledge that runs along the window, sun in her hair and a contract in her lap. She looks beautiful and confident and happy, and while I'd (probably) never engage in workplace PDA, there *are* only a handful of us here. We could revisit my earlier fantasy and make out on the table if we wanted, and only have to suffer Becca's fake-horrified groan. I've heard conference tables are good for that sort of thing.

"Hey, you," Evie says, and motions me inside.

I'd like to say I keep it cool, but I practically jog over, bending at the waist to press a warm, lingering kiss to her lips. "Hey."

She runs her fingers down my chest and to my tie before looking up at me with a smirk.

"This tie *works*," I insist.

"I have an important meeting with Paramount in an hour," she says, smoothing it down again. "If it works as well as you say it does, you can wear your lucky tie every day and you won't see me complain."

"Maybe you can wear it later. And *I'll* get lucky?"

She grins. "Maybe."

I tap the pages in front of her. "You ready for this?"

"I have a kickass package and just need their *yes*. Hey, did you hear that Seamus hit a photographer outside LAX last night?"

My eyes go wide. "Like with a fist?"

"Like with his *car*. P&D can have fun with that one; he's their problem now."

"I think they have a long list of problems. I'm just glad not to be one of them anymore."

She straightens my tie and lifts her chin. "Amen."

"What do you think about going to New York with me this summer?" I ask her. "It's miserable and hot, but it's my parents' anniversary, and I want my family to embarrass me in front of you. It might be awful."

Evie tilts her head and studies me for a moment. "Maybe you could come to Burbank with me this weekend? The TV will be on too loud and my dad will hassle you about how much he hates the Yankees. My mom will probably tell you that you need a haircut. You'll probably have a terrible time."

Her eyes meet mine, and I don't have to have known her a long time to know she's never been this happy, or this secure.

"We'll just have to make the worst of it," I agree, smiling as I lean into her kiss.

acknowledgments

We often get asked how we write so quickly. Obviously, it helps that there are two of us, but even so some books come out faster than others. *Wicked Sexy Liar*, for example, seemed to almost fly out of us. *Dirty Rowdy Thing*, too, we wrote in a matter of weeks.

Alas, *Dating You / Hating You* . . . was not one of those books.

Our first draft was completed in December 2015 and looked almost nothing like the book in your hands. We had such a clear idea of what we wanted—two Hollywood agents fall for each other and then have to battle it out for a job—but the book that came initially didn't look like the one in our heads. It was sort of like we attempted to bake a cherry pie and pulled a meatloaf out of the oven. And let's be real: no one wants meatloaf when they're expecting cherry pie.

Enter Adam Wilson, Holly Root, and a whole lot of tracked changes in a Word document. Seriously—there were times when this book looked like someone went to town with an entire box of crayons on it. Our editor and agent, respectively, have spent nearly as much time with this manuscript as we have. Hopefully they know that every time we sit down to write we realize how lucky we are to have such an involved and supportive group of individuals helping us.

Erin Billings Service reads every word about seven thousand

times, giving feedback from the earliest terrible versions to the final polished one, and she still manages to help us find typos in the pass pages. Seriously, Smister, you are a rock star.

Kristin Dwyer, we dedicated this to you because the adventures we've already had seem unreal. Can you imagine the ones yet to come? This is our first book baby we're doing with the new venture, and we are so excited for all parties involved. Let's do this!!

Thank you to our Gallery team: Carolyn Reidy, Jen Bergstrom, Louise Burke, Paul O'Halloran, Theresa Dooley, Liz Psaltis, Diana Velasquez, Melissa Bendixen, the Gallery sales force that works their butts off behind the scenes to get our books in stores and with online retailers, and the wonderful art department who so perfectly captured the next step in the CLo look. You are all fantastic, and we hope you're coming for dinner because we made extra lasagna for everyone.

We can't do any of this without the romance community. Seriously—the strength and enthusiasm of this group is astounding, and we are so grateful for readers, bloggers, graphic artists, and anyone out there who takes the time to send us a tweet, email, or review. You keep us going, and we mean that with all sincerity. We love this job, and we love you.

Finally, to our husbands, who are both patient and lucky. Patient on the days when the words are flowing, and lucky on the days when they're not and we decide to bake all day instead. Thank you for being so proud of what we do.

PQ, this one was a doozy, but I feel like it clicked something between us, made us even stronger. Holy smokes this is fun. Let's do it again.

Lo, this book, man. Some books are easier than others and

some are like giving birth. I'm pretty sure we both had to bite down on a piece of leather with this one. I love you like Bella loves McFlurries, and anyone who knew us in 2009 knows that is a LOT. Thank you for being the Lo to my C. Meet you in the front row.